A Sister of the Brotherhood

Virginia Smith writing as

GINNY PATRICK

A SISTER OF THE BROTHERHOOD

Published by Next Step Books LLC, P.O. Box 4563, Frankfort, KY 40601-4563

Cover Design and Interior Graphics by Dineen Miller
Developmental edit by Catherine Jones Payne
Map by Matthew Van Egmond

Print ISBN: **978-1-937671-44-0**

United States Copyright Registration Number **TXu 2-142-042**

Printed in the United States of America

10 9 8 7 6 5 4 3 2 1

Sister of the Brotherhood is a fast-paced tale of political subterfuge, self-discovery, and what it means to be family. Ginny Patrick's writing style is sleek, dragging the reader from one chapter to the next just to find out what happens next. Recommended for any fantasy lover!

Ralene Burke, author of *The Sacred Armor Trilogy* and Marketing Director for Realm Makers

In *Sister of the Brotherhood,* Ginny Patrick has created a new fantasy world that kept me turning pages. Arien is a compelling young character you will be cheering on through many challenges and adventures as she learns to use her unique gifts. If you like imaginative worlds and leap off the page characters, then *Sister of the Brotherhood* is the book for you.

Ann H. Gabhart, bestselling author of *Angel Sister*

Sister of the Brotherhood is classic fantasy at its best. Villains, heroines, kingdoms, legends, moral dilemmas, and epic stakes. Ginny creates a complex story world, engaging characters, and frightening but apt parallels to contemporary issues. Her heartfelt storytelling pulled me forward with each page.

Sharon Hinck, author of the award-winning Sword of Lyric series

For my sister, Beth Marlowe,
who loved this book from the very beginning.

With gratitude to Sue, Lyn, Shayne, Cara, Melva, Lee, Dave, J.M., Charlotte, and Catherine for their honest feedback. It wasn't always easy to hear, but they taught me how to write.

A Note from the Author

The first question I'll be asked about *Sister of the Brotherhood* is, "Why did you publish under a pseudonym?" As Virginia Smith I've written thirty-eight novels in a variety of genres, and over the years I've been fortunate to have connected with readers who faithfully read every book. But there's a vast difference between mysteries or romance novels and epic fantasy. Some people who enjoy mysteries will also like fantasy adventure stories, but not everyone. With *Sister of the Brotherhood,* I want to make a clear statement: **This. Book. Is. Different.**

I've always loved speculative fiction, so naturally when I started writing I wrote sci-fi/fantasy stories. I attended professional events like the World Fantasy Convention, joined critique groups with other spec fic authors, and tried over and over to publish in that genre. As it turned out, I found publishing success in another genre entirely, and when *Just As I Am* came out in 2006 I focused my efforts elsewhere. But I've never lost my love of well-written fantasy stories.

I'm not hiding behind a pen name. I'm proud of this book! Ginny Patrick is my maiden name, the one I answered to for the first two decades of my life. I decided to publish anything I write in the science fiction or fantasy genres under Ginny Patrick so you, dear reader, will clearly know what you're getting before you spend a dime.

Sometimes life throws us a curve, and every so often that curve takes us full-circle. *Sister of the Brotherhood* is a full-circle novel for me. In recent years I've been fortunate enough to renew my acquaintances in the speculative fiction industry, and I now serve on the board of directors for the World Fantasy Convention. I couldn't have foreseen that all those years ago. Virginia Smith is still actively writing mysteries and historical novels set on Earth and plans to continue as long as people want to read them. But I do hope Ginny Patrick finds an audience for fantasy novels so she (uh … I mean **I** … this can get confusing!) can write more.

Ginny

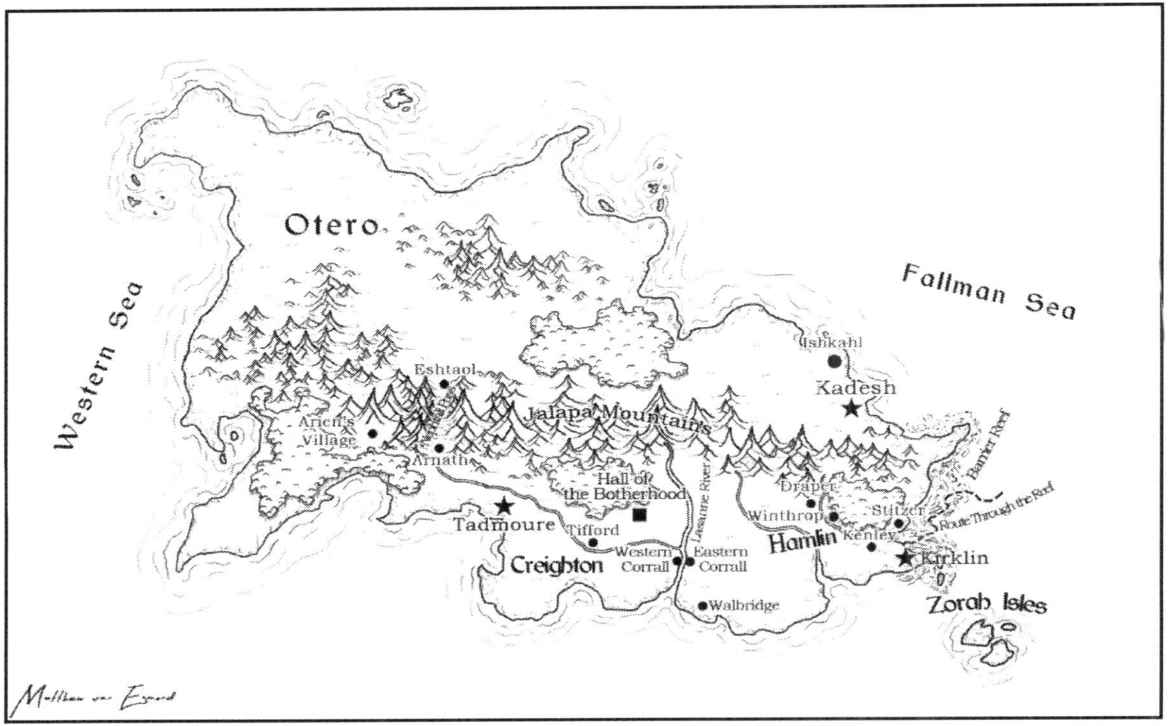
Otero
Western Sea
Fallman Sea
Ishkahl
Kadesh
Eshtaol
Arien's Village
Arnath
Jalapa Mountains
Hall of the Botherhood
Tadmoure
Tifford
Western Corrall
Eastern Corrall
Creighton
Lasanne River
Walbridge
Draper
Winthrop
Hamlin
Stitzer
Kenley
Kirklin
Barrier Reef
Route Through the Reef
Zorah Isles

Prologue

Exhaustion tugged at Lisette's eyelids. She must listen, or Jerolin would chastise her later for not paying attention to the Foretelling. But the babies, a son and daughter of the same birth, had been up most of the night and she was too attuned to their infant minds to sleep through their cries. Though the wet nurse had been on hand to care for them, Lisette insisted upon taking her turn pacing the floor, trying to coax the newborns back to sleep. She clamped her teeth together to suppress a yawn and fixed her eyes on the scene before her.

Gathered around an open area in the center of the room, a dozen or so well-dressed men fixed their attention on an old woman with a face like a prune. The Seer, chanting in a low, coarse voice, unfastened the wrapping from one of two bundles and withdrew a gnarled staff the length of her own leg. She tapped the staff gently, dislodging the excess powder, then turned to the first infant. The staff passed slowly over Lisette's sleeping son once, twice, thrice, while the chanting grew soft, then loud, then soft again. As the staff completed its third pass the old woman dashed it to the floor. One of the watchers jerked at the clatter. Blue powder scattered, and the rod rolled a short distance across the polished flagstones before coming to a stop.

The old woman knelt beside the powder, careful not to touch it, and peered at the pattern through half-closed eyelids. No one in the room dared to breathe, lest they disturb her.

Lisette glanced at her husband. Jerolin stood with his hands resting on a narrow table, a wine goblet before him. His jaw bulged as he watched the Seer, though occasionally he glanced toward the other men in the room as though to assure himself that everyone was attending to his son's Foretelling. His guests, in town to witness tomorrow's Naming Ceremony, all gave proper attention to the ritual.

When she finished her examination of the powder, the woman straightened and turned to face Jerolin.

"The child will come to adulthood strong and healthy." Rheumy eyes fixed on a point somewhere above his head. "He will wear his father's name with pride and add to the wealth of that name. I see opportunities in his life never before available to his bloodline. He will touch three crowns, though none will be his to wear."

The Seer bowed her head. Loud applause burst from the onlookers, and the men flanked Jerolin to clap his back. A successful Foretelling.

Three crowns. Lisette smiled and dipped her head at the congratulations offered to her as well. What could the message mean? Perhaps her son would serve three of this kingdom's monarchs, which may portend either a long life for him or short ones for the kings. Or might they be kings from three different kingdoms? A disturbing thought, though Lisette sensed nothing but pride in her husband's mind. Jerolin was not frustrated at the lack of information in this Foretelling, as she was.

She stifled a sigh. That was the problem with prophecies. Too often they merely hinted at the future, and interpretations varied widely from person to person. A reputable prophet never interpreted, thereby avoiding unpleasant consequences.

And accountability, as well.

"And now my daughter." Jerolin gestured for the servants to clean the powder from the floor.

Lisette signaled for the wet nurse to take the boy to the nursery, and the stout woman bundled the sleeping infant away. The remaining babe slept soundly in her basket, angelic in appearance. Lisette suppressed another yawn. This same child had not been so angelic in the early hours of the morning, when she should have been letting the household sleep.

When every speck of powder had been cleared away, the Seer took a staff from the second bundle. Lisette watched the rod pass over the babe, while the same mysterious chanting echoed in the chamber. Again, the staff clattered to the floor. This time it rolled farther than the last, leaving a trail of powder on the floor the length of a man.

The old woman cocked her head and hesitated before she knelt. Her glazed eyes moved as she inspected every segment of the design, and then repeated her perusal a second time. From her position on the floor, she lifted her face toward Lisette. The prophetic distance in her eyes dissolved, leaving behind an intensity that stopped Lisette's pulse. Something was wrong. Though the woman's outward posture changed not at all, urgency rolled off the Seer in waves. Lisette sent her inner awareness forward, and the old woman's thoughts whispered in her mind as clear as her own.

The babe's life is forfeit unless her mother acts. But to warn the mother is to also warn the father, and to do that is to kill the child.

Breath lodged in Lisette's throat. Fear saturated the woman's mind. Bound by her prophetic gift to speak the truth, she could not hide any part of the child's Foretelling. But Jerolin's temper was well known.

The onlookers became restless. Jerolin fidgeted with his goblet, his gaze fixed on the Seer. Finally, the woman stood and adopted the same stance as before. Amazing that she could exhibit such control given the strength of her fear. Lisette doubted she could manage to look so calm.

"If this little one lives, her childhood will be lonely, but with great accomplishment at the end. The fate of many will rest on her choices and her abilities. I see crowns near her as well."

The piercing blue gaze lowered, and the woman looked directly into Jerolin's face. Muscles in Lisette's stomach tightened into knots.

"My lord, this babe will bring about the downfall of your bloodline. Because of her choices, your name will end with her generation."

Someone gasped, and every gaze fixed on Jerolin. An angry flush suffused his face, and his hands drew into tight fists. Lisette heard murder in his thoughts. If she didn't interrupt, the Seer was dead.

She stood and nodded to the nearest guard. "Escort her out and see that she is paid."

The man glanced toward Jerolin, and when he made no move to counter Lisette, obeyed. Visibly relieved, the old woman hurried to gather her empty pouches and scuffled after the guard.

Aware that a dozen pairs of eyes were fixed on her, Lisette walked to the center of the room, took her daughter from the basket and laid her in the arms of a servant.

"Take her to the nursery." She rubbed a finger tenderly across the baby's soft cheek, then turned to face her husband and his uncomfortable guests. "You were right to worry, my lord, about finding a proper Seer in this uncivilized area. This near the mountains, the commoners are poorly bred." The words tasted sour on her tongue, but perhaps tossing Jerolin's own prejudicial opinions back at him would convince him of the prophecy's inaccuracy. "The woman no doubt did the best she could, but she is obviously inept. Perhaps even envious of her betters. I don't believe the Foretelling is accurate."

One of their guests rushed to agree. "She's right, Jerolin." The man nodded with energy. "You should take the child back to the city and have the thing re-told by a prophet with real talent."

Several others murmured agreement, and Jerolin's fists relaxed. At least on the surface, he appeared convinced.

Lisette sent her awareness toward him. His thoughts shouted at her across the room, heavy with fury. *I have my son, what need have I of a daughter? If the girl dies the prophecy will never come to pass.*

Now the meaning of the old woman's thoughts became clear. If Lisette didn't leave tonight, and take her daughter with her, the baby would die at the hand of her own father.

Is this why Lisette had been gifted with the ability to hear unvoiced thoughts? Was this the reason she had known from childhood that she must hide her ability, even from those she held most dear? So that she could save her daughter's life?

As the men followed Jerolin out of the room, a plan began to form in Lisette's mind. In the city she could think of half a dozen people to help her, but here in the country she was days away from anyone she could trust. The villagers in the nearest town were all terrified of Jerolin, and rightly so. She couldn't put any of them in danger by begging refuge. And there was no one in the household she could trust. They were all Jerolin's servants, hand-picked by him and paid well for their loyalty. In the single year since her marriage, she had learned that their loyalty to her was given only because of her position as the lord's wife.

Which meant she must go unaccompanied. And because she was still weak from the double birth, she couldn't take both babies alone.

Pain assaulted her like a knife through the heart. She must leave her son to save her daughter. Her hands clenched, nails piercing the soft flesh of her palms. There had to be another way. A way to take them both. But she could think of nothing.

At least she could take scant comfort in the Seer's Foretelling. The boy would grow to manhood, and provided Lisette did not hesitate, the girl would live as well. When they were adults, their choices would be their own. She couldn't help with those. Her duty was now, and her daughter's need outweighed her son's.

She turned her mind to the details of her escape.

Part One

One

The unmistakable trace of Power resonated in the air, as clear as the sparks of flame that rose from the bonfire into the night sky. A telltale tingle had begun to vibrate in Petro Tyler's mindsense the moment he entered this remote mountain village, tantalizing with promise. Elusive, though, unusually so. So far, his efforts to locate the source had proved unsuccessful. He'd sensed it at odd times throughout the afternoon, brief flashes of mental exertion gone too quickly for him to trace. But unmistakably Power.

He sat close to the central bonfire surrounded by villagers who were doing their best to ignore him. Their disregard didn't bother Petro in the least. He had grown accustomed to the awe in which people held those in his position. These villagers had been friendlier this afternoon when he first arrived in the company of a traveling trader, but that was before he changed into the black robes and medallion of the

Brotherhood. Now the ones who'd been most talkative had removed themselves to positions as far from him as possible. He didn't have to Perceive their thoughts to know their fears. They thought he was spying into their minds.

If only they understood how little he desired to hear their thoughts.

As the trader entertained the adults with tales of the princess's upcoming marriage to the crown prince, Petro tuned the man's voice out. He'd heard that tale so often in the past few weeks he was sick of it. Besides, at last all the children were in one place, including the ones from the orphanage. He could finally test them all.

The orphanage was the reason he had journeyed to this tiny village in an isolated corner of the kingdom. In the past months he had searched every town and most of the villages tucked into this far-flung section of the kingdom but was no closer to selecting a new trainee than when he started. It was depressing. Where did his fellow masters find their trainees? Were there no boys with the necessary traces of Power left in all of Creighton?

So far, this excursion, too, had proved unrewarding, orphanage or not. In the hours since his arrival Petro had tested every boy he encountered and had not found even one trace of the qualities for which he searched.

But there *was* Power here. It had an odd feel to it, slightly different than anything he'd ever felt, like an apple with the taste of a pear. Frustrating, yes, and discouraging. This elusive wisp of Power might even be coming from a man, an untrained rogue who had somehow gone unidentified all his life.

He turned his attention to the smaller bonfire, the one closest to the well. Thirteen children clustered around that fire, a fair number for a village so small. Eight boys, all of them taking advantage of the adults' attention focused elsewhere. They had drawn closer to the fire than they should and were busily throwing twigs and leaves into the flames, watching sparks rise to the sky. One had found a long stick and was attempting to create a makeshift torch by setting the end on fire.

Petro didn't see any that he hadn't already Perceived.

None displayed even a wisp of Power. Disappointed, he stifled a sigh. Maybe this was a sign. He should forget about finding a new trainee. There were other things he could do with his time and talent. He was still a young man, not yet past the fortieth anniversary of his birth.

The problem was he *wanted* to train another child. He'd enjoyed it so much the first time, had found its challenges and its rewards fulfilling. And while he could try his hand at any number of trades and be almost guaranteed success, there was nothing he felt particularly led to do except teach.

Now that he'd tasted that elusive vein of Power, he could not deny a stir of hope. Though he didn't see any boy he hadn't yet tested, he might as well try again.

He fixed his gaze on a lad of around eight, and Perceived.

Disgusted, he quickly withdrew from the child's mind. It was full of plans for petty cruelties, and thankfully not even a touch of Power. True Power in the hands of a cruel person was a frightening thing. Thank goodness he didn't have to report discovery of a potential problem.

He shifted his gaze and Perceived the next child. This one was stupid, his mind full of nothing but greedy thoughts of sweet cakes without even the ambition to obtain them. Depressing.

The next boy sat with an arm around one of the girls. Too old, by the looks of him. Petro sent his Perceptive thoughts forward. Intelligence and a kindness of spirit, but no Power, not even a glimmer. Yes, he remembered this one from earlier in the day. A shame, for he would have been good to work with.

He shifted his glance to the smallest boy. Here was one he hadn't yet Perceived. The child was too young, clearly little more than a babe. The Brotherhood didn't normally accept them until they began their sixth year, but Petro was growing desperate. If this boy was an orphan with no tearful parents to contend with, well, rules were made to be stretched.

Petro Perceived, and his hopes inched upward. Not raw Power, no, but an unmistakable glimmer of potential. More than any he had yet encountered on this search. And intelligence, with a curious and adventurous nature. This child had possibilities. He wasn't the perfect candidate, to be sure, but what did Petro expect? Another Jothan? He'd been spoiled by having such an exceptional trainee the first time. He would never find another Jothan.

The boy clutched a bundle of rags, his eyes drooping with sleep while he watched the older children toss debris into the fire.

Let's see how you respond to a Command, my boy.

He sent a thought. The boy's hand, the one holding the bundle, began to move. It came up before him slowly, grasping the rags in chubby fingers.

Good. Now another.

Petro sent a Command: *Toss that bundle into the fire.*

He sensed compliance. The child's arm pulled back as he prepared to toss the rags toward the flames.

In the next instant, a rush of Power nearly bowled Petro over. From the boy? No. Petro shook his head. *Toward* the child. Another Command sent to countermand his own. The chubby arm dropped once again into his lap, still clutching his bundle of rags.

That was it! The Power he'd felt all day, but with such an odd flavor to it.

His head jerked upward. Now he could trace the Power back to its source. His eyes followed the trail his mind blazed, and they lit on the sender of the Command.

The air in his lungs deflated, and his excitement along with it. A girl. That explained the odd quality. And she was old, almost through adolescence by the looks of her. A funny-looking thing, too, with pale splotchy skin stretched tight over lanky arms and legs. The firelight glinting off a mop of bushy hair made it appear an unlikely shade of orange. Her eyes blazed brighter than the flames, and even from this distance he detected a spark of fury in them.

Why was she so angry? He Perceived her thoughts.

Ah, the boy was a favorite of hers, and the bundle of rags a doll she'd fashioned for him.

"How can he be so cruel to make Blaine burn up his only toy? Everyone knows orphans got nuthin'."

Her opinion surprised Petro. Was he cruel? That certainly

wasn't his intention. His only thought was to see if the child would recognize the Command and try to resist it. He did not, but she did.

And what Power he had felt in her Command. More even than Jothan.

Of course, she was much older than Jothan when he began his training, and that explained some of it. But she'd never received any instruction, which meant her Power had developed to this extent alone. Amazing for a boy *or* a girl. Had there ever been a girl who developed Power past the rudimentary stages? Not that he knew of.

What a shame she was female.

She glowered at him across the bonfire flames.

Perhaps he should test her, just to see how far developed her gift was.

He gave her a brief smile and sent a mild Command. *"Stand Up."*

Her legs twitched and began to unfold from their cross-legged position. Creases appeared on her forehead as she struggled to control her body. She closed her eyes, her face a study of concentration. Her legs relaxed. When she opened them again Petro was smiling, but she didn't return the smile. Instead she sent a Command of her own.

"Stand up yourself!"

He laughed out loud. Truly amazing. He saw the thought advancing toward him, a bright spark in his mindsense. He intercepted it and easily discarded it before it reached him, but he was impressed. This girl had not only Perceived his Command—which in itself was truly remarkable—she actually tried to imitate it. Her effort was completely ineffective, of course, wild and untrained, but the Command had resonated with raw Power.

He Perceived her mind, tested its quality while she glowered at him from across the distance. Most in evidence were intelligence, strength of character, and hunger for knowledge. Kindness, too. A gentle, compassionate heart.

But also, a deep and powerful longing. She was an orphan, like the boy. But unlike the child, she possessed a Power she instinctively knew no one else did. This girl had spent a lonely life in this village, set apart by those abilities.

Petro probed more deeply, and uncovered her strongest desire—to belong, to be part of a family. Natural for an orphan. And perfect for his purposes. Someone who desperately wanted to belong to a family would be willing, even eager to take the opportunity he offered.

He jerked upright. What was he thinking? He had no intention of taking her on as his trainee. A female trainee? Impossible.

But, oh, if she were male, and younger, she would be ideal.

He glanced toward the cluster of boys. The little one seemed dull and uninteresting after the Power he'd sensed in the mind of the girl.

Perhaps...

No. The Brotherhood wouldn't stand for it. Parnell would have a seizure.

He studied her once again. Her attention had shifted to the little ones, the shadow of an almost-adult smile playing about her lips as she watched their antics. The girl was far too old to begin training with the Brotherhood of Power. In fact, he doubted if she had ever been a child. She had a seriousness about her that would invite people to rely on her, even adults.

What kind of life must she have led here? What kind of life lay waiting for her?

In a flash Petro made up his mind. Demons could take Parnell in his sleep, and anyone else who argued against her. Custom or no, Petro had come looking for true Power and had found it. He had searched long enough to realize that the gift was rare. While his fellow brothers might not all agree with him, Petro believed the gift to be divinely bestowed, and therefore when it was discovered one should not question the package in which it came. Female or not, he wanted to train this girl, and when Petro made up his mind to do something, not even the full membership of the Brotherhood could convince him otherwise.

Still, if he was going to be the master, he'd better show her who was the most Powerful right now. He sent another Command, this one stronger, and indulged in a smile when she leaped to her feet. The boy sitting next to her looked up and asked a question. She shook her head, bewildered, and stared across the bonfire at Petro.

Normally the trainee was young, and the choice given to his parents. But here was a different case. This was an adolescent, and without parents. The choice would be hers to make.

"Come with me." Her head jerked upright when she heard his mindspeech. *"I'll take you to a place where everyone has the same abilities you have. I'll show you how to use the Power you've been given."*

She stood beside the fire, bafflement fading from her expression as the meaning of his offer sank in. Her gaze traveled toward the boy, and then to a man and woman seated in the group surrounding the trader.

Petro projected an image of the Hall of the Brotherhood and of the students and masters who lived there. They devoted themselves to the training of their minds—to harnessing and developing the Power within them.

"What holds you? No one here can teach you the things I can. No one understands what you can do, and they would be afraid if they did."

Her gaze returned to his, and she gave a nod. She knew he spoke the truth.

Petro climbed to his feet. The offer had been made. The decision was in her hands now. With a farewell smile for those around him, he left the circle of flickering light and headed toward his tent. The night air chilled his skin where the fire had warmed him moments before.

"I'll come for you at first light," he told the bewildered girl still back at the fireside. *"And then I will take you to your new home."*

The pounding on the door echoed inside the house, like a drum beating in Arien's ears. She jerked upright and nearly upset the bowl of porridge before her, nerves flaring to full force in an instant. Her gaze flew to Mora's face. Tears glistened in her guardian's eyes. The woman turned to her husband, who slowly rose from his chair. He stood still a moment, hands planted on the scarred wooden surface of the table and studied Arien. She couldn't remember seeing such a grim expression on jovial Guy's face in all the years she had lived in his house.

"Be ye sure, girl?"

Much of the night had been spent wrestling with the question. Could she leave this village and the people who had taken her in as a helpless babe? Put her life in the hands of a stranger in hopes of finding a place where she fit in? Where she wouldn't be the odd one, the outsider with a knack for making unusual things happen. Not that she'd ever confided her abilities to a single soul. Still, when she was younger and first learning to talk, the entire village had been shocked and frightened to have their thoughts announced in the chattering, sing-song voice of a toddling orphan. She'd learned to control her tongue, but no one really forgot. She saw the way they looked at her after the rotted tree almost fell on Darin but skittered away at the last moment. Or the time she pulled little Blaine, coughing and sputtering, from the creek mere seconds before he was carried downstream. Those incidents accomplished something good, but they only emphasized the shameful fact that she was different from everyone else. Unusual. Strange.

Until last night. Imagine, a man who was like her. Who could talk without speech. And he said there were others, too.

Arien squared her shoulders and looked steadily into Guy's face. "I'm sure."

His jaw firmed, and he gave a curt nod before crossing the room to open the door. The man standing on the doorstep had changed into traveling clothes, which relieved her. The black robes he'd worn last night had been imposing and a little frightening. It was harder to be intimidated by a traveler in worn and patched trousers, a homespun shirt, and a scratched leather jacket. The oddly shaped silver medallion still dangled from a rawhide strip around his neck. His brown and gray locks were caught neatly into a clasp at the base of his neck.

"Good morning." His greeting boomed in the room as loudly as the pounding had a moment before. Mora glanced toward the stairs, where the other children still slept above, but Arien detected no movement from that direction.

"G'day to yer." Guy stepped back and swept a work-roughened hand inside. "C'min fer a bite o'somethin'."

"No thank you. I broke my fast an hour ago."

He stepped inside, eyes moving as he glanced around the room. His gaze fell on Arien, and a warm smile lit his features. The nerves jumping in her stomach calmed at the appearance of that smile. Though he addressed the three of them, his gaze remained fixed on her. "I neglected to properly introduce myself last night. I am Petro Tyler, Master of the Brotherhood of Power."

"Master, ye say?" Mora asked, her voice tight.

"That's right, madam." He took up an easy stance, arms folded across his chest. "I earned the rank some years ago. I've successfully trained one student and launched him on the world." His smile toward Arien deepened. "You will be my second."

Mora crossed to stand behind Arien's chair and placed a hand on each shoulder. "Will our Arien be a master too?"

"That will be her choice. It's an arduous process that some of our fellowship choose not to follow." He shrugged. "She won't have to make that decision for quite some time. She has plenty to learn in the meantime."

"Are you ready to leave? We have a lot of ground to cover today."

The words were so clear that at first Arien didn't realize the others could not hear them. How did he do that?

"That's one of the first things I shall teach you. We'll discuss it as we travel."

The thought carried a hint of impatience. Arien pushed back the half-empty bowl of porridge, her appetite banished by another fit of nerves. She picked up the bowl to take it to the wash bucket, but Mora snatched it from her.

"Leave it to me, girl. Best be on your way." The gruff voice didn't fool Arien, who caught sight of tears once again pooling in her guardian's eyes.

Arien picked up her travel bag and slung the strap over one shoulder. She glanced at the stairway. Last night she'd said her goodbyes to the other children before they went to bed. Better to let them sleep rather than risk another tearful farewell session. She came to Master Petro's side, blinking to clear her vision.

When they turned toward the door, Guy stepped in front of them. His hulking frame towered a full head above Petro. "Ye pledge yer oath you mean her no harm?"

Petro raised a hand, palm facing out. "On my honor."

Guy's eyelids narrowed as he weighed the man's word. Then he jerked a nod and opened the door. Petro strode outside, where he stooped to pick up his own pack and sling the straps across his shoulders.

Arien turned in the doorway. Her gaze swept the room. Every day of her life had been spent in this house. With these people, and the little ones slumbering upstairs. She managed a smile for Guy and Mora, whose tears now flowed freely. Then she faced Petro.

"Ready?" he asked.

The answer was trapped behind a painful lump in her throat. Instead she drew a breath, lifted her chin, and started down the cobbled path.

Master Petro set a brisk pace, and for the first candlemark or so the journey was pleasant. Arien had rarely been permitted to venture into the woods, and then only in the company of a half-dozen others under the watchful eyes of a pair of adults. Sunlight filtered through the canopy above them in a kaleidoscope of autumn colors. A slight breeze stirred the leaves, and their feet kicked up more on the forest ground. She followed behind Petro and enjoyed the rare time of silence without the constant chatter of young voices that filled Mora and Guy's house from breakfast to bedtime.

Not that the woods were silent. Leaves rustled, birds called to one another, and squirrels chattered at them from above. She spied the white tail of a deer as it fled through the trees to their right. Delighted, she watched it dash away as gracefully as a dancer. After that she kept a careful watch, eager for another glimpse.

By mid-morning the novelty of a walk in the woods had worn off. Underbrush grabbed at her skirts more than once, and she'd somehow managed to collect a patch of burrs in the hem. Her feet burned, the muscles in her legs cramped, and her stomach protested the unfinished porridge at home. And still Petro maintained his silent stride beneath the trees.

She aimed a glare at his broad back. Did the man expect her to walk all day without even a short stop to take care of nature's call?

He halted and turned, a look of surprise on his face. "I don't expect any such thing. If you need a break, say so."

Heat burned in her cheeks. She'd forgotten he could hear what she was thinking.

"I could use a rest as well."

He gave her a kind smile, and relief flooded her. At least he didn't take offense easily.

The thick trunk of a fallen tree lay on the ground a short distance away. He perched on it, issuing an audible sigh when he sat. "That thicket will afford you some privacy." He pointed to a dense copse of brush. "And you should change into something more suited to travel."

Arien looked down at her dress. Besides the one in her pack, it was the only article of clothing she owned.

He stretched his legs out in front of him. "I wear the robes of my position almost always. They're comfortable, and they let everyone know who I am. But they're a nuisance to travel in. Get caught on every sticker bush I pass, and the brambles go up inside and scratch my legs. I find it easier to wear trousers when traveling."

The sting of a thousand scratches on her calves gave testimony to his words. "I don't have any trousers."

Petro looked surprised, and then sighed. "Of course you wouldn't. Trousers are hardly appropriate garb for village girls." He shrugged. "No matter. We'll get you a pair as soon as we can."

Arien picked her way through the undergrowth and around the thicket. Yes, plenty of privacy here. She let her pack slide off her shoulder and set it to one side, then turned to the business at hand.

"My plan is to head east to Arnath, and on to the Hall of the Brotherhood from there."

Arien gasped, leaping up and whirling to face Petro.

He was not there.

"I'm still seated where I was. Don't worry, I can't see you."

She scanned the area. The twisted branches of the thicket lay still and lazy, bathed in shafts of sunlight. Not a soul in sight.

Forcing herself to relax, she directed a question through the thicket. "How do you do that?"

"Haven't you ever heard someone's thoughts?"

There had been times, such as when one of the children planned mischief. But that happened only rarely, and she had to put forth an effort that left her head pounding. Even then, she'd only understood impressions. Not words. "Not like this. Not like your voice is in my head."

"You'll get the trick of it soon enough."

The telltale niggle of an ache in the base of her skull denied his claim.

"As I was saying, we'll head for Arnath and buy traveling clothes. We should arrive sometime tomorrow. From there the journey will be easier, since I plan to buy a horse if there's a decent one to be had."

A horse. An image flashed into Arien's mind, the memory of a dream. She was perched on the back of a strong, muscular beast, its short fur wet with lather. They were running, but there was something wrong with the ground. It sucked at the animal's hooves each time they hit, like a freshly plowed field, but different somehow. Arien straddled the creature's back, her fingers wrapped in its coarse mane for balance. They were running…somewhere. Speed was vital. If she didn't hurry something terrible would happen.

Of course, that was tame compared to some of her childhood dreams. For a time, she'd been plagued with night terrors and had awakened screaming and inconsolable. Thankfully, those horrible dreams stopped a few years back.

"Interesting. We'll examine those dreams in more detail

once we get settled in the Hall."

The Hall of the Brotherhood. Her breath caught in her chest. "How long will it take to get there?"

"You needn't talk. Just form the thought and send it my way. You can see where I am, can't you? Look."

Arien peered into the thicket, squinting to catch a glimpse of him.

"Not that way. It helps at first to close your eyes. See your surroundings. Feel them. And then find my mind."

She obeyed. For a moment all she saw was darkness. Then she remembered how she had known exactly where to look the day little Blaine almost drowned. He'd wandered away from the village, no one knew where. She'd run directly to him because she had sensed where he was.

With her eyes closed the sounds of the forest became sharper, more noticeable. Wind in the treetops. The nearby rustle of feathers. Running water further away, like the creek at home, splashing against rocks. With an effort she ignored the noise and peered deeper into the darkness behind her eyelids.

A pinprick of light gleamed in her mind, just beyond the darkness her eyes could see. It twinkled like a single star in the night sky.

"Is that you?"

"Don't you recognize me?"

Oddly enough, she did. The light *felt* like Petro.

"Good. Now, think of what you want to say, and send that thought toward me. Don't say it out loud. Just think."

She did. *"I'm hungry. Might we have some bread and cheese?"* She directed her thought toward the light that was Petro.

"Excellent!" Praise warmed his mental tone.

A flush of pleasure washed over her as she made her way around the thicket to find him standing in the middle of the clearing.

"What about lunch?" He eyed her bundle with the eagerness of a boy. "What did your foster mother pack for us?"

The afternoon walk held little of the morning's charm. Arien's legs had gone from stiff to tired, and a pulse throbbed in her thighs in response to the exercise she was putting them through. Worse, her feet were horribly sore from the ill-fitting sandals she'd been given by Mora and Guy at the onset of summer. Dirt stained her toes black, and she had to stop often to clean debris from beneath her soles. Her guardians could never have foreseen this kind of travel, else they would have fitted her with more suitable footwear.

A hiss of pain escaped when a prickly burr found its way between the tender skin on the inside of her ankle and the leather strap. Forget the trousers Petro promised. What she needed were boots. Sturdy ones.

A chuckle resounded in her mind. "*We can arrange for both.*"

She dropped to the ground to dig out the burr and snapped a reply before she could stop herself. "Do you plan to listen to my every thought forever?"

He halted and turned an amused smile on her. "*Only until you learn to erect a suitable mindshield.*"

"Mindshield?" The word provided a welcome distraction from her discomfort. "What's—"

He jerked upright, cutting her off with a raised hand. His gaze grew distant as caution crept over his features.

"*Someone approaches. Be silent. Stand behind me.*"

His thought held the unmistakable tone of a command, and one to be obeyed quickly. Arien slid her foot back into her sandal and leaped up. Petro planted his feet shoulder-width apart and seemed to grow taller, his stance rigid. She glimpsed the stone-like set of his jaw as she scurried around him, tension twisting her stomach muscles into knots. She'd heard tales of vagrants lurking in the forests, waiting to pounce on travelers, rob them of their belongings, and leave them maimed or dead. Guy made sure all the young ones in his care knew the forests were unsafe and roaming any distance from the village was strictly forbidden. She'd half-assumed his warnings were made up to discourage the children from wandering away and becoming lost. Now, she wasn't so sure.

Her ears strained to detect sounds unnatural to the forest. Nothing. Why, then, did Petro believe—

The answer came to her in an instant, and she closed her eyes. Petro was easy to locate, a now familiar mindlight in the swirling darkness of her mind. She expanded her search to sweep the area. Breath froze in her chest. There. Just ahead of them, another blaze of light, this one flashing with an intensity that outshone Petro's. Arien noted the difference but had no time to wonder about the reason. A third presence shone in the darkness, this one moving toward them from the opposite direction.

"Two of them," she whispered.

"I know. Stay near me."

She opened her eyes and huddled so close to his back that the earthy scent of his sweat filled her nostrils.

A few heartbeats later the sound of footsteps rustling the leaves on the forest ground reached her. The first newcomer approached from directly ahead. Hearing nothing from behind, she shut her eyes long enough to note that the second person had halted a short distance away. To sneak upon them unawares?

A man stepped from the cover of thick pine trees into the clearing. Tallish, though he stood at least a handbreadth shorter than Petro. His hair hung in matted tangles to his shoulders and the seams of his shirt were split and ragged. But what drew Arien's attention were his eyes. They glittered with a wild intensity that sent a new chill down her spine.

"Greetings, my friend." Petro's tone held none of the caution she sensed in his tense bearing. "What an unexpected pleasure to meet a fellow traveler this far into the forest."

The man started at the words, his entire body jerking as though someone had taken him by the shoulders and given him a shake.

"Who are you?" he asked in a high-pitched voice. "What are you doing out here?" He swung one arm in a wide ark to indicate the surrounding woods. His hand balled into a fist and flexed repeatedly, and he lifted his other hand to scratch the back of his head, then fumbled with his shirt laces while tapping dirt-incrusted fingers together rapidly. All the while he shifted his weight from one worn boot to the other.

Something about the constant movement seemed…wrong. As though he'd been possessed by a frenetic energy he couldn't control. Was he sick, then? Or maybe—she gulped—insane?

"Traveling," Petro answered. "The same as you, I suspect. On your way to Corral, are you?"

The man's eyes moved as rapidly as his body, his gaze barely landing on Petro's face before darting away. Arien shut her eyes and located the second person, who had crept closer behind them. She grasped Petro's shirttail and squeezed it in her fist.

"Never you mind," the traveler snapped.

"A wise man holds his business close to his chest." Petro dipped his head in tacit approval. "Regardless, our meeting is well-timed. We've just stopped for a rest. Perhaps you'd care to join us for our meager meal of bread and cheese?" He paused to half-turn and gesture behind them. "You and your companion."

The relentless fidgeting halted long enough for the man to give them a startled stare. "How did you—"

He broke off when a second man emerged from behind a thick trunk. Arien pressed herself even closer to Petro, her cheek against his back. This one held a knife.

"Never mind that." The newcomer gestured with the long blade. "You just give Ned here your purse."

Ned thrust his arms into the air. "Now you went and told 'em my name."

"Won't matter none." His companion's lips tightened into a chilly smile. "They won't be telling nobody."

Arien twisted Petro's shirt tighter in her fist. Guy had been right. These men were bandits, and they were going to kill her. *I shouldn't have come. I should have stayed home, where it's safe.*

"You may have my purse." Petro's spine stiffened beneath Arien's cheek, and a stern note crept into his voice. "But the girl and I will be on our way."

Ned's shrill laugh held a wild tone. "You hear that, Gabe? That's the easiest coin we ever stole."

An unseen sensation slammed into Arien like an ear-splitting crash of thunder. She wavered on her feet beneath the force of it. Few times in her life had she felt such an intense onslaught of emotion from another person, almost like a physical attack. Her mind struggled to overcome a wave of malice, of such cruelty as she'd never imagined.

He wants to kill us. Not for money, but for the satisfaction of taking our lives.

"*Don't be afraid.*" Petro's thought pierced the swirling chaos, his mental tone saturated with confidence.

"You'll find my purse in here." He unslung his pack from across his shoulder, which forced Arien to step back though she did not release her grip on his shirt.

He tossed the canvas bag toward Ned, who dove for it and began rummaging inside.

Gabe did not take his gaze from Petro. His eyes glinted with an eagerness that sent bile swirling in her stomach.

Petro held up his hands, palms out. "You've no reason to harm us. Take our belongings and let us go."

"And have you set the guard on us?" Gabe brandished the blade. "Ned, hold the girl."

Ned jumped to his feet and took a step toward them, his hands outstretched. A cry escaped Arien's throat. She squeezed her eyes shut and threw her arms around Petro's waist, her face pressed hard against his back.

A brilliant beam of light blazed in her mind. Like a shaft of white-hot lightning cracking across the sky, it rushed from one side of her brain to the other. At the same instant, the sound of rushing wind filled her ears. She opened her eyes in time to see Ned standing waist-deep in a hole in the ground that had not been there a moment before. As she watched, the soil around him churned and collapsed inward, burying his lower body in a narrow grave.

"Wha—"

Gabe's jaw dangled as he stared at his companion, but only for a moment. Before Arien's eyes the ground beneath his boots parted. He gave a startled shout as he sank into a crevasse that filled again as quickly as it had opened. The knife fell from his hand, and he stared in stunned disbelief at the prison of soil that trapped him.

Ned began to scream, his terrified shrieks piercing the forest. His upper body writhed as he slapped at the tightly packed dirt with frantic hands.

Petro ignored them both. He strode forward to pick up his pack where Ned had dropped it, and calmly retrieved the contents strewn around the ground. When he'd slung it once again across his shoulder, he turned to Arien.

"Shall we be on our way?" He left the clearing at an unhurried pace.

Her mind numb, Arien snapped her mouth shut and followed him.

Two

"But *how*?" Arien repeated the question for the thousandth time. "One minute the dirt bubbled like water, and the next it packed around them as if they were tree roots."

She walked at Petro's side, her mind full of the event she'd witnessed. The bandits' screams had faded behind them some time ago. The trail through the forest had grown wider and easier to navigate.

"I've told you all I can," Petro answered in a patient tone. "Movement is one of the three foundational Powers you'll learn during your training."

The idea that she would one day possess an ability like that seemed like a wild fantasy. A thrilling prospect, but also intimidating. What if she couldn't do it? Would they turn her out? Send her back to her village in disgrace?

"If you fail, then I fail. And that, my dear, is unthinkable. Trust me. You will not be turned out."

The confidence that saturated his thought did much to

ease her worries, though a sliver of doubt remained.

"Will I learn about mindshields too? Because I think I need one."

He stopped and faced her, his expression curious. "You do, but how did you come to that conclusion?"

Once again, the malice in the would-be thief's thoughts slammed into her, and she shuddered. "Because that man, the one called Gabe, was cruel and it was horrible to feel. And the chaos in the other man's mind was…" She swallowed, hard. "I don't want to feel those feelings."

Petro's face went blank. He stared at her with such an intensity she struggled to keep from looking away.

"You felt their feelings?" he finally asked. "Not only their thoughts, but their feelings too?"

"I—" She bit her lip. Had she done something wrong? "Y—yes. I didn't hear what they were thinking. I didn't want to. But I could feel what they felt."

He didn't take his gaze from hers. "And what about me? Can you feel my emotions?"

"Only when you talk to me in my head. The rest of the time it's like there's…" She grasped for words to describe the difference between what she'd seen of the thieves' minds and what she saw of Petro's. "Something like a wall around you. I mean, I can see you when I look for you with my eyes closed, but I don't know what you're thinking. Or feeling," she added.

Another long pause, and then he gave a slow nod as if satisfied. "That wall is a mindshield. People without Power are incapable of shielding their thoughts, but creating a mental barrier is one of the first lessons you will learn from the Brotherhood."

"And that will block the bad feelings from people like those two?"

Again, she found herself the subject of a penetrating stare before he answered. "Yes, a strong shield will safeguard your mind from outside influences."

She released a pent-up breath. "Good. That will be a relief."

He looked like he might say something else, but then thought better of it. Instead, he continued the journey. Arien followed, a dozen questions circling in her mind. But she didn't voice them, and Petro either didn't hear her thoughts or chose not to answer.

The edge of the woods took her by surprise. They stepped from the cover of the trees into dazzling sunlight. Arien blinked to clear her vision.

"Here we are," Petro announced. "Welcome to Arnath."

A wide, packed-dirt road stretched before them, lined on either side by the largest collection of buildings Arien had ever seen. And people! Never had she encountered so many strangers. Everywhere she looked she saw people. They walked singly or in pairs down the main road, their feet stirring up clouds of dust. A trio of children appeared from between two buildings, raced across the street, and disappeared behind another. Women with shopping baskets dangling from their hands talked with a shopkeeper wearing a stained apron. Arien's mind whirled. How did they keep track of one another? How did they remember so many names?

She must have looked dazed, because Petro smiled down at her. "It might look big to you, but it doesn't compare in size or industry to some of the kingdom's larger towns, like Corral or Tadmoure."

She tried to picture something bigger but failed. Clutching her pack to her chest, she hurried to keep pace with Petro as he strode down the center of the street. Her head turned from side to side, taking in the unusual surroundings. Many of the buildings were shops, permanent ones that didn't move around on wheels. Real glass shone in the window frames, allowing the people walking by to look in and see the goods for trade. And the goods she saw through those windows! Bags of grain, bundles of vegetables, and copper pots in every size. On a table in front of one shop lay a half-dozen bolts of brightly colored fabric that would have dazzled the women in her village. One shop displayed ready-made dresses and trousers.

A scent tantalized her nose, and she closed her eyes while she inhaled the delicious aroma of spicy meat being roasted nearby. Other odors blended with the appealing ones, some not so pleasant. Everywhere she looked the townsfolk stared at her, some openly curious while others gave the visitors a friendly smile.

At the end of the street Petro stopped before a huge house, twice the size of any structure back home. A sign hung from a post in front. Arien's training at home included ciphering and letters, so she easily recognized the single word: *Inn.* She followed him onto a covered porch where a row of rocking chairs lined the whitewashed wall. Beside the door hung an embroidered strip of fabric. Arien was about to ask about its purpose when Petro tugged on it. From inside the house came the tinkling of a bell. Moments later the door opened to reveal a petite woman.

She tilted her head to look up at Petro. "You lookin' for a room?"

"We are."

Her cheeks dimpled with a smile and a twinkle sparkled in her eyes. Dark hair hung in a silky wave down her back, held in place by a bright blue bow fastened at the base of her scalp. She wore a dress of an incredibly smooth fabric, dyed the same blue as the bow and stitched with dainty flowers all around the collar and sleeves. Arien thought her the most elegant woman she'd ever seen.

"I've a few empty rooms." She stepped back and gestured for them to enter. "I'm Kalinda Medwin, wife to Jarrett."

Inside, Arien found herself standing before a wide stairway with a polished railing. A door on their right was closed, and directly in front of them stretched a long corridor with several more closed doors. A cheery light shone from a room at the end of the hall, and her mouth watered at the delicious aroma wafting from that direction.

"It's five coppers a night. You'll be wantin' two rooms or one?" The woman arched a delicate eyebrow at Arien.

"Two, if you have them," Petro replied. "Is supper included or should we find it elsewhere?"

"It's included, such as it is. There's only me, and I do the best I can. We take meals in there."

Kalinda dipped a head toward their left, and Arien peered

around Petro into a room with a giant table of shining wood and more chairs than she could quickly count. On the mantle above the fireplace hung a brightly colored painting. A map, perhaps? She couldn't make out details from this distance.

"I serve right at sunset, but if you're late I'll keep a plate on the hearth for you."

She led them down the hallway. Opening a door on the left, she gestured for Arien to precede her inside. A narrow bed occupied most of the space in the tiny room, covered with a yellow quilt. At the foot stood a narrow frame for a pitcher and basin, and a wooden stool. Kalinda crossed to a window and, with a shove, thrust the framed glass outward. A cool breeze rushed in.

"If you have clothes you want cleaned, I'll do 'em for a copper. Just dump 'em outside your door and I'll have 'em ready before supper."

"Thank you, madam. You are a most gracious hostess." Petro made a polite bow, which brought a blush to the woman's cheeks.

She brushed past him. "You're right next door."

When they'd left, Arien removed her sandals, lifted her feet to the bed, and lay back with a relieved sigh.

"Our hostess seems to have gotten the impression that you are my daughter. Perhaps it would be better to let her think so."

Petro's comment didn't startle her this time. She had grown accustomed to his thoughts echoing around in her head over the past several days.

"All right." She rather enjoyed the idea of having a father, even if it was only pretense.

"I intend to purchase a few items in town, and then return for a nap before supper. I suggest you get some rest. But first put your clothes outside your door.

A nap in the middle of the day, and someone else to wash her clothes? Mora would be scandalized.

Tiredness dragged at Arien's limbs as she stripped down to her undergarments and set her dirty clothes in the hallway. Then she returned to the soft bed and was asleep within minutes.

She awoke to a room filled with dusky shadows. How long had she been sleeping? She closed her eyes and located Petro's presence in the room next to hers. Asleep. Not far away she sensed another presence, this one easily identifiable as Kalinda. Thoughts darted around the woman's mind like a nest of fireflies caught in a whirlwind. Most of them centered on food and worries that her guests would enjoy the supper she'd worked hard to prepare.

At the foot of her bed Arien found her dress, clean, dried, and draped across the stool. Kalinda had added a green scarf and a pair of slippers so soft and light Arien could hardly wait to slip her feet into them. The water in the pitcher was warm, proof that not much time had lapsed since it had been filled. Arien rubbed her eyes. She must have been sleeping soundly to have heard nothing of the innkeeper's presence.

Clean and dressed, Arien left her room to thank Kalinda.

"Don't speak of it." The woman eyed the slippers. "I know your poor feet must be terrible sore after all the walking you and your Pa been doing."

"Well, yes," Arien admitted. Actually, several places on her soles stung like she'd stepped on a hornet's nest.

"Don't you worry none. I got something to help." Kalinda disappeared into the larder and returned with a fist-sized jar. "Sit there."

Arien sank into the sturdy chair before the hearth, where the contents of a pot bubbled and emitted an aroma that made her mouth water. With lightning-quick movements Kalinda removed her slippers and began rubbing ointment on the soles and sides of her feet. Relief came almost instantly. Arien closed her eyes and released a long sigh.

"I got the ointment from one of them mind-magic fellows that stayed here a while back." Kalinda lowered her voice, her eyes wide. "They use their magic to make it, you know."

Before Arien had time to question the statement, the woman pressed the jar into her hands. "You take this with you. I have plenty more. And you keep them slippers too. I have so many I'd be embarrassed to count 'em."

Arien sensed in the woman's thoughts that her protests would be ignored. "At least let me help you serve supper."

A protest burst from her lips. "But you're a payin' guest. It wouldn't be right." Despite the words, pleasure at the offer colored Kalinda's thoughts.

Arien stood. "Please. I'm used to working, not to being waited on."

"Well." She made a show of considering, and then nodded. "You could help me cart the food to the table."

At her direction, Arien picked up a tray of covered dishes. The delicious aromas streaming from beneath the lids stirred up a hungry rumble in her stomach. In the dining room a man and woman stood before the hearth, gazing at the painting above the mantle. The couple turned as they entered.

"Supper's almost ready now," Kalinda told them, bobbing her head. "Take whatever seat pleases you."

A second couple, obviously companions of the first, arrived and took chairs at one end of the table. Two men clad in travel clothes occupied the far end. The ladies smiled kindly at Arien, and the men ignored her completely.

When their hostess untied her apron and gestured for her guests to be seated, Arien decided to rouse Petro.

"Supper is ready," she directed toward him. *"Do you want me to wait for you?"*

"I'm on my way."

A few moments later the sound of a closing door echoed down the hallway. Arien selected a seat near the dining room entrance and turned a smile of welcome on Petro when he appeared. He looked clean and rested, with his hair tied neatly back and his clothing fresh.

"I don't believe it." One of the leather-clad men leaped from his seat, his jaw dangling, and stared at Petro.

"Jothan!" A wide smile creased Petro's face. "Well met. Well met indeed."

The two embraced, thumping each other soundly on their backs. Then they stood silent, staring at one another for a moment that stretched uncomfortably long. The two ladies at the other end of the table exchanged curious glances, and one of the men cleared his throat.

In a flash, Arien realized the reason for their unusual behavior. They were communicating by mindspeech. She closed her eyes and, sure enough, saw bright thoughts dancing back and forth between them. To her surprise, the younger man's mind was surrounded by a wall similar to Petro's. This man possessed a mindshield.

Suddenly he turned and looked directly at her. His eyebrows arched, and he laughed out loud. The sound held a note of…something…that sent a surge of heat into Arien's face. Petro, also chuckling, clapped Jothan on the shoulder and together they approached the table.

Before he sat, Petro bowed in Kalinda's direction. "Mistress Medwin, I find myself constantly pleased by the discoveries I make in your excellent boarding house, not the least of which are the other guests."

A dimple appeared in one smooth cheek. "If all my guests talked as pretty as you, I'd find my head swelling' every day. Sit down, now, I'll serve the supper."

"This is an old friend of mine," Jothan told his companion as he slid into a chair directly across the table from Petro.

Petro selected a seat beside Arien and smiled at the roadworn man in travel clothes. In return he received a cautious nod. The man seemed less than pleased at Jothan having met an old friend. But why would that be?

She turned her attention to Jothan, curious. How did Petro know him? With a mindshield, he was obviously from the Brotherhood. He was of average height with a tanned face and shining almost-black hair that fell to his shoulders. Handsome in a rugged way, and quite a bit younger than Petro.

The other man was older, with a thick beard and a suspicious expression. He was heavier than Jothan, with muscular arms and a broad chest, and wore a silver ring in one ear.

"Petro Tyler." Petro nodded as he introduced himself, first to Jothan's companion, and then to the others around the table. He placed a hand on Arien's shoulder. "And this is Arien."

The others went in turn giving their names. On Kalinda's right were the Colbys, and the Hiltons on her left. Jothan's companion hesitated when his turn came.

"Quinn Parkin," he said in a voice that sounded like a growl.

Kalinda distributed plates piled high with food. Arien eyed hers with dismay. It held enough food to feed four orphans at home. There were mutton chops with a thick, savory gravy and potatoes drenched in goat's butter. Those were the only items she could identify. She eyed a mound of green chunks and a pile of yellow paste. Potatoes had been a staple at the orphanage, and she'd eaten mutton all her life, but those other things? Hesitantly, she picked up her fork. She'd better get used to trying new things.

Kalinda stood behind her chair and addressed her guests. "My man Jarrett's helping with a house-raisin' out past town. We won't wait for him." She took her seat. "Lots of folks heading south these days, going to the sending-off for Princess Serena. I daresay the inns in Tadmoure will be full to busting."

"That's where we're going," said Mrs. Colby.

Mr. Colby tore off a piece of bread and added in a heavy mountaineer accent, "Our youngest girl's in service to the princess. Likely the last time we'll see her before she takes off out of the kingdom."

His wife looked disturbed at the thought.

"It's hard on a mother to send a child such a distance." Mrs. Hilton reached across the table to place a comforting hand over her friend's. "No doubt the queen feels the same."

Petro speared one of the green chunks with his fork. "This is an important marriage, one that has been long coming. Your daughter will see the fulfillment of the long-awaited reunion firsthand."

Quinn shook his head, scowling. "This ain't no reunion. Ain't nothing but a political agreement." He sopped his bread in gravy. "The split ain't about to be mended over a wedding. Nothing can make Creights like Hamlers, or Hamlers like Creights."

"Maybe not," Jothan said, "but it's a step toward a reunion."

"Yes, and don't all the townsfolk here just love to gab about what might happen," put in Kalinda.

Mr. Hilton swallowed a mouthful. "I can't see either king

giving over his kingdom to someone else, no matter how many princes and princesses get married."

"It's hard to imagine." Jothan nodded agreement. "But any child of Sarana and Millard's will be a child of both kingdoms. There hasn't been one of those in time out of mind."

Frustrated, Arien tried to follow the conversation. Who was Millard? Hamlers she had heard of. Who hadn't? They were the people from the kingdom that had split away from Creighton a long time ago. Was Millard their prince?

"I don't know." Doubt rested heavy on Mr. Colby's features. "I can't see our Prince Thaine giving up his throne once he gets it from the old king, and I surely can't see him giving it to his sister's child. He already has little Prince Roddy and probably a dozen more by the time he becomes king."

"So, you don't believe there will ever be a reunion?" Kalinda's fork halted before her lips.

The man shrugged. "I can't see it happening easy. Terrible things will have to take place in this kingdom before something like that will come to pass."

Petro picked up his cup. "Perhaps this marriage won't mend the divided kingdoms. But King Mendel of Hamlin approached our King Hubert for this union, and I see it as a wise move. Doesn't seem to be one an evil man would make, though Creights like to believe all Hamlers are bad."

Mr. Colby's eyes narrowed. "Might be his way to get control of Creighton."

Petro conceded the possibility with a dip of his forehead. "I think it more likely he is doing exactly as he says—attempting to heal the conflict between the Twin Kingdoms."

Several expressions around the table became stubborn. Clearly the two couples didn't believe the King of Hamlin could act honorably.

"I doubt King Hubert would have given his daughter to Hamlin's prince if he suspected the gesture was made maliciously." Jothan pointed at his companion with a fork. "This union is important because it is exactly what you say, Quinn, a political agreement. It's the first of its kind since the split, and it sets the stage for future ones like it."

Kalinda stood, breaking the tension. "Those are matters

for smarter folks than me. No good's done by fretting over it, I say. Now, who's ready for another chop?"

Dishes were passed around a second time, though Arien couldn't imagine how anyone could eat more food. For a while the only sounds were forks scraping pottery and the occasional slurp from a mug. Petro ate with quiet enthusiasm, relishing every bite as though it were likely to be his last. Across from him, Jothan devoured his meal with gusto, taking huge bites which would have gotten him a scolding at the orphanage. Arien concentrated on eating slowly, as she had been taught was proper.

Petro eyed Jothan across the table. "What have you been doing with yourself in the half-year since we parted?"

Jothan, having forked a gigantic amount of potatoes into his mouth as Petro spoke, hurried to chew with bulging cheeks. He swallowed heavily, then sipped from his mug to wash the food down.

"After I left you, I made my way down to Corral and looked up my brother. He and his wife have a house there, near the river so Jarlath can work the barges. I didn't see much of his wife. She's expecting their first child soon, and not carrying it well. Home in bed most of the time."

"It was the same for my Hester." From the far end of the table, Mrs. Hilton leaned forward to deliver her comment. "Had to stay abed all the day, but she was fine after the babe came."

Jothan directed a distracted smile at the woman, and then turned back to Petro. "I looked around, did some odd jobs, but couldn't find anything I wanted to settle to. Took a job on a barge with the idea of crossing over to Walbridge, and maybe even to those Zorah Isles where the silk and the teaspice come from."

"Ah, that new silk is *so* nice," put in Kalinda, and the two women nodded agreement. "Old Whit carries some in his shop, but the price is out of my reach."

"Last time Hanna came home she told us the princess has a dozen dresses of it," Mrs. Colby confided, and the ladies *ooh'd* at the idea of such extravagance.

"I aim to look for some when we get to Tadmoure,"

announced Mrs. Hilton, "so I can make my middle daughter a gown for her bride-night."

"A bride-night coming up?" Kalinda clapped her hands. She launched into a list of questions about the wedding, which Mrs. Hilton answered with enthusiasm.

Arien, watching Jothan, saw the slight upward roll of his eyes. He focused his attention on Petro and continued in a low voice so as not to disturb the animated conversation at the other end of the table.

"I found a barge leaving within a few weeks for Walbridge, but then I met Quinn here. He's got a successful trapping business and needed a second hand, so I've decided to give it a try."

Jothan was staring at Petro with an odd look, and Arien closed her eyes briefly to Perceive him. As she thought, he and Petro were exchanging thoughts, bright lights dodging back and forth between them with rapid-fire speed. How could they talk and mindtalk at the same time?

She opened her eyes to find Jothan watching her, an almost imperceptible smile twisting his lips. He winked at her, one eyelid closing so quickly no one else could have seen it. Cheeks burning, she lowered her gaze to her plate. Had he caught her watching their conversation?

"And what do you trap?" Petro directed the question to Quinn.

"Anything," the bearded man replied. "Beaver mostly, though I have gotten a fair share of lynx. The cats pay best."

Arien watched him. Something in the way he looked at Petro made her think he wasn't pleased to run into a friend of Jothan's. She closed her eyes and sent her mind in his direction. No mindshield here, just an open brightness alive with thoughts. She drew close enough to hear them.

"—old man better just mind his own damn business. What is that young idiot Jothan thinking of, talking about our business like—"

"Arien!"

Petro's thought chopped into her mind on a wave of anger so strong it nearly knocked her off her chair. She opened her eyes. A furious flush reddened his face, and his gaze snapped toward her. What had she done to make him so angry?

He must have realized her confusion, because his expression softened.

"I'm aware you don't know this, but it is expressly prohibited to listen to someone's thoughts without permission or cause."

She swallowed, guilt-ridden. Of course, it would be. It must be akin to listening to private conversations behind closed doors, only much worse. People think things they would never say or do. What if someone listened to *her* thoughts? What if Jothan, for instance, had heard her thinking that he ate like an unmannered child? Or that she thought him handsome? She squirmed uncomfortably.

"I'm sorry. I...didn't think about it before I did it."

Petro watched her for a moment before giving a brief nod. *"I have not explained the rule. No harm has been done."*

During this brief mental exchange, talk of the wedding of Mrs. Hilton's daughter had continued. Only Jothan seemed to realize anything else had occurred. He studied Arien and Petro, his expression speculative. Heat warmed her face a second time. Had he overheard her being chastised?

Who was this man? And why did he have a mindshield as sturdy as Master Petro's? Of course, he had been trained by the Brotherhood, or he would have no mindshield at all, like Quinn. But he was young, not old like Petro.

Maybe he was like her, a trainee, only more advanced. Or maybe even no longer a trainee, maybe he had graduated. Petro had mentioned his previous trainee, but Arien couldn't remember a name.

"Very good, girl." The thought came to her from across the table, the tone lighter and recognizably younger than her master's. *"I am his former trainee. His first, I might add. And you're his next. How odd."*

Her cheeks flamed. *"I thought it wasn't good manners to listen to other people's thoughts."*

The conversation at the far end of the table had changed from Mrs. Hilton's daughter's wedding to memories of Kalinda's wedding, with comments thrown in by the others. The men focused on their plates, so no one paid them any heed.

"It isn't, nor to Perceive the mindspeech conversations of others. You've been rude since the beginning of the meal."

"I didn't understand what you said."

"Only because you're too slow, but rudeness is still rudeness, even if it fails in the attempt. By the way, you kept your eyes open that time. That's better. You may be older than most trainees when they're first recruited, but at least you're trainable."

Arien narrowed her eyelids. She refused to be soothed with a compliment following so closely upon an insult. Besides, what did he mean about being older than most? That was something she needed to talk to Master Petro about. Pasting on a polite expression of interest, she turned her attention to the ladies and preceded to ignore Jothan.

He chuckled and turned back to Petro. "And you? How have you kept yourself busy?"

The older man pushed his plate away and leaned back with a contented sigh. When he answered, his voice was low enough not to be overheard by those at the other end of the room.

"I helped around the Hall for a while. Thaddeus has begun an index of the library, and he doesn't trust anyone except a master to help with it. I worked on that until I got bored, then helped Calder with his trainee. A lad named Norbert."

"I remember him. Little fellow, half the size of the others, and ill-tempered as a mule."

Petro nodded. "The very one. He's not only belligerent, he's slow with Command so of course he's having trouble with Movement as well. Several of the masters have suggested that he be sent home, but Calder is stubborn about him."

Quinn kept glancing toward Jothan as he ate.

"Quinn is listening to your conversation," Arien warned Petro.

"He is aware of Jothan's abilities, and therefore mine as well. He can be trusted."

Maybe that explained why a cloud of distrust hovered around him. Arien studied his scowling face for a moment, then returned to her food.

"Send Norbert home? Seems drastic, from what I

remember." Jothan tore a slice of bread in half. "The boy's got a cantankerous streak, but I don't think he's cruel. Besides, he's young still. Perhaps he just needs time."

Petro appeared unconvinced. "We'll see how he progresses. We don't want another Addison to haunt the Brotherhood."

A wave of animosity accompanied the name. Surprised, Arien looked up to scan Petro's features. He wore a scowl nearly as deep as Quinn's.

Jothan seemed unperturbed. "Addison wasn't cruel, was he?"

"No," Petro admitted. "Just self-focused. The only time in the history of the Brotherhood that one of its trainees deserted, and a scant year before his final trial. And robbed the Hall when he left. Whatever became of him, it can't be good."

The unfamiliar names clogged Arien's head. Who were these people? If this Norbert was a trainee, she would soon meet him. And Calder and Thaddeus as well. But who was Addison, the one who haunted the Brotherhood and elicited such dislike in her tolerant master? The question left her uneasy. Apparently not all the members of the Brotherhood were as honorable as Master Petro.

Darkness shrouded the yard around the boarding house when Petro stepped onto the porch. He Perceived Jothan's presence inside moving in his direction, so he sank onto one of the rocking chairs. The street was deserted, but bright lights shone through the windows of an establishment down the road. The local tavern had attracted a crowd, and the merry makers had apparently settled in for a lively night of drinking. Their voices covered the distance, not loud enough to disturb sleep but a faint accompaniment to the night.

The door behind Petro creaked open and Jothan slipped through carrying a tray. He closed the door with his foot, taking care to do so quietly.

"What's this?" Petro nodded toward the tray.

"A jug of local wine, compliments of our hostess."

"A woman of unsurpassed hospitality." Petro eyed the jug, pleased. "I'm surprised she hasn't considered opening an inn in Tadmoure or even Corral. With her talents she could make a fortune in a bigger town."

Jothan set the tray on the wide railing and pulled a cork from the jug. He splashed a generous amount of the liquid into two mugs and handed one to Petro. Taking the other, he dragged a second rocker close and sat.

Petro sipped with caution. As he expected, the wine was somewhat harsh but palatable. The flavor was sweeter than he preferred, but surprisingly good for a small-town vintage.

"Not bad," he told Jothan. "Much better than fighting the crowd at the tavern."

Jothan agreed. "Quinn is there. He'll crawl home in the early hours of the morning and collapse into his bed, snoring loud enough to wake the people across the street. Then he'll sleep until the afternoon."

"Am I to understand by your tone that you're not overly fond of your…associate?"

Jothan shrugged. "Quinn's okay. But he does like his drink."

"And you're traveling with him through the Nephtali Pass into Otero?" Petro gave him a skeptical look, which he wasn't sure Jothan could see in the dark.

"Not too loud, please. Relations with Otero being what they are, it isn't the kind of thing we want to advertise."

"I certainly understand that," Petro responded. *"And now that we can talk, are you going to tell me what you're planning to do once you get to the kingdom of the barbarians?"*

"Quinn has a contact in place who will help us obtain a load of anodyte."

Petro double-checked his mindshield, unwilling to let Jothan sense his discomfort. Anodyte was an opiate, highly valued among physicians for use in surgery and prescribed for those suffering severe pain. But it was rare. Derived from a plant that grew only in extremely high altitudes, the drug was so difficult and expensive to make that many who tried ended with a spoiled crop and bankruptcy, or worse. From what he understood, the distillation process involved repeated washing of the plant's seeds in a series of chemicals, each more volatile than the last. Explosions were common. Toward the end one drop in excess of the required amount would ruin the entire batch.

He hated to ask the obvious question, fearful of the answer. "What is your part in this endeavor?"

"To make sure our northern business associates treat us fairly. I'm to watch for traps, both physical and fiscal."

Petro worked hard to keep his mental tone clear of the disappointment that stabbed at him. *"In other words, you're to spy upon the minds of your suppliers and make sure they don't intend to slaughter you and your partner after you've given them their money."*

"That's the basic idea."

"Not exactly a wholesome use of your Power."

Petro took a long pull from his mug. Jothan's one downfall from earliest childhood had been a desire for personal wealth. It stemmed, no doubt, from early memories of the extreme poverty of his family. In all the years they had spent together, Petro hadn't been successful in ridding him of the deep-seated need to accumulate riches. In his final trial, the masters had pronounced Jothan's integrity intact, but note of his greed had been taken. The one bruise upon an otherwise perfect apple.

It was a weakness of the Brotherhood, in Petro's estimation, that when training was finished, the new brothers were sent from the Hall with no further ties except whatever feelings of loyalty they had managed to pick up during their time there. Many times, he and others had argued that there should be a lasting connection—a sense of continuity for the remainder of a brother's lifetime. Was there a better incentive to noble behavior than having one's peers on hand periodically to examine one's actions? Or if not incentive, at least a deterrent to misbehavior. But since such a bond wasn't outlined in the ancient writings, the older masters would not consider the suggestion.

"I don't plan to make this a full-time occupation." Jothan's chair squeaked when he rocked back. "But you know I've always been fascinated with Otero. This is a chance to see it for myself."

Petro shook his head. "An unhealthy fascination with a dangerous people, and I can't imagine where you got it."

"Thaddeus' library, of course." Jothan laughed quietly. "The old man has books in there he doesn't realize. Some he'd probably burn if he found them."

"He did." Petro allowed himself a chuckle. "That's why he's undertaken this new index. A trainee was caught reading…let's just say questionable material."

"Must have been the drawings of Amahd."

Petro stopped rocking long enough to give his former student a surprised stare. "You know about that book?"

"Every boy who goes through the Hall knows that book. You mean you didn't see it when you were a trainee?"

Petro shook his head. "Must have surfaced after my training."

"What do you expect?" Jothan laughed. "Young boys sheltered away from the world with only a bunch of wrinkled old men to talk to. They're starved for the sight of a woman, and most of them don't remember anything except their mothers and sisters, which isn't exactly the best material for nighttime fantasies."

Petro drew himself up in the chair. "I take offense at being referred to as a wrinkled old man." But he grinned to take the sting out of his words.

They rocked for a moment. When Jothan spoke again caution filled his tone. "Will you tell me what you're thinking to take a girl as trainee?" He held up a hand in the dark to forestall a quick answer. "I trust your judgment, but have you considered the trouble you'll cause when you bring her into the Hall with all those boys and old men? And young men, too, which will cause the biggest problem."

With a sigh, Petro continued rocking. Jothan was right. He'd thought about it many times since leaving Arien's village. "Not to mention the ruckus the old masters will raise when we arrive."

"Even the young ones, I suspect, and any brothers in residence at the time." Jothan turned his head to hold Petro's gaze. "They may reject her."

Petro didn't look away. "You've felt her mind. You know how strong she is."

Jothan shrugged. "They'll say you should have stripped her Power and left her where you found her."

A distinct possibility. "Her Power is too advanced for that. More than any boy I've tested, including you."

"She's a lot older than I was when you tested me."

Petro set his jaw stubbornly. "She has as much potential."

"But she's a *girl.*" Jothan lowered his voice even further. "Does she have the other ability as well?"

The question was bound to arise, and would no doubt be voiced many times more when he reached the Hall. His conversation with Arien in the forest replayed itself in his mind. She not only heard thoughts, she *felt.*

Petro shifted in his seat. "I…believe so." Jothan opened his mouth, but Petro cut him off. "I can manage it. I'm certain of that."

"Hmmm." Jothan looked unconvinced. "They might strip her Power and send her back, have you thought of that?"

"I have," Petro acknowledged, "and I'm prepared to argue against it." He set his jaw. "Strenuously, if need be."

Jothan stared into the night sky for a long moment, sipping wine. When he spoke, it was with a quiet voice, and he did not look at Petro. "Do you really think she has as much potential as I did?"

"Jealous?"

The thought amused Petro, but Jothan shook his head.

"No. But you're right. I did feel strength in her, though I don't have much to compare her to. The only testing I've done is on boys half her age. If she does grow in Power, what will she do with it when she leaves the Hall as a grown woman?"

Now Petro laughed outright. "What do any of us do with it?"

Jothan refused to let the matter be laughed off. "We are men and trained to be level-headed. She'll be a woman, full of the natural whims and moods of a woman. I've had a little experience with women in the months since I left the Hall, and I've discovered that the old masters were right. They are irrational creatures." He held up a hand to forestall an argument.

"I'm fond of my sister-in-law, but the thought of her with Power is frightening."

Petro didn't bother to hide his smile. "In all your nineteen years, you've spent a half-year in the company of women, and you consider yourself an expert?"

Jothan grinned, shaking his head. "Any man who claims expertise about women is either a liar or a fool." He sobered. "But can this girl be trained to exercise the control necessary for one who holds so much Power? Can she be made to understand the responsibility?"

A valid question, and one Petro would soon have to answer before the Hall. The only women of Power mentioned in the writings of Devland had ended in disaster. For this reason, Devland and the early brothers recommended that future generations of the Brotherhood exclude women. A rather intolerant attitude, in Petro's opinion. He preferred to believe those documented accounts were due to a flaw in the training process rather than in the minds of the women themselves.

Still, Arien possessed the same enhanced level of empathy that had caused others of her gender to fail. Was he, a man, capable of teaching her to harness and control a Power he did not possess?

"I think she can." His poured as much certainty into his voice as he could.

Jothan stared at him for a long moment, then raised his mug in salute. "I hope you're right and that you have the opportunity to prove it."

"And I hope," Petro replied, ready to leave a subject that he preferred to think no more about at the moment, "that your venture enjoys success. And that you're not slaughtered while attempting to execute it."

Jothan snorted a laugh. "I'll drink to that."

Three

The morning crept up on Arien like a cat stalking a mouse. One moment she was deep in sleep, and the next she started to full wakefulness, confused by the bright rays of sunlight shining onto her bed.

Petro spoke to her from his room. *"I know the bed is comfortable, but you've got to get up."*

Arien shook her head to dislodge the fuzziness left over from sleep. She rubbed her eyes and yawned, her stomach rumbling. How could she be hungry so soon after last night's delicious supper? *"When is breakfast?"*

"An hour ago. You were so tired you didn't react to my attempts to rouse you, so I let you sleep. But I do want to leave soon."

"I'll hurry." She directed her voice to the wall that separated their sleeping quarters.

The trousers Petro bought yesterday hugged her legs in a

way no skirt ever had. Would she ever get used to the odd feeling? She put the rest of her belongings in the center of her travel blanket and secured it in her bag in readiness for their departure.

The boots had been a fraction too tight when she first tried them on, but Petro used his Power to stretch them to a perfect fit right on her feet. Arien grinned as she slipped them on. The more she saw of these Powers, the more excited she became to learn.

After a quick breakfast of fresh bread and hot, creamy grain sweetened with honey, they took their leave of the boarding house. Kalinda stood on the front porch to see them off, smiling brightly and waving as they retreated down the dusty path.

The shops were open, and tables with trade goods lined both sides of Arnath's main street. Petro led her to a stable on the southern edge of town where they picked up the horse that would carry them to the Hall of the Brotherhood.

He inspected the animal, which fixed mournful eyes on Arien over his head. An old harness hung loosely around its head, the leather worn and cracked. In place of a saddle, a thick rug had been thrown across its back. As Petro ran his hand along the beast's neck and side, the stable owner leaned against the side of the stall, chewing on a piece of straw.

"The poor beast is old," Petro told her. *"A work horse who can no longer pull the plow, if I'm any judge. We'll be lucky if it doesn't die on the way."*

Arien started to ask him why he was buying the animal if it was in such bad shape. She glanced around the nearly empty stable. There didn't appear to be much choice.

He straightened from his inspection of the horse's hoofs and extended a hand for her bag. This he fastened, along with his own, to a leather strap which he belted around the horse's middle. The animal kept its woeful eyes fastened on Arien during the procedure.

Did horses have minds like people? Arien closed her eyes and Perceived. Petro's shield shimmered in her mindsense, the stable owner's more chaotic presence nearby. Like Quinn's at supper, his was not shielded. Bright specks of thought flew here and there, whirling around a glowing center. Mindful of last night's reprimand, she avoided examining any of those thoughts too closely.

Though it took an effort that caused a pinprick of pain deep in her head, she found the horse. Its light shone dully, more reddish than white, and with much less activity. Not nearly as vibrant as either of the men's, but still distinguishable as a presence if she looked closely enough.

"Are you ready, Arien?"

She had never ridden a horse, or even a donkey, though there had been several in the village. With a nervous nod, she watched Petro heft himself onto the animal's back. The stable owner lifted her so she could throw her leg across and clutch Petro around the middle. His legs squeezed, and the animal moved. Muscles beneath her bunched and loosened as it walked. Panic seized her. The ground looked far away. If she fell, she'd break a bone for sure. She tightened her grip on Petro's waist.

They headed south, following a path that ran alongside the forest. When they topped a hill, Arien turned to get one last look at Arnath. Then they descended the other side, and the town was lost from sight.

After a half-day's journey, she decided riding wasn't nearly as bad as she feared. It was certainly preferable to endless walking on sore feet. Even wearing boys' trousers wasn't so bad. Riding in her dress with her legs a-straddle would have been indecorous at best and probably painful. Her only complaints were a numb backside and boredom.

Lazy, so named in recognition of his personality, moved at a slow but even pace. His flank muscles bunched and rippled with each step. Petro didn't push the animal to a faster pace out of fear that it might collapse from the effort.

"Who is the princess marrying?"

At last she was free to ask all the questions she wished, though it was embarrassing to admit ignorance about so many things.

"Prince Millard, the son and heir of King Mendel of Hamlin. Did you get no news in that village of yours?"

"Not much," Arien admitted. "I have heard of Prince Thaine, but I didn't know there was a princess until yesterday. And I've never heard of King Mendel. Where is Hamlin?"

Petro half-turned on the horse's back to stare at her in disbelief. "Have you had no formal schooling at all?"

"Not much." She ducked her head. "I do know how to write all the letters and I can do sums if they're not too hard. I can sew and cook and even do some fancy stitchery. I can cure skins to leather, and spin wool, and—"

"Yes, I see. You've been taught the skills you need to live in that village for the rest of your life." He heaved a sigh and faced forward. "That's as it should be, I suppose, but we'll have a lot to do before you're ready to join the rest of the trainees for classes."

He grew silent, and Arien prodded him. "About Prince Millard?"

"Ah, yes. He is the son of King Mendel of Hamlin. If you are to understand the significance of this match, you need to learn a little history."

He kicked his heels into Lazy's side, prodding the horse to resume a reasonable pace, then settled himself more comfortably on the rug. Arien shifted her weight as well, trying to ease the numbness in her rear.

"In Olney Devland's time—"

"Who?"

A soft sigh escaped his lips. "The founder of the Brotherhood. You'll learn a lot about him in the coming years. As I said, in his time only one kingdom lay south of the Jalapa Mountain Range. It was called Bayland and stretched from the Western Ocean all the way to the Fallman Sea in the east. We refer to it now simply as the kingdom. The king's name was Jasper, of the house Valerien.

"Jasper had twin sons and was unable to choose an heir between them. In what is now considered a mistake of unheard-of proportions, he divided his kingdom in half, with the boundary being the Lusanne River, and set each of his sons as overseer to half. He hoped they would gain experience in ruling, and that one would rise to prominence so that the decision would be made for him."

It sounded like a logical solution. "Why was that so terrible?"

"Because King Jasper died unexpectedly. He should have foreseen the possibility. With no clear instructions as to an heir, each brother declared himself king. They argued, and when kings fight, kingdoms fight. That is how Bayland split, and Hamlin and Creighton came to be. And that is why they are called the Twin Kingdoms."

"We aren't at war now." At least she didn't think so.

"The two eventually reached an uneasy truce, but relations between Hamlin and Creighton have never been good. That's why this marriage between Princess Sarana of Creighton and Prince Millard of Hamlin is so important. This is the first real attempt at a reconnection between the kingdoms since the split."

Arien fell silent. What must the princess be thinking now, as she prepared to leave her home and live the rest of her life among strangers? She must be very frightened.

A laugh burst from her lips. Arien was doing exactly the same thing. She wasn't frightened.

Well, not much.

"I have another question. Does the Brotherhood make medicine?"

That clearly surprised him. He turned to reveal an arched eyebrow. "Not the Brotherhood, no, but that is an occupation sometimes practiced by our members after their training is complete. Why do you ask?"

"Kalinda had an ointment for my feet, and said she'd gotten it from a mind-magic man. She said the medicine must have magic in it, because it worked so well."

Petro's back rumbled with a laugh. "Most people think so. We have no magic, but they don't believe us. Some have used their skills in the making of medicines. When two ingredients are blended with Power, they stay blended. Also, we can Perceive what problems can be cured by which mixtures."

"If you can Perceive sicknesses, why can't you just heal people?"

"Blending ingredients is one thing. Bodies are far more complex, and not intended to be toyed with by human Powers. Even if those Powers are divinely bestowed."

Arien sagged against his back. "I have so much to learn."

Petro reached back to pat her trouser-covered leg. "That's why the trainee period lasts so long. You have plenty of time to learn everything you need to know."

Jothan's comment during last night's supper returned to her. "Am I older than most trainees?"

Lazy walked a dozen paces before he answered. "Ye—es."

She sensed so much hesitation in him that her stomach tensed. "How much older?"

"We like to recruit trainees who are around five or six."

"I'm twelve." She did a quick calculation on her fingers. "That means I'm six years older than the others?"

"Only the newcomers. There are several trainees at the Hall older than you. Most don't pass their final test until they are twenty, some even older. Don't worry. It will all work out."

Twenty years? If trainees entered the Brotherhood at six and left when they were twenty, that meant Arien would be… she didn't have enough fingers and toes. Quite old, anyway.

A chuckle rumbled in Petro's chest, and she felt it through his back.

"Each trainee moves at his own pace. I have no doubt you'll complete the training before you're ready for the grave, my dear."

The Hall of the Brotherhood towered four levels high, by far the tallest and most intimidating building Arien had ever seen. The stones forming the bottom story had long ago darkened from exposure. In an odd-looking arrangement of layers, three more floors had been added after the initial building, these of weathered wood. Windows yawned open on each floor, none with glass but all with wooden shutters. From her vantage point the top floor looked slightly off-kilter, much like the uneven block towers the younglings back home used to make. On the ground floor, double doors opened in the center to create an entrance large enough that Lazy and two of his brothers could have gone through side by side

Into the stone above the entrance the symbol of the Brotherhood had been carved. An encircled triangle. Petro wore a smaller replica on a chain around his neck. The first day of their journey he had described how the three sides of the triangle signified the three types of Power—Perception, Command, and Movement—and the circle represented a human mind.

Arien eyed the gigantic doorway. What would she find on the other side? Terrible mind-wizards who would refuse to accept an orphaned girl too old to join their ranks? Silent teachers who pried into their trainees' thoughts and stared with hard, glittering eyes?

When the door opened, she almost laughed in relief. A wizened old man hobbled through, leaning heavily on a cane almost as crooked as his back.

"Petro, my friend." Watery eyes sparkled with joy. "You've returned. I Perceived you a few moments ago on the road, and your new trainee as well."

He turned to inspect Arien, still seated on Lazy, and started visibly. He came closer, squinting up at her, and she gave him a hesitant smile. His mind approached hers, and she closed her eyes to Perceive him in return. A strong, shining aura towered before her. Surprised, she opened her eyes to look again at the shriveled figure.

"*Don't judge by appearances, missy. The mind and body aren't dependent on each other for strength. A pity more don't understand that.*"

Petro slid off the horse and embraced him with more strength than Arien would have dared.

"Good to see you so fit, Thaddeus. Arien, this is my own master, the man who trained me in the ways of Power." His lips curled into a grin for Thaddeus. "And what do you think of my new trainee?"

The old man shook his head. "You were a trouble-maker as a trainee, Petro, and you've not changed." His chuckle held a touch of mischief. "I can't wait for Parnell to meet her."

Something in the tone sent a ripple of discomfort to Arien's stomach. What did he mean, a troublemaker? And who was Parnell?

Petro laughed, and clapped Thaddeus on the back. "I hope you saved some dinner. I'll need strength to face the ordeal."

Ordeal? Her discomfort deepened.

Thaddeus shouted for someone to come and take the horse, and several boys appeared from inside the Hall. As Petro lifted Arien off Lazy's back, she found herself the object of wide-eyed stares. She barely had time to notice that all the boys were younger than she by several years before she was pulled into the Hall by her master's strong hand.

The Hall's interior was not as impressive as its outside. Arien followed the men through a series of sparsely furnished rooms, none of which she had time to examine properly. Bare stone walls echoed their footsteps, and she self-consciously lightened her step. She followed Petro into a huge refectory, only half-listening to Master Thaddeus describe his findings as he re-catalogued his library. Half a dozen long tables filled the room, each with a row of stools tucked neatly beneath them. A gigantic map spread nearly the length of one wall. She had never seen a map so large and craned her neck to inspect it as she was ushered past. A river ran top-to-bottom, dividing the land in two. This was a map of the Twin Kingdoms.

Petro and Thaddeus led her through a door in the opposite wall, and she found herself at last entering a room that looked familiar. The kitchen was three times bigger than Kalinda's in Arnath, but size was the only difference. A giant roasting pit took up nearly one whole wall, the embers beneath two of the four cooking arms little more than smoldering ash. Suspended from the ceiling were pots and pans, bags of onions and other vegetables, giant slabs of cured meat. A long worktable ran the length of the room.

A man sat at the table, large and muscular, but with a huge belly that told Arien he enjoyed eating, and often. He wore his hair slicked back away from his forehead and gathered into a clasp. When he recognized Petro his face broke into a smile.

He stood, arms thrown wide for an embrace, and then caught sight of Arien. The smile faded.

"What the blooming hell have you done?"

Though he spoke to Petro, his gaze remained on Arien, and again she detected the feather-light touch of Perception on her mind. This time she did not attempt to Perceive him. This man was too big and rough, and her knees began to tremble so that she feared they might not hold her up.

Seeming completely at ease, Petro responded with a smile. "Brother Bayard, let me present my new trainee, Arien. I found her in an orphanage, so she has no surname."

The mental touch withdrew, and Brother Bayard swung around to Petro. "Are you crazy, man? She's a girl."

"I realize that," Petro said dryly. "But Perceive her. You'll sense the Power in her."

The man waved a huge, red hand in dismissal. "What does it matter how much Power she has? Girls can't be trainees."

Arien glanced sharply at Petro. No girl trainees? Why hadn't he told her about this rule?

Petro's smile did not waver, but his lips tightened. "I will discuss this once only. For now, my trainee and I are hungry."

Brother Bayard served them bowls of thick stew without speaking, though disapproval lay like a dark cloud around him. After one glance at his tight-lipped face, she was afraid to look again. She took her bowl and a cup of cold milk without a word and followed Petro to the refectory, her appetite lost amid a jumble of knots in her belly.

"What did he mean about girls not being allowed?"

Petro sat on a stool and began to eat. *"There are no official rules forbidding females. But it has been the experience of the Brotherhood that most women are unsuited to a lifestyle of controlled Power."*

"Unsuited?" She shifted on the hard seat. *"How so?"*

Petro kept his eyes directed forward as he chewed, not looking at her. *"There have only been two in the last seventy-five years, and they both went insane."*

Her spoon clattered onto the table's surface. "Insane?" The word echoed in the huge room. "What do you mean?"

"Just that. One committed suicide during her training.

The other snuck away in the night. She was found weeks later barricaded in a primitive lean-to deep in the forest. She refused to return, refused to accept help, and eventually starved to death."

Horror crept over Arien, leaving a trail of gooseflesh in its wake. "But why? What did the Brotherhood do to them?"

He looked offended. *"Nothing but try to teach them to control their Power."*

A desert had invaded her mouth, and she snatched up her cup to gulp milk.

Petro patted her shoulder, his smile confident. *"The Brotherhood has learned a great deal in the seventy or so years since then. You'll be fine."*

The thought carried such confidence that some of the tension seeped out of her muscles. She retrieved her spoon and scooped a morsel from her bowl.

"There's one other thing we probably should have discussed before now." Hesitation drenched his thought.

"*Something bad?"*

"Not necessarily." He continued to chew, his outward expression impassive. "*The two female trainees possessed an ability not common among males. They were both empaths."*

The unfamiliar word rolled around in her mind. *"What is that?"*

"They could feel emotions as well as thoughts."

She twisted sideways to stare at him. She'd always been sensitive to the emotions of others, sometimes uncomfortably so. Was that what drove those other girls insane? The milk curdled in her stomach.

"My personal opinion is the girls were unable to control the ability of feeling the emotions of so many others."

Arien nodded slowly. Understandable. At times the force of so many feelings back home had been hard to take, especially during storms when the children were terrified. Though Arien herself wasn't afraid, the combination of all those fears sometimes made her *think* she was.

"I...think I've learned to handle them. I can feel others' feelings when I want to, but I can ignore them. Well, most of the time. That's why I want to build a strong mindshield."

His eyebrows arched. *"If that's the case, the argument against accepting you into the Brotherhood loses impact. The problem lies in the fact that I, as a man, do not have that ability, and therefore can't train you in its use."* A smile twitched at the corner of his mouth. *"It's actually something I'm hoping we'll be able to explore together."*

He returned to his meal. The idea that she possessed a talent her master didn't was more alarming than soothing. What if he were wrong, and she went insane here?

Maybe she shouldn't stay. There was still time to change her mind. She'd taken no vows, made no commitments except to Petro. Would he hold her to a promise made without understanding the risks?

Her gaze strayed to the far wall and the map hanging there. The Kingdom of Creighton was huge, much bigger than she realized. Since leaving home she'd seen only a tiny part of it. Could she return to one isolated corner? Would she be happy there, married and raising children who also never knew anything of the world beyond the borders of their tiny village?

A family. Longing filled her at the thought of a house full of her own babes. Yes, she would be happy raising children. But families were not confined to mountain villages. Maybe if she returned to Arnath, Kalinda would give her work and a place to live until she met someone who wanted to marry her.

But if she did that, she would never learn to control the Power she possessed.

If I stay, will I end up like those two women? Crazy enough to kill myself?

Petro set down his spoon and turned to look at her. "If I thought there was the slightest chance of you losing your mind, I would have left you where I found you. I Perceive strength in you, more than enough to control the Power you've been given. Also, I have faith in my own ability to train you."

Before she could answer, Thaddeus and four others entered the eating room. Long black robes billowed around them. They stopped just inside the doorway to stare at her. Of the five, only Thaddeus smiled.

Petro slid his bowl across the table. "*Remain calm and let me talk."*

"I didn't believe it." The sternest looking of the four stared at Arien as though she were a puppy who'd made an unforgivable mess on the floor.

"Parnell." Petro wiped his lips on a square of cloth and tossed it on top of his bowl. "I see news of my new trainee has spread. What do you think of her?"

In answer, Parnell's mouth became a hard slash. The five approached. Should she rise so that they did not tower over her? But Petro did not move, so she remained seated. The men came to a halt on the other side of the table and glared down at her. Disapproval rolled off of them like heat from a fierce fire. Disapproval, and also a hint of … humor? She glanced at Master Thaddeus, whose eyes twinkled.

A severe-faced man folded his arms across his chest. "You are a disgrace to your robes, Petro. What do you mean by this?"

Petro propped his elbows on the table. How he could remain calm in the face of such admonishment? "I mean to train this girl to use her divinely-bestowed Powers."

The touch of several minds pressing against hers felt like a distant tickle. Frantic thoughts raced in her mind. *What do I think about? How do I make them like me?* Her hands beneath the table trembled so violently she squeezed them between her knees to steady them.

The tickling ceased, but one presence lingered.

"There is nothing you can think to affect these men. Trust your master. He can handle them."

Thaddeus winked at Arien, and the kindness in the gesture loosened some of the knots in her stomach. At least one master wasn't against her.

"You should have stripped her and left her where she was," said a slender man with patches of brown speckled throughout his grey hair.

Petro's expression did not change. "You've Perceived her, Sinclare. She's too old to strip without damaging. Besides, she's done nothing wrong with her Powers."

"That does not matter, and you know it," snapped the man next to him, an angry flush coloring his face. "Stripping isn't just for the misuse of Power."

"I know, Dorian, and I've always argued against it. It should be a last resort, when all other attempts have failed."

Stripping? What were they talking about? She didn't dare voice the question, or any question.

"Let us not begin a philosophical discussion." Parnell cast a glare toward Dorian. "Stick to the matter at hand. The only females ever accepted have failed."

"Besides," said the fifth master, who had been silent until now, "she's too old. Look at her, she's almost a woman."

Thaddeus turned a reproving look on him. "Age is not a requirement, Avram. You know that. Nowhere in Devland's writings is age specified."

"Don't quote the writings to me, old man." Avram glared at Thaddeus. "I know what they say."

Parnell interrupted. "And they say that females are not to be trusted with Power. It's been proven time and again."

"Weaklings, all of them." Petro's shout startled her, and she jumped. "You feel the strength in her. She has more potential than any trainee we've seen in years."

"Potential doesn't mean a thing," snapped Dorian. "Can she learn the discipline required? And exercise it?"

Petro straightened his spine and held the man's eye. "I believe she can."

Dorian's eyes narrowed. "And what of the … emotional aspect?"

"Exactly." Avram turned to the others. "We can't take the chance. I say we strip her now and send her home."

Whatever that meant, terror stabbed her at the threat she detected in the man's mental tone.

Petro rose, and Arien hurried to stand beside him. He towered above her like a giant, his face flushed and his eyes flashing. The transformation from calm to furious was swift and not a little intimidating. Fury rolled off him like a blast from a furnace.

"I will not permit you to strip my trainee." The glare he settled on Avram would have sent Arien scurrying into hiding. "I will block any attempt. You'll have to destroy my mind to get to her." The words surprised all of them, even Thaddeus, whose eyes went round. “If the Brotherhood will not approve my choice, I will take the girl away and train her without the aid of the Hall.”

“But— but— you can't!” Judging by Master Dorian's shocked expression, the threat must be a serious one. The others stared at Petro with varying levels of disbelief. Parnell’s cheeks flushed such a deep red that Arien feared he would choke with rage.

Master Sinclare’s chest inflated as he drew in a deep breath. He lifted his hands, palms out, and spoke in a placating tone that still held the edge of emotion. “Be reasonable, Petro. You can't split from the Brotherhood. What about your oath?”

“What about yours?” he shot back. “When I swore to support the Brotherhood, the Brotherhood swore to support me in return.” He draped an arm across Arien’s shoulders, his touch communicating comfort. Encouraged, she straightened. “Rest assured, Masters, that I intend to train this girl. I will do it with or without your help.”

The announcement was met with much sputtering, but Petro returned their scandalized looks with an unbending stubbornness that reminded Arien of little Blaine back home.

Master Parnell’s hands fisted. “It must be put to a vote.”

Petro shrugged. “I expected that.”

Without further arguments the four marched out of the refectory, leaving Thaddeus behind.

The old man stared after them, and then turned a searching gaze on Petro. “Do you mean it?”

“I do.” His shoulders slumped. “I don’t want to, but I will leave the Hall if they force my hand.”

Thaddeus shook his head slowly. “Let's hope it won't come to that.”

Petro’s removed his arm from Arien’s shoulders. “We’ve had a long day on the trail. Will you show Arien to a room? At least one of us should get some sleep tonight.”

The mention of sleep leeched the last of Arien’s strength, and she wavered on her feet. What she wouldn’t give to return to Arnath and crawl beneath the quilt on the little bed in her room at Kalinda’s inn.

“Only one of us?” She looked up at Petro.

He rubbed his eyes with a thumb and forefinger and gave way to a yawn. "The Masters will meet after the trainees have gone to bed. I don't look for it to end before dawn. Between now and then I have some persuading to do. You sleep. I'll wake you when the meeting's done."

Hours later, though still well before dawn, Arien woke with tears on her cheeks. The dream had been so real, so overwhelming, that her heart ached with a loneliness that threatened to shatter her. Sobs racked her body, wrenched from deep within. She rolled onto her side and hugged her knees close to her chest.

No. Wait. This anguish wasn't hers.

She forced sleep from her mind so she could think clearly. The heartache that invaded her dreams came from someone else, someone close by. Closing her eyes, she reached out to locate the source.

There. A child, sobbing in his bed. In the midst of his intense loneliness she sensed a longing. He missed the warm, comforting arms of his mother, was desperate for the sound of her voice singing him to sleep.

He wasn't alone. She sensed a second presence. Stretching her perception, she encountered a mindshield similar to Master Petro's. A member of the Brotherhood, then. Though his thoughts remained hidden, she felt sympathy radiating from him as he tried to comfort the boy.

She could help. Hadn't Mora always said she had a way with the little ones? When Blaine awoke frightened, Arien soothed him. When Sammy was angry, she calmed him. And no one could settle a restless orphan like Arien.

She did so now. A wave of comfort washed toward the crying child, a sense of well-being, of belonging. Almost instantly the sobs ceased. The intense homesickness faded, and the boy relaxed. Within minutes, he slept.

Satisfied, Arien rolled over and did the same.

"Did you see that?" Parnell's face flushed purple, his eyes bulging so that Petro feared he might burst a vessel.

They sat in the main meeting room, the twelve Masters in residence and six brothers who happened to be in the Hall at the moment. Parnell had claimed the chair at the head of the long wooden table, though he had yet to occupy it. Instead, he stood with his fists planted on the table and his body thrust forward in Petro's direction.

Petro maintained a calm exterior, though his thoughts roiled within the privacy of his mindshield. If he'd any doubt Arien possessed the empathic abilities mentioned in the writings of Devland, the scene they'd just watched destroyed them.

"I saw it," he replied calmly while inspecting a fingernail. "We all did."

The meeting had progressed as Petro expected, with Parnell leading the argument against him taking on a female trainee, and Petro displaying his most stubborn side. Most of the others sat silently on the sidelines, waiting to see the outcome between a clash of two of the Brotherhood's most determined Masters.

Then Master Shellie had jumped up from his chair and proclaimed that he needed to tend to his trainee. The boy was new, having only arrived at the Hall a few days before, and was overcome with homesickness. It happened fairly often among the new trainees, especially the youngest ones. But what a perfect opportunity to see how Arien would react to the flood of emotions from an unhappy child. Petro himself suggested that Master Shellie take the boy to the bedchamber nearest Arien's. He had rushed off to comfort the sobbing child while the rest of the Brotherhood sat back to Perceive Arien's reaction.

"She Commanded an emotion to that boy." Parnell sputtered, his fists pounding on the table. "She has the ability we're warned against in the writings. There can be no doubt."

Petro glanced at the faces around the room. Sinclare, one of the senior Masters, refused to meet his gaze, but he wore a stubborn expression similar to Parnell's, as did several others. Of the younger brothers, only one appeared to have had a negative reaction to the scene they'd just witnessed by Perceiving the activity in the rooms above them.

"She comforted the child." Petro acknowledged the comment with a slight nod. "Would anyone here call that a negative emotion?"

Around the table, everyone remained silent.

"Negative or positive, it doesn't matter." Parnell's glare was nearly as harsh as his voice. "This time she acted benignly. But what about the next time? With an ability like that she could be the ruin of us all."

"She can learn to control it," Petro insisted. "I know I can teach her."

"And if you fail?"

Petro hardened his voice. "Then I suggest we all learn how to strengthen our mindshields, because sooner or later someone with empathic power *will* surface." He rose, planted his fists on the table and leaned forward. "What better chance will we have to learn than having a trainee of our own with the ability?"

A few of them looked thoughtful, but not nearly a majority. Petro stifled a sigh. This was going to be a long night.

Arien woke to a tap at the door and a light mental touch. As she struggled to rouse herself, Petro stepped into the room and perched on the foot of her cot.

"Is it over?" she whispered, mindful of the deep silence in the Hall.

He nodded. "You've been accepted as my trainee."

"I have?" She was too sleepy to feel the joy she should at the news. "They want me?"

His lips settled into a tired smile. "Let's just say not all of them don't want you. But we won't be living here in the Hall. I will conduct your training elsewhere."

She shook her head, her brain too foggy to understand. Wasn't that what he'd threatened to do if they *didn't* accept her?

"We're leaving the Brotherhood?"

“No, only the Hall. The Brotherhood lands include several cabins, out of mental reach but still an easy walk to the Hall. We will live in one of them and come here when your training requires it. That decision was made to ensure your safety.”

So. She was to be an outcast, isolated from the other trainees. If her mind were clearer, she might be more upset. At the moment, all she felt was relief that she wasn’t being stripped—whatever that meant—and sent home.

But if she was to be exiled, so was Master Petro. “Do you mind?”

She peered at his face, but the only light in the room came from a wall sconce in the hallway, and his eyes were hidden in shadows.

“Not so much.” He heaved a loud sigh and stood. “The worst part is that I’ll sorely miss Brother Bayard's cooking.”

Part Two

Four

Seven Years Later

Jothan sat at a rickety table with a half-full mug of wine in the Oteran town of Eshtaol, his eyes and mind scanning the crowded marketplace. Illan was late, an unusual occurrence for one so meticulous about exchanges. In the seven years he and Quinn had been doing business with the man, only one time had an exchange gone awry, and it started with Illan being late.

Add to that the uneasy feelings he sensed in the townspeople since his arrival that morning, and the rumors of the impending arrival of an Oteran lord. Combined, they were enough to make Jothan extra cautious, his mind doubly busy as he searched the surface thoughts of those in the street.

Perception at this level was tiring, and he hid a yawn behind his mug. All those people, each with a dozen thoughts bouncing back and forth, and none of them very enlightening. Worry over food, over coin, over a spouse's fidelity. The same theme repeated mind to mind in this poor section of town, wearying beyond belief.

A memory from his trainee days surfaced. Petro always stressed that listening to the thoughts of others was wrong. How long ago had Jothan stopped feeling guilty about spying?

Never, really. Guilt still stabbed at him when he inadvertently overheard highly private thoughts which had nothing to do with him and were none of his business.

And yet, his ability had saved his hide and Quinn’s on more than one occasion. Scanning the surface thoughts of those in a crowd had once pinpointed a thief and saved a struggling merchant from the loss of his business. The merchant had never known the source of the warning, only that the thief appeared at exactly the time the note indicated and attempted to pocket the exact items listed.

Was it wrong to use his Power to help people? Wasn’t that what Olney Devland intended all those years ago when he established the Brotherhood?

Of course, Jothan and Quinn had profited by his Power as well. He shifted in his chair. When he’d first partnered with Quinn, Jothan had used his abilities to get the most from his anodyte bargaining. It was easy to peer into a man’s thoughts and know exactly how much dickering he would engage in before the sale was lost. But after the first year, he’d flatly refused to use his Power in that manner. It left him feeling dirty and low. It was one thing to use Power to protect yourself and your partner, another completely to get the best of a customer.

Even so, Quinn and Jothan had done well during the seven years of their partnership.

His thoughts turned to his own prosperity. Anodyte had become extremely popular among medical practitioners in Creighton, so popular that Illan, their Oteran supplier, was hard-pressed to manufacture enough to meet their demand. The opiate was still hard to get and that allowed Jothan and Quinn to keep their prices high.

Quinn. Jothan turned his head to glance at the window of

the inn behind him. He couldn't see Quinn through the closed shutters but knew that he was inside talking to the innkeeper. When Illan arrived, the three of them would withdraw to Quinn's room to conduct their business.

A commotion down the street drew Jothan's attention. He straightened in the chair, straining to see over the heads of the crowd. A small troop of armor-clad men were making their way through the street, elbowing the townspeople roughly out of their way.

Uh oh.

He'd been doing business in Eshtaol for a number of years, and the locals assumed him to be city dweller who visited occasionally. But he couldn't prove it, and any brush with Oteran soldiers was sure to be disastrous. He considered going inside the inn, but decided he'd only draw attention to himself by moving. The smartest course was to remain where he was.

In the next moment Jothan knew luck had deserted him. The soldiers approached the inn, their leader eyeing him alone among the six or eight customers seated at tables in the front courtyard.

Yikers! They're after me.

As they approached, Jothan sent his mind toward Quinn watching from a crack in the shuttered windows. The man's surface thoughts were easy to hear. His primary concern was the money hidden in Jothan's legging.

"You there!"

Jothan looked up from his mug. He did not attempt to stand, to move at all, or even to set the mug down.

"Me?" Thankfully his voice didn't crack.

The soldiers crowded around his table and the other patrons edged quietly away. The leader looked down at him through small eyes. "Yeah, you. You here to meet a man named Illan?"

This seemed like an excellent time to ignore the prohibition against Perceiving others' thoughts. Jothan scanned the man's mind. They knew who he was, and his business here. He also saw that Illan was dead, and that they had been sent to take Jothan to their lord. The soldier did not name the lord in his mind, but Jothan sensed a great deal of fear associated with thoughts of the man.

Better not resist.

"I am."

"There's someone who wants to talk to you." The gruff voice left no room for argument. "You're to come with us."

None of the soldiers had drawn their swords, though the leader's hand rested lightly on the hilt of his. Jothan Perceived that he would not hesitate to use it.

"Of course." He rose and fished in his pocket for a few coins, which he tossed on the table, then turned to his escort. "When you're ready."

They headed down the street, Jothan flanked on all sides. These men did not wear the colors of the Oteran king. They were privately hired fighting men, with the symbol of an Oteran House emblazoned on the left shoulder of their armor. The billowing red flag with a white stripe through a black emblem was unfamiliar. Even after seven years of frequent trips into Otero, Jothan did not know all the names of the Oteran Houses, nor their family crests. Not many of those noble families kept estates near tiny Eshtaol. They preferred Kadesh, the country's capital and the home of the king. Only very wealthy Houses kept a private guard.

The soldiers led Jothan through the town's streets, while people scurried to get out of their way. They stopped before a large stone inn on the prosperous northern edge of town. He'd passed the inn many times but had never stayed there. They stepped into a hallway brightly lit from the early-afternoon sun, but he was not given time to admire the furnishings. His escort led him through the main common room and into a smaller meeting room. There he encountered three more guards in identical armor to his escort, and one unarmed man seated in a comfortable chair near the fireplace.

"Lord Lucian," announced the leader of Jothan's guard, "this is him."

The man was young, even younger than Jothan himself. Gold flashed on his fingers, and a silky shirt billowed around his slender frame. His chiseled features wore a condescending expression of arrogance. Jothan took an instant dislike to him.

While he smiled a greeting, Jothan Perceived. The smile

nearly fell off his face.

Lord Lucian possessed a natural mindshield.

He'd learned of them during his training with Master Petro and had even encountered a few over the years. When a man gifted with Power went undiscovered, the mind often constructed a natural shield instinctively as a protective measure. In such cases, untrained Power often faded with disuse, but the mental barrier lasted a lifetime.

Never had Jothan seen a mindshield like this one. Its surface was thick and scarred, not smooth like `those trained in the Brotherhood. It had obviously been constructed by one possessed of at least a rudimentary untrained Power.

"Ah, my guest has arrived." Lord Lucian extended his hands in the Oteran gesture of greeting, his lips carved into a chilly smile. "Illan's partner, Jothan Kearney from Creighton."

Jothan took the hands in his own and received a squeeze from icy fingers. The words proved that Illan had been tortured before his death. He would never have betrayed Jothan's name or the fact that he was a foreigner otherwise.

"I'm afraid you have me at a disadvantage, my lord." He gestured at his dusty travel garments, which he'd not changed since arriving through the Nephtali Pass. "Illan did not mention a change in our plans, so I wasn't expecting to meet a member of an Oteran House."

Lord Lucian waved one of those cold hands in dismissal. "No need to dress for your meeting with Illan, and therefore no need to dress for me. Please, sit down. Orran, send for the wine. We have business to conduct, and I prefer to do it with a wet throat."

Jothan sat in the chair opposite Lucian's. "Business? I hope Illan is not ill."

The chilly smile deepened. "Illan is no longer in the anodyte business. As of this morning he has sold out."

"Sold out?" Jothan kept his face polite, but he silently cursed his inability to hear this man's thoughts. He attempted to probe the mindshield, but it was too sturdy to penetrate.

"Yes. To me, in fact. And the sale included his partnership with you as well."

Jothan was saved from replying, for at that moment the wine arrived. A serving woman, her eyes downcast, offered them each a glass. Fear emanated from her, obvious even without Perceiving her mind. Her hands trembled so violently he feared the wine might slosh over the side. Lord Lucian didn't seem the sort to treat servants kindly.

When she left, the guards withdrew as well, leaving them alone.

Lucian sipped from his glass. "I am constantly surprised at the quality of the wine in these little backwards towns. Living in Kadesh, one tends to think that is the only place of culture in the world."

Jothan sipped but tasted nothing. He was far too busy trying to stay alert.

Lucian set his glass on the table beside his chair. "As I was saying, since Illan is no longer manufacturing anodyte, you and I have become partners. I have acquired his business and am prepared to continue to supply your needs."

Jothan cleared his throat. "Excuse me, my lord, for not knowing more Oteran law than I do, but I am surprised that a member of an Oteran House would do business with someone from Creighton. Isn't such commerce forbidden by your king?"

"Oh no," Lucian assured him. "King Kuriel doesn't mind an Oteran making a little profit from Creighton. In fact, he is happy to have the commerce, even if it is beneath the blanket, so to speak. I myself have heard the king mention his desire for closer relations with the Twin Kingdoms south of our border."

Jothan doubted that but tucked it into a corner of his mind to think about later. If he was fortunate enough to have a *later*. "I am happy to hear that."

"Yes, I suspect you are. We are all the same, beneath our kingdom loyalties. Take anodyte, for instance. Our King Kuriel enjoys it, and I've heard your Prince Thaine does as well. Do you partake?"

Though he knew that the drug had found an audience among the wealthy who procured it for other than medicinal purposes, Jothan didn't condone such usage. To fog one's mind with opiates was, in his opinion, a fool's pursuit. He shook his head. "Never have."

"Pity. You really should, you know. It's quite enjoyable." Lord Lucian smiled, an expression Jothan was beginning to dislike rather intensely. "But enough chatter. Shall we get down to business? I have Illan's latest batch of anodyte here, ready for exchange. But you must understand that my costs are significantly higher than Illan's."

"Oh?" No surprise there. Any fool could see that coming.

"Of course. My family's nearest manor house is a two-day journey west of here, and naturally I cannot travel this way alone. I must hire servants and guards and the like. Plus, I will be employing a manager for the plant, since I cannot be away from Kadesh for extended periods of time. All this means that the prices will necessarily increase."

Jothan took another sip from his goblet to hide his frown. "How much?"

"Your arrangement with Illan was for five units?" Jothan nodded. "The price for that quantity is twenty-five gold coins."

"Twenty-five." Jothan controlled his voice with an effort. "Illan charged less than half that, two golds for each unit."

Lord Lucian's chilly smile actually warmed, as if he was enjoying the exchange. "Ah, but my costs, as I explained, are significantly higher. Plus, due to my connections with other Oteran Houses, my market is much wider than Illan's. By tomorrow I could sell all Illan's stock to my friends alone, and they'd think they'd gotten a bargain."

Not to mention the fact that Lord Lucian's friends were using the drug for recreational purposes. They would pay more than Skelly's customers, who wanted it for medical reasons.

"But twenty-five." Jothan raked his fingers through his hair. "I don't have that much. I came prepared to pay ten."

Lord Lucian shrugged. "In that case you may have two units."

"But I have demand for five, plus more. How can I go back and tell my customers I can't deliver?"

"That, Jothan Kearney, is your concern. My position is

simple. Next time, come prepared to pay my price." A hard glint appeared in the man's green eyes, and any further arguments died on Jothan's tongue unsaid. "Do we have a deal for two units?"

Inwardly fuming, Jothan schooled all emotion from his expression. He nodded, then swallowed several large gulps of wine as Lord Lucian called into the hallway. "Bring it."

One of the soldiers returned with a leather pack, which he handed to his lord. Lucian pulled two bundles the size and length of his forearm from the pack and placed them in his lap. He looked expectantly at Jothan.

Jothan rose and propped his right leg on the chair. He unstrapped the leather bindings around his ankle and rolled up his travel legging. Using his knife, he cut the strap that held the coin pouch to his leg, and then tossed the pouch to Lucian.

Lord Lucian counted out the ten gold coins before he surrendered the bundles. Jothan hefted them in his hands. Should he ask to have them weighed? No. The insult would certainly not go unanswered.

"I'll need the pack to carry them in."

"Of course." He removed the remaining three bundles and extended the empty pack. Jothan tried not to look at the remaining bundles as he stowed his two. Straightening, he turned to go. He half expected to be stopped by the guards, but no one made any move to restrain him.

"I look forward to our future business dealings," Lucian called after him by way of farewell.

Jothan awarded him a curt nod, and then left. In the moment before the door clicked shut behind him, he heard Lord Lucian's quiet laughter.

Jothan strode through the streets of Eshtaol, toward the southern edge of town and the forest beyond. He would love to stop at Skelly's inn and wash the bitter taste of Lord Lucian out of his mouth, but he knew Quinn would have headed to the safety of the forest the moment he was out of sight. His partner wouldn't like this new development any more than he did.

Arien Perceived. Her eyes told one part of her brain that the object was a branch, as big around as her thigh with smooth patches where strips of bark had fallen off. It lay on the ground, atop an overturned metal tub.

Her mind saw something else entirely.

A million tiny particles whirled around one another, forming patterns as they rotated in an intricate dance that was dizzying as well as fascinating. Arien *saw* them, felt them, stepped into their midst and watched them revolve around her.

"Go on," said Master Sinclare at her side. "I'd rather not stay out here all day."

Still Perceiving, she issued a Command. It left her mind-shield and sped toward the whirling mass of particles, a pinprick of light carrying her thought to the branch. She *saw* it received, saw the particles absorb it, and watched as they began to obey. Their rotating dance accelerated, and within seconds whirled even faster than she could Perceive. A glow began deep within the mass and quickly spread outward.

Master Sinclare took a step backward as the branch burst into flames.

She glanced at his thin face, his expression impassive as the branch was reduced to ash. He had changed in the seven years since she first came to the Brotherhood. Still slender, even more so, and there was no longer even a trace of brown in his hair.

But at least now he spoke to her on the few occasions she was permitted in the Hall. For the first few years he had simply glared.

"Not bad." He gave a nod. "In fact, acceptable. Better than last time, even. If only it didn't take you so long to Perceive."

"I'm sorry, Master," Arien told him. "It's not that it takes long, it's just that I get caught up in the movements."

"Movement is just what you need to master here, and I mean the Power. Let's try it again, and this time I want to see how quickly you can do it."

He knocked the still-smoldering branch off the barrel and set another in its place.

Arien Perceived. This time she did not allow herself to

commune with the particles, did not waste even a moment admiring the intricacy of their dance. She watched her Command speed away, and almost instantly the branch erupted with fire.

Master Sinclare's expression did not change. "Quite acceptable." He turned and began walking toward the cabin, speaking over his shoulder. "Continue to practice, and I will see you next week."

But before he turned, Arien thought she saw a flicker of something—approval?—flash across his narrow face. Warmth flooded through her. That glimpse rewarded her better than any verbal praise.

She placed another log next to the first and sat nearby. She Perceived again, and this time gave herself liberty to enjoy the dance of the particles, to study their pattern. She shifted her Perception to the embers beneath the branch. The particles were the same, but with a different pattern and a faster dance. The ashes, too, were composed of the same particles, but that pattern was looser and the movement much slower.

Shifting back to the branch, she stepped close in her mind. The pattern was tight, much tighter than the ashes, but there was still a good bit of space between the particles. This was what she found so fascinating, these differences. The pattern of everything she Perceived was different from any other, the clusters tighter or looser depending on the consistency of the object. In certain kinds of rock, for example, the particles clustered so closely together that discerning a pattern was almost impossible. While the pattern for soil was loose and practically unconfined.

What would happen…

She sent a Command to force air between the clusters, disrupting their pattern—

—and dove for cover when the branch exploded into a million splinters.

Dinner in the Hall that night was roasted venison, and Petro, upon hearing the menu from Sinclare, decided they would go. Their custom was to eat alone in their cabin, but in the past year Arien had noted a relaxing of the stern glares she received on the few times they did venture up to the Hall. It wasn't that the rules had changed, but that some of those who had insisted upon the rules seemed to have lost their enthusiasm for enforcing them. So, every few weeks Petro and Arien ate in the Hall.

She didn't particularly enjoy those meals. The refectory, which wasn't nearly so big now that she was older, seemed uncomfortably crowded. The eye of everyone under thirty was invariably directed toward her. The older ones ignored her completely.

Her training had been conducted almost completely away from the Hall. Master Thaddeus had been a frequent visitor from the beginning, bringing volumes from his library to instruct her in writing, reading and history. In the past half-year Petro had arranged informal classes with other masters. His reason, he explained, was to show the Brotherhood that Arien had adapted to the training as well as any male trainee. Master Sinclare and Master Dorian had begun working with her on an irregular basis, helping her with the finer points of the three Powers. Master Sinclare's Movement lessons helped her a great deal, and Master Dorian seemed pleased with her Perception abilities.

The only trips to the Hall Arien enjoyed were when she came to work with Thaddeus in the library, usually during the middle of the day while the rest of the trainees were occupied elsewhere.

A disdainful expression still overtook Master Parnell's features whenever he caught sight of her, and the one time Master Petro had persuaded him to work with Arien on Command had been a disaster. Nothing she did pleased him. She had come to terms with the fact that the man hated her, and there appeared to be nothing she could do to change his mind.

They arrived at the Hall a few minutes before Brother Bayard rang the dinner bell. Arien felt the difference of her gender as keenly as if she had paraded through the Hall naked. Tonight, she dressed as unobtrusively as she could manage. Her hair, which had darkened from its childhood pumpkin-orange to a slightly less flamboyant shade of red, was caught back in a braid and hidden inside her blouse. The trousers she wore were oversized and baggy, as was her blouse, in an attempt to camouflage the womanly curves no other member of the Brotherhood possessed. A floppy hat, the kind customarily worn as a sun shield, hid most of her features and gave her a barrier behind which to hide if the stares became too uncomfortable.

Not for the first time, she spared a wish that she could eat in the kitchen instead of this crowded room. She had no friends here except Master Petro and Master Thaddeus. At the beginning of her training Master Parnell had made it clear that she was not to attempt to befriend any trainee. Though Petro assured her this was a precaution to ensure her safety, she thought it more likely that Master Parnell believed she would somehow pollute their minds simply by being female.

So, she stayed close to her master, and ate at the master's table nearest the kitchen. Occasionally a trainee attempted to hold a mental conversation with her, but she had rebuffed most of them at one time or another, and they no longer tried.

Even the masters did not often speak to her. Every so often Thaddeus or Dorian attempted to include her in the dinner conversation, and on those occasions, she spoke only enough to be polite.

Not that she wouldn't have liked to join in. Her conversations with Thaddeus were immensely interesting. But even after seven years, she knew that she had never been fully accepted. Petro spoke often about her trial, where her abilities would be tested and her full membership as a brother approved. She needed as many masters as possible on her side before that time. Fear of that test gnawed at her insides. Would she be found lacking and sent in disgrace back to the tiny village where she grew up?

At the ringing of the dinner bell, Arien followed Petro to the master's table and sat beside him. She hunched down on her stool to be as inconspicuous as possible. He settled in and engaged in a jovial conversation with the brother sitting across from him while they waited for the food to arrive from the kitchen.

Arien stared at the table's scarred wooden surface and watched her master out of the corner of her eye. How he enjoyed their visits to the Hall. And how unfair to exclude him from fellowship with his friends just because he had chosen a girl for a trainee. One of the brothers made a comment, and he laughed without restraint while Arien battled guilt.

Roasted venison was one of her favorites, and she helped herself to a large slab when the platter was passed. Brother Bayard had also prepared a dish of mixed squashes simmered in butter as well as fresh bread and cheese. She ate, relishing the luxury of a meal she hadn't cooked herself, while trying to identify the seasonings in the squash dish so she could replicate it back at their cabin. Though her cooking wasn't good, she possessed far more skill than Petro so the chore had fallen to her.

The meal had almost concluded when a ringing *clank* cut through the noise in the refectory. Thaddeus left, and returned moments later followed by a stranger in travel clothes. He glanced around the room and pointed to a pair of trainees.

"Norbert. Elden. See to this man's horse."

The two disappeared through the doorway while he led the stranger to the master's table. Silence descended over the room. Mindspeech darted back and forth in frenzied activity, but no one spoke aloud until Master Thaddeus announced, "This is a rider from King Mendel in Kirklin, Hamlin's royal city. He tells me he has ridden here to deliver a message to the Brotherhood. And a request."

The messenger held his arms drawn tightly across his chest, and he cast uncomfortable glances all around, nerves apparent. No doubt he was unaware of their proscription against Perceiving the thoughts of others and assumed his mind was being scanned by everyone in the room. He cleared his throat, shifting from one foot to another while his face flushed deep red.

"Go ahead," prompted Thaddeus with a smile. "Deliver your message."

The man cleared his throat. "I come with bad tidings, sirs. Master Edsel, who has been a valuable and trusted advisor to King Mendel Valerien for many years, has died."

A few gasps sounded around the room, but at the master's table Arien saw only a few bowed heads in response to the news.

After a respectful silence, Master Parnell asked, "How did he die?"

"Old age, sir," the messenger replied. "He was getting on, and his heart stopped in his sleep. He wasn't sick, and the king's healers said they couldn't find anything wrong with him. His stomach showed no signs of poison."

"Poison?" Brother Charnal rose, hands planted on either side of his plate. "Why would they check for such a thing?"

"It's standard, sir," the man assured him hurriedly.

"I'm sure it is." Parnell motioned for Charnal to be seated. "After all, Edsel was quite old."

Standing beside the messenger, Master Thaddeus drew himself up to his full height, his expression indignant. Beside Arien, Petro chuckled.

"Edsel was a few years my junior," Thaddeus informed Parnell.

"Yes, but not nearly as healthy as you are," Petro assured him. "I'm sure he lived a life of luxury in the palace and had not taken care of himself as you have."

The messenger nodded, anxious not to offend. Thaddeus allowed himself to be mollified, though Arien glimpsed a twinkle of amusement in his eyes.

The messenger cleared his throat. "The king considered Master Edsel a friend as well as an advisor. He was laid to rest in the royal tomb."

Nods all around the table, then Master Dorian asked, "And what is the king's request?"

The messenger shifted his weight from one foot to another. "The king has grown accustomed to taking advice from Master Edsel, advice he will sorely miss. He sent me to ask if someone else with the same abilities might be willing to come to Kirklin."

The buzz of trainees' whispers erupted around the room. Arien stole a quick glance around the master's table. Many eyebrows arched high.

"An interesting request," murmured Sinclare, and those

seated nearby nodded.

"A salary would go along with the position, of course," the messenger said. "Plus, rooms in the castle and meals from the king's own kitchen." He cast an earnest glance toward the impartial faces before him and added, "Nice rooms."

Master Parnell rose. "Thank you for the message and your excellent delivery of it. It is far too late for you to think of beginning your return trip tonight. Will you share our meal and our roof?"

"Thank you, sir." The man glanced at the half-full platters. "Whatever you're having smells good."

"And tastes as good as it smells," Parnell assured him as he led the man to a seat at the opposite end of the table from Arien. "We will discuss your request after dinner and inform you of our answer in the morning."

"Thank you, sir."

"I'll want to stay for the discussion," Petro told her. *"I can ask Thaddeus to ready a room for you, if you like."*

She had not stayed in the Hall since that first night, years before. Their cabin, isolated and cozy, suited her tastes far more. *"It's a mild evening. I don't mind walking back alone. I'd rather sleep in my own bed."*

Petro nodded, then turned to listen as the messenger answered questions concerning affairs at Kirklin Castle. Arien finished eating, slipped quietly out the door, and left the Hall through the kitchen exit.

The moon cast a white light over the landscape, its brilliance only slightly subdued by millions of stars studding the black sky. A sparse forest surrounded the Hall. She made her way between the trees, enjoying the rustle of the leaves above her, stirred by a gentle breeze.

She had covered half the distance to their cabin when the snap of underbrush sounded from behind. She Perceived two people, both with mindshields, approaching from the rear. Discomfort stabbed at her. Were they following her? She turned toward them before stepping behind a large tree trunk.

As they came into view, she recognized the two trainees Master Thaddeus had sent to tend to the messenger's horse. They approached Arien's tree.

"Why're you hiding?" asked Elden.

She stepped into view. Elden ran a hand through a thick thatch of dark hair, watching her through narrowed eyelids.

"I'm not hiding."

"Nah, Elden, she ain't hiding." Norbert's gaze lingered on Arien, and her muscles tensed.

Elden grinned. "Then what were you doing back there, taking a pee?"

His friend thought that uproariously funny, and loud guffaws filled the woods. Elden smiled, but kept his gaze on Arien. She stood still, her heart beating in her ears. What were these two up to? They were older trainees, though not as old as Arien herself. Elden was as tall as she, nearly as tall as Master Petro. Norbert was short, almost dwarfish, with sandy hair and a pudgy face.

"We've heard about you," Elden told her.

"Yeah," said Norbert, "we heard you were the masters' whore and they keep you tucked away in a cabin where they take turns giving it to you."

Heat flamed in her cheeks. "That's a lie." She shifted her glare between the two of them. "I'm a trainee, like you."

"You don't come around much," Elden countered. "If you was a trainee, we'd see you around the Hall, or in classes in the library. Don't you think, Norbert?"

Norbert nodded. "You can't be a trainee. You're a girl."

She didn't reply. Arguing with this pair would serve no purpose. They probably just wanted to harass her. If she remained silent, they might give up and go away, so she said nothing.

A new thought seemed to appear to Elden. "Maybe we're wrong. Maybe she's not really a girl after all."

"Whadda you mean, not a girl?" Norbert gave Elden a confused sideways look. "Sure she's a—"

"We don't know for sure." The gleam in Eldon's eyes sent sticky sweat rising along the back of Arien's neck. "There's only one way to be certain, huh?"

A sinister grin spread across Norbert's face as fear spread in Arien's belly. They couldn't mean—

In the years since her arrival at the Brotherhood, Arien

had practiced keeping a tight rein on her ability to sense the feelings of others, a practice Petro approved. She'd managed to extend her mindshield to include blocking out emotions as well as thoughts. But in this instance, a discrete peek seemed advisable.

She shut her eyes and concentrated on relaxing the tightly held ability so she could probe the emotions of the two facing her. A fraction of a second later she snapped her shield shut, revolted at the sensations rolling toward her. Lust, to be sure, but also a gut-wrenching cruelty. Especially from Eldon. Though his thoughts lay hidden behind his mindshield, his intentions were laid bare to Arien in his emotions.

"Yeah, we got to check." Norbert took a step toward her.

She backed up, her heart pounding. It was forbidden to use Power against another member of the Brotherhood, but how could she get out of this without it? Her mind reached out, searching for anyone within mindspeech distance, but she was too far from the Hall.

Maybe she could outrun them.

Glancing to her right, she plotted a path through the trees. Elden advanced another step, Norbert a pace behind him. Arien whirled and ran.

They were after her in an instant. She dodged between trees, ducked below branches and hopped over debris on the forest floor. Fear lent her legs energy, and she ran faster than she ever had.

But not fast enough. She could have eluded Norbert, but Elden was too quick. Long before she was within mindspeech distance of the Hall, he tackled her. She went down hard, his arms wrapped around her knees. Her hands broke some of the impact, so her face didn't receive more than a scratch from a stray stick, but the heels of her palms stung from cuts and scrapes, and she gasped for breath as the impact knocked the air out of her lungs.

"Got her." Elden's triumphant shout filled her ears as Norbert came puffing up beside them.

Elden crawled over her and grabbed her arms from behind, then rolled and sat up so that she was perched awkwardly between his legs. She struggled, but barely managed to gasp for breath, much less break his hold. By then he'd wrapped his legs over hers. His grip tightened on her arms, and no amount of struggling could shake his hold.

"Now." A wicked grin crept over Norbert's face as he knelt beside her. "Let's see if we have a boy or a girl here."

He grabbed her blouse and ripped. His eyes widened as he caught sight of her breasts. Arien's scream reached no one, no help within earshot.

"Just what I thought."

He grabbed one breast in a painful grip. She struggled, but it was no use. She hadn't the strength to repel him.

She grew still. Norbert chuckled, apparently assuming she had given up, but she had not. Far from it. She Perceived and with a speed that would have made Master Sinclare proud, sent a Command.

Instantaneously, Norbert's clothes dissolved to threads.

The unwoven rags dropped from his body to lay in a heap around his shoes, leaving him far more exposed than Arien was. He gasped, and a second later so did Elden.

"What happened to your clothes?" Elden asked, his voice shocked.

Arien took advantage of the distraction and with a giant effort, rolled out of the young man's grasp. She was on her feet in an instant, ready to fight. But not with fists. While Elden stared at Norbert, Arien Perceived. The same Command sped toward him. An instant later his clothing lay in a heap similar to Norbert's.

Then she constructed a different sort of Command. This time she delved deep into the long-suppressed Empathic ability she alone possessed. When the Command was ready, she flung it toward her attackers.

Both trainees stared at Arien, stunned. Eldon's face flushed purple, and mortification emanated from him in palpable waves. Norbert jerked back as if struck, and tears of humiliation sprouted in his eyes.

Clutching her blouse together with dignity, she lowered her gaze and allowed a deliberate smile to spread across her face.

"I started to suggest that you cover yourselves, but there

isn't much to cover, is there?"

She had the satisfaction of watching both faces turn blood-red and then of seeing a pair of white rears as they ran from her, leaving behind two heaps of colored thread.

Five

The meeting room was practically empty. Twenty-eight masters and five brothers clustered around the table, not many compared to even a few years ago. Petro selected a seat next to Thaddeus. It seemed more and more that the trainees who passed their trial chose to leave the Hall and make their fortunes in the world. Like Jothan had. Only one of the brothers currently in residence had chosen to remain permanently. The other four had only recently completed their training and would probably leave soon.

What are we doing wrong? When Petro passed his final trial, he could hardly wait to find his first trainee and come back to the Hall, to claim the title of Master and begin his life's work. *Now they leave and never show up again.*

He inspected the solemn faces around the table. Not an inviting bunch, to say the least. Many were gray and grizzled. What did it benefit a young man to stay once he had the ways of Power about him? Or an old man, either. This offer from King Mendel presented an interesting opportunity for someone tired of life within the constricting confines of the Brotherhood.

Master Parnell entered the room and closed the door behind him.

"Is everyone here?" His gaze circled the table and he nodded. "Good. Let us discuss King Mendel's request."

When did he become our spokesman? The Brotherhood had no acknowledged leader, but it seemed that Parnell always stepped to the front when it came to making decisions, and no one ever challenged his right to do so. It certainly had nothing to do with his abilities. Many of the younger masters surpassed Parnell in the wielding of Power. And age wasn't the deciding factor, either. If so, Thaddeus would enjoy the honor. Except he wouldn't want it. Perhaps it was simply Parnell's personality to be in charge.

"An unusual invitation," said Dorian.

Seated to Dorian's right, Avram shook his head. "Not really. We've received requests for assistance before."

"Yes, from people who are having trouble. Like healers who need medicines or a village that needed help finding a new water supply. But those were requests for help with a specific problem, not an offer of employment."

One of the younger brothers, Tirrell, leaned forward displaying a confused expression. "How did Master Edsel get to be the king's advisor to begin with?"

"Family connections." Parnell had not yet taken his seat but stood at the head of the long table. "Edsel's brother was in the King's Guard and got him a position as a guardsman when he left the brotherhood. With his abilities, he performed his job well enough that he attracted King Mendel's attention. The result was predictable."

"Nothing wrong with that," said Brother Medwin. "If we can't use our Powers to help us in our everyday lives, what's the purpose of learning to use them at all?"

Parnell turned on him, his expression stern. "Control is the purpose. To prevent an inadvertent misuse."

Several side conversations began at this point, everyone

expressing his own opinion. Petro exchanged a grin with Thaddeus at Parnell's frustration. He hated losing the attention of a group.

"Can we get back to the discussion?" Parnell slammed a palm down on the table.

The room quieted.

"What's wrong with sending someone to Kirklin?" asked Brother Tirrell.

Brother Bayard lifted a shoulder. "Nothing that I can see."

Dorian clasped his hands and rested them on the table before him. "We must consider the matter of fairness. King Hubert of Creighton has no one with our abilities to advise him. Would we put ourselves in the position of apparent favoritism by sending someone to Mendel?"

Sinclare shook his head. "King Hubert has never asked. Perhaps he hasn't thought of it, or perhaps he doesn't want someone with Power living in his castle. But that is not a valid reason to refuse Mendel."

Dorian tapped on the wooden surface. "Suppose we decide to honor the king's request. Who would we send?"

Parnell's lips pursed as he considered. "Of the masters in residence, twenty-two have trainees. That leaves five brothers and six masters." He lifted his head and let his gaze circle those gathered. "Are there any volunteers?"

Petro glanced around the table. Masters Parnell, Sinclare, Thaddeus, Dorian and Avram would never again leave the Hall. They'd had enough of dealing with the world and had no desire to submerse themselves in it again. Brother Bayard disliked appearing in public so much that he refused to even make the day's journey to Oswald for supplies. Tirrell, maybe, or Medwin?

But both shook their heads.

"Simon, how about you?" Sinclare addressed the young brother who sat quietly at his side. "This presents a good opportunity for a young man, better than your family's shipping business."

Simon shook his head. "I'm going back to Tifford."

"Brother Werner?"

"Kings and the like make me nervous." Werner flashed a

shy smile around the table. “I've been thinking of finding a trainee and becoming a master.”

Petro nodded, as did several others. A logical decision for the studious Werner.

“Is there no one who would like to counsel a king?” Parnell swept the room with a gaze.

No one answered.

Petro let the silence drag out, waiting for anyone else to speak up. When no one did, he cleared his throat. All eyes turned toward him.

“If no one else wants to,” he said, flashing a bashful smile around the assembly, “I think I'd like to do it.”

A surprised gasp echoed in the chamber. Every face wore an expression of astonishment.

At the head of the table, Parnell sputtered and spat like an angry cat. “You can't. You have a trainee.” He rolled his eyes. “Such as she is.”

“I was thinking of taking her with me,” Petro said, and enjoyed the choking he heard from several throats around the table.

Avram seemed to have caught the sputtering malady. “B—b—but you can’t. It isn't done.”

“Avram is right,” said Dorian. “Trainees must be trained on Brotherhood lands.”

Petro cast a sideways glance toward the man. “I'm glad you didn't say 'at the Hall,' since she hasn't been. But why must they be trained on the lands?”

Dorian’s spine stiffened. “Because they always have been.”

“Petro,” said Sinclare in a placating tone, “when we accepted Arien as your trainee you agreed to train her here. Remember your threat to take her away for training? We allowed her to begin the training on the condition that she remain here.”

“That's right.” Parnell’s lips tightened into a righteous knot. “Have you no sense of obligation to the girl, if not to the Hall?”

“In that case,” Petro said, ignoring Parnell's question as beneath his dignity, “I have a request of the Brotherhood. My trainee, Arien, is ready to stand the trial."

The shocked silence that met his pronouncement lasted a long moment before the assembly erupted.

"What?"

"Impossible!"

"Out of the question."

Petro struggled to keep a grin off his face as he watched the outraged reactions of his peers. He glanced toward Thaddeus and was pleased to see the old man smile and give a slight nod of agreement.

"But what about the Empathy?" Parnell demanded. "Who knows what will happen if we turn that girl loose on the world?"

A glance circled between the masters who'd worked with Arien. Finally, Thaddeus cleared his throat. "I've worked closely with her, and I will attest that I have never Perceived even a hint of Empathic ability from her. I don't believe we need be concerned that Empathy will be a burden to Arien, if she even has the Power."

The others nodded agreement. Petro remained silent. He knew full well that Arien possessed a strong Empathic ability, but she'd learned to control it. The fact that several Masters of the Brotherhood had never seen a sign of it was proof.

"You have lost your mind," Parnell told Petro. "She's been here only seven years, not nearly long enough to have been trained properly."

The man's attitude irritated him. "How do you know?" Petro shot back. "Have you worked with her? Have you tested her? You've refused every opportunity to spend even a moment with her, so I do not accept your ability to judge her readiness. Ask Sinclare or Dorian about the status of her training."

Parnell turned to Sinclare, who looked distinctly uncomfortable.

"I know it is unusual," he said in a low voice, "but I have worked with the girl for several months now, and I would agree with Petro's assessment of her abilities. Perhaps it is because she was older when she began the training or because she possesses an extremely strong natural ability." He drew in a breath and straightened in his seat. “Whatever the reason, she is ready to stand the trial. More than many I've seen pass.”

Parnell stared at the man for a moment, then turned wordlessly to Dorian.

“I agree.” Dorian shrugged. “In fact, I was hoping to convince her to stay and work with me after her training was over. She has one of the keenest senses of Perception I've ever seen.”

Sinclare turned to him. “I've thought the same about her Movements.”

Petro ignored Parnell’s sputtering. “I'll ask her,” he told both Sinclare and Dorian, “but I really would like her to come with me to Kirklin. She needs exposure to culture, to civilization. She was stuck in a tiny, backward village for her childhood, then in that cabin with me for the past seven years. It's no wonder she's underdeveloped, socially.”

“Wait.” Parnell pounded a fist on the table. Everyone turned to him, astonished at his outburst. His face was blood-red, and a vein throbbed above his temple. “You can't make this decision, Petro.” His struggle to keep his voice below the shouting level showed on his face. “I haven't given my approval.”

“Since when does the Brotherhood need your approval, Parnell?” Thaddeus eyed the master with something that could almost be taken for dislike. “The writings say that a trainee's master will inform the Brotherhood of the trainee's readiness for the trial. Then it only takes three masters to conduct the trial and approve the results.”

Petro suppressed a satisfied smile. “So…if Sinclare, Dorian, and Thaddeus will agree to the trial, we can conduct it as soon as tomorrow.”

Parnell looked around the room. No one met his gaze. With a deliberate gesture, he pulled out his chair and sank into it, his face red.

Master Avram leaned forward in his chair. “But we haven't decided if the Brotherhood *wants* to send someone to Kirklin.”

“The Brotherhood isn't sending anyone.” Petro spoke in a tone that allowed no room for argument. “I'm going on my own, just as Edsel did. This is the perfect way. The Brotherhood will not appear to be showing favoritism since the decision is mine, and mine alone."

"Master Petro?" Arien's voice broke into his mind.

"This is not a good time," Petro told her, then he felt the flavor of her thought. The girl was upset, extremely so. *"What is wrong? Are you hurt?"*

In answer, his trainee sent a scene, a block of memory of an incident that occurred a few moments ago. Hot fury blazed through his veins. Barely aware of his actions, he rose from his chair, face burning. Everyone at the table turned expectant gazes on him.

"Something serious has happened."

Now he was the one struggling to control his voice. He broadcast the scene to all the minds in the room. In light of the current conversation, he left out the display of Arien's empathic abilities. Poor Arien would be horrified enough that they all knew of her misfortune, but there was no help for it. A violation of this sort must be punished. A punishment agreed upon by every brother and master in the Hall.

The expressions around the table were as shocked and horrified as Petro could have wished. Masters Calder and Hugh were especially disturbed, since the trainees who had attacked Arien were under their tutelage.

Parnell slapped his hands on the arms of his chair. "I knew something like this would happen." He glared at Petro. "I told you when you brought her here you were courting trouble. You have only yourself to blame."

Petro was in no mood to be diplomatic. "Shut up, Parnell." He addressed the rest. "I formally demand discipline on those two…criminals."

"They will be disciplined," Master Calder assured him, though a little sadly. "Norbert is aware that his behavior has been under examination since the incident with the cat. Speaking as his master, I see no recourse other than to strip him and return him to his home."

"They should both be stripped." Petro pounded a fist on the table. "This behavior is inexcusable."

"Leave it to us, Petro," said Sinclare. Hugh sagged in

obvious relief. "Arien is safe, though understandably shaken. We're all thankful she wasn't hurt. But this does prove your point."

Several of the masters nodded agreement.

"My point?" asked Petro.

"I've never seen anyone who could issue such an intricate Movement so quickly." Sinclare shook his head slowly, obviously impressed. "I couldn't have done it as well with the kind of pressure she was under. And her judgment was superb. Any one of us would have defended her if she'd really hurt those boys." He leaned forward to catch and hold Petro's gaze. "She's an asset to the Brotherhood, Petro. I hope she decides to stay and work with me after you leave."

"If she does stay, I'll want equal time," Dorian announced.

Petro glanced to the spot where Parnell sat fuming. His tense muscles relaxed.

Arien sat in the center of a round room, surrounded by walls devoid of windows, paintings, or tapestries. The only furnishing was the straight-backed chair in which she sat. The walls and the floors were of the same rough-cut stone as the exterior of the Hall, though without the advantage of sunlight to give them warmth. She shivered, whether from external chill or internal she didn't know.

Surrounding her, their backs not quite touching the stone, stood four masters. She'd spent a half-day in their company individually as they tested her abilities, her control of Power, and every aspect of her training. She'd Perceived everything in the forest and the hall, from trees to rocks to tableware. She had issued Commands, performed Movements, and undergone a thorough examination of her knowledge of the writings of Devland. None of the masters had given her the slightest indication of their judgments, either by word or expression. Even Master Thaddeus had been abnormally solemn. And Petro, usually so supportive and encouraging, had absented himself to pack their belongings in readiness for the trip to Kirklin, which they would begin in the morning.

If she passed her trial.

Only this last part to go. Her stomach gave a queasy lurch at the thought of the test she was about to undergo. The hardest test, the one that broke the minds of ill-prepared trainees, including the only female to ever get this far in over eighty years.

Well not me.

She took a deep breath, gathering courage as her lungs gathered air, and shifted her weight to a comfortable position on the hard wood. Success meant she would finally be accepted as a full member of the Brotherhood of Power. The right to wear the robes and medallion of the Brotherhood would be hers. The ability to choose her own future.

Failure meant being stripped of all Power and turned out in disgrace. And the stripping process may result in death or insanity.

Teeth set firmly together, she raised her chin. Let them try to break her. She would succeed.

"I'm ready," she told the waiting masters, pleased that her voice remained steady.

Standing directly in front of her, Master Sinclare glanced toward the others and then lowered his gaze to her.

"In this final test we will examine your mindshield for any sign of weakness. We will also test your resistance to deception and hostile Commands. And finally, if you withstand those ordeals, we will examine your mind for any qualities unbecoming a member of the Brotherhood of Power. Do you have any questions?"

Taking special note of Master Sinclare's choice of the word 'ordeals,' she swallowed against a dry throat. Did he mean she might pass every trial perfectly and still be expelled from the Brotherhood?

"What qualities do you consider unbecoming?"

Master Thaddeus answered. "Cruelty, excessive greed, malice, dishonesty. Even excesses of positive traits, such as fierce loyalties which might be a temptation to misuse Power. Anything that, in our opinion, would be contrary to our beliefs that Power is a natural gift, though a dangerous one that requires a lifetime of restraint."

In other words, anything they decided they didn't like about her. At least Master Parnell had not been included as one her examiners. She tried not to review every expression she'd seen Master Avram wear during the day. She was fairly confident the other three didn't dislike her, though their feelings on women as members of the Brotherhood might play against her. Well, there was nothing she could do about that.

She nodded a second time. "I'm ready."

"Then we will begin." Master Sinclare clasped his hands loosely in front of him. "Prepare yourself by making your mindshield as solid as possible."

Arien closed her eyes, not because she couldn't strengthen her shield with her eyes open, but to guard against distractions she might detect in the faces of her examiners. She sat rigid in the chair and focused all her attention on presenting a solid, impenetrable mindshield.

The first Command, sent by Master Avram, hurtled toward her, easily seen and easily deflected. Next came one from Master Thaddeus, then Master Dorian, Master Sinclare, and back to Master Avram again. They were simple Commands such as she had been practicing for seven years: *raise your arms*, *open your eyes*, and *make a fist*. She parried them quickly and efficiently.

The speed increased. Not difficulty, for there were even some repeats, but the quantity multiplied until they seemed to be flying toward her from all directions at once. Arien saw them as pinpoints of light, racing through the dark void around her. She reinforced her mindshield and deflected each Command. Despite the chill in the room, a bead of sweat slipped down the side of her face.

And still the Commands came, battering against her mindshield, waiting for the moment she lost control.

The instant Arien felt her strength begin to slip, they ceased. She waited a long moment, just in case it was a trick, then cautiously opened her eyes. The masters stood exactly where they had been, their expressions unchanged. The first part of the test was over. She heaved a sigh and sagged against the hard chair back.

From his position a few feet away from her right shoulder,

Master Dorian spoke in a tone devoid of emotion. “Compose yourself for the next test. Let us know when you are ready.”

How long had that gone on? It could have been a few minutes or several hours. More importantly, how had she done? Her shield weakened at the end, but had it remained strong long enough? Not one Command had gotten through, but if they'd continued, one would have. Her stomach muscles trembled with the onset of exhaustion. Could she muster enough strength for the next test?

No choice now. They're not going to let me come back tomorrow.

She rubbed her forehead, not surprised when her fingers came away wet, and drew another fortifying breath. Eyes closed, she checked her shield again. Still in one piece, which was a good sign. And she still felt in control, though very tired.

With the next breath, a measure of calmness returned.

“I'm ready,” she told them.

“Open your mind to me.” Master Avram’s voice held an almost hypnotic singsong quality. “I will show you a scene. Let yourself live there. Make it your home.”

She sensed his approach and opened her shield to receive his thought.

A foul odor struck her. She looked around and found herself no longer seated on the hard chair but perched atop a pile of stinking straw. Cold stone, black with slime, rose high on all sides around her. From far above, a dim, white light shone through a shutterless window with an iron grate. Filthy, lice-infested people pressed against her on all sides. The odors rising from herself and those around her made her eyes sting and water, and her throat ached with breathing the stench. Something crawled in her hair and when she raised her hand to dislodge it, saw that her arm was covered with open, oozing sores.

A scratching sound to her left caused her to turn that way, and she located the source of at least part of the stench. The body of a child lay in the corner. It’s grey, decaying skin was covered in the same sores as her arm. A rat sat perched on the child's chest, gnawing at an exposed bone.

I'm in a plague house. Her stomach twisted with revulsion. The thought brought no fear, only the deep dread of the certain realization of a slow, agonizing death.

She'd heard of this plague. The lesions oozed poison, and everywhere the pus touched, new lesions would begin until her whole body was covered with them. Then the poison would work its way inward, to eat away her life-sustaining organs. The pain that was almost intolerable now would become excruciating. Her bloodstream would fill with the burning poison, and the pain would torment her until it took her mind. The disease was incurable, the victims isolated in plague houses. Left to die.

I can't do this. If I'm going to die anyway, I'd rather do it quickly while I still have a little strength and before the pain gets any worse.

She examined her surroundings, searching for something, *anything* she could use as a weapon. An end to the torment even now working its way inside her body.

Something tickled the back of her mind, something she should know. What? Pain vibrated along her nerve endings, destroying her attempt to concentrate. All she wanted, all she could think about, was to stop hurting.

Something flashed to her right. Metal. She raised herself up on agonized knees. A knife, placed there by compassionate attendants who knew that some would choose a quick end. Too weak to stand, she crawled across the people who lay moaning on the straw. A woman screamed as Arien's hand raked an oozing leg sore. With a flash of sympathy, she continued her mission.

An eternity later, she arrived at the corner of the cell. She picked up the hunting knife and found it already filthy with the dried blood of those who had chosen the same escape before her. Inch by agonizing inch, she pulled herself into a sitting position, her back against the slime-covered wall. Taking the knife in both hands, she pointed it inward, toward her chest and the heart that lay beating within. A silent prayer floated through the pain-filled haze in her mind. *Give me enough strength to pierce skin and bone.*

Before she thrust the weapon home, she glanced around

the stinking cell one last time. Moonlight reflected off the wet sores covering every inch of flesh she saw, the evidence of pain and suffering made even more real by the tortured moans that filled her ears. A hell, a nightmare, and yet…

Something stopped Arien's hand. How had she come to be here? An elusive memory taunted, something important, something she *must* remember. She closed her eyes to concentrate, trying to ignore the burning pain that threatened to overpower her. Where was she right before…

The trial.

Now she remembered. Master Avram's thought. This was all part of the trial. It wasn't real, it was an illusion. A test to see if she would be fooled by the deception.

She Perceived and saw that she had been deceived by a thought not her own. She had accepted it, had taken it into herself and believed it to be true. Had almost let it convince her to take her own life.

She rejected the thought, pushed it away and closed her mindshield with a snap.

When she opened her eyes, she found Master Avram watching her.

"I failed, didn't I?" Her heart sank as she struggled to hold back the tears that stung her eyes.

His smile softened. "Not at all, my dear. You did very well." A note of compassion in his voice sent tears streaming down her cheeks.

"I almost did it." A sob cracked her voice even as relief washed over her like a strong wind. "I almost used the knife. I believed it, believed that I was dying of the plague, and I wanted to take my life."

"Of course you did." He laughed gently. "A pretty poor master I would be if I couldn't construct a realistic mental illusion. The thought of suicide was mine, not yours, and part of the test."

"But you recognized it," Master Dorian continued. "It didn't feel real to you, did it?"

Arien shook her head. "Not at the end. But at first."

"Of course it did. Avram told you to open to him and you did. But thoughts of suicide are contrary to your own deepest, innermost nature, so you weren't fooled for long."

Arien swallowed, relieved to find that her throat, though dry, did not sting with sickness. She couldn't help a quick glimpse at her hands, just to make sure the skin was smooth and unmarked. It had seemed so real.

"Are you ready for the last part of the trial?" asked Master Sinclare.

Was she? She clutched her knees with shaking hands, glad for the chair. Thank goodness, she didn't have to stand.

"May I have a drink of water first?"

"Of course." Master Thaddeus left through the single door.

"The last part of the trial is not at all taxing," Master Dorian assured her with a smile. "We will ask you a few questions and Perceive your thoughts in answer. The hardest part will be letting us inside your mindshield to hear the answers."

That was certainly correct. Her mindshield had snapped shut like a slammed door after the last test. It would take an effort to let down her defenses again.

Master Thaddeus returned and handed her a cup with a smile.

"Citrus tea," he told her. "It will fortify you."

The mug was warm, and a wisp of sweet-scented steam rose from the surface of the liquid within. She sipped the spicy tea, the dry tissues in her throat quenched. The trembling in her hands lessened. When she'd drained the mug dry, she set it on the floor and managed a tremulous smile at her examiners.

"I'm ready."

Master Dorian approached to stand before her. He wore a kindly expression, which did as much to calm Arien as the tea.

"You must open your shield to us," he told her. "We will each make a few simple requests. There are no trick answers, so do not be concerned at hidden meanings to the questions. The requests are designed to prompt you to recall specific memories or thoughts, and your feelings about those memories. That is all."

Arien nodded, then closed her eyes. She Perceived Master Dorian before her and the others as well. Master Dorian approached and she opened her mindshield.

"Don't be nervous," Master Dorian told her. He projected assurance, which encouraged her. *"What is the most fun you've ever had?"*

The most fun. Arien remembered the first snow after she had arrived at the Brotherhood. She and Petro bundled up in several layers of clothing and ventured into the forest. He was teaching her about Movement, and to demonstrate he let her lob snowballs at him, which he deflected with a series of quick Commands. Then, with a wicked grin, he'd insisted that she try it, though he knew her abilities weren't anywhere close to ready for such a test. Arien could still feel the force of the snowball as it hit her square in the face.

"Fine." Master Dorian drew her away from the memory. *"And now remember your saddest experience."*

That was easy. Arien stood before two girls, both older than she. 'You got no mama,' one girl taunted. 'Yeah, your mama's dead,' said the second, giving Arien a shove. Once again, pain stung her, and she felt isolated, alone.

Master Dorian withdrew and another mind approached. Master Avram.

"What do you plan to do after you leave the Brotherhood?"

Do? Why, journey with the only family she knew. Petro was at the cabin even now, the place she thought of as home, packing. Tomorrow they would leave, would travel to a town called Kirklin, a world Arien could not even imagine. What would she do there? Meet people and learn new things. Read new books, ones not available in the limited library here at the Hall. Mostly she would help Petro in whatever way she could.

"But what about the time when Petro has no further need of your help? What then? What are your goals for you, alone?"

"I... I haven't thought that far. I don't know what I'd do without Master Petro."

"Marriage? Children?" prompted Avram.

Oh, of course. That kind of goal. Yes, she always intended to marry, but she hadn't thought of that in a long time. Back in the village there had been nothing else in her mind. It seemed so long ago. Had she stayed, she would no doubt have a husband and several children by now.

But look what she would have missed.

And then, coming to her as though dredged up from the depths of her being, Arien knew what she would do, the one thing she longed to do. One day she would find her family. Somewhere she had a father, and maybe even a mother. Perhaps brothers and sisters as well. Grandparents. *Someone* would know the identity of the woman who had died clutching a red-headed infant on the sides of Mount Caliago, and Arien would find that someone.

Master Avram withdrew, leaving Arien with an uncomfortable feeling. Her goal was personal and long forgotten. Was it enough? Was it the right answer?

Master Thaddeus was next, and Arien smiled when she Perceived his thought.

"What is your favorite book?"

Of course, that would come from Master Thaddeus, who loved books. She *should* say that the writings of Devland were her favorites, but here in her own mind she couldn't lie. She found them extremely boring. So, she thought instead of the histories she loved. Her favorite? It had to be the story of Princes Creighton and Hamlin, of how old King Jasper had split the kingdom of Bayland so each of his sons could reign as king.

"And now, what frightens you more than anything in the world?"

Master Avram's plague scene flashed into Arien's mind. Death frightened her. Another memory, this one of last night's attack. Pain frightened her, and humiliation. But the *most* frightening?

The most frightening thing of all, she realized, was Master Dorian's question a few moments ago. What would she do if she could not find her father? Where would she go when Petro no longer needed her? She would be alone, and that frightened her in a different way. Not heart-pounding, blood-rushing fear, but a long, stomach-wrenching loneliness that was even worse.

Master Sinclare approached. The last one. She breathed a

sigh of relief. Master Dorian had been right that this test was not taxing physically. But dredging up memories and experiencing the accompanying emotions was depleting her energy reserves faster than a foot race. If she had to withstand much more, she was afraid she'd collapse.

"Not much longer now," Master Sinclare promised. *"You know that Norbert and Elden are going to be disciplined tomorrow, don't you? Are you aware of the form of punishment?"*

Arien did know. Petro had told her their minds would be stripped of Power and they would be turned out of the Brotherhood.

"How do you feel about that?"

Oh, unfair! She experienced an anguished moment when her thoughts were jumbled, and she tried to sift through them to find her true opinion. She'd been attacked and might have been brutally raped if she hadn't possessed the ability to defend herself. No one would blame her for hating those two boys, and indeed, she felt a great deal of disgust and loathing. They deserved to be punished. Imagine what they would do if they were turned loose on an untrained girl without Power. The Brotherhood had a responsibility to the Twin Kingdoms as well as its own reputation, to ensure that did not happen.

On the other hand, she herself was afraid of being stripped and turned out in disgrace. Where would she go? Back to the village where she was nothing more than an old, over-aged orphan? Or to Arnath maybe, and try to find a means to support herself? Those were her only options, for she didn't know any other place. What options did Norbert and Elden have? They'd been taken from their families as little boys, much younger than Arien. Their families were strangers to them. What would they do?

That was assuming they survived the stripping process. Petro had told her that sometimes the mind was left so deformed that all mental abilities were lost. Sometimes the person was unable to perform even the simplest functions.

"I'm glad you understand the serious decision we faced," Master Sinclare told her. *"But you should not feel guilty. You are not to blame."*

His words did nothing to relieve Arien's guilt over her attackers' fate, but she appreciated Master Sinclare's consideration.

Was that it? Was the trial over?

"There is one more question. Would you consider remaining here, in the Hall, to work with some of the more advanced masters on perfecting your skills?"

What? Move to the Hall and not go to Kirklin with Master Petro? A stab of fear knifed her in the stomach. Had she failed the trial? What had she answered incorrectly? Were they upset that she found the writings of Devland boring, or were they displeased at her personal goals? Or had they found a deficiency in her control of Power during the morning tests?

"No, no, my dear, none of those things. Don't be alarmed." Master Sinclare saturated his thought with comfort to soothe her. *"The opposite is true. You have passed your trial, and after dinner this evening you will be presented as a full member of the Brotherhood. You will take the oath we have all taken and will be entitled to wear the robes and the medallion of the Brotherhood of Power. But many of us were impressed with the control you displayed during the attack last night, and your performance today has reinforced our impressions. We wondered if you'd like to stay and become even more proficient. Maybe even teach us a thing or two!"*

He chuckled, and Arien felt his pleasure as she heard his laughter.

"I see in her mind that she is determined to go to Kirklin, Sinclare," Thaddeus said aloud. His voice sounded odd, distant. Mindspeech was so much more intimate.

"If you ever change your mind, my dear," Master Sinclare said as he extended his hand to help Arien to her feet, "you have a place here."

As she stood, all four masters congratulated her. Happy tears blurred her vision. Master Thaddeus embraced her. With his lips near her ear, he whispered, "No matter what happens, you always have a home here with the Brotherhood."

She smiled, grateful beyond words. Then she laughed as a sudden thought struck her. "What will they call me? Brother Arien? Sister Arien? How about Brother Sister?"

"Brother Arien," said Master Sinclare with a definite nod. "Anything else and we'll have Parnell to deal with."

Six

Kerman Sein cowered before Lord Lucian, his hands shaking so violently that he was afraid he'd spill the powder as he placed it on the scales.

"Be careful, you idiot." At Lucian's snarl, Kerman's knees trembled. "I don't have all day to waste in this pathetic, underdeveloped town. I wish to get out of here and back to my manor house, which at least possesses some semblance of civilization. As much as can be had in this loutish posterior of the kingdom."

With luck, Lord Lucian would get his wish, and quickly. His presence in the laboratory was nothing short of terrifying. Yesterday he had ordered a man whipped to death for splashing the floor with a vat of boiling fernroot, saying he would not have clumsy clods working for him. The man had been one of Kerman's best workers, if a little slow.

Kerman suppressed a sigh as he carefully scraped a bit

more powder onto the scales. Things had changed drastically with Illan's death. Illan would never have treated his helpers with such disrespect, as though they were merely slaves to be discarded with no more consequence than killing a wild dog.

And he gets away with it. A bitter taste rose in the back of Kerman’s throat. As son to the powerful Lord Jerolin, Lucian could do practically anything he wanted. As long as he didn't offend the king, no one dared stop him.

Kerman tapped a few more grains onto the scales, peering closely at the needle. Perfect. He gathered the edges of the treated paper into a bundle, not breathing, careful not to spill even a speck, ever conscious of Lucian's watchful gaze.

“At last.” Lucian snatched the eighth and final bundle. “The next time I expect you to have it finished before I arrive.”

“Yes, my lord.” *It would help if you'd tell us when you are coming.* He dared not voice the comment.

Lord Lucian placed the last bundle into a pack and handed it to one of his personal guards. Then he turned back to Kerman.

“Oh, yes.” He snapped his fingers, as though he had just remembered something. “Have you heard from the southerner? The one from Creighton?”

Kerman shook his head. “No, my lord. The innkeeper hasn't mentioned that he's returned.”

Lord Lucian considered that with narrowed eyelids. “Isn't it time for him to contact you?”

“Yes, my lord. Any day. For several years he has arrived every season, the only exception being when weather through the Ir’Shemath kept him away.”

“Hmm.” A harsh smile twisted the young man’s lips, and Kerman repressed a shudder at the sight. “Perhaps he has had trouble convincing his customers to meet the higher price.”

A higher price? News, but not really surprising. Lord Lucian expected the alchemist laboratory to add to his personal wealth and add generously. The lab’s legitimate business of providing powders, ointments, and potions for the common ailments of the people of Eshtaol did not generate enough profit for the greedy lordling. Since Illan’s death, anodyte production had grown to the point that Kerman could barely keep his regular customers supplied with the medicines they needed.

"One final question." Lucian turned to face Kerman fully.

"Yes, my lord?"

"Is it true that if the fernroot is contaminated by snowseed in the final wash, the anodyte is harmful?"

Kerman tensed, then gave a cautious nod. "It is."

"And what happens if that anodyte is used?"

His heart began an uneven pounding. The eager look on Lucian's face made him uneasy. "It eats a man's brain away, until he's got no more reasoning than a child."

"Oh." Lucian looked disappointed. "I'd heard the person would die instantly."

Kerman shook his head. "It has been known to cause death, depending on how much is used. But not instantly."

"I see." The disturbing smile returned. "No matter. Insanity will serve me as well. I want you to make a batch of anodyte using snowseed."

Kerman swallowed against a suddenly dry throat. "But Lord Lucian—"

The look on Lucian's face stopped the protest before it left his lips.

"You will do it," Lucian said in a voice that left no room for argument, "and you will keep quiet about it. And when that southerner shows up, you will send word to me at my family's house in the mountains. Is that clear?"

Eyes wide, Kerman nodded.

"Good. And here is a little bonus for you and the others. I am pleased with the work you've done."

He tossed a leather pouch onto the mixing table. The clink of coins sounded when the purse landed on the wooden surface. Then he swept from the room without a backward glance.

Kerman picked up the pouch with trembling hands. He poured out a handful of silvers. Lord Lucian was not the kind of man to give bonuses, nor to pay for a service he wanted. But he was the kind to pay for silence.

And if he did not receive what he paid for, he was the kind who took revenge.

Jothan followed Quinn through the door of the Bed and Bitters Inn, blinking in the dim light. His mouth watered at the aroma of roasting meat, and he smiled in anticipation of one of Skelly's meals. The inn's common room was deserted, and Jothan doubted there were any customers in the rooms upstairs either. There were almost never visitors to this out-of-the-way Oteran town so close to the dangerous Ir'Shemath, what those of the Twin Kingdoms called the Nephtali Pass. *Ir*, meaning *not* and *Shemath*, meaning *easy way*, was a good description of the deep canyon through which Jothan and Quinn traveled every season or so. History taught that the barbarous Oterans had once invaded Creighton through that pass, and when the Oteran army had finally been defeated, Creighton filled the pass with a rockslide to make it impassable. It could still be crossed, but not without a lot of climbing. Not even a pack mule could be led through the mountainous debris, which meant Quinn and Jothan traveled with their supplies on their backs.

But no more. This is the last trip I make, one way or another. It's time to move on to something else. I won't deal with a man like Lord Lucian for any amount of money.

"Ah, my southern friends." Skelly emerged from the kitchen and greeted them with a smile on his round face. "I thought it was time for you to turn up. How about a plate of roast boar and some of my wife's potato pie? I expect the whole town's been smelling it cook all afternoon, so you'd best say yes while I've got some left to offer."

"The aroma has tempted me since the moment I came into town," Quinn told the man with a laugh. "We'll each take a plate, and an ale as well."

"Good, good."

Jothan and Quinn chose a table near the rear exit, as was their custom. In the years they'd been coming to Otero, and to the Bed and Bitters, they'd never been forced to use the escape route, but it didn't hurt to be cautious now that Illan was dead and Lord Lucian in control.

Skelly pushed through the kitchen door backward with an overflowing plate of food in each hand. He set them in front of Jothan and Quinn and then drew two mugs of ale from the keg on the counter. When he delivered those, he spoke in a lower voice.

“I've been asked to send a messenger the minute you arrive.” His normally jolly expression looked serious. “Since it's late in the day, the man should be able to come right away. I won't be long.”

“The messenger?” Jothan glanced at the door, suddenly uncomfortable.

“A friend,” Skelly assured them. “Stay here, and don't go wandering around the streets.”

Quinn glanced at Jothan, and Jothan understood the unspoken request. He Perceived Skelly's thoughts and found no malice in them.

“We won't go anywhere except right here, as long as there's this to keep us occupied.” Jothan raised his mug and drank deeply.

As soon as the door closed behind Skelly, Quinn asked in a low voice, “What was that all about?”

“Someone named Kerman instructed Skelly to fetch him when we arrive. Skelly thinks it an odd request and is worried because Kerman is somehow involved with Lord Lucian. But he does trust this Kerman and knows the man is not fond of Lucian.”

“Can't be all bad then.” Quinn took another long pull at his mug.

Jothan lifted his own tankard. “Still, we’d best be on our guard.”

They ate in silence, and Jothan forced himself to concentrate on the food. It was delicious, as always. Half-way through the meal, a girl came from the kitchen to bring them a basket of hot rolls and to refill their mugs. They were sopping the last of the juices with the bread when Skelly returned with a short, thin man in tow.

“You won't have met,” he said to Quinn and Jothan, “but this is Kerman Sein.”

Kerman executed a half-bow that seemed out of place in

the comfortable but slightly shabby common room of the Bed and Bitters. He clutched the back of a chair, a knot in his throat bobbing nervously.

"Sit," Skelly told the little man, and Kerman obediently sat.

Skelly brought a third mug of ale to the table, and then left them alone. Kerman sat in silence, gulping his ale like a hungry baby tugging at his mother's breast. Jothan glanced at Quinn, who returned the look with one raised eyebrow.

"Mr. Sein," began Quinn, but the little man shook his head with a quick, jerky movement.

"Call me Kerman," he replied in a high tenor. "One of you is Jothan and the other Quinn?"

"I'm Jothan."

"How do you know our names?" Quinn's question was polite but insistent.

Kerman swallowed again, obviously a nervous habit. "Illan was my employer."

Jothan Perceived, then gave a slight nod to Quinn. Kerman was telling the truth.

"Can you tell us what happened to Illan?" Quinn asked.

"He was killed." Kerman swallowed twice in rapid succession. "Lord Lucian had him killed because he wouldn't make anodyte for free."

Jothan's lips twisted upward in a cold smile. "Lord Lucian wouldn't like for anyone to deny a request, I imagine."

His comment was rewarded with a series of convulsive swallows, and then Kerman sucked down a deep swallow of ale. When he spoke, his voice was even quieter. "That's why I'm here. He's asked me to do something. No," Kerman corrected himself, "*commanded* me to do something terrible. And I think it affects you."

Jothan and Quinn exchanged a glance.

"What does he want you to do?"

"Do you know anything about the process of making anodyte?"

Quinn shrugged. "A little."

"Do you know what happens if diced snowseed is added to the last wash?"

"It spoils the anodyte?" Jothan guessed.

Kerman shook his head, his gaze capturing Jothan's. "It *poisons* the anodyte, but you can't detect it. It doesn't even change the taste. There's practically no way to tell that the drug is contaminated."

"And it kills the user?"

"Usually not. It damages the brain so that they're left with no more mind than a babe."

A suspicious look crept over Quinn's features. "What does this have to do with Lord Lucian and us?"

Kerman's throat bobbed like a cork on a swiftly moving river. "Lord Lucian has forced me to make poisoned anodyte. He didn't tell me, but I fear he plans to give it to you."

"But why?" asked Jothan, even as he searched Kerman's mind for the answer.

"I don't know." The little man shook his head, and Jothan saw that he gave a truthful answer. "I can't imagine why he would want to harm his customers. He'll never make any more money from you."

"He doesn't need our money," Jothan said.

Quinn nodded, his finger toying with the handle of his mug. "He has plenty of highly-placed friends who will buy all the anodyte he can provide."

"That's right," Jothan said. "He even told me that Otero's king uses anodyte, so he ..." He stopped, several thoughts falling into place.

Quinn gave him just a moment to think before pouncing with his question. "What? What have you remembered?"

Jothan shook his head, trying to clear it. What had Lucian said, exactly? Something about the king, and prince ...

"Prince Thaine." Jothan glanced around the room and continued in a low voice. "Is he one of our customers?"

Most of their customers were healers known to them both, but he knew Quinn had a few wealthy clients who dealt with him exclusively. They were the ones who used the drug recreationally, and Quinn kept their identities close to his chest.

The man remained silent, his eyes boring into Jothan's as he considered the ramifications of the question. Finally, he gave a slow nod.

"He is," Quinn acknowledged. "I've never met him. He sends a messenger to trade with me, but I've had the messenger followed several times and he always returns to the castle."

"But do you *know* he's acting for Prince Thaine? It couldn't be some other wealthy person there? Maybe even the king?"

Quinn shrugged his shoulders. "That's possible, but the messenger only comes when Prince Thaine is in Tadmoure, and I've noticed that the purchases are larger right before he leaves on a tour."

"Ooohhh." Kerman sucked in a frightened breath. "Do you mean Lord Lucian is trying to kill your prince?"

"I think that's exactly what he's trying to do." Quinn turned back to Jothan. "But why?"

"Suppose that's only part of what he's trying to do." Jothan spoke slowly, his mind busy. "Anodyte is hard to obtain in the Twin Kingdoms. It's expensive, and usually purchased only by healers and well-placed physicians. With our last supply being so small, Lucian knows our customers will be eager to buy any quantity we can sell them."

"But healers aren't our only customers." Quinn shifted in his seat, clearly uncomfortable. "We've gained a faithful clientele among the sons of rich lords. And who are the captains of the King's Guard?"

"The sons of rich lords?" Kerman's voice squeaked on the question.

Jothan and Quinn both nodded.

The implications were staggering. Jothan raked fingers through his hair, his mug forgotten. Was it possible? Was Lucian really plotting to incapacitate Creighton's royal guard?

"Does Lord Lucian have that kind of power? Is he close enough to Otero's king to be involved in a plan like this?"

"Oh, yes," Kerman assured them with a nod. "Lord Lucian's House is one of the most influential Oteran Houses, behind only the Therians. In fact, Lord Lucian's House is a distant branch of the royal family, listed in the Book of Heirs. Lucian's tutor and trusted friend is none other than Lord Zadornin himself, a close advisor to King Kuriel."

Jothan leaned away from the table slowly, a chill creeping up the back of his neck. He caught and held Quinn's eye. "We may have stumbled onto an Oteran plot to invade Creighton."

Arien studied her reflection in the glass while Beryle pulled a brush through her hair. The green of the gown matched her eyes almost perfectly, and her hair glowed in contrast. While she'd much rather wear the black robes of the Brotherhood, she was obligated to dress formally tonight.

"I don't see why I have to go." Arien heaved a sigh. "Prince Thaine doesn't give two shakes about meeting me, and I don't think the princess wants me there."

Beryl's eyes went round as pumpkins. "You should know if she does or not, miss."

"I've told you, I don't pry into people's thoughts. It's considered bad manners."

"Well, anyway," Beryle said with a haughty sniff, "I wouldn't waste a thought on whether Princess Pucker Face wanted me anywhere."

Arien winced as the girl pulled her hair upward and clasped it in a leather strip at the top her head. Having a personal attendant could be a touch awkward, and she had yet to become accustomed to having someone constantly underfoot. Beryl was anything but a proper lady's maid. No doubt Princess Sarana had taken Arien's arrival as an opportunity to rid herself of an unwanted attendant. Still, Arien enjoyed the girl's unruly tongue.

"You shouldn't say that too loudly," she cautioned. "The princess might hear you."

Beryle glanced toward the door. "Is she out there?"

Arien Perceived, then shook her head. "No. She's in her room, attended by the healers."

"That pregnancy is the best thing that ever happened around here." Beryle spoke loudly. She brought the rod from the hearth and wrapped a lock of Arien's hair around it. "It keeps the princess in her rooms where she belongs, instead of listening at doors for snippets of news that's none of her business."

"It's the best thing for other reasons than that, Beryle," Arien commented.

Beryle grinned. "You mean because now Prince Millard has time to look elsewhere, don't you miss?" She winked slyly at Arien's reflection.

Arien jerked around to look Beryle in the face and winced when the movement pulled her hair. "You know how I feel about that." She schooled her voice into a stern reprimand. "It's bad enough everyone thinks I'm Master Petro's mistress. Now they're gossiping about me and the prince as well?"

"Only because he follows you around the castle like a tomcat. You could have him at your feet with a wink." Beryle unwrapped the lock and tested its bounce before she wrapped another.

"I don't want him at my feet," Arien replied, irritated, "or anywhere else. I also don't want to talk about him."

She sat silently as Beryle curled one bright lock after another. Prince Millard was a dandy and an idiot, but since her arrival at Kirklin Castle five months ago, Arien had learned enough decorum to know it was not a good idea to broadcast those opinions about the future king, even if it was only to her personal attendant. Or, since Beryle loved gossip, especially to her personal attendant.

She watched in the mirror as Beryle worked with a curl. *I hope King Mendel lives a long, healthy life.* When Millard took over, the kingdom would fall apart within a few years. He'd deplete the treasury for something useless, like jewel-studded uniforms for the entire King's Guard. As well as dazzling saddlery for their horses, no doubt.

Of course, the king knew all this—she'd seen an expression of concern creep over His Majesty's features when Millard made an especially short-sighted comment. Mendel was careful not to show his concern, but he was an intelligent man. Was he worried about the fate of his kingdom after his death?

That's why he is so anxious for Sarana to have a boy. All kings wanted to ensure that the royal line of succession was fat with healthy, clever heirs. King Mendel had been disappointed in that respect. His queen had given birth to only one son and no daughters. Naturally, he would want a flock of grandchildren.

How disappointed the king must have been when Sarana had suffered one disastrous and unproductive pregnancy after another. How disappointed they all were, the whole kingdom.

If only Millard weren't such a dunce.

"Anyway," Beryle broke the silence with a matter-of-fact tone while she twisted yet another lock of hair around the rod. "You have to go tonight, because everyone expects you to be there."

Arien made an unladylike sound. "No one expects me. No one even knows I exist. Prince Thaine will expect to meet Master Petro, but that's it. Maybe I can go to dinner and skip the dancing afterward."

"Can you heat this again, miss? It's gone cold."

Beryle held out the rod, and Arien sent a Movement that increased the speed of the particles. Beryle gingerly touched a wet finger to it and nodded when it sizzled. She reached for another lock of hair. "That Prince Thaine is a comely one. Shame he's married. I got a glimpse of him in the stables this afternoon when he came down to see to his horses. Doesn't look a thing like his sister."

Arien gave Beryle a stern look in the glass. "You shouldn't say such things. Princess Sarana is very pretty and your future queen."

"Huh." Beryle sniffed. "No queen I ever heard of spent her time peeping through keyholes. And I don't expect I want to live in a castle where someone like her is queen. I'll leave afore then."

Arien ignored the comment. "And furthermore." She turned to give Beryle a suspicious look. "What were you doing in the stables this afternoon?"

A blush crept into the girl's cheeks, and Arien clucked her tongue. "I thought you'd decided not to forgive Hassin when he turned up again. I assume it is Hassin and not someone else?"

Beryle nodded, dark hair bouncing on her shoulders. "He's back and ever so humble. He got called away to take care of the planting, because his pa is sick. It was sudden, and he couldn't get in touch with me."

"And you believe that?"

"I do, miss. He ain't never given me no reason not to believe him." Beryle gave Arien a sly look. "Unless you know something I don't."

"No, I haven't listened in on his thoughts," Arien said. "Though if there was anyone I would suspect of hiding secrets, it's Hassin. Maybe I *should* listen, just once."

Beryle shrugged, unconcerned. "If you do and you happen to hear something about me, I want to know."

Arien shook her head. No matter how many times she assured the girl that she *would not* spy on people's thoughts, Beryle persisted in believing she did just that.

Of course, Petro did. It was part of his job as one of the king's advisors.

How can he throw away the prohibitions he drilled into me without being eaten alive by guilt? The answer remained a mystery to her.

"There." Beryle stood back to examine her work. "Beautiful. And shining like a forest fire atop that green gown."

Arien studied her reflection. A dusting of powder—applied in an attempt to cover her freckles—succeeded only in making her appear pale and sickly. Her hair was pulled sharply into a cluster high atop her head with red ringlets falling on every side like a bouncy waterfall. A short fringe at the hairline above her forehead softened the severity somewhat. She turned her head this way and that. It might look nice on someone else's head.

"If only it weren't so red."

Beryle gave her a truly perplexed look. "But that's what makes it special. Why, there's girls in town who've been trying to find a coloring to turn theirs the same shade."

Arien twisted around to look the girl in the face, surprised. Then she burst into laughter. "To look like me?"

"A'course," Beryle assured her. "You're a pretty woman, and your hair is so different. It's kind of exotic an' all. I've thought of doing it myself."

Beryle put her head next to Arien's and draped one long, red curl over her forehead, studying her reflection in the glass.

Arien laughed and moved her head away. "Don't be silly. You have lovely dark hair. I'd trade you in a minute."

A thought from Petro interrupted their conversation. *"Are you ready to go?"*

"I suppose so. Are you sure I must go? I'd rather stay in my rooms."

"Nonsense. The king invited you. He enjoys your company."

Arien enjoyed King Mendel as well. She spared one last thought of amazement that such an intelligent man could spawn the idiot Millard, then told Beryle, "Master Petro is ready."

Beryle's eyes went round. Petro was the only person who could reduce the verbose maid to speechlessness. She was more awed by him than by the king. Whenever he entered the room, Beryle shrank into a corner or escaped if she could.

Arien met Petro in the corridor outside the door to her rooms. His eyes widened when he caught sight of her.

"Nice dress. Green suits you better than black."

"I'd rather wear my robes." Arien awarded him a scowl.

"The curse of womanhood extends even to wardrobe."

He smiled to take the sting out of the thought and offered an arm to escort her. They wound through the maze of corridors in the residential wing, heading for the ballroom. It was the first time Arien had seen Master Petro alone in days. He seemed preoccupied.

"Is something bothering you?"

"No, but I've seen something in Prince Thaine's mind that I'm thinking about. I want to be ready with a plan when the time comes."

"I don't know how you can do that."

Petro gave her a querying look. *"Do what?"*

"Listen to people's thoughts as though it were nothing."

"But I must, my dear. That's what King Mendel expects of me. It's the reason I'm here."

"I know," Arien told him, *"but you taught me for years how unacceptable it is to eavesdrop on someone's mind. How can your opinion change so suddenly?"*

A thoughtful frown tugged at his mouth. *"I haven't*

changed opinions. I still believe that to spy upon another person's mind is a vile act, an invasion of a person's most private possession. But when dealing with kings, the rules change. I don't tell him everything I see in the minds of his subjects, only the things he needs to know to make the right decisions. And to keep himself safe, of course. Besides, everyone here is aware of my position. If a man is so foolish as to come into my presence with things on his mind he wants hidden from the king, he deserves to have his thoughts exposed."

Arien shook her head. *"I don't think I'd ever be able to tell which things the king needs to know and which he doesn't."*

"You must be discreet and diplomatic," Petro told her as they reached the ballroom.

"It must come with age," Arien muttered.

Petro gave her a playfully poisonous glance as he nodded a greeting for the guards at the doorway. Then he took her arm and led her inside.

The ballroom never failed to intimidate her. Its vaulted ceilings towered overhead, bright from the light of hundreds of lamps. Every inch of the white stone walls was carved and sculpted with elaborate designs, many of them etched in gold. Tables lined the perimeter, the silver goblets and tableware gleaming around colorful centerpieces of fresh flowers. A gold-draped table on a raised dais at the far end of the room was surrounded by ornately carved chairs. It was the king's table, where King Mendel dined during infrequent state dinners, along with Prince Millard and Princess Sarana and any other guests he wished to honor.

When Arien realized that Petro was leading her toward the dais, she tugged on his arm.

"I'd rather sit down here." She nodded toward one of the side tables.

"Nonsense," Petro replied. *"You are my guest tonight, and I've been invited to sit at the high table."*

She would have scowled, but Lord and Lady Aldon quickly approached, forcing her to smile. They were followed by Lord and Lady Fuller, then Lord Cranson.

Petro made the appropriate greetings, then led Arien away

from the chatting noblemen. They took the seats assigned them at the end of the main table. Lord and Lady Curran sat next to them, and Commander Jarvis of the King's Guard at the other end.

They hadn't been seated long when a trumpeter marched ceremoniously through the entryway. He blew an announcement sequence, which lulled the conversations in the room to silence. Arien rose, along with everyone else, and watched as the king entered.

King Mendel Valerien was of average height, with a kind face and dark hair interspersed with stray strands of grey. He was not normally one to stand on ceremony, and Arien suppressed a smile at his kingly costume tonight. That he was trying to impress Prince Thaine was obvious to anyone who had seen him hold court in his gardening breeches. He had assumed a stately walk tonight as well and nodded regally at his guests as he made his way slowly through the crowd. The ladies curtsied and the gentlemen bowed as he passed.

Behind him came First Prince Millard and Princess Sarana, whose bulging belly showed becomingly beneath her sky-blue gown. How in the world could someone with such a sweet face be so calculating and petty? Had Arien not caught her listening when she opened the sitting room door last month, she would not have believed the lovely princess capable of such an ignoble act.

Arien spared barely a glance toward the prince. It had not taken long after her arrival to discover that appearances were deceptive where royalty was concerned. Millard was quite handsome, with black hair and piercing blue eyes, but otherwise completely useless.

Following the first prince and the princess came tonight's honored guest. First Prince Thaine Valerien of Creighton resembled his sister, with golden hair and attractively arranged features. But where Sarana's were delicate and feminine, Prince Thaine's were decidedly strong. He walked with the easy grace that Arien had come to expect from the King's Guard. She'd heard that Prince Thaine held the position of Captain in Creighton's guard, and almost laughed at the thought of Millard in a similar capacity.

Looking at Prince Thaine, Arien remembered Beryle's comment. Yes, he was comely enough. Light, where Millard was dark, but both were handsome. She hoped they had nothing else in common.

As the procession made its way through the ballroom Arien scanned the crowd. Even though these were all guests of the king, and therefore diplomatically minded, Arien caught a few hostile expressions as Prince Thaine passed. Distrust between the Twin Kingdoms was strong, even here in Kirklin Castle. The marriage between Sarana and Millard seven years ago had been a good start, but the princess had done little to ingratiate herself to the people of Kirklin. Her brother's reception was polite, but not altogether friendly.

When he approached the king's table, King Mendel stood before his chair in the center. He placed his son on his left, and Prince Thaine on his right. That put the foreign prince next to Commander Jarvis's wife, and Arien breathed a sigh of relief. She wouldn't be expected to hold a conversation with him.

When everyone had arrived at their assigned places King Mendel sat, and the rest of the assembled followed suit. Millard glanced her way, trying to get her attention, but she ignored him. Tonight, at least, she was not obligated to talk to the prince. She would eat her dinner and leave as soon as good manners allowed.

Introductions were made, for the prince had arrived only that afternoon. The official meeting of the king's council would not take place until tomorrow morning. Beryle had reported that the prince met privately with his sister earlier today and had delivered messages from her parents, King Hubert and Queen Glenna of Creighton.

Upon being introduced, Arien nodded toward Prince Thaine, careful not to dunk her curls in her plate. She smothered a grin at the speculative glance the prince gave Petro, her escort. Outside of Kirklin Castle, strangers had assumed Master Petro to be her father, which irritated him no end. But she had become accustomed to strangers in the castle mistaking her for his mistress.

Dinner was elegant. King Mendel had given orders in the

kitchen for Thaine to be treated royally, and the kitchen staff had obliged. Their normally plain fare was replaced by an elaborate dish of pheasant stuffed with oysters and nuts and accompanied by a huge selection of vegetables and fruits. The fish was smothered in a delicate sauce and surrounded by large pink shrimp. The colorful ices served with dessert were juicy and the display of cakes impressive. Arien made a mental note to compliment the cook later.

After dessert had been cleared away, King Mendel motioned for the orchestra to play. They began a stately dance tune, and the king rose. Both princes did likewise. Prince Thaine extended a hand to Sarana, who beamed as she stood to dance with her brother.

Arien wanted to slouch down in her seat but couldn't do that while seated at the king's table. She'd never even seen a dance before arriving at Kirklin castle five months ago. Though she had tried to learn, her effort was half-given at best. She would much rather spend her time reading or wandering through the king's zoo.

She refused to look toward Millard. Maybe he would take the hint that she did not want to dance. Still, a hand was extended toward her. Resolutely she stood and was pleasantly surprised when she looked into King Mendel's face.

"Would you dance with an old man, my dear?"

Arien grinned. "I would, but since there doesn't appear to be one nearby, I'll dance with you instead."

"We'll make a diplomat out of you yet." Humor flooded Petro's thought.

She allowed the king to lead her down the dais steps into the center of the ballroom. Thaine and Sarana stood politely to one side, waiting for the king to begin the dance. As Arien placed her hand lightly on Mendel's shoulder, she saw Millard lead Lady Curran onto the floor.

"You look lovely," the king told her, his smiling eyes on level with her own. "I've never seen you in anything but men's breeches or black robes."

Arien pitched her voice low, as though whispering a kingdom secret. "I prefer either of them to this. You wouldn't believe how uncomfortable this gown is."

"Yes, I would," Mendel assured her. "I hated dressing for affairs like this when I was a young prince, and when I became King, I promised myself I would never do it again." He sighed. "Diplomacy has made me break that promise on several occasions. It is the fate of a king, I suppose."

Arien laughed but did not reply. The weight of many eyes lay on her from various tables around the room, and she concentrated on moving her feet without picking them up, lest she step on the king's toes. She bumped his shoes several times and flushed with embarrassment at first. But King Mendel didn't seem to mind or to notice. He was busy watching Thaine and Sarana. Arien heard Sarana's laugh and the murmur of the prince's low voice.

"Can you tell what they're talking about?" The king nodded toward the brother and sister.

Arien swallowed. Did he mean…yes, she knew by the look on his face that he did.

She Perceived, then smiled. "He's telling the princess about the antics of his son, Prince Roddy. He stole a horse last year from a member of the King's Guard, and Prince Thaine is describing a mad chase about the castle grounds when the horse bested him."

King Mendel nodded, a smile on his face. "Anything else he's thinking? Anything I should know about?"

Arien swallowed uncomfortably. She sent a quick thought toward Petro.

"He wants me to tell him Prince Thaine's thoughts."

"Just skim the prince's surface thoughts. He's not asking you to probe deeply."

She Perceived again, this time skimming all the prince's surface thoughts. She cleared her throat before speaking in a low voice. "He is thinking that his sister has grown lovely, but that she doesn't seem happy."

King Mendel nodded. "I've often thought the same."

Arien refrained from mentioning that Thaine thought the primary cause of Princess Sarana's unhappiness was her husband.

"He's also worried about something to do with Otero," Arien told the king. "That's the reason he's here, and he's frustrated that he had to come to this dinner tonight instead of meeting with your council immediately."

Now the king smiled broadly. "I feel exactly the same. Protocol does nothing but get in the way of the real work."

She cocked her head. "Then why do you allow it? You're the king. You could refuse to have fancy dinners and ceremonies."

Mendel shook his head. "My dear, the king is a slave to his subjects. The people expect ceremonies and balls and long, formal meetings."

"You don't make it sound much fun to be king."

Mendel smiled. "Part of it is fun. But it's a job that takes half your life to train for, and the rest of your life to accomplish. There will always be people who say you do it badly. Every decision affects someone in your kingdom, and usually a great number of people. If you are a good king, you care about the people, those decisions are … difficult."

He fell silent, his gaze fixed on a point somewhere up among the lanterns. Arien did not speak either, for she was considering what he had said. Would Prince Millard feel the same when he became king?

The dance ended, and the orchestra quickly struck up another tune as all the people stood and moved toward the floor. The king escorted Arien back to her seat and claimed the hand of Commander Jarvis's wife. Arien leaned toward Petro to excuse herself when she became aware of another presence beside her. Looking up, she was surprised to see Prince Thaine smiling down at her, his hand extended.

"If I may have the honor."

Heat flooded her face as she remembered her prying a moment before, but she rose and took his hand.

"My, my, you seem to be the prize of the ballroom tonight," Petro's thought teased.

"Hush," Arien sent back.

"He's quite handsome, isn't he?"

"I said hush," Arien replied with another flush. She had just been thinking how handsome Prince Thaine was and instinctively checked her shield.

They arrived at the center of the ballroom and Thaine

turned, placing his hand lightly at her waist. They were surrounded by dancing couples. Thank goodness they weren't on display for this dance. The prince moved gracefully, and she found herself able to follow his movements without bumping into him.

"I've met so many people here," he told her, "that the names are running together. Please forgive me for asking yours."

"I'm Arien, Your Highness."

"Arien…" His voice trailed off, waiting for her to supply the surname.

"Tyler." Arien took Petro's surname as she had done in the past when pressed.

"Ah, Master Petro Tyler is your… "

She flushed again, and explained, "He's like my father, in a way. I'm an orphan, and he was my teacher. When he came to Kirklin, I came with him."

Confusion creased Prince Thaine's forehead. "But he's a member of the Brotherhood of Power. I thought members of the Brotherhood taught mind Powers."

Arien nodded. "They do—as well as reading and history and ciphering, and other things." She laughed at the dumbfounded look on the prince's face. "I'm sorry, but you look just like Prince Millard when he found out I was a brother."

A fake shudder shook Thaine's shoulders. "I sound like Millard? Don't say that, even in jest."

She suppressed a grin and looked away. It was not diplomatic to enter into a derogatory conversation about the future King of Hamlin. Especially with the future King of Creighton. When she looked back at him, Prince Thaine grinned, and Arien took it as an unspoken apology.

He went on. "I've never heard of a female brother. Are there any besides you?"

Arien shook her head. "I'm the only one. And they almost didn't take me."

"You must have special abilities, then."

Arien shrugged, uncertain how to respond.

"Where were you from, before you went to the Brotherhood?"

"A village in the mountains of Creighton, west of Arnath."

"Really?" Interest sparked in Thaine's eyes. "I've been telling our guard commander we need to go to those mountain villages to recruit. The guard is always looking for men, and the pay's good. I've thought it might appeal to people in those small villages."

Arien smiled and shook her head. "There aren't more than twenty men in the whole village, plus a few mountain men who come down with their flocks in bad weather. You wouldn't find much there to make it worth the distance you'd have to travel."

"Someone found you." A complimentary smile curved his lips, and Arien blushed at the admiration in his tone.

Just then, the music ended and Arien realized they had shifted position during the dance. They were near the entrance.

She stepped away from the prince and nodded her thanks for the dance. When he took her arm to guide her back to the king's table, she hesitated.

"I've had enough ceremony for one night." She flashed a quick smile. "If you don't mind, I think I'll leave now."

Prince Thaine leaned down to whisper in her ear. "I envy you your freedom. Good night, Lady Arien."

"Brother Arien," she corrected with a grin.

He laughed out loud. "It's absurd, but it suits you, somehow. Brother Arien, then. I hope to see you again."

With a final smile, she made her escape.

"Good night," she sent toward Petro.

"Leaving so soon? Millard will be devastated." Petro's tone told Arien the thought pleased him. Did no one like Millard?

"Give him my regrets," Arien sent. *"I'll see you tomorrow."*

Seven

Kirklin Castle contained an entire town within its protective walls, with a few hundred inhabitants and a good selection of shops and services. Though bigger than her old village back in the mountains of Creighton, walking through the town gave Arien feelings of nostalgia. The streets were clean and well-kept, the people industrious. Instead of a man-made moat, a wide deep lake encircled the island on which the castle was located. The lake was brackish, for Kirklin was near enough to the Fallman Sea that the scent of salt wafted throughout the town when the wind blew from the east. The castle itself, located in the center of the walled island, was beautifully built and exquisitely decorated. Its doors stayed open to the townsfolk night and day, with guards posted only at the entrances to private chambers and the king's audience rooms.

Arien was in the zoo the morning after the ball when

Beryle came to fetch her. She had just finished cleaning out the monkey cage, a chore the zookeeper gladly delegated because the monkeys delighted in hanging from the branches of their leafless trees and lobbing bits of fruit rind down on whichever human invaded their space. The first time Arien tossed a banana peel back, they had squealed with glee and then bombarded her with everything they had stored in their treetop nests. The game had become something of a tradition, which she enjoyed as much as the monkeys.

Beryle approached at a run, excited and out of breath. “Hurry, miss! It's a summons from the king. You're to go to the Council Chamber right now.” Beryle skidded to a stop and swept Arien head to toe with a horrified glance. “You can't go like that.”

Arien glanced down at her clothing. She wore old breeches and a loose blouse, both covered with bits of goo from her game with the monkeys. Her shoes were covered with something else, and a decidedly unpleasant odor drifted from them. She put a hand to her hair and came away with a smashed grape.

Beryle's eyes rolled with exasperation. “I told the page you'd be right there.”

“I'm sure the council won't mind waiting a few moments while I get cleaned up. If they could see me, they'd probably insist upon it.”

She laughed at Beryle's obvious distress. It helped to relieve her own nervousness. In the months since her arrival, she’d never been called into a council meeting. What could they want with her?

Beryle stopped off at the kitchens for a bucket of hot water while Arien returned to her room. She was combing garbage out of her hair when Beryle came in. For once, Arien was glad for help during a bath. Beryle cleaned her feet while Arien scrubbed her face, neck, and arms. That was all she had time for. She slipped into her black Brotherhood robes and let Beryle clasp her hair in a simple leather tie. Grabbing her medallion, she almost ran out the door.

A pair of guards stationed outside the council chamber nodded for her to go in. She paused with her hand on the handle and took a deep, fortifying breath.

She'd been inside the council chamber several times, but never with anyone present. The room was more imposing filled with people, all of them seated around a long table and wearing solemn expressions. King Mendel sat at the head flanked by Princes Thaine and Millard. She recognized several lords and also Commander Jarvis. Two guards wore blue uniforms. Prince Thaine must have brought his own guardsmen with him. Petro sat half-way down the table from the king.

Prince Thaine was the first to notice her entrance. "Brother Arien." He rose, a broad smile on his handsome face.

"Ah, yes." King Mendel also smiled as he gestured toward an empty seat. "Thank you for coming, my dear. Please be seated."

Her face heated while every person at the table watched her make her way to the chair.

Petro spoke. "Prince Thaine has brought interesting news, and we are discussing what should be done about it."

Arien glanced toward Thaine. The smile was gone, and he wore a solemn expression.

"What has this to do with me?" she asked Petro.

"Wait and see."

"Yes." The king wore an expression as grave as Thaine's. "King Hubert received a warning several weeks ago that Otero may be planning an assassination attempt in Creighton."

Thaine dipped his forehead in acknowledgment. "I am a target, and apparently several other captains of our King's Guard as well. We can only assume this is part of a larger plan to invade Creighton."

"It may be nothing," Millard put in. Arien didn't need to listen to his thoughts to sense his jealousy at the attention Prince Thaine received from his father's council. The look on his face when he glanced toward his brother-in-law told her that. "The news came from a questionable source."

Thaine nodded. "True. But my father decided that to disregard the warning is more risk than he is willing to take. It has been almost two hundred years since Otero's last attempt to invade our kingdom. At that time, the Twin Kingdoms joined together to defeat them. That is why I'm here."

"I don't see why we should get involved." Millard glanced toward his father. "They can't attack Hamlin. The mountains across our northern border are impassable, and our coast is well protected by the barrier reef."

An embarrassed silence fell on those around the council table.

"Is he really as stupid as he appears to be?" asked Petro.

An unexpected sympathy for Millard struck her. *"I think he's more short-sighted than stupid. But I still don't see what this has to do with me."*

"Have patience."

King Mendel sent an apologetic glance toward Thaine, who sat back in his chair with arms folded and a disgusted glare leveled on Millard.

The King spoke to his first prince in a patient voice. "If the Oterans take Creighton, what is to prevent them from making Hamlin their next target? It is in our best interest to ensure that Creighton remains strong and free from invasion."

"And besides," put in Lord Aldon, "when you married Princess Sarana, we renewed an ancient alliance with Creighton. We promised that we would come to their defense should the need arise, just as they promised us."

"I know that." Millard frowned toward the man. "I merely meant that we're not prepared for a war any more than Creighton is."

"I'm sure that's what he meant." Sarcasm loaded Petro's mental tone.

"Creighton *is* ready," Thaine corrected him. "But, as my father pointed out, we've had no contact with Otero in a hundred years. How do we gauge the size or strength of their guard? That's why we need to send an emissary."

"Here's where you come in. Pay attention."

Arien looked across the table at Petro, startled.

"That is why we asked you to join us, my dear," said King Mendel at the same moment. "Prince Thaine has come with a request that we also send an emissary north, to show the Oterans that the Twin Kingdoms stand together. To attack one of us is to attack us both. Master Petro has recommended you be included as part of our diplomatic group."

Arien gasped, her hand flying to her collarbone. "Me? But— but—" Several smiles appeared around the table, some hidden by courteous hands. Her face burned. "But I don't know anything about diplomacy or how to be an emissary."

"You wouldn't have to," Prince Thaine assured her. "You would go as an escort, and your true position will remain secret. Your unique, uh, abilities will give us a tremendously advantageous position."

They wanted her along to spy on the Oterans' thoughts? She shifted in her chair. That went against everything she'd been taught.

Then another piece of Prince Thaine's comment registered, causing her to frown. "An escort to who?"

Millard leaned forward and sent a grin the length of the table. "To me."

By sheer force of will, she managed not to roll her eyes heavenward.

"He insisted." Sympathy flooded Petro's thought. *"Prince Thaine will be going as well."*

Unconsciously echoing Petro's thought, Prince Thaine said, "I'll be going, too, and members of the King's Guard from both kingdoms."

"Don't you think Master Petro would be a better choice?" Arien glanced toward her master. "He's accustomed to this sort of thing. I wouldn't know what to look for."

"I would gladly go," Petro responded, "except that I will likely be viewed with suspicion. It is well known that King Mendel has an advisor with Power, and if it is known in the Twin Kingdoms, we must assume Otero's king knows as well."

Prince Thaine nodded. "However, it is not known that a female has Power, and that may put you in a position to learn things Master Petro would not."

Arien looked toward the head of the table where King Mendel sat. "Is it wise to send both first princes into a country you suspect of trying to assassinate one of them?"

The king grinned. "You may know nothing about

diplomacy, my dear, but you cannot claim the same about defense."

Though pleased by the compliment, Arien told Petro, *"That's just common sense."*

"We were discussing that when you arrived," said Lord Theobald. "And I agree with Lord Aldon. I think sending the first prince of either kingdom is a mistake."

"My father said the same," Prince Thaine told him, "but I convinced him otherwise. If you have a trained diplomat you'd like to send along, by all means do so. But I feel that the Oterans will not take us seriously unless we send someone of importance to the kingdoms. I have authority to bargain in areas where no diplomat in Creighton does."

Several of the lords shook their heads, not convinced. But King Mendel looked thoughtful.

Petro rested his elbows on the table before him and steepled his fingers. "The choice of emissary relays as much as the message he brings. Consider the prince's mission here. Would you have treated a diplomat other than the king's son with as much courtesy as you have treated the First Prince of Creighton? Would you have listened as seriously to someone else?"

The king considered that, then shook his head. "No, I would not. I would have listened, assuredly so, but the fact that Hubert sent his own son tells me how close to his heart this issue is, and therefore, should be close to mine."

"I will agree," said Lord Fuller with a nod of concession "that the emissary should be of royal blood. But *both* first princes?" He turned toward Millard. "And what if the princess should be brought to childbed while you are gone?"

Millard shrugged. "It's unlikely I'll be of much use to her when that time comes. And if Creighton is to be royally represented in Otero, so should Hamlin."

Arien glanced around the table and noted the disapproving expressions on most of the councilors' faces. She agreed with them. The prince should be here when his heir arrived. But no one voiced their thoughts, and the king did not speak.

Millard obviously considered the matter settled. "What shall we do when we arrive? March into their king's castle and demand to know if they are planning to invade Creighton?"

For once, he had asked an intelligent question.

Thaine answered. "My father suggests that we travel under the pretense of establishing a trade arrangement."

Lord Theobald rubbed his chin. "A logical reason to send an emissary."

Lord Fuller agreed. "As far north as they are, they can't have anything like yellowberries or tandies, or the other fruits that grow in the southern parts of our kingdoms."

"Our furniture is popular with the islands," Millard put in. "And some of our fabrics as well."

"And the wines from the vineyards around Tifford in Creighton are exquisite," added Thaine.

"We must assemble a selection of gifts for their king." Fuller glanced at Thaine. "The finest from both kingdoms."

"But not too much," Thaine warned. "We'll be crossing the Oteran border through the Nephtali Pass, and what we take will be carried on our backs."

"Why don't we sail?" asked Millard. "We have found a way through the barrier reef. That's what has enabled us to set up trade with the Zorah Isles. We could take more on a ship, and it would be much easier than climbing through the Nephtali Pass."

"A good thought." From Prince Thaine's expression, he did not think so at all. "But do we want to announce to the Oterans that there is a passageway through the barrier reef? As long as they think it is impassable, Hamlin is safe from a sea attack, as it has been for centuries."

"Gifts are fine," said Petro, pulling their attention away from Millard's display of ignorance, "as long as we don't forget the primary reason for our visit. We are going to gather information. The more we know about the Oterans, the better our position if it comes to war."

The council began planning in earnest, each determined that his opinions be heard and acted upon. The session lasted far longer than Arien's interest, and her thoughts wandered. Millard constantly leaned forward to glance down the table at her, which made her want to shrink into her chair. Even more disturbing, her own eyes were repeatedly drawn toward the fair prince who sat across from him.

"And remember that you are not expected to Perceive every mind you encounter," Petro told Arien as she and Beryle scurried around the room, folding clothes and packing them in trunks. "Only the ones who are suspicious. And the high lords and the king's, of course. If anyone is aware of a plot, it will be them. You should see it in their surface thoughts. Don't probe further unless you discover something suspicious." His eyebrows arched. "Or unless you *feel* something that causes concern."

Arien took his meaning. Her empathic abilities may tell her things even men's thoughts would not. She folded a black Brotherhood robe. "I'll remember."

"You can't take that." Petro took the robe from her hands.

She sighed, exasperated. "Not even to wear in Tadmoure? I'm not stupid enough to take it to Otero."

But Petro shook his head. "Not even in Tadmoure. It would jeopardize the mission if anyone discovers that you are Brother Arien, and not just Prince Millard's…escort." He had the grace to look embarrassed and turned his head to avoid Arien's glare.

"And have you considered," she almost spat, "how the people in Tadmoure Castle—Princess Sarana's home—will receive me in that role?"

"King Hubert will know your real purpose, and I can't believe you'd be worried about the rest."

"Oh, no." She flooded her voice with sarcasm. "I've grown accustomed to being looked down upon, whispered about, and snubbed. Life at the Brotherhood certainly gave me enough practice. Why should I worry about the gossip of an entire kingdom?"

Beryle, who was filling a small case with toiletry items from Arien's dressing table, turned to look at her, concern plain in the deep creases on her forehead. "And how will we get through that Nephtali Pass, that's what I worry about."

"You'll have to hike, and climb part of the way," he told

her. “It won't be easy.”

Beryle blanched, and Arien turned a kind look upon her. “You don't have to go if you don't want to, I've told you that. Hanna has said she would go. She is from the mountains and more accustomed to climbing than you.”

Beryle raised her chin. “Huh,” was all she said, but Arien took her meaning. Beryle was more excited about this trip than anything she'd ever done, and she wouldn't miss it even if it meant being pulled up a cliff while dangling from the end of a rope.

Petro turned to Arien with a somber expression. “You don't have to go, either, if you don't want to.”

“But I'm the whole reason we're going.”

“Yes, but we could find someone else. Prince Thaine could stop off at the Hall of the Brotherhood on his way to Tadmoure. I'm sure he can convince them to send someone on such an important mission.”

Arien shook her head. “Then we lose the benefit of bringing along a female with Power. You were right about that to begin with. They'll never expect me to be anything but Millard's mistress.”

“I hate for you to feel forced to do anything against your will.”

She didn’t need empathic ability to sense the deep regard in Petro's thought, and she gave him a tender smile.

“Thank you. I appreciate your concern. And believe me, I have no intention of doing anything except pretend at our relationship. And in a way, I do want to do this. It's just that I'm nervous.”

As she projected the thought, she realized it was true. She had never felt more useless as she had since coming to Kirklin Castle. Master Avram's question during her trial haunted her. What had she done since leaving the Brotherhood? Nothing. Except learn to dance and read books and play with animals in the zoo. And what did she plan to do? Nothing. Except read more books, play with more animals, attend social functions, and tag along after Master Petro.

But now she had the opportunity to do something important. And for the first time, she would do it alone, without

Petro to rely upon. It was frightening, and she *was* nervous, but also more excited than she had ever been.

And I get to go with Prince Thaine. She pushed that thought away, refusing to give it any consideration.

Beryle snapped the small case shut. "When are we leaving?"

"Sunrise tomorrow." Petro turned a skeptical eye on their trunks. "You know you'll never be able to get all those trunks over the Nephtali Pass? Everything you take must be hauled on the backs of your escort. You aren't taking the entire King's Guard."

"A lady must be prepared for anything." Beryle thrust her chin in the air, and Arien smiled.

"I said the same thing," she told Petro, "and was informed that while I was in Tadmoure Castle I had to dress like a princess myself." She grinned. "Believe me, I won't take but half of that into Otero."

Petro threw one more glance toward the trunks. "Better make it even less."

For as long as she could remember, Arien had dreamed of visiting Tadmoure Castle. In the orphanage, it was spoken of in such tones of awe she fully expected to see its towers and turrets rising in glowing golden jewel-studded peaks. When they rounded the last bend in the road and the castle finally came into view, disappointment stabbed at her.

Tadmoure Castle had been constructed of huge blocks of grey stone for defense rather than ornamentation. While Kirklin Castle was designed for beauty, Tadmoure had been situated in the wild northwest at a time when the nearby Nephtali Pass was of utmost concern. High, windowless walls surrounded the courtyard. And as the group approached, the only way inside that Arien could detect were huge iron doors, half a spear thick and wide enough for two large wagons to enter side-by-side.

The town of Tadmoure spread out around the castle, its buildings neat and sturdy. The streets were clean and free of debris, and the people who strolled through them appeared to be happy and curious of the band of travelers that passed by. Prince Thaine wore nothing to mark himself as first prince—had not since their departure from Kirklin. But the townspeople recognized him regardless. Word spread, and before they had reached the palace doors a cheering crowd had lined the streets.

Arien and Beryle rode in a wagon with their luggage. It had also served as their shelter at night during the journey, when they unrolled their travel blankets beneath it and hung curtains around its edges. The group had traveled without stopping except to sleep, though Millard argued to stay a few days in Corral. Thaine, eager to return to Tadmoure, prevailed.

Arien kept to herself for most of the three-day journey. She in no way wanted to encourage Millard, for he had let her know the first day out that he desired her for his companion, not simply as a cover on the mission. Her cold rebuff seemed not to affect him at all. She steadfastly ignored him for the rest of the trip.

For different reasons, Arien didn't speak to Thaine either, except when politeness required it. Respect blossomed for his ability to command the guardsmen who accompanied them. His men held him in high regard and not only for his position as first prince. He was an intelligent, caring captain, and the soldiers trusted his judgment. Her admiration for Thaine bordered on something that disturbed her a great deal. Not only was he a prince, he was a *married* prince. So, she maintained a distance between them.

The little party approached the huge doors late in the day, when the sun had begun to set behind the castle. Long shadows gave the unadorned grey walls a dismal, even forbidding look. Arien suppressed a shudder as they passed through the thick wall. Beryle, looking up to see the stern-faced guards posted high above them, shivered openly.

"Makes me long for home," she whispered to Arien, her brown eyes round.

Arien patted her arm. "I'm sure the inside is much more pleasant." At least, she hoped so.

In a wide-open courtyard inside the castle walls a group of uniformed guardsmen stood at attention in two rows. Their leader stepped forward and greeted Thaine with a crisp salute. "Welcome, First Prince." The man's voice filled the silent courtyard and echoed off the surrounding walls. "His Majesty bids you welcome and asks that you hasten to attend Princess Lianne. I will escort your companions to His Majesty's receiving room."

Thaine started visibly. "Is the princess ill?" Concern flooded his voice.

The man's face remained stern, but somehow took on a sad affirmative without changing his features. Thaine gazed first at Millard, and then Arien. He gave them an unreadable glance, and then dashed through a door.

Millard turned toward the wagon with a disgusted grunt and raised a hand to assist first Arien and then Beryle from their bench. "And off he goes, leaving us to introduce ourselves to the king. Hardly the gentleman he appears to be."

Arien let the remark pass. Millard turned to the guardsman with an arrogant expression. "Are we permitted to wash the road's dust from ourselves before being presented to the king?"

She gave him a sharp look. Was he purposefully trying to antagonize the man? She had never heard him speak in so belittling a manner.

If so, it didn't work. The guardsman's face remained impassive. "Of course, Your Highness." He bowed respectfully.

Millard smirked, obviously pleased with the response.

The guardsman turned to one of his men.

"Ask the chamberlain which rooms have been assigned to our visitors. Tell him to make arrangements concerning their luggage."

"We require adjoining chambers," Millard put in, glancing slyly at Arien.

Her face burning, she turned an irritated stare on Millard. A thousand angry retorts flashed through her mind, but she was unable to select an appropriate one. And she couldn't even utter a protest, lest she give away the deception to which she had agreed.

The man hurried into the castle through the same door Thaine had taken, and the guardsmen's leader addressed them with a bow. “If you will come this way, Your Highness. My Lady.”

When the man turned, Arien glared at Millard. His suggestive smirk served to infuriate her. As a further insult, she caught sight of Beryle covering a grin with her hand as she reached up to grab Arien's small travel case from the wagon.

They stepped into a long, dark corridor without windows. A dim light came from sconces along the wall, only half of which held burning lamps. The tapestries appeared at first glance to be dull and colorless in the insufficient lighting, but when she inspected one, she discovered that they were quite beautifully made.

Halfway down the corridor they were met by the chamberlain, a short man with a full head of shaggy black hair. His smile brightened when his eyes fell on Arien, and she couldn't help returning the grin. With a low bow, he addressed Millard.

“Your Highness, welcome to Tadmoure Castle.” Even Millard would not be able to fault his respectful tone. “I am Oren, the king's Chamberlain, and am most honored to serve you while you are here.” He turned to Arien and bowed again. “And welcome to you as well, lady. I hope your room meets with your approval. If you will follow me.”

He led them through several turns in the castle's confusing corridors, and Arien became completely lost. The castle hadn't looked very big from the outside, but they'd already walked farther than it should have taken to cross the length of it twice. Were they traveling in circles? The corridors all looked similar, though she couldn't swear they hadn’t passed through the same one twice.

As though he could hear her thoughts, Oren turned his head to speak to them as they walked. “The private rooms are near the center of the castle and the route convoluted for security reasons. The rooms along the outside walls contain the armory, ballrooms, and audience chambers. And of course, barracks and the servant's quarters.”

“Are there no windows?” Millard glanced around the dimly lit corridor.

"Some, along the back of the castle, high enough in the wall that they pose no security threat. And there is an inner courtyard, open to the sky and quite defensible." Though she could not see his face, Arien heard a smile in the chamberlain's voice. "You probably find our preoccupation with defense odd."

"No," Arien answered. "Living this close to the Nephtali Pass, it would be foolish not to take precautionary measures."

Millard shook his head. "But the Pass has been closed for a long time. Surely there is no need for all these precautions now."

The man shrugged. "Possibly we are foolish, but security becomes a way of life."

Hardly foolish, considering the reason for our mission. Her thought remained unspoken. She had no idea how many people knew the reason behind their visit, but she doubted a chamberlain was privy to kingdom secrets.

A few moments later she revised that opinion. A chamberlain, especially one as alert as Oren, deduced a lot without being told. As he showed Arien her rooms, she glanced nervously toward a side door in the receiving room. It obviously led to the next suite. Millard, seeing her glance, allowed a slow smile to spread across his lips as flames erupted in her cheeks. Oren also saw the glance. As he left to show Millard to his rooms, he slipped a key into Arien's hand.

"For the door," he said in a low voice, nodding toward it.

He grinned, and Arien smiled in return, clutching the key in her fist. Then he was gone, escorting the First Prince of Hamlin to the next set of rooms down the corridor.

She immediately crossed to the adjoining door and twisted the key in the lock. Just to be sure, she rattled the handle. Good. Then she turned to inspect her room. It was furnished, as any receiving room would be, with several chairs and small tables, plus a large set of shelves with a number of books. She selected the biggest, heaviest chair in the room and pushed it in front of the connecting door just as Beryle entered the bedchamber.

"What might you be doing?" she asked as she helped Arien position the chair.

"What does it look like?"

Beryle grinned, her plump cheeks dimpling. "Looks like you're determined to disappoint Prince Millard." When the chair was placed to Arien's satisfaction, Beryle straightened and placed her hands on her hips. "And him your future king and all."

"King he may be," Arien said, "but anything else would be most grudgingly given." Irritation flooded her and spilled over into her voice. "And he knows that. Surely there are any number of willing girls ready to do such a service for their future king. Why does he plague me?"

Beryle laughed, shaking her head. "Being tucked away in that magic school with a bunch of men should have taught you something of their ways. He's after you because you don't want him. If you'd give in once, chances are he'd find another skirt to chase and leave you alone."

Arien shuddered and shook her head. "Never."

Just then a knock sounded, and she started forward to open the corridor door. But Beryle laughed again and pointed toward the door that connected to Millard's room.

Arien approached cautiously, glaring at the wood. "What do you want?"

The handle rattled, followed by Millard's muffled voice. "Someone's locked the door."

"I did," Arien shouted back, "and it will remain locked."

He said something too low for her to understand. She could have Perceived him easily through the wall, but why bother? She didn't want to know what he was thinking.

Beryle's grin irritated her further, so she trounced into the bedchamber to change for her upcoming meeting with the king.

Within minutes of Beryle pronouncing her ready, a guardsman arrived to escort Arien to the king's receiving room. She wore a simple gown of yellow cotton, tied around her middle with a wide sash. Her hair had been pulled loosely back with a bow of the same fabric as her dress, and fell in a mass of soft, shining curls down her back. As she stepped into the corridor, Millard gave her an admiring glance.

"My father won't be pleased to hear that you dress more

beautifully for the court of Creighton than for his own," he said as he offered his arm.

Arien took it with a chilly smile. "Your father understands and approves dressing for comfort."

"Yes, I suppose he does." Millard gave a quiet laugh.

Arien looked sharply at him, but the comment had been made lightly and, she realized, with affection. Apparently, he really did love his father. She warmed slightly toward him. Perhaps this trip would provide an opportunity to understand more about Millard. If she planned to continue living at Kirklin Castle, she must develop some sort of respect for him as a ruler, if not as an individual. Maybe Thaine would provide a model that Millard would want to imitate. Perhaps she could encourage him in that direction.

They followed their guide through the twisting corridors and arrived shortly at the king's receiving room. King Hubert was a tall man, fair like his son, with a muscular body. He sat upon an ornate throne, his bearing regal, and Arien's fingers tightened nervously on Millard's arm. This king was the exact opposite of friendly, caring King Mendel. His subjects probably never saw him in anything other than royal dress.

Queen Glenna sat at his side on a smaller and only slightly less bejeweled throne. Arien would have known her anywhere. That she was closely related to both Sarana and Thaine was obvious, though her face was more heavily lined than either of her children. Her waist was thick, but not unsightly, and her hair was a truly lovely golden color that shone as brightly as the jewels around her neck.

The guardsman stepped forward from his post just inside the doorway and announced, "First Prince Millard of Hamlin."

Millard bowed and kissed the hand the king extended.

"You are welcome, my son," said King Hubert.

"Thank you, sire."

The queen also extended a hand toward him, and he knelt before her as well. She glanced at Arien before asking, "How is my daughter?"

Arien went hot at the implication in that glance, but Millard either ignored it or hadn't seen. He smiled. "She is well,

Your Majesty, though not able to rise from her bed. The healers are taking excessive precautions this time. We have hopes she'll deliver a strong heir soon."

"It is my constant prayer," Queen Glenna assured him.

Millard gestured toward Arien. "May I present Lady Arien, who has joined my father's court in recent months?"

Arien stepped forward and sank low before first the king, and then the queen. Her cheeks burned, humiliated at the purposefully vague reference to her position at Mendel's court.

"Welcome, Lady Arien." King Hubert's greeting was solemn.

"Yes, welcome," said the queen. "My daughter has mentioned you in her letters."

That can't be good. Arien smiled at the queen. "I'm honored to have been noticed by my future queen."

She kept her eyes lowered and was relieved that the king's next words were directed to Millard. "I have given instructions that dinner be served in our private dining room. We can talk less formally while we eat."

"Thank you, Your Majesty," Millard replied with another bow.

At least he knew how to mind his manners in a formal setting.

Hubert rose and extended his arm to his wife. A guardsman pulled back a heavy drapery to expose a door along the rear wall. Millard and Arien followed the king and queen through it and found themselves in yet another dimly lit corridor. A nearby door stood open and from that direction wafted the blended aromas of roasted meat, fresh fruit, and pungent onions.

Private the room may have been, but small it was not. The table, fully the size of King Mendel's council table, rested in the exact center of the room with two glittering chandeliers suspended above it. Six places were set at one end, King Hubert's at the head. After the king and queen had seated themselves, Millard led Arien to the chair on the king's right, across from Glenna. He sat beside her.

A moment later Thaine arrived with a woman leaning heavily on his arm. Arien rose and waited for the prince to lead his wife to the empty chair beside his mother. Though nearly as tall as Thaine, Princess Lianne's frame was thin to the point of being nearly skeletal. Prominent cheekbones protruded beneath hollow eyes, and her chin jutted sharply. Was the princess ill? Signs of a once-lovely woman lingered beneath the severe features. With an effort, Arien kept her expression pleasant.

When he had helped her into her chair, Thaine stood beside her. "Lianne, allow me to present First Prince Millard of Hamlin, and Lady Arien Tyler, from the King Mendel's court in Kirklin Castle."

Millard bowed and Arien executed a curtsey, though the princess barely acknowledged the introduction. She shifted in her chair as though trying to find a comfortable position and then picked up the spoon next to her plate. This she twisted in one hand, while the other plucked at the linen tablecloth. Her gaze darted everywhere, landing only briefly on Arien before flitting away. The constant movement reminded Arien of something. A long-ago memory, but of what?

"Please, sit down." Thaine gestured toward their chairs as he slid into the empty one between the princess and his mother. The skin around his eyes looked tight, and worry lines creased his forehead.

Servants stood along the far wall, each holding a covered platter. At a nod from the queen, a white-clad man standing near a second entrance to the room approached the table. One by one, the servants brought their platters forward so the dining attendant could dish portions of food onto their plates. Arien's was soon full to overflowing, and a blend of tempting aromas stirred up a rumble in her stomach. Their midday meal of travel fare had been a long time ago.

Lianne, who continued to fidget in her seat, knocked the attendant's arm and sent a spray of corn into her lap. A look of horror twisted the man's features, but the princess appeared not to notice.

After more food than Arien could possibly eat had been placed before her, the king spoke to the attendant. "Thank you, Garvey. Please leave us. I will ring for you if we need anything."

As the man turned to leave, Lianne leaped out of her chair. Her eyes wild, she grabbed a lock of her own hair and began to yank on it. "I— I need to leave."

"Are you ill?" Thaine rose too.

"No." She shook her head so violently an earbob came loose and skittered across the floor. "I must go. Excuse me."

With an apologetic grimace flung toward the king, she fled the room. Thaine hurried after her.

Arien placed the elusive memory of that convulsive twitching. The bandit who tried to rob Petro when he was taking her to the Brotherhood to begin her training. The one Petro had half-buried in the forest floor. Was the princess afflicted with the same sickness as that man?

She faced the king. "Is the princess ill?"

King Hubert gave Arien an uneasy glance and nodded.

The queen heaved a heavy sigh. "She's never regained the strength she had before Roddy's birth, though the child is past his tenth year. In recent months she's worsened."

She fell silent, her eyes averted. Questions burned in Arien's mind, but the queen's closed expression told her they would not be welcome.

"And how is my daughter?" She addressed the question to Millard.

"Confined to her bed until the baby comes." Millard pulled a sour face. "She's not taking the confinement easily."

The queen laughed, which eased the tension in the room a fraction. "I can't imagine how your healers have convinced her to lay abed all day."

"She wants a son badly as do I," Millard said. "No doubt her attendants are having a bad time of it."

According to Beryle, they had a bad time of it before her confinement as well.

The king picked up his fork. "Lady Arien, I understand that you have been trained in the ways of the Brotherhood." Though his tone was conversational, his face was serious.

"Yes, Your Majesty. I passed my trial a few months ago, before going to Kirklin Castle with my teacher."

"And what is your position in Kirklin?" With a glance at Millard, he said, "I understand it is not that to which you are pretending during this journey."

Arien shifted beneath his penetrating stare. "I have no real position, Your Majesty, other than assisting Master Petro. King Mendel is kind enough to allow me to call Kirklin my home, since I have no other. I was orphaned as an infant."

Hubert nodded slowly "I did wonder why you had not returned to your home. My son told me you came from one of the mountain villages in the northwest corner of my kingdom, but he neglected to mention the fact that you were an orphan." He turned in his chair to face her fully. "I'm sorry to be rude, but I've never had anyone in my castle who was adept in the Powers of the Brotherhood. Not to my knowledge, that is. To be honest, I'm not comfortable around your people, so I hope you'll forgive what I'm about to say. While you are here, I would like your oath that you will not listen to my thoughts or those of my family."

He thinks I'm sitting here spying on his mind.

"Your Majesty, you have my promise, and it is gladly given." She held his gaze. "Further, I swear to you that I have not listened to any thoughts since entering Tadmoure Castle and that I do not intend to do so at all. I don't listen to thoughts at Kirklin Castle, either. Well." She faltered, heat rising into her face. "Not unless specifically requested to do so by the king. But I was taught at the Brotherhood that it is tantamount to listening at keyholes, and I struggle with guilt whenever I am asked."

Beside her, Millard cleared his throat. Arien wondered if he, too, had surprised his wife in that endeavor. The king relaxed visibly, and Queen Glenna's smile became warmer, more genuine.

When next the king spoke, his voice was almost friendly. "It must have been difficult for you to agree to this trip."

Arien nodded. "But I see the need. In this case, I am uniquely qualified."

"Because you are a woman." The queen displayed an impish grin, one which put Arien much in mind of her son. "My dear, you must have had a fascinating time of it, growing up in that Hall of the Brotherhood. Someday I hope we can find the time for you to tell me about it."

Before Arien could reply, the door opened and Thaine entered.

"My apologies, Father." He hurried forward and returned to his chair. "Lianne isn't feeling well, but she's settled back in her room. I hope I've not kept you waiting."

King Hubert held up his fork. "As you can see, we didn't wait."

"We've just begun discussing the trip," Millard told Thaine.

"Ah, good, then I haven't missed anything." Thaine took a bite of roasted meat. He chewed with his eyes closed, relishing the taste.

King Hubert picked up his wine goblet. "I have engaged the guide you suggested."

Thaine explained to Arien and Millard. "The anodyte seller I told you about."

"Actually," the king said, "there are two of them, and they work as a team."

"Fine," Thaine said with a shrug. "I've never met them, but Oren has been dealing with them for years, and he says they're trustworthy."

The queen set her fork down and turned to face her son. "I wish you would stop buying that horrible drug."

Thaine gave her a sad smile. "I wish I could, Mother."

He turned his attention back to his food. After a moment, Queen Glenna sighed and did the same. Arien remained quiet. She had almost no knowledge of anodyte, except that it was a hallucinogenic, similar to wine taken in excess. Did Thaine indulge in the drug? She glanced in the direction the princess had fled. Maybe Lianne needed it to calm whatever affliction caused that constant restlessness.

"When will we leave?" Millard asked.

King Hubert answered. "As soon as you're ready. Your guides have been here for a week, and your escort has been prepared."

Thaine glanced toward the door, worry lines creased his forehead. "I'd like to delay a few days."

His mother covered his hand with hers, her expression full of sympathy. "You must take all the time you need."

"But not too much." Millard turned toward King Hubert. "If my heir is born while I'm in Otero, will you dispatch a messenger with the news?"

"Of course," Hubert agreed. "In fact, I will have messengers ready to cross the Nephtali Pass with any important news. Be sure you keep a few of our men near the northern side to receive them if the need arises. And of course, I will be waiting for updates. Please keep me informed."

Thaine gave a nod. "We shall leave in two days' time."

He returned to his food, though did not eat so much as rearrange it on his plate. Arien watched him from the corner of her eye, careful not to catch his gaze full on. What was he thinking? She itched to Perceive his thoughts.

Funny that so soon after making the promise to King Hubert she should feel the urge to break it. Maybe her part in this charade would not be so difficult after all.

Eight

On the morning of their departure, Arien donned the trousers and loose blouse that she found more comfortable than even her Brotherhood robes, much to Beryle's disapproval.

"This is far more suitable travel garb than your skirt," she told the scowling maid. "You'd do well to change before we leave."

The girl drew herself up to her full height, which put the top of her head roughly on level with Arien's chin. "I'll not be seen traipsing about dressed like a boy."

As if her delightfully plump frame could ever be mistaken for anything but a woman's.

"All right." Arien shrugged. "But you might change your mind when we get to the Nephtali Pass. Climbing will be hard enough without those skirts getting in your way."

"Hmmph."

With a toss of dark curls, Beryle exited the room. Shaking

her head, Arien followed.

The courtyard where they were to meet the others was a blur of activity. Men crowded the open space, most in uniform and several talking to the women who had come to bid them goodbye. Beryle mumbled something about checking their luggage and wandered off in the direction of the wagon that would accompany them as far as the path through the Nephtali Pass allowed. Millard and Thaine were engaged in a quiet conversation with King Hubert in the far corner, probably receiving last minute instructions.

Beside Thaine stood his son, Prince Roddy. One regret Arien had with their speedy departure was not having an opportunity to spend more time with the boy, a miniature version of Thaine, with hair as white as mountain snow and eyes bluer than the sky. They'd met at breakfast the morning after her arrival. With childlike candor, he exclaimed on the unusual color of her hair and eyes and proceeded to compare her to a variety of vegetables and plants, to the absolute horror of his tutor. Arien enjoyed the child thoroughly. At the moment, he stood bouncing on his toes and looking like a whirlwind eager to burst free.

"I don't believe it," said a voice behind her, and she whirled to see who had spoken.

A face from the past loomed before her. His dark hair was neatly trimmed, and his chin supported a short, thick beard, new since the last time she had seen him. But then, he was older than the last time. He took her hand and kissed it with a flourish, as though she were truly the courtly lady she pretended to be.

"Jothan!" She couldn't stop a wide grin. "Master Petro will be so pleased when I tell him I've seen you."

He looked around eagerly. "Is he here?"

"No, he's at Kirklin. Didn't you know?"

"Kirklin? I expected him to be still at the Brotherhood, training you. Oh." He stopped, a flush reddening his already ruddy cheeks. "They refused to accept you, didn't they?"

Arien laughed. "No, they accepted me. For the most part, anyway. I passed my trial half a year ago, and Master Petro—"

"Passed your trial?" Jothan shook his head, clearly astonished. "After only…" his eyes swept upward as he considered "…only seven years of training? Why, that's even faster than me." Grudging respect crept into his gaze.

"Be careful of your voice." She glanced around their immediate surroundings. Everyone appeared occupied with readying travel gear or checking the saddles on horses that stomped and snorted, eager to get moving. *"Only Thaine and Millard know of my abilities. And the king and queen, of course."*

"We were told that the First Prince of Hamlin was bringing his consort. Is that you?"

Arien flushed hotly. *"A charade, I promise you. Necessary to explain my presence in Otero."*

Jothan cocked his head sideways. *"Not a bad plan. We were disgusted at the thought of having to lug a dainty woman through the Pass."* His gaze swept her man's garb. *"I assume I won't have to carry you over the difficult parts of the trail."*

"Carry me? Are you going, too?"

"Of course. I'm your guide."

She studied him more closely. *"Then you're the anodyte seller."*

Jothan nodded. *"With my partner, Quinn. And don't look so self-righteous, little girl. My clientele are healers and medical practitioners. Besides, it is due to my occupation that we were able to uncover this invasion plan."*

"Possible *invasion plan."*

He dismissed the thought with a wave and changed the subject. "Tell me of Petro. What sent him to Kirklin?"

"Master Edsel died, and King Mendel sent a messenger to the Hall asking for someone to replace him. Master Petro volunteered."

Time enough to go into the details later, when it would make a good tale to pass time during the journey.

"Here comes my partner." Jothan spoke to someone behind her. "Look, Quinn, an old friend. You remember Lady Arien?"

Arien turned in time to see Quinn approach. He examined her face, a confused smile playing about his lips, and then shook his head. "I'm sorry, but I don't remember..."

His voice trailed off as he searched his memory.

Jothan laughed out loud, and Arien smiled. "You can't be expected to remember me. I was a child of twelve when we met, and then only briefly. It was in Arnath, at a boarding house."

Realization dawned on Quinn's face. "You were the funny-looking little girl with orange hair and freckles."

He stopped, embarrassed, but Arien and Jothan both laughed.

"That she was," Jothan agreed, "but no longer. This is the lady who will be traveling with us to Otero."

Surprise erupted on Quinn's face, and his eyebrows rose as his glance slid from her to the corner where Millard stood talking to the king. Oh, how she hated to have anyone think her capable of being the man's mistress, but she couldn't deny it. Not and keep up the deception to which she had agreed.

"It's not what you think," said Jothan in a low voice. "She's only pretending to be the prince's consort for this trip."

So much for keeping the secret.

"Jothan! You're not permitted to tell anyone."

"Quinn's all right," came his reassuring thought. *"And, by the way, I don't want to advertise my abilities, either. It's best if we both travel under cover. Me as a lowly guide and anodyte seller, and you as...whatever you're pretending to be."*

Her cheeks flamed. *"Agreed."*

Beryl approached in the company of a man leading a pair of horses. The stable master, by the look of his clothing and the way he handled the animals. Arien had long since overcome her fear of horses, but preferred to ride only gentle beasts, and not the high-spirited mounts guardsman usually selected.

The stable master, seeing her anxiously examine the horses, gave her an encouraging smile. "This one is yours, my lady." He led a beautiful chestnut mare forward. "She's sweet as chocolate cake and a lady, too. Like you. That's her name, Lady. Here, let her get a whiff of your hand."

She extended her hand, and the horse sniffed her

cautiously. Then it snorted a gentle blast of warm air and ducked its head twice, as though nodding approval. Arien smiled, pleased with the stable master's choice.

He turned to Beryle. "And I've the perfect mount for you, too, miss."

But Beryle planted her feet and folded her arms. "Not a chance for it. I'm planning on riding in the wagon as long as we have it, and I'll walk from there. Or climb, more likely. But I ain't riding no horse."

Arien grinned. "Why, Beryle, as much time as you spend in the stables at Kirklin, I thought you loved horses."

The maid had the grace to blush and turned away, muttering.

Across the courtyard, the royal consultation ended. King Hubert embraced his son and Millard in turn, and then his gaze swept the company. He caught Arien's eye and raised a hand in farewell before disappearing into the castle, Roddy at his side.

Will I see them again?

The thought struck Arien suddenly and startled her. The hazards of this mission had been openly discussed for weeks. A state of open hostility, if not downright war, had existed between Otero and the Twin Kingdoms for time out of mind. Since the closing of the Nephtali Pass there had been no official communication with those who lived beyond the massive mountain range that marked the northern border of both kingdoms. The possibility existed that a diplomatic party may not return. Yet, until this moment she hadn't truly realized the full danger. She might actually die. And not only her, but the princes of two kingdoms. Perhaps Lord Aldon had been right after all, and this was nothing but a fool's errand.

Thaine and Millard joined them and after being introduced to their guides, Millard asked about their route.

"We'll stick to the main roads as long as we can." Quinn's tone announced to all that he intended to lead the party, at least until they crossed into Otero.

Millard responded to the show of authority by adopting a haughty expression. "There must be shorter paths which will get us there quicker."

"Not with that wagon." Quinn pointed at the fully loaded wagon. "And without it, we'd be even longer since we'd have to stop for meals and beds."

The quick glance he shot toward Arien and Beryl spoke volumes. Men traveling alone no doubt ate whatever they could hunt and slept in bedding they carried on their backs. Arien bit back a quick response. If she and her maid were to be viewed as a burden, she'd gladly stay behind. But how could she face King Mendel and Petro and the others, after she had agreed?

Commander Norval stepped in. "Your Highness, we have hired these men as guides. I suggest you let them guide."

Millard turned an arrogant look upon the commander, but at a glance from Thaine, he gave a petulant nod. Thaine smiled at him and turned to Arien.

"And may I present Lady Arien?" he said to Quinn and Jothan.

Jothan grinned at her. "We've met the lady, and I am looking forward to the journey all the more for the opportunity to spend time in her company."

Arien dimpled at him for the compliment and caught a frown on Thaine's lips. It was mirrored on Millard's.

"Oh ho, so both princes are protective of you," Jothan teased. *"How interesting."*

"Nonsense. If they are, it is because I'm a female and you are a scoundrel seller of drugs from whom they think I need protection."

He chuckled, which drew further frowns from the princes.

"I suggest we get on our way, Your Highnesses." Quinn cast a stern look at Jothan. "That is, if we want to make Arnath by nightfall."

"We're going through Arnath?" The prospect of seeing the town again lifted her spirits.

Quinn nodded. "And with luck we'll all find rooms, because from then on we'll be camping."

Thaine gave the order for his fifty or so guardsmen to mount up. Beryl climbed onto the wagon bench beside the driver and began to chatter nonstop. The driver nodded distractedly, straining over Beryle's voice to hear Thaine's instructions to the Guard. Arien chuckled. No doubt the man would be heartily tired of Beryle's voice by the time they reached Arnath.

A crowd had gathered in the streets of Tadmoure, but the cheers were half-hearted as the party passed through. That Thaine was well-liked was obvious, but Arien caught sight of many silent, scowling faces in the crowd.

"I see the people have recognized Millard," she commented to Jothan. Once again, she had someone with whom to hold mindspeech. She missed Petro more than she could have imagined.

"No, actually they've gotten word of your mission and are unhappy about it."

Arien scanned the assemblage. *"But, how could they?"*

"Not the real reason, but the reason the king let out. That you are going on a diplomatic journey into Otero to set up a trade agreement. Here in the north, most of these people have ancestors who were killed fighting the Oterans. They're not happy at the thought of diplomatic relations with a people they consider to be dangerous barbarians. That, and they're not too sure Hamlers can be trusted with their first prince."

"And are the Oterans barbarians?" The very concern King Mendel's council voiced before approving this mission. *"I hear you have spent some time there in the past few years."*

"No, they aren't. At least not the ones I know. They are just like us, for the most part. One or two I count as friends. But they aren't as lucky in their rulers as we are."

She caught an odd flavor in Jothan's last thought, something he was holding back. The Oterans weren't lucky in their rulers. What could he mean by that?

"Have you met their king?"

"No, but I did meet a member of one of the Oteran Houses, which are like our lords, only with more power and more money. He isn't a nice man."

He withdrew, leaving her alone with her thoughts. If Jothan numbered Oterans among his friends, perhaps the mission wouldn't be as dangerous as everyone feared. Not all of King Mendel's lords were kind, and no doubt King Hubert had his share of greedy lords and landowners as well. Perhaps the man Jothan disliked was atypical and the Oteran king as kind and wise as his southern counterparts.

How surprised Petro would be to learn that Jothan was part of this expedition. And what a relief. Peeking into people's minds wouldn't be completely up to her now, as long as the Oterans didn't know Jothan's status as a brother. Presumably they didn't, or he wouldn't have asked that his abilities be kept secret.

But not from Thaine. As leader of this mission, he had a right to know all the facts. She would mention that to Jothan later. Right now, she could see him up ahead, talking with Quinn and Millard, and she didn't want to disturb them. Instead, she dropped back to ride beside the wagon and let herself be lulled by the sound of Beryle's familiar voice.

Arnath had not changed from Arien's previous visit. Though she had only spent one night in the little town, each building rose in her memory, unchanged. She looked eagerly into the store windows, amused at how common everything looked to her more sophisticated eyes. Seven years ago, this tiny town had seemed like a giant city.

The sun lagged close to the horizon, and the shops had closed down for the night. That didn't stop a crowd from gathering to stare as they marched through the center of town. Prince Thaine wore his guard uniform and Prince Millard his travel clothes, so they went unrecognized. Still, a display of any kind was a curiosity, and a few people cheered as though they were a parade come to entertain the town.

They soon came upon the boarding house, and there on the porch stood Kalinda. Apparently, she'd heard the noise and came to see what the fuss was about. She was unchanged. Still a dainty beauty, but now, to Arien's older and more experienced eyes, dressed more like a country wife than a princess.

Kalinda planted her hands on her hips and eyed Quinn and Jothan. "Either your group has grown, or you've gotten yourself into a load of trouble."

Jothan laughed. "Actually, Madame, we are about to make you the most famous boarding house in this part of Creighton."

“Oh? And just how will you be doing that?” Laughter flood her voice and twinkled in her eyes.

Quinn gestured toward the princes, who both dismounted and stepped forward. “Mistress Kalinda, let me present His Royal Highness, First Prince Thaine of Creighton, and His Royal Highness, First Prince Millard of Hamlin. We've described your hospitality, and they’re here to sample it for themselves.”

Kalinda started to give Quinn a sharp retort but stopped as she got a closer look at Thaine. Though Arien doubted that she had ever met him, she’d obviously seen his likeness. Her eyes grew round, and she swallowed convulsively as her gaze slid from him to Millard. Then she sank to her knees and bowed until her forehead rested on the wooden porch. “Your Highnesses.”

Thaine hurried forward and gently touched her shoulder. “Please get up.” He helped her to her feet. “We’ve heard all day how comfortable your house is, and I for one am looking forward to a hot bath, a good meal, and a soft bed. Have you room for us?”

The woman swallowed again, her eyes still round as eggs. “Of course, Your Highness.” She whispered, still too awed to speak out loud. “I have no guests at the moment, and if I did, I’d toss them out in a flash. But I’ve only ten rooms in all. There's another inn in town, run by a good woman, friend of mine, and she has six more.”

“The ten will be more than enough,” Thaine assured her. “Prince Millard and I will each have one, and our guides, and of course, Lady Arien and her attendant will each need one as well. That leaves four for my Lieutenants, but I wager they'll be happier camping with the rest of the men.”

“I have a good-sized yard, but the barn won't hold but twelve horses. There's Old Will's, back down that way, but as to whether he'll be able to house all these animals—” She gestured toward the pack of animals stamping in the dirt. “—I couldn’t say.”

A lieutenant stepped forward and saluted. “Captain, we can put up a pen north of town for the night, and the men can camp there. If we can get feed for the animals, that's all we'll need."

"Old Will should have feed," Kalinda said. "I'll send a boy to fetch him."

Word spread through the crowd that had followed them through town, and as Jothan stepped to Arien's side to help her dismount, a shout went up.

"Welcome, Prince Thaine!"

"Bless the princes."

"Yes, long life to Their Majesties!"

Thaine waved, and even Millard smiled at the crowd and managed to look regal and friendly at the same time. In response, the cheers rose in volume.

One deep voice rose higher than the rest. "Come by the alehouse after supper, and I'll spot you both a tankard."

Thaine laughed and shouted back, "We may take you up on that offer."

The princes followed Kalinda inside, and Arien stepped onto the porch. A smile tugged at her lips when she spied the row of rockers. She'd sat in that one, her feet burning from ill-fitting sandals.

Inside, a tantalizing aroma wafted down the hallway that looked exactly the same, though smaller than she remembered.

Kalinda had apparently recovered from her shock. "If I'da known you were coming I coulda had the best supper you ever ate, Your Highnesses," she told Thaine and Millard. "As it is, you'll have to make do with what I can throw together quick."

"I'm sure whatever you have will be wonderful," Thaine assured her.

She caught sight of Arien, and a puzzled expression settled over her. "I don't forget a face. I've seen you before."

Arien nodded. "Seven years ago, with my…my Pa. We stayed only one night—"

Kalinda interrupted. "On your way to Tadmoure to see the princess off to her wedding. And you, Your Highness," she turned to Millard and sank gracefully into a curtsy, "were the groom."

Delighted, Arien clapped her hands. "That's right. I'm surprised you remember."

Kalinda nodded, then grinned. “An' I see you're still wearing boys’ clothes, even though you're a grown lady now. Am I going to have to lend you my nightdress this time, too?”

“Not this time. I've even brought my own slippers.”

“A good thing,” Kalinda told her, “because mine won't fit you no more, you've grown so. I'll put you in the same room you had last time. You remember where it is?”

“I remember.”

“Good, then you can find your own way while I take care of the gentlemen. And you, miss.” She directed a smile at Beryle. “I’ll put you right next door. She'll show you. If you’d like to visit the bath house before the men, I'll see that you're not disturbed.”

After the day's long ride, Arien wanted nothing more than to sink into a hot bath and soak the stiffness from her muscles. A quick glance into her room revealed that Kalinda had changed the coverings, but everything else was as she remembered. She led Beryle to the bath house. They didn't stay long, knowing the princes would also like to bathe, but they came away refreshed.

Supper was a rich, meaty stew and thick slices of bread smeared with honey and fruit jam. There were also a variety of pickles and a huge bowl of sugared fruit. Arien couldn't imagine how Kalinda had managed such a wonderful meal in so short a time. No matter how Thaine and Millard raved, the innkeeper shook her head and apologized for the poor fare.

Jarrett, Kalinda's huge husband, looked to be much awed by his royal guests. He took two sheep carcasses and a keg of wine to the guardsman's camp and thereby escaped having to sit at the table with the princes.

After the meal, Beryle insisted on helping Kalinda clean the dishes and refused to let Arien help. “You're a lady,” she hissed, glaring. “Go to bed or something, but don't come into the kitchen and do servant's work.”

Arien allowed herself to be convinced rather quickly. The day’s ride had worn her out, and she wanted nothing more than to fall into the comfortable bed and sleep until morning. When Thaine announced that he and Millard were going to pay a courtesy call to the tavern down the road before retiring,

Jothan stopped him.

"I have something to say that I think you'll want to hear." He closed the door to the dining room and sat down in Kalinda's vacant seat at the head of the table. "When I was in Otero back in the fall, I met a lord of one of the Oteran Houses."

"We know this." Millard apparently had not appreciated the interruption to his plans. He sounded irritated. "That's how you discovered news of this invasion."

Jothan shook his head. "No, that occurred a few months ago. But before last winter I met Lord Lucian when he took over the anodyte shop from the man we'd been dealing with for years. Lord Lucian is…" He ran a hand over his mouth. "Well, he's a hard man to describe. Around nineteen or twenty years old, self-assured and powerful. His men are terrified of him and extremely loyal. He won't hesitate to kill if it serves his purpose. He killed Illan, our anodyte supplier, so he could take over his shop."

Thaine cocked his head. "How do you know that? Did he tell you?"

Jothan glanced at Arien. "No. I saw it in the mind of one of his personal fighters."

Spying on someone else's mind. She checked her initial rush of disapproval. After all, her purpose on this mission was to do the same.

"In his mind," Thaine said, his voice low. "You are a member of the Brotherhood of Power?"

Jothan executed a half-bow, still seated. "Brother Jothan, at your service, Your Highness."

Millard turned to Arien. "Did you know this?"

"About Jothan being trained in Power? Yes. He was Master Petro's first trainee." She shifted her gaze to Thaine. "I didn't know Jothan was your anodyte seller until this morning. There hasn't been time to tell you since."

Thaine leaned back against the hard, high back of his chair, his gaze fixed on Jothan. "So, you listened to the man's thoughts and discovered that this Lucian killed your supplier. What did you hear from Lucian's own mind?"

"That's what I want to tell you. His thoughts were hidden.

Blocked." He laid an arm on the table and turned in his seat toward Arien. "He's got a mindshield the likes of which I've never seen."

She straightened, her interest piqued. "A mindshield? Do you mean he's been trained in the ways of the Brotherhood?"

Jothan shook his head. "I don't think so. It was a natural mindshield, obviously constructed by an amateur, but strong nonetheless. Impenetrable, in fact. But do you realize what this means?"

As the question left his lips, their import dawned on her. The presence of a man with a mindshield, even an amateurishly constructed one, meant there could be others. If she encountered a man of Power, he would recognize her instantly. He had only to Perceive her, and he'd detect her shield the way Jothan had detected that Oteran lord's.

Apparently, the same realization had just occurred to the princes as well.

"Then it's settled," Thaine said. "Arien must not go."

Millard nodded, for once in complete agreement with his brother-in-law. "Absolutely not."

Warring emotions rose inside her. This was her chance to desert the mission, to back out with a perfectly valid reason that both Petro and King Mendel would accept. She could remain here in safety, and no one would think the worse of her.

But two first princes will still journey into danger, even though their plan lay in ruins.

If they walked into a trap she could have prevented, she'd never forgive herself. Though she would no doubt regret her actions as she tossed in her bed later tonight, she clasped her hands on the table in front of her and spoke with certainty.

"I am going." Millard and Thaine began a protest, but she raised a hand. "The point of the mission is for me to get close enough to their king and his nobles to hear their thoughts. No one else can do that."

"Jothan can take your place," said Thaine quickly.

She dismissed the suggestion. "If a man would have served, Master Petro would be here." *And we'd all feel a lot better right now.* "No, it has to be me."

Millard leaned toward her, concern darkening the gaze he

fixed on her. "But if you are discovered, you'll be in danger." He glanced around the table. "We all will."

"And how is that different from Jothan?" she countered. "If there are trained men of Power in Otero, they will surely Perceive all of us, and Jothan will be discovered same as me. Quicker, probably, since they'll certainly scan every male's thoughts, but who would think a female consort a threat?"

"Are you sure about this?" Jothan asked.

She saturated her answer with humor. *"As sure as you are. So no, of course not. But I'm going anyway."*

"If it helps," Jothan said to the rest, "I haven't heard even a whisper about anything like the Brotherhood in all the years I've visited Otero. I'll wager Lord Lucian is an anomaly, a rogue talent who unconsciously built a mindshield as a protective instinct. I certainly didn't detect even a hint of him trying to Perceive me."

In the end, Arien managed to convince them, though certainly not with eloquent words. No, she simply folded her arms across her chest in an imitation of Beryle at her most stubborn and refused to budge. Later, when sleep evaded her and fears defeated bravado, she hoped she didn't soon regret her victory.

Nine

During her years at the Brotherhood, Arien studied the infamous Nephtali Pass. As the diplomatic party approached it the next morning, she gazed around with a kind of reverence. History had been made here. Since Hamlin's coastline was protected by a long barrier reef and the rocky Jalapa Mountain Range ran east to west across the northern border of both kingdoms, the Pass was the only avenue of entry to Otero from either of the Twin Kingdoms. Some of her favorite stories included references to the Nephtali Pass. To stand where famous commanders of old had repelled Oteran military forces hundreds of years ago filled her with awe.

When the travelers entered the Pass itself, Arien craned her neck to admire the beauty of the rocky peaks towering on either side of her. The air was crisper here, cleaner than she had smelled since leaving the mountain village of her childhood, and she closed her eyes to enjoy its taste in the back of her throat.

They were able to ride only a half-hour into the Pass before the path disappeared beneath a barrier of giant boulders. She saw immediately why they could not ride all the way into Otero—the horses would never make it over this slide. It was as though someone had carved out huge chunks of the mountain and piled them here, as if to dam the flow of a river.

Arien turned in the saddle and looked back toward Beryle, who was staring ahead, eyes round. She sent the girl a reassuring smile, though she felt anything but confident in her own ability to climb that rocky wall.

"Here's where we leave the horses," Quinn said, unnecessarily.

Several guardsmen began to unload the wagon, piling bags and cases on the ground. Others sifted through them to find their own packs. Arien located both of her trunks easily—they were the only ones on the wagon.

Jothan came up behind her. "What do you expect to do with those?"

Beryle stepped up beside them, carrying Arien's small case and her own. "That's our luggage."

A loud laugh shook his shoulders. "And just how do you propose to get it over that?" He pointed toward the mountain of rocks that blocked the path.

Beryle raised her chin and gave a haughty sniff. "That chamberlain at the castle, Oren, said the guardsmen would carry it for us."

Jothan's laughter increased. "Not likely. Their hands are going to be occupied with climbing. Anything we take must be strapped to our backs. Do you see anyone here big enough to climb with this thing strapped on his back?" He kicked at the nearest trunk.

Beryle started to protest. But Thaine, who had overheard, came up beside Arien. "I'm afraid he's right." The prince shrugged apologetically. "I'm sure Oren had no idea what we'd be crossing, or he never would have agreed to these trunks."

Beryle placed her hands on her hips. Anger blazed in her eyes and Thaine, prince or not, was going to catch the brunt of it.

"And just what do you expect, that we strap our things on our own backs? Lady Arien's a *lady*, and she ain't gonna climb over no rocks with a case on her back. And neither am I."

"Well…" Thaine cast an uncomfortable glance toward Arien. "We've divvied up the gifts we're taking to the Oteran king, but I still have some room in my pack."

Arien was horrified. "That won't be necessary," she said, but just then several of the guardsmen spoke.

"I have some room, too."

"I could fit a thing or two in mine."

Face burning, she smiled her thanks but shook her head. "Thank you, but no."

"Don't be hasty," Beryle cautioned in a low voice. "You don't even have a pack, and how are we going to get your things over that?"

"Well." Arien hesitated, but she really had no choice. "All right, just a few things. And thank you."

Embarrassment churned in her stomach. These men already thought she was Millard's mistress, and now they were going to carry her undergarments into Otero.

She and Beryle selected two gowns and a few essential toiletries. Beryle herself hadn't brought much. Arien also pulled out her spare trousers and blouse for the remainder of the journey. These they portioned out to polite guardsmen, some as red-faced as Arien as they stowed the more private garments in their packs.

When all was done, Beryle shook her head. "I don't know what them Oterans will think of you, coming to meet their king with only two gowns to your name."

Arien sighed. "I'm sure they'll understand that we were traveling under constraints."

Once they had put their mounts in the hands of those assigned to remain, the group turned toward the mound of boulders that clogged the narrow Pass.

"How long will it take to get over this blockage?" Millard asked as they all stared at the monumental pile of rock.

"The rest of the day, for sure." Quinn shielded his eyes and gazed toward the peak. "Jothan and I've done it in five hours, but with all these men and the ladies, going will be slow."

"It must be a huge barricade," commented Millard.

"Oh, it is," Thaine assured him. "And impassible, except on foot. Which was the reason for building it. No army can get through here, not without a lot of trouble. And an army on foot wouldn't be much good against our guard."

"How was it built?" Beryle asked.

Arien answered with a grin. "That's a secret."

"A poorly kept one." Thaine's lips twitched with humor. "It was put around that the King's Guard went up into the mountains and worked for weeks to throw every movable boulder they could find down into the Pass."

Beryle looked around, noting the size of some of the boulders and shook her head. "I don't see how even a whole army of men could move some 'a these rocks."

"They couldn't," Arien agreed. "The secret is that a group of men from the Brotherhood came with the guard and, let's say, helped a little."

"But why is that a secret? All the people would have been grateful to them."

Jothan answered. "Because the Brotherhood didn't want anyone to become aware of them, or their abilities. At that time, the Brotherhood had only been in existence a short while, and people with Power were viewed with suspicion. Only a handful of them existed, and Power was a huge mystery to most people."

"Still is, to some of us," murmured Beryle, eyeing the barrier with apparent awe.

Quinn, who carried a walking stick, tapped it impatiently on the ground. "Are we going to stand here talking? I'd like to get over this rough part before sundown. You don't want to camp up there."

They started to climb. Jothan and Quinn went first, then two guardsmen before Thaine, Millard, Arien, and Beryle. The rest of the guard brought up the rear. At first, several men tried choosing their own paths. But before long, they realized that the route Jothan took was the best and safest way. Soon they had spread out into a long line, single file behind Jothan.

The climbing wasn't difficult. At first, in fact, Arien enjoyed it as a welcome change from riding. But it didn't take long for her hands to become sore, and later, raw. Some of the men, Jothan and Quinn included, wore thick leather gloves. If she'd been warned, she would have done the same. She almost mentioned it but knew if she did one of the guardsmen would certainly give her his, and she was already embarrassed that her belongings were being carried for her.

Beryle performed better than Arien expected. The effort of the climb silenced the normally chatty attendant, and Arien kept looking back to make sure she was keeping up.

"Not as bad as I thought," she puffed, red-faced, with a characteristic grin. "But I see what they mean. I couldn't make a bed after climbing these rocks, let alone pick up a sword."

They stopped after a few hours for lunch, and the guardsmen produced slabs of dried meat and hard bread from their packs. Arien, still full from breakfast at Kalinda's inn, would have preferred something to drink, but there was no water this high on the rock barrier. She sipped from the pouch offered her and tried not to wish for more. The moment she stopped moving, exhaustion dragged at her limbs.

"There's a stream at the end of this," Jothan promised, and she couldn't muster the strength to answer.

After a rest that was too short, they continued over the sharp boulders. Jothan and Quinn did not stop at the peak, but Thaine did. Arien came to a halt beside him and followed his gaze. From this vantage point she saw the true length of the barrier and again marveled that men of Power had created this obstacle. What a tremendous task that must have been.

"Impressive," Thaine said, to which she could only nod.

The descent was harder than the climb. Her raw hands ached, the skin torn and bleeding in places. Twice she almost lost her grip and managed to maintain her balance only by grasping a sharp rocky edge with nearly numb fingers. One thought kept her going—they were almost at the end.

They stepped off the last of the boulders and onto the packed dirt just before sunset. The shadows had lengthened so that it was hard to see where to put her feet. Arien was certain that, had they been required to climb over the treacherous rock barrier much farther, there would have been injuries to deal with. But now they were safely on the other side—if being inside a possibly hostile kingdom could be considered safe.

"Thanks be," Beryle shouted between pants of breath, as though trying to make sure she was heard in the heavens.

But they couldn't rest yet. Quinn and Jothan led them away from the barrier, continuing northward along the pass into Otero. At least the ground was even, which made walking almost a pleasure after the torturous day. Even so, Arien stumbled with exhaustion when they finally came out of the pass itself and into a sparse forest. Quinn stopped barely inside the tree line.

"We'll camp here," he announced. "There's water nearby and plenty of wood and game."

Arien had never received any piece of news with more gratitude. Her legs had ceased aching long ago, but now trembled alarmingly while her feet were almost completely numb. Beryle was so exhausted she sank to the ground, heedless of the dirt, and leaned against a tree trunk with her eyes closed.

"Lars, take a few men and check out the area," Thaine directed. "Prince Millard, if you will oversee setting up camp, I'll take a crew to gather firewood and see if we can flush any game, though it's doubtful this late at night."

Millard nodded, and Thaine tapped a few guardsmen to accompany him deeper into the forest.

There wasn't much to do, setting up camp. They had not brought tents, so would sleep in the open beneath the trees. The men spread their pallets directly on the ground, then began clearing a central area for a campfire. Someone produced pallets for Arien and Beryle, but Arien was too tired to do more than nod her appreciation, and Beryle had fallen asleep leaning against the tree. After settling his own pallet, Millard helped Arien unroll hers and Beryle's.

"I think you should sleep here, nearest the fire," he told her. "The men will be spread out all around you, and you'll be safer that way."

Arien managed a weary smile in return. "Thank you." For some reason, Millard didn't seem nearly as annoying as usual tonight. Nor as talkative. "You've been very quiet today."

He gave her an embarrassed grin. “Truth to tell, I couldn't spare the breath for speech. When we started to climb, I couldn't seem to get enough air. Thaine is so fit I didn't want anyone to hear me panting for air.”

Arien chuckled. With his guard down and his pretensions forgotten, she could like this man who would one day be king. “I felt the same, and I've never heard Beryle so quiet.”

“It has hit the three of us harder than the others. Jothan told me it has something to do with living near the sea, that the air is different here in the north.”

The hunters enjoyed limited success, snaring six wild hares and a pair of fat fowl, while Quinn and Jothan netted a dozen or so fish in the stream. These were speared and roasted over three campfires. With fifty traveling in the party, the fresh meat had to be supplemented by the travel food the guardsmen carried to make enough for everyone.

Arien ate a small piece of fish and drank her fill from the stream. Hunger still rumbled in her stomach, but she'd made many meals in her life with far less. She fell asleep huddled next to Beryle and didn't move until morning.

Waking was torturous. Her legs protested when she tried to force them into action. At least they weren’t shaking and threatening to dump her on the ground as they had been the night before.

“My feet are nothing but blisters.” Beryle’s whine grated on Arien’s exhausted nerves. “My legs feel like they’re gonna fall off.”

“We'll be in Eshtaol by mid-morning,” Jothan promised. “And I hope Skelly at the Bed and Bitters Inn has room for us and a good lunch as well.”

“And a decent bath,” Beryle mumbled, with which Arien heartily agreed.

The morning's march was almost pleasant compared to the struggle of the day before. They came upon the little town of Eshtaol before the sun had truly begun to warm the night's chill from the air. It was small, as Jothan had promised, though larger than Arnath. They approached the town's southwestern corner, and from this angle it looked pleasant enough. The path upon which they walked widened and became a street with buildings lining both sides. Other streets led off the main one, and the structures on this end of the town stretched a good distance to the east.

She would have liked to change into a gown, but Quinn assured her fancy garb was unnecessary. "There's no one to impress in Eshtaol," he told her, "except plain, everyday people like you'd find in Arnath or Tadmoure."

"I thought Lord Lucian kept a house here," Millard said.

"Near here," corrected Jothan. "He spends no more time in Eshtaol than necessary, and the townspeople are grateful for that. I think the only reason he comes at all is because of the anodyte laboratory."

Thaine peered toward the buildings. "I find it hard to believe we've not encountered an Oteran Guard, or even a sentry. Do they not watch the pass at all?"

Quinn laughed. "What for? Creighton is no threat, never has been."

Thaine's lips pressed together to form a thin line. Arien was close enough to hear him mumble, "We may have to change their minds about that."

As they drew closer to the first building—a blacksmith's shop and stable—the party finally attracted some attention. The smith stopped his work while they were still a good distance away and turned to speak to a boy working the forge. The boy looked toward them, then dashed up the street where he disappeared behind a building.

The town bustled with activity, people running their various errands and conducting business. They all stopped whatever they were doing and turned to stare as Jothan and Quinn lead the party toward the town. The smith stepped into the street as they approached. His scowl disappeared momentarily as he recognized Jothan and Quinn, then deepened.

"What's going on here?" the large man asked, his voice a growl.

Jothan stood with his back to Arien, with Thaine, Millard, and two guardsmen between them so she could not see his expression. She angled herself so that she could watch the smith's face and noted the deep suspicion apparent there.

Time to begin the job for which she was recruited.

Fighting a stab of guilt, she Perceived. Deep worry colored the smith's thoughts. He feared the party was the advance troop of a larger army sent to take possession of the town. He worried that the town's militia wouldn't be able to handle so many soldiers, even if the boy were able to rouse them in time to do any good. Fear colored his thoughts, and Arien saw the mental image of a woman with two babies inside the house behind his shop.

She stepped forward to stand between the princes and spoke in a low voice. "He thinks we're here to attack and has roused the town's militia."

At the same time, Quinn spoke to the smith. "We're here as guides to their highnesses the First Prince of Creighton and the First Prince of Hamlin. They've come on a diplomatic visit to meet with your king."

Disbelief shone plain on the smith's face. Thaine stepped forward. "It is true, I assure you." His manner was calm, yet unmistakably regal. "I am Prince Thaine Valerien, first prince and heir to the throne of Creighton. This," he gestured toward Millard, who gave an arrogant nod, "is Prince Millard Valerien, first prince and heir to the throne of Hamlin. We have come to meet with your King Kuriel to establish diplomatic relations between our kingdoms."

The man's expression relaxed a little, though another quick peek into his mind told her he had strong doubts that Millard and Thaine were who they claimed to be.

"I would have thought you'd send a messenger or something first, so the king would know you was coming."

"We could have." Thaine gave a tight-lipped smile, his manner clearly stating that he would not explain his actions to a small-town smith.

The bearing of the princes began to win the smith over. The man recognized authority and responded to it. At that moment, a group of six men came running around a corner, each carrying a weapon. Two swords, but the rest carried bows with arrows nocked and ready. Behind Arien, the guardsmen drew their own weapons in response, and the little militia halted, fear and determination plain on their faces.

The smith held up a restraining hand. "Hold up there,

Natty," he said to the man in front. "This here is a diplomatic group, come to see King Kuriel. There's a couple of princes from the south with 'em. They don't mean no harm." He eyed Thaine. "Leastways, that's what they say."

Thaine raised his voice to speak to the cluster of armed men. "We apologize for our abrupt appearance. Naturally you are startled and suspicious, but I assure you our intentions are peaceful. We request lodging in your town until a message can be sent to King Kuriel. We've brought gold and will pay for whatever services we use."

At the mention of gold, several of the men as well as several of the observers who had begun to line the street lost much of their suspicion. The leader considered Thaine's words before nodding slowly.

"All right, then." The man lowered his sword. "Though I doubt if we have enough rooms for all of you. There's only two inns in town and not but ten rooms between them."

"Our guard will camp," Thaine announced. "We will gladly purchase any available gear for them. We are traveling with two ladies who will need rooms, and His Highness of Hamlin and myself as well. Ten rooms will be more than adequate for our needs."

A man stepped forward from the crowd lining the street. He was tall and thin, with dark hair and sunken cheeks. "Your Highnesses." He bowed first to Thaine and then to Millard. "My name is Natan Maren. I have six rooms at The Roadside Inn on the north end of town. I would be happy to have you and your ladies stay at my inn while you are in Eshtaol."

Another man came hurrying forward as well, this one the exact opposite of Natan Maren. His body was as round as Natan's was thin, and the top of his nearly bald head came barely to Natan's chin. The man's round face was anxious.

"I'm Skelly Engle." He bobbed toward Thaine and Millard. "I run the Bed and Bitters Inn, as these gentlemen here can tell you." He nodded toward Jothan and Quinn. "I have rooms, too. Four of them, if you've a mind to stay. Mine ain't near as fancy as Natan's here, but the bedclothes are clean, and my wife is the best cook in Eshtaol."

Jothan turned to Thaine. "I can speak for the cooking."

Thaine smiled toward the fat Skelly. “I'm sure we can find volunteers to stay in your excellent inn and sample your wife's cooking.” He turned to Natan. “And yours as well, sir. Thank you both for your hospitality.”

Skelly nodded, relieved.

Lieutenant Curran, standing protectively beside Thaine, cleared his throat. “Is there a place nearby where my men can camp?”

Natan nodded. “There's a grain field, spent at this time of year, just next to my inn. I'm sure the farmer will be reasonable to deal with.”

Meaning that he could be paid for the use of his land.

They decided to house Arien, Beryle, both princes and the two lieutenants at the Roadside Inn, while Jothan and two other guardsmen stayed at the Bed and Bitters.

“If you'll come this way, Your Highnesses.”

Natan lead the southerners up the street. The watching crowd wore suspicious and sometimes fearful expressions, and more than once Arien felt curious eyes fastened on her. Beryle had been uncharacteristically quiet during the exchange with the militia, and a glance toward her showed Arien that she was as suspicious of the Oterans as they were of her.

But when she caught Arien’s glance, she admitted in a low voice, “They don’t look like barbarians.”

“No more than we do to them.”

She turned her attention to their guide and Perceived Natan Maren. His chief concern of the moment was which Prince would receive one of the two rooms he considered appropriate for royalty. The other he planned to reserve for Lord Lucian, to whom he would send a message as soon as he got his guests settled. She sensed no loyalty to Lucian in the man's thoughts, but a great deal of fear. Natan was holding Lucian’s room in reserve because he did not wish to suffer the lord’s wrath if he arrived and found that his regular room had been given to a foreigner.

So, Lord Lucian stayed at Natan's house when he came to Eshtaol. And Lucian would be made aware of their presence immediately. A good thing to know.

She Perceived Skelly and found a blur of activity that

skipped from worry that his wife could make a passable lunch at such short notice to frustration that Natan's Inn was so much more suitable for royal visitors. He was pleased that Thaine had spoken for all four of his rooms and wondered if he could somehow arrange to feed the entire guard at their camp, thereby earning a tidy profit from the visitors' presence. He also planned to send a boy to fetch someone named Kerman as soon as he had the chance.

They passed the Bed and Bitters Inn first, where Jothan and Quinn, accompanied by two guardsmen, left the group. Arien smelled a delicious aroma wafting from inside the somewhat shabby inn and spared a brief wish that she was staying there with Jothan and Quinn.

"Keep your ears open," Jothan sent as he followed Skelly through the door. *"The Roadside Inn is where I met Lucian."*

"Don't worry," she replied. *"I'll be careful."*

"We'll come up later," Quinn told Thaine, then followed Jothan inside.

The Roadside Inn was nicer than Skelly's place, though not as welcoming from the outside as Kalinda's house. There was no porch, only a covered stoop fronting a large stone house with an abundance of shuttered windows. They stepped into a spacious common room filled with wooden tables and chairs. Through double doors to the rear of the room, Arien glimpsed the kitchen. A smaller door to the right was closed, as well as another beneath a narrow staircase to the left of the kitchen entrance.

"My wife and I sleep beyond the kitchen." Natan pointed toward the door on the right. "That room is for private conversations, and you are welcome to use it. The bathing room is through there." He nodded toward the other door. "I'll make sure the water's hot."

A woman came out of the kitchen and stopped in surprise when she caught sight of the group of people.

"This is my wife, Yulene." The man smiled for the first time as he gazed at the pretty, plump woman who stood wiping her hands on a towel. "Yulene, we have royal guests from the south. They are Their Highnesses, Prince Thaine and Prince Millard, and two of their soldier guards, and…." He paused as he looked at Arien and Beryle.

Millard stepped forward and took Arien by the arm in a possessive gesture. “This is the Lady Arien of Kirklin Castle, and her attendant.”

Yulene sank into a curtsey before Thaine and Millard, mumbling a barely heard welcome. What a contrast between this woman and Kalinda, who had quickly recovered from her shock at royal guests arriving on her doorstep unannounced. Yulene was much too shy to ever run an inn virtually alone, as Kalinda did.

“They will require a midday meal, and soon,” Natan told her in a gentle tone. “And send the boy to Karl and ask him to come and meet with their Highnesses immediately. They want to set up their soldiers’ camp in Karl's field.”

Yulene nodded again and disappeared into the kitchen. Natan lead them up the stairs. At the top, a narrow corridor ran the width of the house with doors on each side.

“These first five rooms are all but identical,” Natan told them, “and the last one there is larger and better appointed.”

He glanced from one prince to the other, confusion apparent on his face.

Millard’s suggestion surprised Arien. “Lady Arien will take the larger room, and her attendant next to her. The rest of us will make do with the smaller ones.”

Thaine agreed, and relief softened Natan’s features at the solution.

Lieutenant Curran pointed toward a seventh door, across the corridor from the one just assigned to Arien. “Do you have other guests at the moment?”

Natan’s throat bobbed up and down. “No, but that room is reserved for the Lord of an Oteran House who stays here when he is in Eshtaol. When he discovers that Otero has royal visitors from the south, I know he will come to greet you.”

At least he didn't lie. Arien noticed that both Curran and Lars cast uneasy glances toward the door. No doubt they worried about someone else staying so close to the first princes.

Had they heard Jothan describe Lucian, they would have been more than uneasy.

Natan opened the door to Arien's room and gestured for

her to enter. It contained a large bed and a chest, and a small writing table with two chairs. Natan crossed the room in five steps and pushed open the shutters, flooding the room with sunlight and fresh air. The view from the window was of the stables to the rear of the house and the smell that entered the room pungent with horse sweat and manure.

"If there is anything you need, just ask me or Yulene. Or the boy you'll see running about the place."

He retreated, and Beryle bustled around the room, inspecting the furnishings. She jerked a grudging nod of approval. "I'll collect your things from the men. And while I'm down there I'll ask about a dressmaker. I hope there is one in this town."

The maid gave a haughty sniff, which Arien took to mean she doubted if Eshtaol could produce a suitable seamstress. Then she left, closing the door behind her.

Arien sank onto the bed, grateful for the opportunity to rest her weary legs and feet. She leaned against the pillows and was asleep in an instant.

A soft rap on the door jarred her into full wakefulness. She Perceived and saw Beryle on the other side.

"Come on in, Beryle," she called, and relaxed against the pillows once again.

"How'd you know ... oh." Beryle shook her head. "'Course *you* know. Here."

She dumped a pile of clothing on the chest, and Arien recognized her own green gown.

"I'm going to have to steam the wrinkles out of the yellow one. That oaf wadded it up into a ball before he stuffed it in his pack."

"At least he brought it." Arien didn't bother to suppress a yawn. "Did you find a dressmaker?"

"Yes, and she'll be here quick." Beryle grinned. "I don't think they have much to do in this town, so she'll be eager for your business. I just hope she can make something suitable for you to meet that king in."

Beryle had not yet finished hanging Arien's clothing in the wardrobe when another rap on the door heralded the arrival of the dressmaker. Beryle let her in, then stood watching closely while the woman measured Arien from all angles. When she was satisfied that the Oteran knew her business, Beryle began her normal flow of conversation, which kept up until she had ordered five gowns. Arien smiled at the eagerness on the dressmaker's face as she departed. It was a good thing Petro had given them a pouch full of gold and silver coins.

When Beryle had gone off to see to the yellow gown, Arien slipped out of her room and into the corridor. A quick Perception showed her that the princes were each in their rooms. She rapped on Millard's door softly, then Thaine's. When the doors opened, she motioned for them to come into her room.

"Did you hear something?" Millard asked, his expression eager.

"Not much," Arien admitted, "but I thought you should know. Natan Maren plays host to Lord Lucian, as he mentioned. But what he didn't tell you is that he plans to send a messenger to Lucian immediately. Probably already has by now."

"Is he planning treachery, then?" Thaine's brows drawn into a concerned frown.

She shook her head. "No. I Perceived no indication of foul play against us, either on his part or on the part of anyone else he knows. If there's an invasion planned, our host does not know about it. He is more than a little curious about what King Kuriel will make of our presence."

"Then why is he sending a messenger to Lord Lucian?" asked Millard.

Arien sat on the bed, facing them both. "I sensed a lot of fear. I'd say Natan is following orders to notify Lucian of anything out of the ordinary that happens in Eshtaol."

Thaine considered this, his expression thoughtful. "That means we'll be watched so he can tell Lucian everything we do or say while we're here."

They all glanced uneasily around the room, wondering if someone could be listening to their conversation even then. Arien Perceived the general area, and easily located Beryle and Yulene in the kitchen. A guardsman stood on duty in the common room below, gaze fixed on the stairs. No one else.

"One more thing. The other innkeeper, Skelly, plans to

send a message about us as well. Someone named Kerman, who I gathered was a friend. When he pictured this Kerman, he was thinking more of Jothan and Quinn than either of you. I didn't sense any hostile feelings at all, only concern that he has the opportunity to make as much profit from our arrival as Natan." She grinned. "Actually, I rather liked him. And that smith, too, who was only afraid that we were going to harm his wife and babies."

They sat in silence for another moment, both princes considering the things she had told them.

Thaine stood. "Good work, Lady Arien. Did you find it as difficult as you expected?"

Arien considered, then shook her head. "When I listen in on someone's thoughts to protect the two of you, and two entire kingdoms besides, it doesn't seem as intrusive."

Millard grinned. "You haven't seen anything embarrassingly personal yet."

They heard footsteps in the corridor, and Arien Perceived.

"Beryle," she said as the attendant's knock sounded on the door.

Arien opened it to admit her maid, who had the yellow gown draped over one arm and a pail of steaming water dangling from the other hand. She was surprised to see the room full of first princes.

"We were just leaving," Thaine assured her as he edged through the door.

"Lunch is stew and will be served soon." Beryle regained her composure and eyed the still-dirty clothes the men wore. "If you're going to make use of the bathing room, you'd best do it now."

Millard followed Thaine out and turned to give Arien a farewell wave as Beryle shut the door firmly in his face. She rounded on Arien.

"What are you thinking, having them both in your room at the same time in broad daylight?" she scolded, while Arien slipped out of her dirty traveling clothes.

"We needed to have a quick meeting."

Beryle drew herself up, disapproval radiating from her plump frame. "There's a room right downstairs for that."

"We didn't want the whole house to know we were talking. And besides, I knew no one was nearby. Don't be such a chaperone."

Beryle shook her head, clucking her lips like an old woman.

"And anyway," Arien went on, "I'm supposed to be entertaining Millard in my room on a regular basis, or so everyone is being led to believe."

"One prince at a time is acceptable." The girl gave a righteous sniff. "Two at once is courting gossip."

Arien couldn't stop a grin at Beryle's implacable logic. "One is courting gossip as well."

To which Beryle threw up her hands and refused further discussion of the matter.

Lunch was delicious. Lieutenant Curran reported that Skelly's wife had produced enough hot soup and flat bread to feed the entire squad of guardsmen, who were setting up camp in the grain field next door. Several tents had been purchased—all the town had to offer—and several more were being hastily thrown together by the eager townspeople. Lots had been drawn to select the first two men who would take the extra rooms at the Bed and Bitters Inn and would be drawn each day until everyone had been selected or the party left Eshtaol.

The first night, as Arien and the princes finished a supper of plain but well-cooked food, Jothan entered the common room of the Roadside Inn. The few other dining guests sat as far from the princes as possible and watched them the entire time. Jothan helped himself to a mug of ale from the keg on the counter, then slid into one of the empty chairs beside Arien. After a sip, he sighed and licked his lips.

"Better than Skelly's, truth to tell, but I'd wager a gold to a silver that Skelly's wife is the best cook in town."

Arien eyed the remains of the food on her plate. "Perhaps we could have supper at the Bed and Bitters tomorrow and spread our custom evenly around the town."

"Actually," Jothan said, "I was wondering if you'd like to come there now and share a mug of ale with Quinn and me. There might even be some cobbler left."

Millard patted his bulging stomach and Thaine had drawn breath to protest as well, when Jothan lowered his voice and continued. "There's someone we'd like you to meet, but he's afraid to come here. Says Maren is too much Lord Lucian's man, and Kerman is terrified out of his wits of Lucian."

"Kerman," repeated Arien, her voice also low. "The one Skelly sent a message to this morning."

Jothan nodded. "He's our anodyte supplier, since Lucian killed the last one. He's plainly scared to shivers, but says he needs to talk to you, Your Highness."

"Have you any idea what he wants to talk about?" Thaine asked.

Jothan grinned. "Of course. He has a batch of poisoned anodyte ready for me, and he wants to assure you that he prepared it only because he's afraid if he doesn't, he'll be killed, as his predecessor was. This isn't a trap, Your Highness. Kerman isn't the type, and I haven't seen any harmful thoughts in his mind at all."

Thaine nodded. "All right. I'll meet with him." He glanced around the table. "Anyone coming with me?"

"I am," Arien said.

"And I," Millard added.

They stood, as did the four guardsmen sitting nearby. As though on cue, Natan came hurrying through the kitchen door.

"I hope everything was satisfactory, Your Highnesses." He rubbed his hands compulsively, his expression eager.

"Perfectly," Thaine assured him. "Please compliment your wife on an excellent meal. We're going to check on the rest of our party now and will return shortly."

Natan nodded as he began removing dirty dishes from the table. Arien, Millard, Thaine, and Jothan left the common room, followed by two of the guardsmen. The remaining two stayed to watch the inn.

The sun had not completely set, but the night breeze blew with a chill. The lights from buildings along the street cast a warm glow against the approaching twilight. The few Oterans they encountered spoke pleasantly as they passed.

The common room of the Bed and Bitters was empty but for Quinn and another man seated at a back table. Skelly, hearing the door open, came from the kitchen and smiled broadly at his royal visitors.

"I'd hoped to see Your Highnesses." He beamed. "If you've not had supper, I'm sure my wife—"

Thaine held up a hand. "I'm afraid we have, though Jothan has made us all envious with a description of the meal we missed. We've decided to dine here tomorrow evening, if you'll have us."

"If we'll have you?" Skelly grinned, clearly delighted. "My wife will worry me to death if we don't have the honor of feeding you at least once. Now she'll be up all night planning tomorrow's supper."

Thaine laughed. "I'd hate to be the cause of a sleepless night. Tell her anything she throws together will be fine. But for now, a mug of ale while we talk with our friends would be welcome."

"Of course, of course."

Skelly hurried to fill the mugs while Arien, Thaine, Millard, and Jothan joined Quinn and the thin, nervous man. His throat convulsed as he bobbed his head at Millard and Thaine. After one glance her way, he avoided looking at her completely.

"This is Kerman Sein," Quinn said in a low voice by way of introduction. "Has Jothan spoken of him?"

Millard nodded while Thaine answered. "Yes, we understand he is your anodyte supplier. The one who warned you of the plan to give you poisoned anodyte."

Kerman gulped and spoke in a shaky voice. "I didn't want to do it, Your Highness, I honestly didn't. But Lord Lucian would have killed me. I know he would. I've seen him kill others when they wouldn't do what he told them. He killed the previous chemist, Illan, just because he wouldn't sell his chemist lab when Lord Lucian wanted it."

"You worked with this Illan?" asked Millard.

Kerman nodded. "I was his apprentice for five years. Now I run the lab for Lord Lucian. He doesn't get involved in much of it, he doesn't care about mixing medicines or the like. Only anodyte."

Thaine leaned forward, his arms on the table. "Did he tell you directly that he wanted the poisoned anodyte to go to me?"

Kerman shook his head. "No, but I was told to have it ready before the southerners came back the next time." He glanced toward Jothan. "I didn't have it ready for your last visit, and Lord Lucian was unhappy with me." The man swallowed uncontrollably. "Very unhappy."

Arien Perceived and found memories of the most horrible beating she could imagine. She winced in sympathetic pain at Kerman's memory, and then drew her breath in surprise as she saw something in his mind she hadn't expected.

Lord Lucian's face.

It loomed above the pain of Kerman's memory, the finely shaped lips curved into the mockery of a smile as he watched Kerman being beaten. The man had dark hair instead of red, but besides that the resemblance was striking. Eyes the identical shade of green, matching chiseled noses, the same slender faces.

She had closed her eyes to study the memory, and she opened them to find herself the object of five stares.

"I'm sorry," she stammered. "I must be tired."

"I saw a mental image of Lucian," she projected to Jothan. *"He looks just like me!"*

"You know..." Jothan's thought came to her on a wave of cautious introspection. *"...he really does. I didn't notice before. When I first saw him it had been seven years since I met you, and you were little more than a child then. But now that I've seen you again, the resemblance is rather striking."*

Kerman Sein was watching her strangely, as though he had just noticed her. His eyes widened, and his lips gaped open. "You!" He raised a hand to point across the table at Arien.

Fear leapt into the man's face and sent his thoughts reeling in terror. He started to push back from the table to stand, preparatory to running from the inn. Quinn put a restraining hand on Kerman's arm, and the frightened little man began to tremble visibly. He didn't take his eyes from Arien's face.

"Please." She reached across the table toward the terrified man. "I won't hurt you. You have nothing to fear from me."

Kerman drew back in horror as her hand came close to touching his, but he did not bolt from his seat.

"She's a friend, Sein," Jothan assured him, and everyone at the table nodded.

Kerman seemed to relax a fraction but continued to stare at Arien as though she were a nightmare come to life. Arien Perceived the man's thoughts again and was shocked by the incoherence she found there. She glimpsed Lucian's face again. One thought was primary, though it made no sense to her. The man kept thinking of a prophecy and seemed to link it to her.

"What *is* it?" she asked, hoping to get him to explain without revealing her ability. "Why are you frightened of me?"

When Kerman had controlled his repetitive gulping, he finally managed to whisper, "You're the missing girl, aren't you?"

"Missing girl?" Millard's face mirrored Arien's confusion.

Kerman nodded. "The babe born almost twenty years ago. Lord Lucian's sister."

Her own thoughts stumbled to a halt. Around the table, everyone wore stunned expressions, which no doubt matched her own.

"Sister?" Jothan raked fingers through his hair. "What are you talking about? Out with it, man."

"Have you not heard the story?" The little man's glance circled their faces. "I'm speaking of Lord Lucian's sister, the one who disappeared all those years ago."

Arien's hand rose of its own accord to cover her mouth. Her breath came in short, staccato gasps. Was this… Could it be…?

"Who is this Lord Lucian, anyway?" asked Thaine.

"Don't you know?" Kerman shook his head, his eyes fixed on her. "He's the heir to one of the most powerful Houses in all Otero. The House of Arien."

Ten

No one spoke.

Thoughts whirled in Arien's mind, only one of which she could lay hold. This man was speaking of *her.* Her past. Her family.

He peered closely at her. "You don't know, do you?"

She managed to shake her head.

Jothan caught the man in a stern glance. "What are you talking about, Sein?"

Kerman drew in a slow breath, which seemed to calm him. He spoke in answer to Jothan's question, but kept his gaze fixed on Arien. "Oteran Houses follow the custom of having a Seer perform a prophecy for their newborns. We call it a birth foretelling. A formality, really. The Seer says something pleasant about the child's future, often how it will make the House stronger, more powerful. But twenty years ago, a different sort of prophecy was spoken over a girl child born to

Lord Jerolin Arien and his lady."

Lord Jerolin. Arien leaned back in the chair. Her father's name was Jerolin.

The little man continued. "The Seer said the daughter would be the downfall of the House of Arien and would cause the end of its existence. Lord Jerolin was furious and gave orders for the child to be killed. He justified his actions by saying he had to protect his father's name and his son's future."

A desert invaded Arien's mouth. Could this be true? Her own father had ordered her killed. Her own father.

"And Lord Jerolin's wife?" Her voice came out as a squeak.

"Disappeared, along with the child. Rumor told that she escaped with the babe and left her son behind."

"Dead, then." A breath she wasn't aware she held escaped in a loud sigh. As a girl she'd held out hope that the woman who brought her to the orphanage had been a stranger, maybe a kidnapper or something. Not her mother. "Dead on Mount Caliago. As I always thought."

"And the son was Lucian?" Thaine asked.

Kerman nodded.

This time it was Arien who swallowed convulsively. "My brother."

"He's more than that." Kerman jerked his head toward her. "He's more than that. He's your twin."

Silence descended on the table for a long moment while everyone absorbed Kerman's words. A twin. *Her* twin.

"This changes everything," Thaine said, after they had absorbed Kerman's revelation. "Arien can't stay here any longer. She must return to Hamlin immediately."

She looked at him in surprise. "Why?"

Millard answered. "Because you're in danger. If they tried to kill you as an infant they will try again."

"They certainly will." Jothan nodded, concern etched on his forehead. "You were no threat as a babe, but now you've returned as an adult, and with an envoy from Creighton and Hamlin. They can't help but see you as the prophecy come true."

"And us along with her." Thaine cast an apologetic glance

her way. "Our mission will be viewed with suspicion if we've returned accompanied by someone who was predicted to bring about the death and downfall of one of their most powerful Houses."

Of course, the words rang with logic, but a quiet determination rose within her. She was so close to finding her family. She couldn't let the opportunity slip away, even if her own father *had* wanted her dead. Her brother was horrible, yes, full of violence and hatred. But maybe her father wasn't. He'd only been reacting to a prophecy, after all. Trying to protect his infant son. Maybe Lord Jerolin had changed in twenty years and regretted his actions. He may even have remarried, fathered other children. She might have younger brothers and sisters who weren't as cruel as Lucian. If only she could meet them, could somehow make them understand that she would never knowingly cause their deaths.

She straightened and faced Thaine full-on. "But you need me. Without me, how will you know if there is a plot to invade Creighton?"

Millard said, "Jothan can take your place. He has the same training and abilities."

Arien glanced toward Kerman, but the little man seemed confused, and obviously didn't know what abilities Millard referred to.

"We've been over this. He can't go the same places I can." She kept her tone low but insistent.

Thaine glanced at Kerman and spoke in a louder voice. "We will discuss this later. For now, we owe our thanks to our new friend for his warnings." He raised his mug in an informal salute to Kerman. "You have my gratitude, and that of my kingdom."

Kerman seemed flustered by this, and swallowed several times in succession, ducking his head. Everyone remained quiet, watching him for a long moment before he realized he was being dismissed.

"I'd best be going before someone sees me here." He rose and glanced toward the door and uttered anxiously, "You won't mention to anyone, Lord Lucian in particular, that you've spoken with me?"

"Of course not," Thaine assured the little man. "I hope we can count on the same from you."

Kerman gave a tight half-smile, then nodded. With one more uneasy glance around the inn's empty common room, he left through the rear exit.

When they were alone, Arien stiffened her spine and faced the others. "I want to stay."

Millard shook his head. "Arien, be reasonable."

His placating tone infuriated her. With a firm grip on her patience, she responded in a voice as calm as she could manage. "I'm already here, and the entire town has seen me. I've ordered dresses made, and Beryle has spent the day pestering half the shop owners in Eshtaol on my behalf. How suspicious will it be if I leave now?"

An uncomfortable silence descended around the little table. Quinn cleared his throat to speak, and Arien braced herself for another argument against her.

To her surprise, he agreed with her. "If we send her back now the Oteran King will certainly hear of it, and I'm afraid it will look suspicious."

A quick glance around the table told her everyone saw the wisdom in this argument, though none looked pleased.

"Could we change her name?" Millard asked. "Call her Lady Elsa, or something like that? Maybe it will throw them off."

Jothan shook his head. "Lord Lucian will still be certain to recognize her when he sees her."

Quinn toyed with his mug. "Maybe we can arrange to keep her away from Lucian."

Jothan snorted. "Eshtaol isn't that big. If Lucian shows up here, as we suspect, keeping them apart will appear contrived. Too many people have already heard her called Arien. I'm surprised Maren or Skelly haven't questioned it yet. They're probably afraid to. If we suddenly change her name, it's sure to cause talk."

Thaine agreed. "Jothan is right. We'll have to be open about the whole thing and act surprised when Lucian recognizes her. And be ready to defend her, in case he tries anything."

They were all looking at her, and Arien tried to maintain a serious expression to match their own. But inside a smile threatened. Now that she was so close to finding her family, nothing was going to make her leave before she'd seen them face to face.

Thaine arranged for runners to go to the Oteran capital of Kadesh carrying their request to King Kuriel for a formal diplomatic meeting. Kadesh lay near Otero's coast. The king would need time to consider their request, so they did not expect to hear from him in less than a full seven days.

To their surprise, an official messenger returned four days later. He delivered a document sealed with an impression in purple wax. Thaine read the message while the runner refreshed himself with a mug of ale and dinner from the Roadside Inn's kitchen. He passed it to Millard without a word, and Arien read over that prince's shoulder.

To Their Most Gracious Majesties, First Prince Thaine and First Prince Millard,

Welcome. I am surprised and honored to learn of your arrival within our humble borders. If I were able, I would hasten to greet you in person, at the point of your entry into my kingdom. Alas! State matters prevent me from leaving Kadesh at this time.

I am most eager to receive you, my friends from the south, at my palace in Kadesh as soon as arrangements can be made for your travel. An escort is being assembled as I pen this missive and will arrive shortly.

I trust that you have found your stay in Otero pleasant thus far, and I look forward to welcoming you personally.

His Royal Majesty,
Emperor of Otero and the Western Isles,
Kuriel

Arien looked from the message to Thaine's face.

He shrugged. "Much the same message my father would draft if the circumstances were reversed."

"Still, it is pleasant enough." Millard rolled the scroll so that the broken seal fit together again. "He could have returned an armed escort to take us in chains."

"That's not how political games are played," Thaine replied absently, while he stared up into a corner of the Roadside Inn's meeting room.

Millard bristled at the implication that he didn't understand politics, and Thaine seemed to realize his mistake. He went on in an approving tone. "Still, that's a good thought. We should probably have been ready for just such a response. We're lucky we weren't faced with it."

Millard calmed visibly, and Thaine glanced at Arien, the only other person in the room. She smothered a grin at his almost-wink.

"We're lucky," Thaine repeated, "but now we must be ready to answer this message. I admit I expected to be confronted by Lord Lucian, or maybe even the senior Arien, Lord Jerolin, since they have lands nearby."

"Perhaps my father and brother are in Kadesh with the king," Arien said.

Both princes gave her a sharp look at her reference to her family members, which she ignored. "After all, Kerman did say this is only one of their houses, and Jothan and Quinn were not expected for another anodyte purchase for months. It stands to reason Lucian wouldn't be nearby."

Thaine nodded, though he continued to eye her. "I suppose you're right. And that does make things easier as far as your presence is concerned. That's one problem we won't have to face until we've had an opportunity to meet the king, and maybe by then you will have discovered something from whoever he sends to escort us."

Thaine's words, and the hope they expressed, were proven wrong three days later when Kuriel's soldiers arrived to escort the southerners to Kadesh. The group was led by Lord Lucian Arien.

Arien was in her room when the party arrived. Beryle rapped on the door and opened it without waiting for an answer.

"It's the soldiers from the king." Awe saturated her whisper. "And with them is a man who looks like you."

Beryle had accepted the news of Arien's parentage with philosophical indifference, but now that one of Arien's actual relatives had appeared in the flesh, her normally unflappable manner was subdued.

Arien's heart began a wild tattoo. "A young man, or old?"

"Young," Beryle answered, "and not bad looking, but cold-like. With green eyes, like yours."

"My brother." Arien Perceived the common room below her.

"Prince Millard sent me up here with a message that you're not to come down until you're sent for. He wants to get more guards inside."

She nodded, distracted by the thoughts that raced through the minds below her. Though banished from the room, nothing could stop her from knowing what went on.

"Go downstairs and watch for an opportunity to let Thaine know I wish to come downstairs and meet Lord Lucian."

Beryle nodded and left.

With only a slight twinge of guilt, Arien peeked at Thaine's thoughts. They were colored with distrust as he spoke to Lucian. Most of the prince's discomfort centered on thoughts of her, and his strong desire to protect her. She ignored that, searching instead for his impressions of her brother.

Thaine considered Lucian's manner properly formal, as the situation required. His welcome speech, delivered on behalf of King Kuriel, was eloquently given. Thaine noted the astonishing resemblance to Arien in the man's face, and she smiled at Thaine's opinion that the features were more suited to a woman than a man.

She turned her attention to Millard. That prince remained silent, as he had done more and more often since the beginning of the mission, but his thoughts were as active as that of his brother-in-law. Millard regarded Lucian with even more suspicion than Thaine and wondered at Thaine's friendly response to the man. Millard was determined not to speak kindly to this proven murderer. Arien shook her head. How like him, to be completely ignorant of the need for diplomacy in a potentially volatile situation.

With some hesitation, she turned her mind to that of the newest presence in the room below. Her brother. What would she see in his mind?

Please, don't let him be as horrible as everyone says. Let me find something to redeem him, something I can take comfort in.

But, as Jothan warned, she encountered only an oddly constructed mind shield. Not a thought, or even a glimmer of personality slipped through. She had no experience with natural shields but saw instantly that this one was composed differently than those she had encountered at the Brotherhood. Instead of the smooth surface to which she had grown accustomed during her training, this wall rose in an uneven pattern, the surface twisted and scarred. Some areas were thicker than others, and almost no glimmer escaped from within. It was as though Lucian had built a fortress around himself and at every attempt by outside forces to approach him, he had fortified his mental wall tighter and thicker.

No wonder he is cruel. He has closed himself away, refusing to be touched, or to touch anyone else. His thoughts are completely centered on himself at all times, because that is all he senses.

He must have possessed a great amount of natural ability to begin with. A pang of sympathy struck at her. How badly he must have been hurt at a young age. Why else would his mind have taken this form of defense? Would she have done differently, given a different upbringing? True, she had been without a family, without the loving parents she so longed for, but she had not lacked love in the orphanage.

While Arien had been studying Millard and Lucian, Beryle must have had an opportunity to speak with Thaine, for the door opened and the maid slipped through.

"Prince Thaine says no." Beryle folded her arms across her chest. "He says they're going into the meeting room, and there's no reason for you to be there. He says we don't want to give away the real reason you're here, and if you really were Prince Millard's consort, you wouldn't be included in meetings. He says you can meet Lord Lucian at supper."

Arien dropped onto the bed with a bounce, irritated. Thaine was right, of course. As Millard's mistress, she would have no reason to attend a diplomatic meeting.

Beryle patted her knee sympathetically. "Nothing to be done but wait." She brightened. "You're welcome to come along while I do some errands for Yulene. She's rattled by Lord Lucian, to be sure, and having fits at the thought of feeding him, so I said I'd help."

Arien shook her head. "Go ahead, Beryle. I'll just stay here and read." She picked up the book of poetry she'd borrowed from the common room below and smiled at her maid.

When Beryle left the room, Arien put the book down and shamelessly eavesdropped on the meeting taking place below her.

The supper hour came slowly. Arien tried on each of the dresses she'd had made and discarded them one by one as unsuitable. One was too formal, the next too plain. In the end, she wore the yellow gown she'd brought from Hamlin, steamed and wrinkle-free. The color gave her skin a warm luster, and her hair fairly gleamed in contrast. She had planned for Beryle to curl it, but the maid was busy helping the nearly hysterical Yulene prepare supper for Lord Lucian, and in the end Arien simply caught the thick mass back in a clasp.

Millard appeared to escort her downstairs. She'd heard Jothan and Quinn arrive some moments before and knew that Thaine and his lieutenants were already below.

The prince offered his arm as they walked down the corridor toward the stairs. "It will be difficult for you, pretending that you don't know he is your brother."

Arien shook her head. "I doubt I'll have to pretend long. What will be difficult will be acting as though I'm ignorant of the other things I've learned, like the reason for my mother's escape. I'm curious to hear how Lucian explains it."

They descended the stairs side by side, Arien's hand resting lightly on Millard's arm. At the bottom, she paused to look around the room.

Four soldiers stood in the corner to the left of the main entrance, two dressed in red uniforms, their bearing crisp and military. They wore a crest on their helmets and patches on their shoulders bearing an embroidered golden crown. Probably King Kuriel's guardsmen. The others had donned chained armor over blue uniforms without helmets and wore shoulder bands displaying a symbol—a large A on a red background. An odd twist wrenched at her stomach. Her family's crest.

To the right of the door stood four of Thaine's guardsmen, their blue and white uniforms fresh and crisp. They stood stiffly, their eyes scanning the room as though they expected trouble and were determined to prevent it.

Jothan and Quinn lounged near the ale keg, having just filled two mugs from the stack on the counter. Thaine stood nearby talking to a tall, slender man with dark hair, whose back was turned to Arien and Millard.

My brother. My twin. Again, her stomach gave a nervous flutter.

Thaine caught sight of them, and his lips tightened. He expected trouble. She sensed fierce feelings of protection emanating from him, which normally might have flattered her. Time enough to think of that later, after her family had been confronted. Right now, her focus was on the man before her.

Lucian, seeing Thaine's gaze lock on someone behind him, turned.

Millard whispered, "Here we go," and led her forward. He approached Lucian and stopped, nodding politely. "Lord Lucian, allow me to present Lady Arien, who has traveled with us from Hamlin. My lady, this is Lord Lucian Arien, of the

Oteran House of Arien, who has come on behalf of King Kuriel to escort us to Kadesh."

Lucian's eyes, as green as mountain grass, pierced hers, and his elegant lips parted slightly as his jaw dropped.

"It seems we have a name in common, my lord." She sank into a brief and graceful curtsey.

"Yes." Thaine stepped forward. "We thought it odd this afternoon, when we learned your name."

Lucian remained silent, his gaze intent on her face. An emotion lay buried in his features. Cautiously, she employed her empathic ability. No thoughts, but a strong sense of displeasure hovered around his tight mindshield.

Disappointment stabbed at her. *I expected that,* she reminded herself.

"If I were to guess," he said in a calm voice, his green eyes locked onto hers, "I would say we have more in common than a name, lady."

"You are right, Lord Lucian." Millard looked from one of them to the other. "I've never seen anyone with eyes the shade of Lady Arien's until now. Without a doubt, there is a similarity."

"More than a similarity." Thaine looked from one to the other. "They are exactly the same hue. And that's not the only resemblance. Look at them. Their features, too, are remarkably similar."

Lucian's gaze became more piercing, and his eyelids narrowed slightly. Arien tried to maintain an expression of amazement, and hoped she succeeded, for Lucian looked suspicious. Their gazes locked for a long moment, and then he appeared to come to a decision.

He broke the visual contact as he searched the room. "Where is Maren?" The words trembled. "I feel the need for wine, the stronger the better."

"I'll find him." Jothan left the room in the direction of the kitchen.

"Would you care to sit, my lord?" Thaine asked.

Lucian nodded. "Let us all sit and work out this puzzle. My lady." He gestured toward a chair at the nearest table.

She sat, and Millard and Thaine leaped to take the seats

on either side of her. Lucian circled the table and sat facing her.

"Is Arien your family name?" His eyes narrowed as he watched her.

Arien shook her head. "I am an orphan, my lord. I was found as an infant, just moments before my mother died of exposure during a mountain snowstorm. She whispered the name Arien, and the man who found me assumed it to be my given name. He took me to the orphanage where I was raised."

Jothan returned, followed by Maren carrying a large tray with several bottles of wine and an arrangement of glasses. "Just put them there." He waved toward the table. "We'll serve ourselves."

Jothan poured wine for Arien, Lucian, and Millard. Thaine waved aside the offer, pointing to his ale mug. Lucian lifted the glass Jothan placed before him and gulped half of the liquid before speaking.

"Prepare yourself for some news." He set the glass on the table and folded his hands before him. "I was born at my family's manor house not far west of here, the oldest of twins. The second babe was a girl. But before our Naming Day, my mother took childbirth fever. She became hysterical and insisted that someone was trying to kill her baby. The healers assured my father that such a reaction was normal. She was young and the birth a difficult one. They convinced him that she would recover, as other young mothers had done."

Lucian took another sip of wine, this one smaller. He kept his gaze fixed on the table. "But instead of recovering, my mother ran away, taking my twin sister with her. She left in the night, and by the time her escape was discovered, she could not be found. Trackers followed her trail into the mountains, but a fierce storm blew up and they were unable to pursue her further. She never returned."

Lucian grew silent and peered into Arien's eyes. The pain she saw there, the same she had lived with her entire life, moved her to compassion. They had both grown up motherless. At least she had the benefit of knowing her mother died. What must it have been like for him, knowing his mother left him and took his sister? Had he felt rejected, unloved? Was that why he built his sturdy mindshield?

She swallowed against a cluster of lumps in her throat. "Are you saying that I am your twin? Is it possible?"

Lucian nodded. "It is more than possible. When you see my father, you will know without a doubt."

"Does he look like you?" Millard asked.

Lucian shook his head. "Not especially. Everyone always told me I bore the looks of my mother. But she is unmistakably his daughter."

"Oh?" Thaine twitched one eyebrow up. "How so?"

"He has bright red hair. In fact, I am the only child in memory of our family's history to be born without it. Father used to tell me he would have doubted my parentage, except that he had seen my twin sister himself, and she had hair as bright as a carrot."

A lump of tears lodged in her throat. It was true, absolutely true. She had found her family.

"I admit," she managed to whisper, "that when I heard your name…" She cleared her throat and blinked, then went on in a steadier voice. "Earlier today, when my attendant brought news of you, I wondered if it could be true. And now I find that it is."

"Hey!" Jothan's thought reached her. *"What is this? I hope you're a better performer than I'd anticipated, and half of this is put on for Lucian's benefit."*

"Some of it certainly is. But I have been eager to find my family since I was a child."

Jothan looked uneasy, and his thoughts were colored with discomfort. *"You haven't put your personal quest first, before our mission, have you?"*

"Of course not." Arien stiffened her spine. *"I have no intention of doing anything to jeopardize the mission. But while I'm here, I see no harm in meeting my family."*

"No harm? Your father tried to have you killed as an infant. And you know what kind of man your brother is. You've seen proof of his cruelty in Kerman's mind. And he just lied to you about your mother's disappearance. The rest of your family may be no better."

"Maybe he doesn't know the reason our mother ran

away," Arien argued. *"He was only a days-old infant, after all."*

"A lowly village chemist knows the story, and he doesn't?" A hint of alarm crept into Jothan's mental tone.

She answered with a thought as soothing as she could. *"I know you're right, but it is possible that his is the true version. Regardless, I promise to be careful."*

To cover the brief time during which their conversation had taken place, she blotted at her eyes with a handkerchief and turned her attention to her brother. "Will your father be in Kadesh when we arrive?"

Lucian nodded. "Our primary residence is there."

"And did he ever remarry? Do you have brothers and sisters?" She could not keep an eager tone from creeping into her voice.

An odd expression crossed his features. Was he considering not answering her question? Then he smiled. "Yes, though not until a few years ago. His wife gave birth to a second set of twins, a boy and a girl, both with bright orange hair. They are around four years old, I believe."

Natan and his wife entered the room then, each carrying a large platter piled high with food. They served their guests silently, placing ample servings of roasted venison, broiled fish, spiced vegetables and fresh fruit on each plate. Arien glimpsed Beryle standing in the kitchen doorway, staring intently at the back of Lucian's head as though trying to find a resemblance to her mistress from behind.

When the plates had been filled and distributed, the innkeepers escaped to the kitchen with obvious relief.

Thaine turned to Jothan and Quinn, his expression strained. "Lord Lucian tells us that we have no further need of you as guides, as the king has kindly assigned him to accompany us to Kadesh."

That shocked both Jothan and Quinn. Jothan tossed a look of dismay toward Arien but didn't follow it with mindspeech. He didn't have to. Having been involved in this mission from the beginning, indeed before the beginning, she knew how he would hate being excluded now.

"But..." Quinn's voice trailed into silence.

Lucian spoke to Jothan, his manner as condescending as Millard's had ever been. "You are, of course, welcome to stay here in Eshtaol to guide the princes back across the border when they return from their visit with King Kuriel. I trust you will find your stay comfortable."

"And you can act as relay for messengers from home." Millard gave Lucian a self-conscious grin. "My wife is due to deliver a babe soon. Our first."

"Of course." Lucian dipped his head. "I have brought a team of message dogs from Kadesh. I will leave them here for any missives that need to be relayed to us."

"Message dogs?" Arien asked.

"Yes, they are trained to carry messages from anywhere in the kingdom back to their home station. Their ability to find Kadesh, even from the most remote mountain village, is rather remarkable. We've never had one go astray, except, of course, in the case of an accident. They can't be trusted with confidential missives. Unscrupulous men have been known to interrupt the dogs' missions."

"How fascinating." A broad smile appeared on Thaine's face. "That's why King Kuriel was able to respond so quickly. We've never thought of using animals as message carriers. But dogs are territorial, and I would think they could easily be trained to return to their home."

Lucian nodded. "We've bred them to heighten the instinct over the years, that and for speed. They're remarkably fast and much cheaper than a man traveling by horse."

Millard grinned at Thaine. "It appears we have already discovered something worth taking back to our kingdoms from this trip."

Thaine agreed. "Indeed, and that is the primary purpose of our mission. I imagine there are a good many Oteran developments that would greatly benefit our kingdoms. And, of course, we are bound to have practices or customs to benefit Otero as well." He smiled at Lucian. "If this meeting with King Kuriel goes well, I hope you will allow us to return the favor and play host to you in Creighton."

"And Hamlin," Millard put in.

Lucian nodded. "I would find it an enjoyable mission,

should the king allow me to go. I confess that I have long had a fascination with the kingdoms that lay across our southern border."

"Forbidden fruit, perhaps?" Thaine smiled.

"Perhaps." He looked at Arien. "But now I have even more reason to discover all I can about your kingdoms, since they have until now been home to my long-lost sister."

At the slight emphasis he placed on the words *until now*, Arien's stomach gave an odd leap. Did he expect that she would leave her home, and Master Petro, to live in Otero with a family she did not know and probably wouldn't even like? Hardly.

And yet, a vision of orange-haired tots played through her mind. Oh, how she looked forward to meeting the brother and sister she had always longed for but had not known existed until today.

Eleven

"I don't like it." Jothan glared at Lucian's back over Thaine's shoulder.

They stood in the street in front of the Roadside Inn. Around them guardsmen readied themselves for the journey, checking their packs and equipment. King Kuriel's escort had arrived with enough horses for their guard. A wagon had been purchased in Eshtaol and packed with everything that could not be carried on horseback.

"I know you don't," Thaine said, "but we have no choice. I have no valid reason to bring you along. You are here as our guide through the Nephtali Pass and we're through that. Besides, Lucian doesn't trust you."

"I feel the same toward him," Jothan assured the prince. "Plus, I don't like the idea of Arien going off to his house to meet his family without me there."

Thaine grinned. "Are you Lady Arien's self-appointed bodyguard?"

"Of course not, but—"

Thaine interrupted. "We can take care of Arien. And it is natural for her to want to meet her family."

Jothan didn't answer. He watched Arien mount her horse with assistance from her brother. His stomach gnawed at itself, as it did each time he saw them together.

"I know that." He pitched his voice just above a whisper. "But there is something odd happening. I can't put my finger on it, but I feel it whenever I think of that family Lucian talked about."

"I will watch her." Thaine grasped his arm in a firm grip. "If Lucian or his father try anything, my guardsmen will be on hand to protect her."

"And what could they do?" Jothan allowed his gaze to sweep the assembly and return to the prince. "What could they do to protect any of you? You're in the middle of a possibly hostile kingdom with no escape route, surrounded by thousands of loyal Oterans. If King Kuriel decided to take you hostage he could do it easily enough, and your guard won't be much hindrance to him."

"I know." The prince's lips thinned. "I heard the same from my father's council and King Mendel's as well. We're relying heavily on unwritten rules of diplomacy, but there's no other way. I prefer to look on the top side of the coin. If there *is* an invasion plot, this diplomatic visit might at the least forestall it. Or even give Kuriel cause to re-think it. Perhaps peace and a diplomatic trade agreement with our kingdoms will appeal to him more than war."

Unlikely. Bad enough being entrusted to guide two first princes into Otero. Now they wanted to run off deeper into the kingdom to places Jothan had never been and knew nothing about, with a man he did not trust—Arien's long-lost twin brother. And she was behaving as though she'd like to clasp him to her bosom.

But what could he do about it? Not a thing. He stepped to the side of the street and watched Thaine and Millard mount their horses. Lucian was already on his and spoke with Arien, no doubt telling her some enchanting tale of his home.

"*Be careful,*" he sent to her.

She turned in the saddle and smiled when she caught sight of him. *"I will. And you behave yourself here."*

"I have no choice. In case you haven't noticed, there isn't much in Eshtaol that could get me in trouble. In fact, there isn't much in Eshtaol at all."

"Don't pout." Her grin reached him across the distance. *"It makes you look childish. I'll see you when we return."*

Jothan replied with a shrug as he watched her prod the horse forward so she could speak to Beryle who was perched atop the wagon near the driver. Quinn came up beside Jothan and together they watched the troop of guardsmen and princes ride out of Eshtaol.

Jothan stared at the back of the last guardsman. "This feels wrong."

His partner shrugged. "No use worrying. They are their own responsibility now. There's nothing to be done but wait. At least Prince Thaine paid for our room and board for a month in advance."

"And left a few guardsmen as well," Jothan added glumly. "But I still wish I were going along."

Quinn shrugged again. "So, go."

Jothan turned to him. "What do you mean?"

"If you're hankering to run off after them that bad, do it. I'm sure they won't be hard to track. Not like they're riding covert."

"But Prince Thaine said—"

"Said what? Not to follow him? If he did, I didn't hear it."

Jothan gave him a thoughtful look. "What about you?"

"Who, me?" The man laughed. "I plan to stay right here and let the prince pay for my meals and ale for the next month. I don't see any reason to run across Otero chasing a group of people who are capable of looking out for themselves. And besides, I plan to get friendly with Kerman Sein. If I can convince the man to come back with us and set up his alchemist shop in Arnath, we'll control the anodyte prices ourselves, as well as the rest of the chemist trade."

He couldn't blame Quinn. If Jothan was smart, he'd be concentrating on profitable possibilities too. If Thaine's mission was successful, the Nephtali Pass may be opened soon and there would be rich profits to be made in Arnath, the closest town to the major trade route.

But he couldn't shake the nagging feeling that something terrible was about to happen in Kadesh.

Otero's capital city was a shock to the southerners. Oterans had always been referred to as barbarians, but with one look at Kadesh Arien revised her opinion. The city was huge by southern standards, at least three times the size of Corral, which was the biggest town in the Twin Kingdoms. Long before they approached the gates, they encountered clusters of shops, homes, factories, and inns in one small village after another with only a few horse lengths between them.

"They're called the burgs of Kadesh," Lucian explained as they rode through. "Most of them have no name, and their only reason for existing is to hold the overflow from the city, both visitors and inhabitants. The planners of Kadesh didn't expect the city to grow so large, and space inside the wall is limited."

Arien gazed at the people they passed. The streets bustled with travelers, but the passage of their large company drew the shopkeepers out of their stores to stare. She spied one or two frightened expressions when they caught sight of Lucian's banner, the large A on a red background. *Are the people afraid of the Ariens, then?*

A quick peek inside the mind of one burly man verified the fact. But she saw that he was not only afraid of the Ariens, he was terrified of drawing the attention of anyone who belonged to an Oteran House. He had no wish to risk their quick displeasure and lose his home and business.

Interesting.

Although today, the man need not have feared. Lucian rode with his gaze fixed on the city gates before them, not deigning to notice the people who lined the streets.

The crowds thickened as they neared the gates. People scrambled to get out of their way but moving was difficult. Oxen, carts, wagons, and horses clogged the streets. And, of course, people. More people than Arien had ever seen or dreamed of seeing. They were everywhere, all kinds of them—old and young, clean and filthy.

Getting through the gates took an eternity, and when they passed through the thick wall, they encountered even more confusion. Inside the walled city the streets were just as crowded, but far narrower than those outside. Thaine's guardsmen became nervous, and, after a struggle, arranged themselves to encircle her and the first princes. The crowds crushed in on all sides so tightly that she rode with her legs actually touching her escorts' horses.

What seemed like hours later the crowds thinned and they could spread out on the road. At last Arien could look around and formulate some sort of opinion about Kadesh.

The buildings that lined the street when they first entered the city were made of timber and gradually became sturdier and bigger. Closer to the palace, most were constructed of stone, and more ornately decorated. For the most part, they stood flush against one another, with an occasional narrow alley running between. Many dwellings stood here, though she passed several shops as well. The wares she saw in one window almost took her breath away. Gold and jewels glittered in the sunlight, rings and arm bands, necklaces and even goblets were prominently displayed for all to see.

But by far the most eye-catching sight in the city loomed directly before them. Kuriel's palace was enormous, with no less than twenty towering spires rising high into the sky, some of them with rounded rooms and colored glass windows near the top. The turrets pointed upward like huge arrows aimed at the heavens, each one cut from pink crystallized stone. Together with the rainbow-hued windows they made a colorful display. She glimpsed the glint of gold atop the highest spire.

A guard stood waiting to question them when they approached the palace gate. He recognized Lucian and bowed.

Lucian sat straight in his saddle. "This is the delegation from the southern kingdoms to see King Kuriel."

"Yes, Lord Arien." The guard hurried to swing the double gates open, to allow them to pass through with their mounts.

Inside, they came upon a courtyard similar to that at

Tadmoure Castle, though many times the size. Arien gazed around the massive space with interest. Soldiers in crisp red uniforms stood at attention, stationed at even intervals. A few curious locals took the opportunity to stop and stare at the visitors. The horses' hooves clopped across flat, polished paving stones. Elegant arches led into different parts of the palace grounds or into the palace itself. Such an area might have appeared formal or cold, but not this one. Statues and benches placed here and there formed cozy conversation nooks, and well-tended patches of red and yellow flowers made a lovely effect. Maybe she would be able to lounge here on one of those benches and chat with the Oterans of the area.

Lucian drew his mount to a halt, and stable hands ran from one of the archways. Glancing that way, Arien glimpsed another outdoor courtyard through a high arched tunnel. Her brother dismounted and turned to lift her to the ground. He tossed the reins of her mount and his to one of the attendants as the others circled the party, collecting the horses from the southerners. Thaine and Millard moved quickly to stand near Arien. Beryle, climbing down from the wagon, hurried over as well.

"You, there." Lucian pointed at one of the soldiers. "Inform the king and Lord Zadornin that our southern guests have arrived. And send someone to show them to a guest house."

The soldier bowed, then disappeared through another of the arches.

Thaine raised his brows. "Lord Zadornin?"

Lucian smiled. "The king's most trusted advisor and a close friend of my family. An amazing man, quite intelligent. He looks forward to meeting royalty from the south."

"We're to be lodged in a guest house?" Millard asked.

Lucian turned to face him. "Yes, the king maintains a number of houses within the palace walls to host guests who stay for an extended period. You'll be assigned one of those while you're here."

Arien noticed that Lieutenants Curran and Lars wore relieved expressions. It would be much easier to guard the princes if they weren't inside the palace itself.

A man hurried toward them from the direction the soldier

had gone. He approached Lucian and bowed. "The king wishes to see you at once, Lord Arien. I will show Their Highnesses to their house."

Lucian nodded his head toward Thaine and Millard. "I will see you soon, then. Your Highnesses." Then he turned to Arien and took her hands. "I will send word to my father at once. He will want to meet you without delay."

Impatience jumbled within her as she returned his smile. "Please tell him I look forward to meeting him and the rest of his family as well."

Lucian's smile held secrets, but when she attempted to Perceive him, she found only his impenetrable, awkwardly constructed mindshield. Not even an emotion this time. He walked without hurrying through an arch and into the palace.

They turned back to their guide. He stood a full head shorter than Arien. A nervous-looking fellow, his eyes continually shifted from person to person but never settled on anyone.

"I am called Gannon, Your Highnesses." He bowed nearly double. "I will see to your comfort during your stay in Kadesh. Please come this way."

Thaine gave Arien a glance full of meaning as they trailed along after the little man, and she understood that he wanted her to read Gannon's thoughts. She Perceived.

He was unusually nervous, though she assumed that was rather a normal state of affairs. His taskmaster, of whom Arien caught only a glimpse with no name associated, was a harsh man whom Gannon feared. She assumed the taskmaster to be comparable to the chamberlain at Tadmoure Castle and Gannon to be one of his underlings. His thoughts concerned the swift accomplishment of his duties and hopes that these foreigners were kind and would not report any oversights on his part.

Odd. Why would King Kuriel send an underling to see to the comfort of his royal visitors? Would it not be more appropriate to send the palace chamberlain himself? Perhaps the ways of courtesy were different here than at home.

She caught Thaine's eye and shook her head, letting him know there was nothing to fear in this man's mind.

They entered the palace courtyard from the west, and Gannon led them north through yet another stone arch. A short tunnel let onto a smaller courtyard in which stood four guest houses—all of them large and handsome. Statues and benches had been placed about the yard, the result charming and even cozy. To their left the outer palace wall, made of stone, towered above the roofs of the guest houses. Another wall at the back served to enclose the guest houses in their own private yard.

Curran and Lars studied their surroundings. Arien looked again, evaluating the area from their perspective. The only visible entrance into the courtyard was the arched tunnel through which they had just come. The walls stood high enough to make scaling difficult, though certainly not impossible.

"The guest houses are empty at the moment." Gannon led them across the paved courtyard. "I'll put you in this one because it is the largest. There should be room enough for all of you. You've also been assigned a staff to see to your domestic needs. They will arrive soon. If you will make your tastes known to the cook, she will prepare your meals accordingly."

"We won't be taking our meals with King Kuriel?" Millard asked.

Gannon's eyes widened. "The king eats only in private."

Thaine smiled at Gannon's startled expression. "Please forgive our ignorance. Our ways are different. My father normally dines with at least a dozen of his councilors and lords, and their wives, and even merchants from the surrounding village. An invitation to the king and queen's table is viewed as an honor and highly prized."

"The king *and* the queen?" Gannon shook his head, eyes rounded as oranges. "King Kuriel's queen is never seen in public, nor are any of his wives. It is considered a great insult to look upon one who has—" His voice dropped to almost a whisper. "—lain with the king."

"Wives?" Millard's eyebrows arched. "How many does he have?"

Gannon placed a finger to his lips. "It is unseemly to speak of such things. But since you are unfamiliar with our customs, such breaches in courtesy are to be forgiven." He lowered his voice even further. "It is rumored that the king has forty-four wives. We know that he has ninety-seven children, and so such a great number of wives is not beyond belief."

Millard gave a low whistle, and then threw a wicked grin, reminiscent of his old, lustful self, toward Arien. "Perhaps we have stumbled upon something else which bears consideration in the south."

Thaine chuckled. "I doubt my mother would agree."

Arien lifted her nose to the sky and ignored Millard completely. She was supposed to be posing as his mistress, therefore could not risk an unadoring comment before their Oteran host.

Gannon led them to the guest house nearest the outer wall, and Curran appeared about to protest. His gaze circled the other options, and then he shrugged. Apparently, he considered them all equally defensible.

Their guide pushed the door open and stepped aside. Lieutenant Curran went first with three guardsmen, and Lieutenant Lars motioned for the other guardsmen to remain outside.

Arien entered and stopped just over the threshold, blinking at an assault of colors. She stood in a large, wide room that doubled for entry hall and public room. Huge, colorful pillows lay scattered about the floor, along with several gold-embossed chairs and an ornate writing table. The ceiling arched high above them, hung with bright tapestries and friezes etched in gold. A set of stairs spiraled upward in one corner, a most interesting effect. A quick mind scan showed no one in the house besides themselves.

"The large sleeping rooms are above." Gannon indicated the circular staircase.

He led them through the kitchen and outside into another small courtyard, this one completely enclosed. A wall separated the yard from the one next to it.

"This courtyard is nice for meditations." He nodded toward a secluded bench in a well-flowered corner.

"Where is the bath house?" Beryle had been so uncharacteristically quiet during the tour.

Gannon turned to her. "The bath house?"

"Yes." Beryle slowed her speech as though talking to a child. "The place where you take a bath, get clean, soak in hot water."

Gannon actually blushed, and stammered, "In the sleeping rooms." He brushed past them and retreated into the house, obviously embarrassed.

"Well!" Beryle planted her hands on her hips and stared after him. "They must not speak of baths either in this barbaric kingdom."

"You should be careful about calling it a barbaric kingdom." Thaine glanced after their guide. "The Oterans might not take that as a compliment."

The maid drew herself up. "Hmph. I'll just have myself a look at those sleeping rooms."

She marched back into the house and after a moment's pause, Arien and the princes followed. Gannon stood in a corner of the public room. Thaine stayed below to speak with him while Arien, Millard, and Lieutenant Lars followed Beryle up the spiraling staircase.

A sitting room met them at the top of the stairs. A long corridor led toward the rear of the house, with doors along each side. Beryle opened one of them, and she and Arien stepped inside.

They entered a spacious room, easily as big as Arien's back in Kirklin Castle. Sunlight filtered through a wide window, fringed by a thick, green curtain. The coverings on the enormous bed were also of green, with gold trim. Arien ran her hand across it. The fabric was silky, softer than any covering she'd ever felt. In a corner of the room stood a moveable set of wall panels with an intricate floral design. Beryle peeked behind it and turned to Arien, grinning.

"The bath," she verified, "and a chamber pot. They must heat water in the kitchen and bring it up. That won't be fun."

"We'll manage," Arien told her.

Millard and Lars stood in the doorway, peering in.

"This will do for us," Beryle told Lars. "Have someone fetch a pallet for the floor, and I'll stay in here with Lady Arien."

Arien started to protest that Beryle should have her own

room, but then she realized that beds would probably run short before they all had one. This room was easily big enough to accommodate them both.

Before he pulled the door shut behind him, Millard awarded her a sly wink. “I'll be next door.”

Arien frowned after him. “He has certainly perked up since we got here.”

“Been a long time since Tadmoure,” Beryle commented.

Arien gave her a questioning look. “Tadmoure? What do you mean?”

Beryle shrugged. “Just that the prince found himself a bed warmer in Tadmoure, and it's been a long time since he left her. He'll be lookin' around soon, I expect.”

Arien was astonished. “Prince Millard? Are you serious?”

“Are you surprised?” She ran a finger over the ornate bed curtains and then tested the mattress. “He's not exactly hideous to look at, and he *is* a prince. There's lots of ladies who would like to keep him company on a cold night. This one was a chambermaid to Princess Lianne, a timid little thing, but pretty. She was quiet about it, which showed she had good sense. I wouldn't be surprised to see her turn up at Kirklin Castle.”

“But…” Arien trailed off. Why should she be surprised that Millard, of all people, would take a mistress?

What about Thaine? Arien felt a pang at the thought. His wife was ill and apparently had been for some time. Did he take mistresses? Beryle would know.

“And what of Prince Thaine?” She assumed a casual expression. “Did he leave behind a bed-warmer in Tadmoure as well?”

Beryle shook her head. “Talk around Tadmoure Castle is that Prince Thaine don’t go in for that. Seems he's all wrapped up in the princess, the poor thing.”

Relief washed through her, followed immediately by a stab of irritation. What did she care if Thaine took a mistress?

Another thought occurred to her, and she turned a suspicious look upon Beryle. “And just how did you manage to get these interesting little pieces of information?”

The girl blushed. “Well, Oren did like to chat a bit.

Especially after he was nice and relaxed, if you know what I mean."

The girl's cheeks grew redder as Arien said, "Ah."

That explained a lot. Beryle would make an excellent spy, even without Power. So far, she had discovered more on this trip than Arien.

Beryle opened the door. "I'm going to go see about our things."

"I'll go with you."

She was suddenly unwilling to be left alone. To be alone forced one's mind to work, and there were too many things she didn't want to think about right now. Like Lucian, her father and his family, and also Thaine, and his love for an invalid wife. And how much she missed Master Petro back at Kirklin Castle.

The cook and housekeeper arrived while Beryle unpacked their trunks. Arien scanned the thoughts of both and found nothing with which to be concerned. The cook, a large, loud, red-faced woman with grey hair stood on stocky legs bigger around than Arien's waist. She insisted on being called simply Cook. Mila, the young housekeeper, rarely spoke, probably due to an inability to make herself heard above Cook's incessant speeches. No doubt the household was in store for a few epic verbal battles for speech time between Beryle and Cook.

Arien and Beryle had unpacked the two trunks purchased in Eshtaol when a soft rap at the door sounded. Beryle opened it and listened for a moment to the housekeeper's whispered comments.

"Lord Lucian is downstairs, waiting to see you," Beryle announced to Arien.

Arien smiled. "Perhaps he has already had news of our father."

The girl shrugged. "I just hope the father's cut from a different piece of fabric than the son."

Arien turned an amused glance on her. "Am I to understand that you're not fond of my brother?"

"Not by far." Beryle sniffed. "You should hear the stories Yulene told of him beating his attendants and even other people's servants. He actually had a man killed just so he could have the wife. And then he didn't even marry her, but just used her and took her dead husband's property."

A disquieting piece of news, if it were true. "Some of that might be rumor. Especially the part about taking property. Surely that's against the law."

"Hmm." Unconvinced, Beryle pursed her lips. "I wouldn't know about that, but any man that beats people who serve him don't get none of my good thoughts wasted on him."

To that, Arien had nothing to say. Very probable those tales were true. Even given the heartache and hardship of a motherless upbringing, she refused to defend him. Brother or not, she would not condone beatings.

I hope the little twins are being raised by a loving, caring mother. That will make all the difference in their lives.

An image rose to mind of orange-haired tots running into the arms of a young woman, full of smiles and laughter. A comforting idea, and she still wore a smile as she faced Lucian in the common room.

"Ah, there you are, as lovely as ever." Lucian pecked her cheek with a brotherly kiss.

Thaine frowned behind Lucian's back. Arien tossed him a smile, which he met with a scowl.

"I have news of our father." Lucian led her to a seat next to Thaine's. "He is away at the coast for a few days. I've sent a messenger after him, and no doubt he will return as soon as he can when he reads my note."

"And his wife?" Arien asked. "Is she here in Kadesh?"

"No, I'm afraid she and the twins have gone with him. They love the coast, and when Father has business there they often accompany him."

"Oh." Disappointment stabbed at her, but she covered it with a smile. "No matter. Later is as well as sooner after so many years."

Thaine spoke up, and she detected a note of annoyance in his tone. "It seems that customs are different here than in the south. Vastly different, in some respects."

Arien turned toward him. “Oh? How so?”

Lucian answered. “His Highness mentioned how eager you've been to meet King Kuriel, and I had to correct a misunderstanding in that matter. Women in Otero are not permitted to roam openly in the halls of the palace. Nor do they attend meetings of state, either formal or informal.”

She drew herself up, surprised. “They don’t?”

“No.” A heavy frown darkened Thaine’s fair features. “You will not be able to meet the king or his advisors.”

Though he looked calm enough, he broadcast waves of frustration. Lucian watched her closely, apparently trying to gauge her level of disappointment.

She didn’t bother to hide her own frustration. “But surely the king encounters women at *some* time.”

“Oh, certainly. In fact, he announced that he will host a formal ball in seven days to honor his royal visitors.” Lucian nodded toward Thaine, who responded with a brief smile. “At that time, you will be presented to him in your role of advisor to Prince Millard.”

Arien's breath stopped. “Advisor?” She glanced toward Thaine.

Spots of color appeared on his cheeks. “Consorts are not openly accepted in Otero. We must present you as a female advisor, something also unheard of in Otero but at least not offensive. As diplomats, we dare not risk insulting the king's dignity.”

Arien Perceived Thaine's surface thoughts. They were so colored by frustration that she was immediately frustrated herself. *So, it seems that all our careful planning and the embarrassment Arien has gone through was more harmful to our mission than helpful. It would have been far better to bring the old man. At least he would have gotten to see the king and his top advisors, and we could have learned something from them.* Thaine glanced toward Arien, unaware that his thoughts were being heard. *On the other hand, I wouldn't have enjoyed the journey nearly as much.*

The last was tinted with so much admiration Arien’s face warmed. She glanced quickly at Lucian and saw that he had noted the blush.

Hopefully, he attributed her embarrassment to her position. Truly, the idea that her brother—and soon the rest of her family—would think her Millard's mistress was embarrassing enough to fan the warmth in her face to full flame.

That Lucian had mistaken it in exactly the manner she hoped was proved by his next words. "Please don't think I or our father will hold your, ah, position against you. I understand that you have been raised in a kingdom with different views on that sort of occupation. The rest of the family will come to understand that as well, given time."

Face burning, she could only manage a quick nod. His contempt for her assumed occupation showed plainly, though his desire to appear tolerant was also apparent. Would her father and his wife be as quick to accept her? Would they welcome her into their home, or would they be horrified and choose to ignore her claims that she was Lucian's missing twin?

Millard descended the steps at that moment, and Lucian rose to greet him with a bow. Arien glanced toward Thaine and found him staring at her. He smiled, apology apparent in his face, and shrugged.

"The other reason I came," Lucian told the princes, "is to inform you that King Kuriel has called a meeting of his advisors for this evening. You will be officially presented to them."

"Splendid." Millard rubbed his hands together, casting a glance at Arien. "Then we can get the diplomatic talks underway."

"Yes, well, we will fill you in on the rest of Lord Lucian's news later," Thaine told him, and then addressed Lucian. "Where will the meeting take place?"

"In the king's advisory hall, at the southern end of the palace. I will arrange for an escort to arrive after dinner to escort Your Highnesses."

"We will be permitted to bring our guard?" Thaine's request held a touch of steel that said he intended to, whether they were permitted or not.

Lucian spread his hands, smiling. "Of course, though they will be expected to wait outside the hall, as the king's soldiers do."

Thaine nodded, though his expression clearly showed his displeasure. Millard tossed a questioning glance at Arien. She gave her head a slight shake and looked pointedly toward Lucian. Millard took the hint and remained silent.

Lucian stood. "I hope you are finding the guest house to be satisfactory."

The three southerners stood as well.

"Everything is very nice," Arien told him. "Please express our appreciation to the palace chamberlain for the attendants he's sent us. They've been most helpful."

"My lady." Lucian took Arien's hand and bent over it in a charming salute. "I will notify you the moment I hear from our father." He then bowed toward Millard and Thaine. "Your Highnesses, until this evening."

When the door had closed behind Lucian, Thaine let his frustration vent with an angry exclamation. Arien Perceived the location of the others in the house and, confident that they would not be overheard, nodded toward the princes. Thaine filled Millard in on Lucian's news.

"So." He threw himself into a chair. "Our plans have played against us. It would have been just as well to bring that drug peddler."

Arien leaned against the edge of a sturdy table. "Not him, because Lucian knows him. You should have brought Master Petro or practically anyone else with Power. I won't be able to do much for you now."

"How about this meeting?" Thaine straightened. "Maybe it will be close enough for you to pick up something from here. You don't have to be within sight to hear thoughts, do you?"

Arien shook her head. "No, but there's a limit to the distance I can Perceive sightless, and it isn't very far. Plus, the more people between me and my target, the less likely I'll be able to Perceive anything worthwhile. After a certain distance, I can't see more than a blur of light, much less pick up individual thoughts."

"Have you tried?" Millard gestured toward the palace. "Have you been able to hear anything inside the palace since we arrived?"

Arien looked toward the window. Her eyes unfocused as she Perceived the immediate area. She knew everyone within the guest house, as well as the guardsmen outside. Beyond that, she located a dozen or so people in the main palace courtyard, their thoughts fairly easy to detect. Broadening her range, she reached further inside the palace. The number of people increased, their thought-lights nothing more than a blur.

She shook her head again. "There are a lot of people in the palace. The courtyard is pretty easy, but beyond that it gets difficult. I can try, and I will, but unless someone happens to walk into our courtyard thinking about a plot to invade Creighton at the same time I'm Perceiving him, it's a useless effort."

Millard cocked his head. "They have to be thinking about it for you to see it in their minds?"

"I can see surface thoughts without touching the person's mind. I can push deeper, but that can be uncomfortable to the person being probed. It's even been known to cause damage if the person resists."

"A surface thought is one that someone is thinking?" Thaine asked.

She nodded.

Millard scratched his chin. "If that is so, how did you expect to catch them thinking about the plot to begin with?"

"I was to be there, Perceiving King Kuriel's mind as you and Thaine were presented to him. If there is a plot against the south, he won't be able to prevent himself from thinking of it when he sees you. It's only natural."

Silence settled in the room. Arien lowered herself to one of the huge cushions, obviously placed on the floor for that purpose. If only they could come up with an idea to redeem their mission.

"Perhaps I could stand in the courtyard," Thaine suggested, "and as people pass and recognize me, you could watch their thoughts."

Arien shook her head. "Too dangerous. Lars and Curran would have a fit. Princes don't put themselves on stage anywhere, especially in a foreign kingdom. But I could go sit in the courtyard and watch people as they come in."

"And hope they just happen to be thinking about Creighton as they enter the palace?" Thaine shook his head. "I'll not bet the odds on that one."

Still, after several moments of silence, no one came up with another solution. Arien's suggestion was the closest thing to an alternative plan they could come up with. At any rate, it would only be for seven days, then Arien would meet not only the king, but Lord Zadornin and all the other Oteran lords as well.

That decided, Thaine rose. "I'm going to get some rest before dinner so I'm fresh for this meeting."

Millard, who had already rested, left the house to wander the area, and Arien followed Thaine up the stairs. At the top, he turned a weary smile on her. "I'm sorry for the embarrassment you must be feeling. Especially since it's turned out to be unnecessary."

"The situation couldn't be predicted." She shrugged. "A little embarrassment won't kill me."

"I appreciate all you've done for this mission. You've suffered a lot, and you should know that someone has noticed."

He placed a hand on her arm. Warmth radiated where his skin touched hers. A loud pounding began in her ears, and a flutter erupted in her stomach. His face hovered only inches from hers, so close she smelled the musky scent of him. If she leaned forward just a bit, and tilted her head, their lips would touch.

She stepped sideways and averted her eyes to break the contact. "I've not contributed anything yet, so suffering doesn't count for much. But I haven't given up. Rest well, Your Highness."

She slipped into her room and closed the door behind her. Safe inside, she leaned against the wood, heart pounding, and strained to hear Thaine's footsteps. She was tempted, sorely so, to Perceive his thoughts.

No. Her own thoughts were erratic enough.

A long time passed before Arien heard his footsteps retreating down the corridor to his own room.

Twelve

After their encounter in the corridor, the idea of facing Thaine over dinner left Arien fidgeting with discomfort. Feeling like a coward, she asked Beryle to bring a tray to her room with the excuse that the journey had tired her. No doubt Millard would assume her to be pouting over being left out of the meeting. Let him. What Thaine thought she couldn't guess and dared not Perceive. She spent the evening arranging her wardrobe and purposefully *not* thinking about Prince Thaine.

When a page arrived to escort them to the meeting, Arien followed their progress mentally. She traced them through the courtyard without any trouble, scanning the thoughts of those they passed without encountering anyone who even knew who they were. Then they entered the palace. Dozens of minds surrounded them, and shortly afterward, hundreds.

Was some sort of gathering in progress? When she'd Perceived the palace interior earlier there hadn't been nearly so many people. She selected an individual at random and Perceived his thoughts.

A merchant by trade. She filtered through several surface thoughts concerning a fabric shop in the outer city. He worried that his workers would fall behind in their production, but had he forbidden them to attend the king's banquet they would have thrown down their aprons and left him. Ah, here was an appropriate thought.

"What's it mean, this banquet? Kuriel ain't never done nothing like this afore. All that talk in the invitation about the king's goodwill toward us who work hard to make Kadesh a thriving city is cow flop. But the food's good, anyway.

Similar thoughts crowded the other minds she Perceived. She lay in the ornate bed and nestled beneath a thick pile of soft blankets, occupying herself by searching for the reason behind King Kuriel's unexpected and uncharacteristic generosity.

Interesting that such an unusual gesture of goodwill should occur at the same time Millard and Thaine were to be presented to the king and his advisors. According to the thoughts she Perceived, an invitation of this sort had never been issued from the palace. The banquet must be connected with the southerners' visit, but how?

She continued to scan various minds in the crowd. Almost no one was aware of the princes' presence, though a few had heard rumors. She focused on those. One man supposed King Kuriel was attempting to put on a show of generosity in front of the royal foreigners.

A likely reason, but something still didn't feel right. There was something else, something she should be aware of but couldn't grasp. Something threatening, perhaps?

Or was she merely reacting to the frustrating situation in which she had been placed? If only she could talk to Petro, he'd be able to pinpoint whatever disturbing fact evaded her.

She needed to stay awake to discuss the situation with Thaine and Millard when they returned. Maybe between the three of them they could reason out any sinister purpose behind King Kuriel's actions tonight. Besides, she itched to know what they learned in the meeting.

But the bed was soft and warm, and the day had been long and full of new things. Try as she might, Arien could not stay awake.

When she awoke it was full night. She sat up, instantly and completely awake. Something had awakened her, and she listened for the sound to repeat. The room was silent but for Beryle's slow, even breath on her pallet in the corner.

She Perceived and saw no concern in the guard stationed in the corridor hallway, nor in the one at the bottom of the steps. A quick scan of the perimeter showed her a dozen guardsmen alert and on duty. No one had seen or heard anything unusual.

She narrowed her search to check the rooms surrounding her. Curran slumbered across the hall, as did Millard in the room next to hers and Lars across from him. Arien sent her mind toward Thaine. He was awake and deeply upset. His feelings radiated from him as though projected directly to her. Ah. This was what had awakened her. A deep and unrelenting grief colored his mental presence.

Grief?

Should she Perceive his thoughts? No. Whatever disturbed Thaine so deeply must be intensely personal. If it concerned the mission, she would not have hesitated, but personal thoughts were different.

Still, the depth of his emotions stirred her. To suffer so while alone in a foreign land? Maybe he would appreciate a welcome ear, as he certainly would not appreciate a prying mind.

Beryle sighed and rolled over, immediately settling back into a deep sleep. Without considering her actions further, Arien slipped out of bed. She paused before her traveling chest. The wisest course of action would be to don a casual gown, but that would wake Beryle. The thick robe she had purchased in Eshtaol was modest enough to be an overcoat. She slipped it on.

As the catch clicked softly closed, Arien waved a hand at the guard. He peered intently at her in the flickering light from the wall sconces before returning the gesture. She crept down the corridor to Thaine's room and tapped on the door, careful to make no more noise than necessary.

After a pause, the door opened. The grief Arien had sensed in his mind showed plainly on his face, his features ravaged by it. His clothes were rumpled, and his hair looked as though he had spent several hours scrubbing his fingers through it.

When he spoke, his voice held a weariness that made her heart ache. “I can assume by your presence that you have heard the news.”

Arien shook her head. “I've been asleep. What news?”

Thaine threw the door open wider and gestured for her to enter his room. She hesitated. What would the guardsman at the end of the corridor think? With a glance his way, she stepped inside but left the door standing half open.

Thaine crossed to a writing desk in the corner and retrieved a piece of thick parchment, which he handed to Arien. Then he threw himself into a chair and stared at the ceiling while she read.

> *Dearest Son,*
>
> *I regret to send this terrible news by letter, but circumstances do not permit me to tell you in person. Princess Lianne has died. My healers tell me her heart has been weakened by misuse of the drug and that this end has been inevitable for some time. The pen cannot express the pain I feel, and the distance between us prohibits me from lending my arm for you to lean on as you learn of this crushing news.*
>
> *You must return at once. Roddy needs you here. I will send Erskine to take your place as diplomat. He and Prince Millard must carry on the mission you have begun.*

It was signed simply *Father* and stamped with the royal seal of Creighton.

Arien looked up, her throat tight. “I am so sorry.”

Thaine continued to stare at the ceiling. “I knew it would happen. The healers told me the drug would kill her but withholding it from her suddenly would kill her as well.”

At last she understood how he could hate the drug and yet continue to buy it. “You bought anodyte for the princess.”

He nodded. “I tried to wean her from it, tried giving it to the healers to administer, but she found other means to buy it.” He stopped, his eyes closed at a painful memory.

“Aren’t there any other remedies for her condition?” she asked. “No safer medications?”

He looked startled. “You don’t understand. The drug *was* her condition. She started taking it after Roddie’s birth, and she never stopped, even though it was destroying her.”

The convulsive twitching was caused by anodyte? Then the bandit who tried to rob them long ago had been using that drug too, or one similar to it. He’d wanted Petro’s money to buy more of it.

Thaine went on, his voice ragged. “She needed it. Her body depended on it, and she wasn't strong enough to withstand not having it. And I was not strong enough to withstand her begging.”

What could she say to ease the pain she sensed in him? The sight of his shoulders slumped in defeat tore at her heart.

Thaine broke the silence with a small voice. “I killed her.”

Arien crossed the room and placed a hand upon his arm. “No. You loved her. You couldn't stand to see her suffer.”

Thaine dug at his eyes with a thumb and finger. “I didn't love her, not at the end. I did at the beginning, loved her so much I would have done anything for her. And she loved me, too. Not my title—me.

“After Roddy was born anodyte became her lover. The only thing I was good for was getting the drug for her.” He stopped, took a deep, shuddering breath. “But I loved the memory of her, of what we had been together. And because of that, I couldn't say no to her, even though I knew it would kill her eventually.”

Arien swallowed against sudden tears. No wonder he suffered such great anguish. He not only felt responsible for the princess's death, he also grieved the loss of his love. She looked down on the top of his head, on the disheveled blonde hair, and let tears roll down her cheeks. Then she knelt before him, her hand still on his arm.

"I don't have your father's strong arm." She tilted her head back, looked up into his face. "But you can lean on mine in place of his."

Fresh tears sprang to his eyes at the sight of hers and weeping wracked his body. He dropped to his knees before her. Arien put her arms around him as he wept, his face buried in her hair. She whispered in his ear the way she had seen mothers do for their children, gentle words of comfort which he probably didn't even hear. Her fingers traced circles on his back with a soft, light stroke.

Finally, his tears slowed as he succumbed to the comfort she offered. When the change happened, Arien felt it in herself and in him. The gentle motions of her fingers and the comfort of her words drove away his grief. Or perhaps grief stepped aside, giving way to a stronger emotion. He turned his face, and his lips found hers.

A wave of passion flooded her senses. Hunger she'd never known threatened to overwhelm her. She returned the kiss with abandon, rising on her knees and clutching his head with both hands, her fingers buried in his hair to pull his lips even more firmly against hers. His ardor fed hers until she wasn't sure which controlled her, only that she wanted more of him, more—

The kiss ended as suddenly as the it began. Thaine grasped her wrists and pulled them gently from his hair. For one long moment he gazed into her eyes, and then he stood abruptly. He crossed the room and stood staring out the window into the darkness, his back to her.

Newly awakened emotions vibrated along every nerve in Arien's body. She stood, her chest heaving. The sight of his stiff frame, his hands clasped behind his back, acted on her like ice water on a fire. What was she doing? This man had just lost his wife.

"I'm sorry, Your Highness." Flames burned in her cheeks, in her heart. "Please accept my apology."

He whirled to face her, and his gaze locked onto hers. "Arien, you have no reason to be sorry. I should apologize to you."

Coming toward her, his step hesitant, he raised a hand to

touch her face. It stopped before she felt his fingers on her skin. His eyes were intense, and Arien found her breath held captive by the passion in them.

"On the night we met and danced together, I knew. Since then my feelings have grown so that I can't sleep for thinking of you. Even my dreams are full of you. I want…" His hand dropped to his side. "But I cannot dishonor Lianne on the night I learn of her death."

Arien nodded, though he had turned away again. She sensed his turmoil even without Perceiving him. Though her lips still tingled from the press of his, he was right. She hurried to the door.

Thaine spoke again, his voice soft. "I would not have this thing between you and me begun in the shadow of her death. I want more from you than tonight."

Her heart thudded heavily in her chest. What was he saying? *Yes*, she almost shouted. *I want more, too.* Instead she gave the briefest of nods before she slipped through the doorway.

In the corridor, she leaned against the wall, willing her thundering heart to still. Her mind whirled with thoughts of Thaine—his lips, his hair, the touch of his hands on her skin. Of the passion they had both felt. And denied.

She became aware of the guardsman at the end of the corridor, watching her. Could he see her burning face across the distance? With a casual wave, she slipped quietly down the hall, through her own door, and closed it behind her with a soft click.

Jothan selected an inn fairly close to the palace gates, but off the main thoroughfare. Located on a busy side street, a variety of shops boarding houses surrounded the place. Beggars in filthy, tattered clothing littered the area, their palms outstretched. Some of the people coming out of the nearby taverns didn't look much better than those who approached them to beg for alms.

The innkeeper eyed him with open suspicion at first but

accepted his coin gladly enough and showed him to a closet-sized room with a tiny window looking over the street. Jothan spared a thought of gratitude for Skelly. The Eshtaol innkeeper swapped Jothan's southern coins for Oteran ones, though he emptied his coin box and even dipped into his private purse to do it. From the window, Jothan watched the shadows of the beggars below him as they moved between those hurrying on their way.

After stowing his pack in the chest, he checked the security of his coin belt and went below to join the crowd in the common room. The princes arrived yesterday. The offer of Skelly's horse had been unexpected and welcomed—due in large part to Quinn. Without it, Jothan would have been forced to follow on foot. He sold the animal in the outer city for a good price and planned to return with a younger, stronger beast to reward the fat innkeeper.

Patrons sat at a good number of the tables in the common room, though plenty remained empty. Jothan chose one near the center of the room, next to a pair of men who looked as though they'd been drinking ale the better part of the evening. He signaled to the serving girl for a mug and a plate of the night's fare, then settled in to listen.

The inn appeared to be frequented by the locals. He wasn't surprised when, after a few moments of polite silence, the men from the next table spoke to him.

"New to the city, are you?" The man nodded his dark, tousled head toward Jothan.

"I am." Jothan modified his speech pattern slightly to take on the mountain twang used in Eshtaol.

The second man nodded, noting his accent. "You here for a visit?"

His manner was friendly, even talkative. Good. Exactly what he'd hoped to find.

Jothan took a drink from his mug before answering. "Looking to find work. Been aiming to come to the city my whole life, but Pa always needed me on the farm. When the foreigners was coming here, thought I'd tag along. Better 'n traveling alone and getting robbed on the way."

"Foreigners?" The light-haired man cocked his head,

curious. “What foreigners would that be?”

They hadn’t heard of the southerners’ visit? Interesting. “Foreign princes from the south. Came through the Ir'Shemath down by home, coming to see the king.”

The first man nodded. “I heard of them. Some say they're the reason for this so-called banquet in the first place.”

“Banquet?”

“Yeah, the king’s putting on a banquet tonight, to say thanks to the merchants of Kadesh.” The man shrugged. “Or so he says.”

“I still don't believe it.” A scowl furrowed his friend’s brow. “But if there’s foreign princes here, that makes more sense than believing Kuriel suddenly found a generous streak in his miserly old soul.”

“Shh.” The first man cast a frightened glance around the room. “Men are charged with treason for saying less.”

Supper arrived, and Jothan applied himself to it while the pair returned to their ale. As he ate, he scanned the surface thoughts of those in the room. Nothing interesting, except more speculation over King Kuriel's uncharacteristic act of gratitude. Since none of the thoughts centered on the southern princes, he ignored them.

He had finished his food and was half-way through a second ale when a new customer entered the inn. The man wore a uniform, and from the crest on his breast Jothan took it to be palace livery. The occupants of several tables hailed him in a friendly manner.

“Kindin,” shouted Jothan's dark-haired neighbor. “Join us, and your first ale's on me.”

Not about to pass up such an offer, Kindin made his way through the room and clapped both men’s shoulders in a hearty greeting. He appropriated an empty chair from Jothan's table and joined his friends. The serving girl set a mug before him.

He picked it up and eyed the foam with appreciation. “I've not known you to be so generous with your coin, Posper.”

“Perhaps he's caught the spirit of generosity infecting the town tonight.” The light-haired man lifted his mug and laughed.

"Ignore Ximun," Posper told Kindin. "He's miffed at not receiving an invitation to the king's banquet."

Ximun half-turned away from Posper. "Now that you're here, what's the real reason behind this banquet? Surely you've heard something while running about the halls of the palace. And don't tell me Kuriel's been overwhelmed by admiration for the hard-working people of Kadesh, because I won't believe it."

Kindin shook his head. "Can't tell you a thing. I'm as bewildered as anyone, including the rest of the palace staff too. But take hope, Ximun. I hear there's to be another banquet tomorrow. Perhaps you'll be included then."

"Another?" Ximun and Posper whistled in amazement. "What's he up to?"

Kindin glanced around, his manner secretive, and Jothan made much of studying the serving girl across the room.

The man spoke barely above a whisper. "Something interesting did happened. A group of foreigners arrived this afternoon. Claim to hail from the kingdoms south of the Jalapa Range. Before I left, right after the banquet started, they came to a private meeting in old Kuriel's *small* audience room."

His audience stared, uncomprehending.

"Yeah?" Ximun asked. "What of it?"

"Just that the king never uses his small audience room, and especially not when all the Houses have been summoned. They must have been sitting on top of each other in there. The king always uses the big one."

Posper shrugged. "Maybe the big one was dirty or something?"

Kindin shook his head. "It wasn't. And these foreigners have a woman traveling with them. I saw her today when they arrived. She's got hair as red as Lord Arien's, and I've never seen hair that color anywhere except in the House of Arien."

Though Posper and Ximun appeared unimpressed, alarm klaxons sounded in Jothan's mind. He Perceived Kindin.

Idiots. Can't see past their next ale. 'Course, they didn't hear those two lords talking about that red-headed witch like I did. But that didn't make sense. How could a woman have anything to do with which audience chamber the king used?

And what about that red hair? Such an unusual shade could only come from the House of Arien. A by-blow of Lord Arien's, maybe? If so, how did she become associated with foreign royalty?

Jothan withdrew from Kindin's mind, disturbed. The term 'witch' revealed much. At least some people in the palace suspected, or even knew of, Arien's Power. How? A few possibilities came to mind, none of them reassuring. And why was King Kuriel using a different meeting room than normal? The location of this all-important first meeting was too much of a coincidence to be ignored.

The more he thought about the term 'witch,' the greater his alarm. A rumor that Arien possessed Power spelled disaster, not only for her but for the mission. How widespread was knowledge of that birth prophecy, and how long would it take for people to start putting the two together?

The serving girl approached to clear his empty plate, and he handed her enough coin to cover his meal. He needed to do a little investigating at the palace.

Outside the inn, he crossed over to the city's central, and thus more populated, street. More people meant safety after dark. He wandered toward the palace, seemingly aimless in his destination, glancing through the windows of the shops he passed. The people ignored him, and in short order he arrived at the palace gates.

A row of guards stood in front of the gate. Jothan had no official reason to enter the palace walls, nor did he need to. Instead, he paced back and forth, an awed expression on his face as he gawked up at the towering spires like the country-boy tourist he pretended to be. The guards, accustomed to sightseers at all hours, ignored him.

Now within the range of mental contact, Jothan Perceived. A crowd of a hundred or so drew his inner sight. Attendees at the king's banquet. He didn't have time to try to pick thoughts from them, not without alerting the guards by lingering too long at the gates. Perception to any point beyond the crowd was rendered impossible due to the vast number of people. Instead, he scanned the perimeter. He searched for a mind to Perceive, one specific mind.

As expected, he found it almost immediately. He recognized Arien as easily as if he had spied her bright head in a sea of dark ones.

She was asleep. He could wake her with mindspeech, but to what end? At this late hour, he couldn't enter the palace gates without drawing attention to himself, and she couldn't leave for the same reason. He turned and wandered aimlessly back down the street he'd just traveled, his face clear of the worry he now felt in abundance. His worst suspicions had been confirmed. Unless he missed his mark, Arien was being kept purposefully away from King Kuriel. Not only that, but the king had flooded the palace with a multitude of people, placing them between her and those of his lords whose minds he did not want her to see.

Which could only mean one thing—King Kuriel was not only aware of Arien's Power, but also of its limitations. How? Were there men of Power in Otero?

Irritation washed over him. They should have expected to encounter men of Power in Otero. *Arien* came from here, didn't she? And while Jothan had not detected Lucian using Power, he definitely possessed a strong shield. That could only mean that at least some Oterans recognized Power and had even learned to control it. If so, they would know its limitations. Or even if they had access only to the occasional rogue Power, they could have learned enough to enable them to set up this mental barrier under cover of the banquet.

But how had Kuriel known about Arien? The answer was obvious. Someone told him. But who? Someone from Creighton? Or someone within the group traveling with her? Either way, the mission and everyone connected with it was in danger.

Jothan forced himself to relax. Panic threatened to get the better of him, but he fought against it. Maybe King Kuriel was simply averse to having his thoughts Perceived, as was King Hubert. Would Kuriel go to such extremes if he had no invasion plot to hide? Unlikely, but possible. And Kindin told his buddies that another banquet was scheduled for tomorrow evening, which meant that the king planned to keep up the deception for a while. The princes weren't in any immediate danger, at least not tonight.

But at first light, he would approach Arien and the princes. They had to know what he had discovered.

He turned the corner into an alley that cut across from the central street to the one where his inn was located. Racing thoughts distracted him. In an instant, he became aware of the presence of two men following him. Thieves, he saw in their minds. Before he could do more than begin to turn, they were on him. His struggle lasted only a moment. Pain exploded in his head, and Jothan knew no more.

Thirteen

Preparations for Thaine's departure kept the guest house staff and guardsmen busy the next morning. Embarrassed over their passionate kiss, Arien held her tongue and avoided looking at him whenever they were in the same room. How should she act toward him? What if he regretted his words and their kiss in the stark light of morning? She remained quiet and tried not to watch him as he instructed the guardsmen in preparation of his departure. Lieutenant Curran and seven Creighton guardsmen were selected to accompany him. The rest would remain in Otero with the diplomatic mission.

As Thaine's packs were being secured to his horse's saddle, Arien slipped inside the house. Upstairs, she sat on the bed and stared at the wall. Would the spark that flared briefly between them in the night flicker out before she saw him again?

A soft rap at her door a few moments later set her heart

pounding in her chest. She opened the door to find him in the hallway. Her throat constricted. It might be a very long time before she saw him again.

He spoke quietly. “I couldn’t leave without seeing you once more. I spent all night trying to think of a way to take you with me, but—”

“I know.” Arien forced a smile. “But I'll be useful here, at least I will be in a few days when I am able to meet the king.”

“And Lord Zadornin.” His eyelids narrowed. “That man knows what’s going on if anyone does. He’s got a calculating look about him that I don’t like. If we could only arrange for you to meet him now.”

He fell silent for a moment, and then, with a quick backward glance, stepped into the room and closed the door behind him. “I thought of something else last night. I want you to consider it while you’re here. When the mission is over and you come home, I’d like you to stay in Tadmoure.”

Arien caught her breath. “Stay in Tadmoure?”

“If you will. My father may not see the need for a counselor with Power, but I have learned on this trip that I don’t wish to be without one.” He grinned. “And if I am permitted to choose my advisor, I'd choose you over a gray headed old man any day.”

Arien started to laugh, but she found herself suddenly in Thaine’s arms, his lips locked onto hers. Her knees trembled and she leaned into him, holding herself upright beneath their embrace. Their kiss was full of longing and the sadness of goodbye, and when he pulled away, she reached for the wall to steady herself.

“I must go.” He fingered a stray lock of hair on her cheek, his gaze tender. “No doubt everyone wonders where I am.”

Arien nodded and opened the door. With one last piercing gaze, he was gone. She ran to the window and watched him and his guardsmen march through the tunnel leading to the palace's main courtyard.

A wild urge to weep almost overtook her. She couldn't bear to go down to the common room and listen to Millard's chatter. Instead, she picked up the book she had browsed the night before, a book of Oteran poetry, and pulled a chair near the window. Every poem she read reminded her of Thaine, and she found herself staring dreamily out the window.

There she remained most of the day, leaving her room only for lunch. Beryle fussed but appeared to accept Arien's explanation of a restless night. After trying without success to lure her to a shopping trip in the city, the maid threw up her hands and left the guest house in the late afternoon.

Still at her post by the window, Arien saw Millard, Lars, and several guardsmen leave for the evening meeting with King Kuriel. The lateness of the day surprised her. She had spent hours in dally-dreams. The sun had just begun its descent behind the city. Millard was leaving early.

She roused herself and went downstairs to find a guardsman. "Why did the prince leave so early?"

"He received an invitation to dinner from some lord or other an hour past, lady."

A dinner invitation? Interesting. "I see."

She wandered down the corridor and into the kitchen. Oterans were a strange people. The king couldn't eat in public, but his lords could invite visiting royalty to dinner on a moment's notice.

In the kitchen, she found Cook chopping vegetables while loudly instructing Milia in the proper measurements of spices to be added to a simmering pot. She turned to glare at the intruder entering her domain but brightened when she recognized Arien.

"Ah, the lady. Your girl feared ye was sickening. Feeling better, then?"

"I'm fine," Arien assured her.

"And even finer ye'll be when ye has a cup o' my peacock stew."

"Peacock stew?" Arien sniffed in the direction of the pot Milia stirred.

Cook nodded, her hands still busy with a paring knife and a rapidly diminishing mound of brown vegetables. "Aye, it's been credited for curing ails what no one else could cure. I've made it for lords and ladies who was sickening, and most o' them got well."

"But not all of them?" Arien asked.

Milia turned a mischievous grin on Cook before answering. “Nah, some 'a them died.”

“That,” said Cook, her voice stern as she shook her knife at Milia, “weren't no fault o' the stew.”

Arien smothered a grin. “I'm sure it wasn't. It smells wonderful. Is there anything I can do to help?”

Judging from the horrified look turned on her by both Cook and Milia, Arien guessed that Oteran ladies did not stoop to cooking.

“Then I'll go outside until it's ready.” She slipped out the back door.

The sun had sunk lower, and long shadows chilled the air in the rear yard. She sat on the corner bench and breathed the fragrant aroma wafting from flowers that had already begun to close for the night. Once again, her thoughts turned to Thaine, and she resolutely thrust him from her mind.

I've already wasted the entire day in dally-dreams. I should have gone with Beryle into the city. There I'd have something else to think about.

But how could she thrust Thaine from her thoughts when her heart was so full of him?

The sun had dropped out of sight when Arien heard footsteps. She looked up to see a guardsman coming toward her from the house. “Lady, Lord Lucian Arien is inside to see you.”

Her brother, there for a surprise visit. Maybe he had news of their father's return. “Thank you.”

She rose and brushed a few stray blades of grass from her skirts. When they passed through the kitchen, she winked at Milia, who giggled. She entered the common room, where Lucian turned to greet her with a smile, a wine glass in each hand.

“I hope you'll join me.” He crossed the room with a glass extended toward her. “Our father has returned from the coast.”

Arien took the glass. Lucian held his aloft in a toast to their father's return, and she raised hers in salute as well before taking a sip.

“Please sit down.” She indicated a chair, which he took.

“He returned today and insisted that I bring you to him this evening,” Lucian told her, still smiling.

He peered at her with an intensity that left her uncomfortable. Something about his manner didn't feel…right. She cocked her head. If only his mindshield weren't so impenetrable. "He was pleased at news of my sudden arrival?"

"Pleased?" Lucian laughed. "He was joyful. When I described you he nearly danced with delight."

Arien sipped her wine, and then again, trying to gain time to think. Why was he watching her with such a forced expression? "Why didn't he come with you?"

A slight frown tugged the corners of his lips downward. "My dear, he returned from the coast only a short while ago. Do you expect him to leave his house and family?"

"No, of course not." Though that is exactly what she expected. She took another sip of wine.

"And besides," Lucian went on, "the house has been empty but for servants, since I stay at the palace most nights. When I left, he was shouting orders for rooms to be cleaned and food prepared in readiness for your visit. He intends that you be impressed with your family. And the children, of course, were jumping about, shouting their eagerness to meet their sister."

Sister. Arien imagined two orange-headed tots leaping into her arms to welcome her into the family. She smiled, suddenly eager to go.

"I should change." She started to rise.

"There's no hurry." Lucian waved her back to her chair with a gesture. "We must give them time to prepare, after all. Let us finish our wine, and then you may change into whatever you wish."

Arien sat, not because of Lucian's words, but because a sudden dizziness overtook her. She'd eaten only a light lunch, and the wine must have been stronger than she thought. Leaning against the back of the chair, she set the glass down carefully on a small table beside it.

Lucian's smile faltered. "Are you ill, my dear?"

She opened her mouth to respond, but no words came. In fact, she could not even be sure her mouth had opened, for her body seemed not to be her own. She tried to raise a hand to her head, but her hand refused to move from its resting place in her lap. Her gaze fixed on Lucian, she saw him nod toward one of his soldiers, and then saw a swift movement from the tail of her eye. But she could not turn her head.

Lucian rose and crossed the room to stand before her. She tried to look up at his face, but her neck remained fixed, unresponsive. And her mind was quickly following her body. A weight weighed her down, rendering her insides dull and dead. She could not even muster the energy to issue a Command.

"Bring her." Lucian's voice sounded different, muffled, as though he spoke from behind a closed door.

Someone grasped her arm and pulled her forward. Then her eyes closed and she sank into darkness.

Jothan turned his head. The pain had finally receded enough to allow that small action without sending him immediately into oblivion again. Much encouraged, he opened his eyes. Just a crack at first, and then wider as he encountered success without further blasts of pain.

He lay prone on a cot in a room he'd never seen. A window above him stood open and through it he glimpsed a snatch of glittering stars. The room itself was dark. The sounds of slow, even breathing nearby told him he was not alone, and that the breather was asleep. He Perceived the person's thoughts and saw her dream. Not interested in her nighttime endeavors, Jothan probed deeper to discover her identity.

But the effort proved too much for him. Sharp pain in his head surged in warning just as his grip on consciousness loosened. He withdrew from the woman's mind and settled himself once again for sleep…or what passed for it at the moment.

When he woke the next time, the pain had dulled to a persistent and unpleasant throb. He opened his eyes more confidently than before, and then shut them against the bright sunlight flooding the room. But the movement had been observed, and he heard someone scurry to his side.

"Are you awake, then?" asked a low and familiar voice.

"Please, Master Jothan, wake up."

"Not Master," he whispered. "Brother."

He opened his eyes slowly and saw an anxious face hovering above him.

"I know you." The words sounded scratchy, with hardly any volume.

"I'm Beryle, Lady Arien's attendant." Beryle whispered the reply, glancing with apprehension at the door.

"Lady Arien?"

A fog clouded his mind, making it hard to focus. Beryle's words produced a picture. A skinny, orange-haired girl with green eyes. *No, that's not right.* Another image appeared, a woman, hair dark red and skin pale, but with the same startling green eyes. That felt right, and he breathed a relieved sigh that he'd gotten the picture right. He closed his eyes again and started to drift off to sleep.

"Oh, please, Brother Jothan." Beryle's voice held a tearful plea. "You've got to wake up. Lady Arien needs you. They've taken her somewhere, and the princes, too. I don't know what to do."

Jothan's eyes flew wide open as the rest of his memory returned. The princes! They were in Otero, *both* princes and Arien and a small company of guardsmen. And somehow King Kuriel had become aware of Arien's Power. He must warn Thaine and Millard.

He struggled to sit up, and pain pounded like a mallet inside his skull. He ignored it while allowing Beryle to help him into a sitting position. A wave of nausea almost conquered him, but he focused on her face.

"Taken them where?"

The maid stood before him, ringing her hands. "I don't know. It was two days ago—"

"Two days!" Jothan winced as the sound of his own voice echoed between his ears. "But just last night I sensed Arien inside the palace walls."

"I don't know when that was, but it weren't no last night. We found you yesterday in an inn not far from here. You'd been coshed on the head and robbed. The innkeeper was keeping you until he could get word to your relatives in Eshtaol.

Some of his customers found you on the street and told him that's where you said you was from."

Jothan put a hand to the back of his head and felt a tender spot there. "I remember talking with some men at the inn. And I remember going to the palace walls and Perceiving Arien. I was going to come back the next day and tell her and the princes that Kuriel knows about her Powers. That was the day I arrived in Kadesh."

Beryle nodded. "Then you don't know about the princess."

"Princess?"

"Princess Lianne died, and King Hubert sent a message to Prince Thaine to come home. He left the next day after we got here, right after first light. And it was that night Lord Lucian took Lady Arien."

"Lucian." Jothan swore under his breath. "I *knew* that bastard meant us harm."

"He's a bad 'un, all right, but Lady Arien couldn't see it. She was too took up with having a brother." Beryle sniffed, and tears sprang to her eyes.

"Tell me what happened." Jothan adopted a commanding tone. They didn't have time for emotions.

Beryle swallowed and began. "Lady Arien was tired that day, so she stayed in her room reading. I tried to get her to come out, but she'd have none of it, so I left and went into the city to do some shopping." She sniffed again. "Prince Millard and some of the guard left for the palace and when he'd been gone a bit, Lord Lucian came asking for Lady Arien. He fed her drugged wine right there in the common room, in front of the guardsmen without them any the wiser. When she was drugged, his soldiers killed our guardsmen and took her away. I got back late because of all the shops and goodies I saw, so I wasn't there. That's the only reason he didn't kill me, too."

"If you weren't there, how do you know what happened?"

"Because of Milia, the housekeeper. Before I got to the gates, Milia comes up behind me and grabs me by the arm and pulls me into an alley. She tells me what happened and brings me here, to her mama's home."

Beryle glanced toward the door once again. "Her mama

don't know who we are," she whispered. "Milia told her I was from the country, trying to explain my accent, and then when Mama Peli heard about a man from Eshtaol being kept at that inn, it turned out that was a good thing to say. She thinks you're my brother, and you were coming after me to try to get me to come back home when you got coshed."

"You said they had taken the princes." He would have shaken his head to clear his thoughts, but pain held him in check. "How do you know that?"

"Milia heard from Cook, who heard in the palace kitchens that Prince Millard was arrested by soldiers when he went to have dinner with one of their lords, the same day as Lady Arien. Milia goes up to the palace every day, because she works there. She says she's looked everywhere, and she can't find no sign of them. She says the guest house where we was staying is empty."

Jothan rubbed his temples. All this information flew at him too quickly. He couldn't sift through it.

"And Prince Thaine?" he asked. "When was he taken?"

"Mama Peli told me the other day she heard talk in the market that some foreign prince was killed outside Kadesh. But Cook said the same one who told her they'd taken Prince Millard said they captured Prince Thaine when he left the city and killed all his guard."

Jothan dropped his head into his hands. "Prince Thaine dead or captured? Yikers, I hope he's captured, and I never thought to hear myself say that."

"There's more." Tears appeared in Beryle's eyes again. "Milia says Cook says there's talk about a war with the southern kingdoms. She says Lord Zadornin is in charge of it, along with Lady Arien's father. She says the army's been training for a long time, and they marched out of Kadesh a month before we came."

"Then we were right. And we must have passed their camp as we came to Kadesh. No wonder the king sent Lucian to guide the princes. He didn't want them to blunder onto the path of his army."

Jothan fell silent. His head hurt horribly, but he had to ignore the pain and concentrate. Somehow, he must get word to

King Hubert in Creighton, if it wasn't too late. Since they hadn't encountered the army when they crossed the Nephtali Pass, he had to assume they were camped somewhere between Kadesh and Eshtaol, awaiting Kuriel's order to attack. If that order hadn't been given yet, he had to warn King Hubert.

But he couldn't leave Kadesh, not until he knew whether Arien and the princes were dead or alive. Could he trust Beryle to take a message to Quinn? He looked up at her, noting her tear-stained cheeks and anxious eyes. No. She couldn't travel to Eshtaol alone. He'd have to go himself.

But first he had to see if Arien and the princes were still alive. If he could find the right mind to Perceive, he wouldn't lose more than an hour or so. And maybe a quick rescue would be possible.

If not, he'd have to leave them.

"This Milia," he asked the maid, "can she take us to Lucian's house?"

Beryle shrank visibly. "Why do we want to go there? If Lord Lucian sees either of us, he'll kill us."

"I need to get close enough to Perceive the minds of his guardsmen. One of them is bound to know where Arien is being held. The one thing we have in our favor is that Lucian doesn't know I'm in the city."

Though clearly reluctant, Beryle agreed. She brought Jothan a mug of hot soup and insisted that he sleep after he had eaten while she went after Milia. Jothan allowed himself to be convinced. Pain pounded in his head, and he had no more strength than a babe. He drifted off to sleep listening to the sounds from the street beneath his window.

"At least it's a busy street." Jothan eyed Milia and Beryle. "Let's stand here like we're looking in this shop window. Act as though we're gawking, not really buying, and that way the shopkeeper won't bother us."

"No fear of that." Beryle fixed her gaze on the diamonds glittering in the necklace behind the glass. "We're not dressed like people with the coin to buy *that*."

"Look there." Milia sighed, pointing to a ruby bracelet. "Ain't it the prettiest thing you ever saw?"

Jothan's eyes followed Milia's fingers, but his mind tuned them both out as he studied the house behind him. A large manor house, as were all the homes on this street, with a walled entryway almost as elaborate as that surrounding the palace. Inside the wall, two guards stood sentry by the front door, their uniforms signifying they served the House of Arien. He Perceived their thoughts and found nothing useful other than the fact that Lord Jerolin was at home.

A quick scan revealed no less than two dozen people inside the house. Their mind-lights shone clearly, most of them located in one room in the lower floor of the house. A dozen more scattered here and there, and three in a back room above—

Wait. He located the familiar mind he sought. Dim, as though in sleep, but undoubtedly enclosed in a mindshield. Jothan tested the shield and sighed in relief. Arien. And alive.

"I've found her," he whispered.

Milia's eyes went round with awe, but Beryle was past being impressed by Power.

"Is she all right?"

"Keep looking at the window," Jothan ordered. "No, in fact, let's move down to the next store. I don't want the guards to become suspicious."

They walked a short distance down the street to the next window and gazed at the beautiful crystal figurines displayed there.

His attempt at mindspeech went unanswered. Then he tried a Command to awaken her. No response.

"There's something wrong with her," he told them. "I can't rouse her. They must have her drugged."

"Drugged." Beryle and Milia both shuddered.

Jothan Perceived the two minds nearest Arien, not surprised to discover more private soldiers. They knew nothing more than that they had been set to guard the foreign woman whose hair flamed as red as their lord's, and to report her slightest movement.

Jothan turned his scrutiny to the well-occupied lower

room. His Perception swept the area and located Lord Jerolin Arien. The elder Arien possessed no trace of a mental shield, and his thoughts shone like beacons in the night. Unfortunately, his surface thoughts concerned the accountant on the other side of his desk and the quantities of coin tallied on a document before him.

Jothan scanned the others in the room. Soldiers mostly, their minds busy with thoughts of security and, not unexpectedly, Lord Jerolin's coin balance in comparison to their own.

Then he touched a mind that was preoccupied with a far more interesting subject. The soldier was worried about his brother who served in the Oteran army. This soldier was grateful that he had been lucky enough to be hired by Lord Arien and felt guilty that he had not spoken to the lord concerning his brother. Now the army had left for the south and his brother with it. He prayed nothing happened because his brother couldn't swim.

Swim?

Jothan detected a picture in the man's mind of huge ships, eighteen of them, each with multiple companies of men on board. The ships floated on a vast expanse of water. The sea, obviously. But there was no sea between Otero and Creighton. The only sea near Otero was…

"Blooming hell," Jothan whispered in a horrified voice.

"What is it?" Beryle stood before him, her eyes demanding. "Have they done something to Lady Arien?"

Jothan shook his head. "It's much worse than that. Hush a minute."

He continued his scan of the minds in the Arien home. He caught a few other references to a floating army and not a few thoughts of envy for those lucky enough to be included on the ships. One man's thoughts were of the plunder he would miss by staying behind as a hired soldier for the House of Arien.

Jothan withdrew from the man's mind. How did they hope to navigate an army that size through the barrier reef protecting Hamlin's coastline? He didn't know, but he sensed no doubts in the minds he touched.

Unable to discover any further helpful information, Jothan turned to the women. He was about to suggest that they go back to Milia's house to plan their next move, when Beryle gasped. Jothan saw her shocked expression fixed on something behind him. Instinctively, he turned and saw a man entering the gates of the Arien home. He was dressed in black trousers, a spotless white shirt, a long cape, and a hat similar to the one Jothan had seen Lucian wear. The man nodded toward the guards, one of which hurried to open the door for him.

"It's Hassin. But I never saw him dressed all fancy and looking like a lord and all." Beryle stared, eyes wide.

"Who is Hassin?" Jothan asked.

"He's a stable hand back at home." Beryle shook her head, clearly confused. "I went about with him a bit, but Lady Arien never liked him none. He'd disappear for long times, and then show back up again and expect to take up where he left off, if you know what I mean."

Milia spoke then, her voice so soft Jothan had to bend down to hear her. "Seen him, I have, in the palace. He ain't no stable hand. I never heard no name. He ain't no lord, but he's friendly with Lord Lucian."

"A spy, then," Jothan said, and Beryle shrank visibly.

He straightened, and then glanced behind him at the door. They'd attracted the attention of one of the soldiers. "Time to move on."

He guided them down the street at a leisurely pace, though he didn't want to get too far from the Arien household. He needed to hear what this Hassin had to say. They gazed into the windows they passed until they were out of sight of the soldiers. Then Jothan led them across the street where they walked back toward the manor house. No shops stood on this side of the street, but the risk had to be taken. At least high walls enclosed every home, which enabled Jothan to stay out of the soldiers' sight.

Beryle and Milia remained quiet while he Perceived. He located the new mind easily enough, and by watching the thoughts as they skittered back and forth between him and Lord Arien, was able to follow the conversation inside the house.

"Is she still unconscious?" the new man asked without

preamble.

"Do you think me an idiot?" Lord Jerolin Arien answered. "Of course she's still unconscious. My soldiers report every move she makes and give her more lenitin before she comes fully 'round. I'm taking no chances with the witchcraft that one can work. Not until Zadornin gets here to question her, which should be any day."

Hassin—whose real name appeared to be Darrin—didn't think much of Lord Jerolin but maintained a respectful attitude. He considered Jerolin a wily, dangerous man and had no desire to cross him. Jothan also saw a great deal of ambition connected with Darrin's thoughts concerning Lord Jerolin.

"Do you think that's safe?" he asked. "How long can she go without eating?"

Darrin suppressed a cringe at the scathing look Lord Jerolin gave him.

"We feed her." Disgust colored the lord's reply. "We pour soup down her throat three times a day. Not that it matters. We're going to kill her anyway."

Jothan updated Beryle and Milia in a whisper. "They've given her something called lenitin, which must be a sedative, but they're planning to kill her after someone named Zadornin questions her. I don't know when."

Beryle gulped, and Milia gave a little whimper. Jothan ignored them, intent on his mental spying.

Darrin thought that Lord Jerolin must be as cold as the king himself, talking about killing his own daughter without so much as a hint of regret. Though Darrin considered her death a pity, her being so lovely.

Lord Jerolin's thoughts centered on the prophecy pronounced at Arien's birth. He believed his daughter would somehow fulfill the prophecy and bring about the downfall of the House of Arien. Killing her would put an end to the fear that had nagged at him since his wife disappeared with the infant brat.

"Brother Jothan." Beryle linked her arm through his and prodded him to continue down the street. "That fellow over there has been watching us. We'd best be gone."

Jothan switched his Perception from inside the house to

the man Beryle indicated. Thankfully, the man was nothing more than a clerk for the jewelry shop, nervous at their loitering.

"I've learned enough for now." He guided the women toward Milia's home. "Enough to make a plan for Arien's rescue."

his partnership with Quinn he'd broken the rule that forbade a brother to spy on the thoughts of others, but issuing an actual Command to injure someone? And yet, if he didn't, Arien was as good as dead. Gathering his nerve, he tracked the soldier's progress and when he was far enough away from the front gate, issued a third Command. This one hurled toward the soldier's mind, and unconsciousness overtook him. He fell to the ground.

After a quick glance around the street to make sure no one was watching, Jothan casually sauntered around the wall. Mentally, he watched those inside while Beryle greeted him with round eyes.

"Is he dead?" Her voice held awe as she glanced at the collapsed soldier.

"No, just sleeping."

Inside the house, he tracked the approach of the second soldier and grinned. "Here we go."

When Jothan opened the door, the soldier stood in the middle of a large entry hall. He halted, confusion creeping over his features. Before he could sound an alarm, Jothan issued a Command. The soldier dropped to the floor in the act of reaching for his sword. Beryle shut the door behind them with a quiet click.

"There are ten others." He pitched his voice low. "Give me a minute."

He scanned the minds of the ten remaining in the house. If only there were a way to issue a Command to more than one mind at a time. Why hadn't someone in the Brotherhood worked that out? He sent a Command toward each one in sequence, and when they all lay unconscious on the floor, nodded at Beryle.

"This way."

He led her up the stairs in the entry hall and made his way toward the back of the house, Beryle tiptoeing behind him.

"There's no need to be quiet." He grinned at her. "No one's awake to hear us."

With a fearful glance at the prone body of a chambermaid in the upstairs corridor, she shuddered and continued to creep along silently. At the back of the house they found two soldiers tumbled into an unlikely heap before a door. Jothan stepped over them and into the room.

Arien lay on a bed beneath a quilt, her face pale. Her hair had been brushed and braided into a long rope which lay across her shoulder and atop the bedclothes. She wore a soft bed gown with lace at the neck and wrists.

She looked, for all the world, like a corpse.

Beryle heaved an audible sigh. “At least they took care of her. I feared we’d find her beaten and in rags.”

Crossing the room, Jothan pulled a vial from his vest pocket. “See if you can find her clothes.”

The chemist he’d visited in the outer city this afternoon assured him that this concoction would safely counteract the effects of lenitin. He held the vial to Arien's lips and pressed her chin to open her mouth. When he had poured a sufficient amount of the liquid onto her tongue, he clamped her lips shut and massaged her throat until she swallowed.

“They're not here.” Beryle pointed toward an empty chest.

“Search the other rooms.” He pulled Arien into a sitting position. “She can't walk the streets in a bed gown.”

Beryle nodded and scooted through the door, hopping over the prone guards on the threshold. Arien stirred and Jothan, impatient, took her by the shoulders and shook her.

“Arien, wake up.”

She moaned and lifted a hand to her head.

“Arien!” He repeated, giving another shake.

She protested, her voice cracked and raspy. “Stop it.”

“Beryle.” He turned his head and shouted toward the door. “Find some water.”

Arien opened her eyes, squinting. “Jothan?” Her thumb and forefinger pressed her temples. “What are you doing here? In fact, where is here?”

“A long story, and one better told elsewhere.” Without ceremony, he began to strip the clothing off her body.

A strange voice behind him nearly startled him out of his wits.

“On the contrary,” boomed a baritone, “this is the perfect place to tell your story.”

Jothan turned. In the doorway stood a dark-haired man

he'd never seen. He stood almost as tall as the door frame and wore well-cut clothing. Jewels glittered on his hands, neck, and wrists. The fingers of one hand clamped around Beryle's upper arm and were long enough to encircle it completely. Beryle's expression held a blend of fear and outrage.

Jothan Perceived, in preparation to issuing another Command, and then stopped cold, confused. He encountered a mindshield, strong and smooth, as well-constructed as his own.

This was no natural shield. This man had been trained in the use of Power.

A brief smile hovered about the stranger's lips. "It's been a long time since anyone tried to Perceive me. Not since I left the Hall of the Brotherhood, in fact, over twenty years ago."

"The Brotherhood?" Arien shook her head, her voice still slightly slurred.

Jothan stared at the stranger. Twenty years ago? This man had left the Brotherhood before Jothan arrived. Petro must know him.

"Yes. I went through the training." He gave each of them a chilly smile. "The same training as you both, so your Commands will not work on me."

Jothan bit his lip. What was that story he'd heard long ago? Something about a man who left the Brotherhood. The memory surfaced, and he allowed his lips to curve into a smile that held no warmth.

"Of course," Jothan answered Arien, his eyes locked onto those of the stranger. "Didn't Petro ever tell you about Addison, the only trainee in the history of the Brotherhood to abandon before standing his final trial?" He deepened his chilly smile. "I assume you're known here under another name. Lord Zadornin, perhaps?"

Addison mirrored Jothan's smile. "Very good. You're not slow, whatever else you may be. I've often wondered what they said of me after I'd gone."

"Only that you were a greedy coward," Jothan told him evenly, "and that whatever became of you, it couldn't be good."

Addison's smile didn't dim in the slightest. "I assumed

something like that. They couldn't understand how contemptuous I had grown of their little organization. All those men, studying the Powers of the mind, but to what purpose? Not for their own gain, certainly. Not even to further their own interests as a group. There was no reason for it, no ultimate goal."

"People with Power must learn to control it." Arien's tongue sounded thick and dry, but her eyes appeared more alert. "That is the goal."

"Yes, but to what end?" Addison shook his head. "That's the question they refused to consider. What good is controlled Power put to no use?"

Jothan remained silent, uncomfortable. He'd had the same argument with Petro many times.

Arien straightened in the bed, apparently becoming more coherent by the second. "Without control, unscrupulous people might use their Power to hurt others. That cannot be allowed."

Addison laughed outright. "But it happens. It happens all the time among people with or without Power. In war, the slaughter of others is the only measure of success, a fact that the Twin Kingdoms are about to discover. To their own grief, I can safely say."

"War?" Arien glanced at Jothan.

He nodded. "Otero is planning to attack Hamlin by sea." He leveled a hard gaze on Addison. "Their army left Kadesh for the coast only a few weeks before we arrived."

"And will shortly be on their way south on a new fleet of fighting ships." The irritating smile twisted into a smirk. "My idea, by the by."

Jothan narrowed his eyes, not sure he believed the claim. "Yours?"

"Certainly. King Kuriel is proud of his new war ships. They were going to sail eastward to find other lands to conquer. But when one of my spies obtained a copy of a map tracing the route through the barrier reef, I suggested that we begin with Hamlin instead. You see, I've done something with my Power, something worthwhile. I've become King Kuriel's personal advisor."

"King Mendel has a personal advisor with Power," Arien

said. “He has for a long time.”

Addison nodded. “That's where I got the idea.”

Jothan shook his head. “I'd wager a month's meals the advice you give King Kuriel is designed to benefit one person only. You.”

The man actually smirked. “Do you think me that ignorant? That short-sighted? I am intelligent enough to find a king with my own values, one who would not be bothered by scruples if they got in the way of his goals. Neither of the southern kings met my qualifications. I considered befriending Hubert's or Mendel's sons, but training isn't one of my strong points.”

Training? Another piece of the puzzle fell into place. “You’re certainly right about that. Lucian’s mindshield is a disaster.”

“So, you've noticed Lucian's shield. He was the first person I encountered in Otero who possessed even a trace of Power. But, as I said, teaching is not something at which I excel, so I wasn't able to get very far. He'd already half constructed it himself. I was able to teach him a few tricks, though, and he learned well.” The man turned to Arien, the smile on his face unpleasant. “Lucian possesses an uncanny ability. He can convince others to believe whatever he wants. He instinctively knows what they desire most and twists it to his own use. Often, he isn’t even aware of what he is doing. Your longing for a family undid you.”

Arien didn’t answer, but she swallowed convulsively.

The arrogant smile deepened. “Jerolin has no wife, no other children. Lucian invented them when he saw how badly you wanted to believe and projected his invention toward you. You were pathetically eager to receive it. He succeeded in his goal, to build your expectations such that he could separate you from your princes.” His chest inflated with a breath. “I never stood the trial myself, but I understood that the old masters tested the trainee's ability to recognize a mental illusion. Obviously, they aren't as discriminating as I expected.”

Arien's body wilted, as though her strength had just been stripped. Jothan glanced at her. He didn’t need to hear her thoughts to know them. Her face broadcast her devastation at the news that she had been deceived by Lucian, that her own training and trial had proved useless.

Or perhaps she was disappointed to discover that there was no family after all, that her own twin brother would plot her downfall. That her father would keep her a drugged prisoner.

Welcome home, Arien.

"You still have Petro, and Beryle, and me. We're more family than any strangers ever could be."

He sent the thought quickly, and then turned his attention back to Addison in time to see Beryle jerk her arm free of his grasp and hurry toward Arien. Addison shrugged, and watched the maid gather Arien in a hug.

Jothan stiffened his spine. "I see you have grown wealthy by using your Power."

Addison laughed outright. "I'm not the only one. According to Lucian, you've become a seller of anodyte, and I have no doubts you used your training and your Power to assist you in that endeavor."

The accusation took Jothan back a pace or two. It was true. He *had* used his Power for purely personal gain. How was he different from Addison?

I haven't started a war lately. I've tried hard to prevent one, in fact.

The thought gave him scant comfort.

Then he stiffened. He wouldn't stand here and let this man take him to task over anything. Time to change the subject. "How do you expect to benefit from this war?"

"I assisted King Kuriel in the selection of those who will act as regent in the southern kingdoms, in his name. Jerolin, as Lord of the House of Arien, will be named Ruler-In-Proxy in Hamlin, and Lucian after him. The Lord of the House of Perfili will serve the same function in Creighton once our army has taken that country as well." He dipped his head in false modesty. "Since I am a trusted friend and advisor to them all, in effect I will rule all three kingdoms."

Arien roused herself. "You're awfully confident of your ability to defeat the combined Guard of the Twin Kingdoms."

A smirk twisted his lips. "Hamlin's Guard is no match for

King Kuriel's army. And the Creighton Guard will be demoralized by the death of their king."

Fear clenched Jothan's stomach like an iron fist. "What?"

"The assassins have been in place in Tadmoure and have been for months."

Arien cast a look at Jothan. *"We've got to warn him."*

"I know. But first we've got to get away from Addison."

"And what are your plans for us?" Beryle asked.

How did she muster the courage to ask the question? She must have nerves he hadn't guessed at.

Addison folded his arms across his chest and shook his head sadly. "I'm afraid that was decided the moment you crossed the Oteran border. You will be killed, as will the southern princes." His gaze shifted to Arien. "And for you, my dear, your death must occur immediately, before you have the opportunity to fulfill your Birth Foretelling."

"Prince Thaine?" Her voice broke on the name.

"Oh yes. He is in the custody of King Kuriel, along with Prince Millard. They'll, ah, *accompany* the army to Hamlin."

Though their circumstances were grim, Jothan breathed one inward sigh of relief. At least Thaine and Millard were alive, though captured. As long as they lived, escape remained a possibility.

"Why would the princes be taken to Hamlin?" he asked.

The answer never came. At that moment Jothan saw a blur as something swung behind Addison in an upward motion, connecting with his skull with a sickening thud. Surprise flashed onto Addison's face in the moment before he toppled forward to the floor. A quick Perception showed Jothan that the blow had been fatal.

A woman stepped around the door frame, a wooden club in her hand. Straight grey-shot brown hair framed her face above a stump-shaped body.

No one in the room spoke. Jothan was so astounded by the turn of events, he forgot to Perceive her thoughts.

The woman looked at Arien and a tear slipped down her cheek. "I am Illari. I nursed you at my breast the first days of your life." She gulped and dragged in a ragged breath. "When Lady Lisette took you away, I grieved like I'd lost one of my own. I knew why she took you and not Lucian." Her head drooped forward. "I was ashamed. Did she think I wouldn't go with her? With two of us, we could have taken both babes."

Tears dropped to the floor in front of her feet. Then she lifted her head and smiled through them. "When you came back, I knew why I'd been spared. It was so I could care for you one more time. I've been feeding you and dressing you since they brought you here. I wouldn't have let anyone hurt you."

The conflict on Arien's face, so apparent through the woman's speech, cleared. She lifted her arms, and Illari dashed forward to clasp both Arien and Beryle to her ample bosom. They stayed locked in an embrace, all of them weeping.

Jothan stared, bewildered. He had remembered to Perceive her as she spoke and knew her words were true. But he certainly hadn't been reduced to tears, and he didn't have much patience for them now.

"That's all well and good." He shuffled his feet, an awkward observer to the tender moment. "Would you tell us how you came to be here now?"

She wiped her dripping nose on her sleeve before answering. "I've no other home, and Lord Jerolin allowed me to stay on when Lucian grew past the need of me. I tend house for him, train the servants, and the like. Just now I've been out picking up a few things in the market." She sniffed again, mightily. "When I came back and saw the guard asleep in the yard, I thought someone had come to hurt her. I snuck up the stairs, quiet-like, and heard Lord Zadornin saying he was going to kill her quick." She straightened her shoulders. "So, I did what I had to do."

The club with which she had attacked Addison laid on the floor beside him. Jothan grinned. It was the branch he had shaken lose from the tree in the front yard.

In her mind, he saw that she would torture herself if she knew she'd killed the man. Well, he could save her that.

He prodded Addison's leg with a booted toe. "Unconscious," he lied. "I think he'll be out for a while, by the looks of him. But I won't feel comfortable until we're far away from this house. In fact, outside the city. Can you find Arien's clothes?"

After much sniffling and hugging, the women tore themselves apart and began to prepare Arien for her rescue. Jothan stepped over Addison and the still-unconscious forms of the soldiers and found Jerolin's library on the first floor. With luck, the man kept documents here that might help them. He began with the desk drawers.

He had moved on to the bookshelf when Arien and Beryle joined him. Arien looked better in her own gown with her hair in order. Her eyes were brighter, more alert.

"We're ready." She gestured toward the desk. "Have you found anything useful?"

"No." He slapped at a book, frustrated. "Nothing but his personal affairs. He must have documents concerning Hamlin, but either he has them with him, or he keeps them at the palace."

Illari entered the room. "Here's what you're looking for."

She thrust a leather satchel into Jothan's arms, and he set it on the desk to unfasten the clasp. Inside he found dozens of documents, all of them rolled and tied with blue ribbon. Jothan pulled several out and inspected them. A register of Otero's army, including the number of soldiers on each ship. Another listed the supplies loaded in the ships' berths. Then he slipped the ribbon off the end of another and unrolled it.

He sucked in a breath. "Do you know what this is? It's a map of the eastern shoreline." He spread it out on the desk and traced a finger over a line. "That indicates the route the Oteran ships are taking to reach Hamlin."

"Lord Arien came back from the coast in a rush when his daughter turned up," Illari told them. "He'd been seeing to the fighting ships. He's planning to sail with them, but Lucian called him home. He aims to return there tomorrow, and his bags are packed."

"How do you know all this?" Jothan eyed the woman.

She shrugged. "Servants talk."

In her mind, Jothan saw that she spoke the truth. The household servants talked to Jerolin's hired soldiers, who naturally knew as much of their lord's plans as anyone. He rolled the map and slipped it back into the satchel.

"Let's get out of here."

In the entry hall, he discovered that Illari had packed her own bags. Apparently, she planned to go with Arien. Without a word, Jothan hefted the largest bag with one hand, Jerolin's satchel clasped in his other, and led the women from the house.

Once on the street, they turned south, and then cut through an alley to take one of the less-traveled city streets.

"Where are we going?" Arien asked.

She sounded out of breath and was trotting to keep up with him. Her face still had not regained its full color. He slowed until she was walking at a comfortable pace.

"To the outer city. I want to get you as far away from the palace as possible so you won't run into anyone who may recognize your resemblance to Lord Jerolin. When he finds you've escaped, he'll probably send his soldiers looking for you."

Jothan glanced at Illari. No doubt she helped ease Arien's shock. She was proof that someone from Arien's infancy besides her mother had cared about her, and still did.

He led them through the streets of Kadesh, his mind as busy Perceiving as it had ever been. The only attention Arien had attracted thus far was from admiring men, though a few people wondered what a well-dressed lady was doing so far from the palace. They'd have to take care of that soon.

The crowd swelled as they neared the city gates. They struggled through the mass of people entering Kadesh as though marching into a gale-force wind. The gates loomed before them, and Jothan eyed the soldiers stationed there. They were bored, watching the travelers who passed before them with lazy expressions. With any luck—

"Brother Jothan," said Beryle in a low voice behind him, "shouldn't Lady Arien put something on that hair of hers?"

"A good thought, but we don't have time to shop right now."

Illari rummaged in one of her bags and pull out a tattered cape and a scarf similar to the one she wore. She threw the cape across Arien's shoulders, then used the scarf to cover her shining hair. With her locks hidden beneath the cape, perhaps no one would notice her.

They moved on.

For all the tension in his stomach, passing between the soldiers proved to be nothing more than a few west-bound steps. In no time at all they were in the outer city with the gates receding behind them.

He searched for an inn. They didn't have much in the way of coin. Jothan's had been taken by the thieves who clubbed him over the head, and Arien left hers at the palace guest house. All they had was the little bit Beryle had taken with her the day she'd gone shopping, which she had given to Jothan upon his awakening. It amounted to one silver and a few coppers, not enough to keep the four of them long.

Jothan led them almost to the edge of the outer city, then cut south to get well away from the main thoroughfare. They roamed the less affluent side streets until Jothan noticed Beryle and Illari carried a sagging Arien between them. She looked exhausted. Immediately contrite, he sent her a mental apology, and renewed his search for a suitable inn.

The next turn brought an end to his quest. Mid-way down a packed-dirt street stood a building reminiscent of Skelly's Bed and Bitters Inn. As they watched, a stout woman swept dust from the open doorway into the street. A sign, perhaps, that the rooms were relatively clean? A sign above the door read simply, 'Inn.'

He led the ladies there, stepping into the building with one last glance at the street. Thanks be, he saw no one familiar.

Jothan addressed the woman with the broom. "We're looking for rooms."

"How many?" She glanced toward the women.

Jothan didn't look behind him. Was Arien's expensive gown covered beneath Illari's cape?

"We can only afford one." He dipped his head to adopt a humble attitude. "But I'll be happy to sleep in the stable if you have one, or on the floor in the kitchen. So long as my mother and sisters get a decent bed."

The innkeeper eyed him with suspicion.

A breath later, Illari stepped to his side. She announced in a commanding voice, “No son of mine is sleeping in the stable. We'll pay for two rooms. Maybe even three once we find your dear Papa.” Her eyes filled with tears, which she dabbed away with the tail of her scarf. She addressed the innkeeper. “He met up with a pack of no-good rascals who deceived him into thinking there were fortunes to be made in Kadesh. We're here to fetch him home.”

Jothan suppressed a grin. Illari possessed talents he hadn't suspected. She wiped her eyes again before producing a silver coin from somewhere within her bosom. A quick peek into her mind revealed she had others hidden in various places around her body and her bags. She handed the coin to the innkeeper, who bestowed a broad smile upon her new guests. The silver disappeared into the woman's pocket as she led them to the rooms upstairs.

Fifteen

Arien awoke when a delicious smell tantalized her stomach into loud demands for satisfaction. She cracked open her eyes to see early morning sunlight streaming through a window in the small but tidy room where they'd spent the night. Two rolled-up pallets, where Illari and Beryle slept, stood in a corner. They'd insisted she take the bed. The soft mattress on which she lay cushioned her body with its downy filling. Sleep still dragged at her senses, but not the groggy, dazed state to which she'd awoken for what had seemed like months. Her nose promised something more substantial and satisfying than the thin broth her captors had fed her.

Not captors. Her family.

The truth cut deep, but she couldn't shy away from it. Her own father and brother had lied to her, abducted her, kept her drugged and planned to kill her. There was no second wife, no orange-haired twins. No loving father.

And no Thaine.

She shut her eyes against the pain and guilt that accompanied thoughts of the prince. If only she could touch his mind, could somehow assure herself that, though captive, he was unharmed. Their kiss seemed long past, on the other side of her drug-misted struggles for consciousness. Visions of Thaine in chains, beaten and abused, tormented her.

One truth resonated. The fault for his capture lay on her. If she hadn't fallen for Lucian's illusion, Thaine and Millard would still be free.

She forced the accusation from her mind. Wallowing in guilt wouldn't help. She must think clearly and come up with a way to rescue him.

Her thoughts turned to Illari. The woman's presence was comforting, like a mother's would be. Arien saw in Illari's mind that her own baby, a daughter born just days before Arien, died at birth. She loved Lucian, whom she had nursed and raised, but she'd always held a special place in reserve for the two little girls she'd lost.

As if thoughts of Illari had summoned her, the door opened, and the big woman entered. She smiled and placed a tray on a small table near the door before coming to Arien's bedside to peer intently into her face.

"Sleep's done you good." The woman gave a decisive nod. "Now you need to eat."

Arien stretched, then sat up. "It smells wonderful, whatever it is."

"Roast venison, and fairly done at that."

Illari set the tray on Arien's lap. Disappointed, Arien eyed a thin slice of venison, and a quarter-loaf of bread. Only those? She could eat five times as much. The food tasted good, and she devoured every scrap. If Illari hadn't been present, she would have licked the juices off the plate. As it was, she handed the dish to Illari and received a knowing pat on the shoulder.

"Not too much at first, or your stomach won't hold it. It's had nothing but broth for days. Are you well enough to get up? Jothan says we have plans to make."

"He's right." She allowed the woman to help her out of

bed. "And soon is best, in this case. We don't have much time."

Illari picked up a stack of clothing from the corner and held it out to Arien. "Beryle and Jothan combed the nearest shops while you were sleeping, and this is what they brought back."

Arien stood to inspect the clothing. Boy's traveling clothes. A shirt and jerkin looked to be the right size, but the pants would be short. She spied a pair of boots in the corner, sturdy ones with high sides to support her ankles.

"I suppose we'll be posing as travelers." She held the trousers to her hips, testing for size.

Illari nodded. "Until we come up with a plan. But if you ask me, that Jothan already has something in mind."

Arien turned her back to allow Illari to unfasten the gown. "I hope so. I don't have a shadow of an idea, myself." She stepped out of her gown and dressed in the boy's clothing. As she tied the laces on her boots, a thought occurred to her, and she looked at Illari with interest. "Lucian told me I was taken away before our Naming Day. But you were there. Surely you know what my parents had planned to call me."

Illari shook her head. "Names here are held in secret until the Naming Ceremony. Discussing a babe's name before the ceremony brings bad luck. By then you were gone." Illari's expression drooped. "I'd have gone with your mother, if only she'd asked. But she didn't trust me."

Excitement stirred inside Arien as she realized she could at last get some questions answered. Finally, she'd met someone who knew her mother, however briefly. She settled onto the bed and patted a place beside her. "What was my mother's name?"

The woman heaved her body down. "Lisette. Of course, I called her Lady Arien, but her name was Lisette."

"Lisette," Arien whispered. "It's a beautiful name."

The woman nodded, and her expression grew distant. "She was a fair lass, taller than Lord Arien, with hair the color of honey in sunlight. And quiet. She answered Lord Arien's bellows in a voice soft as a kitten's."

Though guilt nagged at her, Arien peered into Illari's

mind and saw her memory. She closed her eyes, reveling in the sight of the lovely girl, younger even than Arien was now, her spun-gold hair disheveled, her blue eyes sleepy. Illari remembered her bending over a wooden cradle to pick up a screaming infant and hold it close to her chest. The infant quieted as the girl rocked it in her arms, singing in a soft voice. Arien's heart raced as she watched her mother comfort her infant self in Illari's memory.

Her memory now. She seared it into her mind, stored it there in a place never to be forgotten. She would have this picture of her mother forever, to study, and ponder, and wonder at, for the rest of her life. Her beautiful mother, Lisette.

She opened her eyes, and they flooded with tears as she smiled at Illari. "Tell me more. All my life I've wondered about her, and I want to know everything."

Her expression sad, Illari shook her head. "I didn't know her long, just a few days before she arrived at Lord Arien's country house, and her abed with the childbirth most of that time. She was young, younger than I, and birthing twins took more strength than she could afford to give. She wasn't strong even before, the servants said, and had spent a long time in bed before you were born."

Illari paused and looked away, as though she'd remembered something she didn't want to pass on.

"What?" Arien demanded. "What is it?"

"The servants didn't like her much." Illari shrugged. "They were afraid of her, though I couldn't understand why. She was such a sweet thing, and so young, not a mean streak in her. But there was talk that she… Well…" Illari's gaze slid sideways. "That she had queer ways."

Arien's heart beat more quickly. "Queer ways?"

Illari nodded. "They said she knew things she had no way of knowing. Like when a housemaid was stealing from Lord Arien and no one, not even the older household staff, had any inkling. Yet Lady Arien told him where to look for the stolen silver, and she had never even been in the servant's quarters. Things like that happened more than once, and the servants whispered about her."

That's where my Power came from. My mother had it, and

she passed it on to her children, to me and Lucian.

Her breath caught in her throat. *Another woman with Power! Was Lisette the first, or did her mother have it as well? Will I pass it on to my daughters, if I ever have any?*

Arien rose and smiled at Illari. "Thank you. You've given me something I've longed for my whole life. A past. But now we should talk to Jothan and figure out whether or not I'll have a future."

Jothan's room lay down a short corridor. Documents from Jerolin's satchel covered a bed identical to hers. He gestured for them to gather close. She came to his side and examined the map spread out before him. Illari perched on the foot of the bed.

"Where's Beryle?" Arien asked.

"Shopping for a few things she said you'd need." Jothan lowered his voice. "I've been studying these documents. The Oterans have a different writing style than ours. They shape some of the letters differently, but I've gotten accustomed to it over the years." He glanced up at her. "It's worse than we thought. Most of the documents are written in code, a complete mystery to me, but some of it isn't, and the markings on this map are fairly obvious. Take a look."

Jothan slid the map around in front of Arien. It looked like a bunch of curvy lines, some thick, some broken, and some jagged. Not at all obvious, no matter what Jothan said. Scrawling letters identified landmarks, and while they looked vaguely familiar, she couldn't read them.

"This makes sense to you?" She gave him a sideways glance.

Jothan pointed to a long, jagged line. "This is the coast, and that word says Otero. These points here are supposed to be the Jalapa Range, and below that…"

"Hamlin." Arien traced the shoreline down the page. "This must be Kirklin, down near the bottom." The word used to label the spot intended to be Kirklin appeared vaguely familiar, now that she knew what she was looking at.

Jothan nodded. "And here are Ashton and Kenley, between Kirklin and the Jalapas. Here's Kadesh, where we are now. "He placed his finger on a large spot north of the mountain range and about a finger-tip inland from the line representing the coast.

"Looks like there's a port town just north called Ishkahl. That's where their ships are docked."

Illari nodded. "That's where Lord Arien was until Lucian called him back."

"Look at this one." Jothan handed Arien a second map. "I'll lay odds a mapmaker from Kirklin penned this."

The words were entirely understandable, written with letters she knew. Before her lay a map of Hamlin's coastline, the barrier reef sketched in great detail. A line had been drawn in red ink to mark a twisting route through it. The line led to a point just north of Kirklin.

Arien looked up. "How did they get this?"

A chilly smile appeared on his face. "Spies. Someone named Darrin, who posed as a stable hand in Kirklin Castle. Beryle recognized him outside your father's house."

"A stable hand?" Arien's hand clenched into a fist. "Hassin." Beryle's wayward love. She should have Perceived him when she'd had the chance.

"The very one. And if the princes hadn't come to Otero when they did, the war would already be underway."

He sifted through the pile of documents behind him and extracted another document for her inspection. At first it looked like so much gibberish, but when she examined closer, she recognized some of the letters. The sprawl at the bottom of the short document was bold and black, the royal seal beneath it unmistakable.

"What does this say?" She handed it back to him.

"King Kuriel sent this to inform Jerolin of our arrival in Otero, and to issue a temporary halt to their departure. Jerolin was told to wait in Ishkahl for further directives. This one," Jothan handed her another document, "is from Lucian, informing his father of your existence. It merely says 'My twin is not dead but has arrived with the southern princes. Return with all haste.'"

Arien stared for a moment at the signature and the seal of the Oteran House beneath it. She handed it back to Jothan without a word.

"Apparently Jerolin was to lead the war party to take Kirklin, following this route." He returned to the original map and traced his finger along a dotted line out from shore. "Eighteen ships carrying a hundred men each."

The number staggered her. "Eighteen-hundred men?" King Hubert's entire Guard consisted of only five hundred men, and poor King Mendel had even less than that. They couldn't possibly stand against such an army.

"That's what these documents say, and I don't find it hard to believe. I've never seen a city as big as Kadesh. Even Corral, which is the biggest thing either of the Twin Kingdoms has, would fit in a corner of this place. Not only that, the ships are not merely floating vessels. They're armed with long-range cannons and catapults that can either be used on board or moved to the shore. I found a cargo list for each ship. The Twin Kingdoms have nothing that can stand up to them."

Fear squeezed Arien's chest like a strap. She gestured to the pile of documents scattered on the bed. "Do any of those say when the ships will sail now?"

His expression grim, Jothan shook his head. "I hoped to find a timeline, but if one exists, it isn't here. It's possible Jerolin has it with him, or he went to the palace today to meet with the king to discuss that very thing. And your escape is sure to have an impact on the timing. But even had you not escaped, they now have the princes. We have to assume they won't delay much longer."

A chill crept up her arms. "We've got to get home and warn King Mendel."

Jothan nodded. "We do, but do we leave the princes here?"

Panic plucked at her insides. What would it mean to the southern kingdoms to have Thaine and Millard, the heirs to both kingdoms, held captive under Oteran control? That would have a profound effect on Mendel and Hubert and would play in whatever decisions they made. Not to mention the guardsmen, who were the kingdoms' only defense. The knowledge would affect them as well.

She swallowed a rising panic. No time for that right now. "What do you think we should do?"

Jothan didn't hesitate. "We have to warn King Mendel about the Oteran ships. We also have to get word to King Hubert and warn him of the assassins who plan to kill him. He'll send at least part of his guard to King Mendel. If we get that done in time, Kirklin might have a chance. If they're taken by surprise, they've none at all."

She opened her mouth to protest, but he stopped her with a hand.

"I know what you're going to say. We also need to find out where Kuriel is holding the princes, and free them. Addison said they were being shipped to Hamlin. That means they will be at Ishkahl soon, if they're not already there."

"Okay," Arien agreed, "How do we get all those things done?"

Jothan glanced first at Illari and then at Arien. He chewed his lip for a moment.

"It's not much of a plan," he told them, "but here's my idea."

Jothan's first reconnaissance mission enjoyed limited success. Lord Jerolin was absent, and the thoughts of the servants had been on Arien's escape, Addison's death, and Illari's disappearance. Not a single active thought revealed the specifics Jothan needed about Lord Jerolin's whereabouts, but he noted one interesting fact. There were only two soldiers in the entire house. Even Jerolin's personal guard was gone. Either the lord, paranoid with the escape of his daughter and the death of Lord Zadornin, had determined to keep himself surrounded, or he'd left the city.

From there, Jothan approached the palace gates. Since the benevolent banquets had been cancelled—Kuriel having no further reason to flood his palace with distractions after Arien's capture—far fewer people congregated inside the palace tonight. Crowds filled the streets, and the guards had not yet noticed him. He attached himself to a group of wanderers who strolled past the palace wall, staring upward in awe, while his mind kept busy scanning the interior.

Most likely, King Kuriel's apartments would be near the well-protected center of the palace, so he sent his Perceptive thoughts there. A small cluster of people in that direction seemed promising. He peered inside a mind on the perimeter of the group.

Ah, a servant to the king. The man's thoughts focused on his duty, taking a second jug of wine to the king's private audience chamber.

Pleased at his success, Jothan switched to another individual. Even better. He'd stumbled upon an advisor to King Kuriel. This man fumed over a recent conversation with the king.

Why ask my advice if only to ignore it? We should attempt a bargain with the southern kingdoms before attacking. If we can take them without bloodshed, so much the better. A simple surrender demand, in light of the fact that the princes are in our custody would be best, but I'll not lose my life and my lands by arguing. Let Lord Arien handle this war, since he's so keen on it. He'll be on his way by morning.

Jothan sucked in a breath at the last thought. He switched into another mind. This man was speaking to the small group.

"Our plans remain the same, then, even with the added advantage of the two princes?" Unless, of course, the man thought without speaking, *you have plans we know nothing about, and I'll bet my oldest son on that.*

Jothan switched to the mind that answered. When he recognized the man, he could hardly believe his luck. Lord Jerolin. If Jerolin was still here, then maybe the princes were, too. Jothan and Arien could ambush them as they marched for Ishkahl.

"Exactly the same," Jerolin replied, *"except we will have the princes' heads on a pike as we march on Kirklin Castle. Their king and soldiers will be demoralized and our victory swift. Then we will march on Creighton, which by that time will be without a leader."*

Acid churned in Jothan's gut. They meant to kill Thaine and Millard within sight of Kirklin Castle.

He searched the surrounding minds and found no trace of a thought concerning the princes' current location. Nor could he locate King Kuriel. If he'd been in the room, Jothan could have ended this war before it began.

He returned to Jerolin's mind, pushing his way past the man's surface thoughts. Without Power, Jerolin was aware only of an uncomfortable pressure. He raised a hand to his head and tried to massage away a dull ache deep beneath his temples. Jothan deftly stepped around his natural defenses and pressed deeper. The man would have a fierce headache for a day or so.

He didn't have to look far.

Triumph swelled within Jothan like a tidal wave. The princes were being held in a small military camp outside Kadesh, chained and under heavy guard. After the theft of his satchel and Zadornin's death, about which he had not informed King Kuriel, Jerolin planned to take no chances that they might be rescued. Fifty soldiers surrounded them, with Lucian in charge. Jerolin would join them at first light. From there they would march to Ishkahl and set sail at dawn the following day.

Jothan abruptly broke contact and left the group with which he stood. He drew curious stares at his haste, but since the guards didn't follow him, he didn't check his pace. He hurried toward the city gates and negotiated the winding, crisscrossed streets of the outer city on his way back to the inn where Arien, Beryle, and Illari waited.

Not a soul sat in the inn's common room, probably normal given the late morning hour. Jothan tiptoed up the stairs and rapped on the women's door.

"Brother Jothan." Beryle pulled the door open.

Upon entering he encountered three anxious faces. "I know where they are holding Millard and Thaine. Beryle and Illari must leave immediately for Eshtaol, with a message for Quinn to carry to King Hubert. Arien and I will move tonight. If we don't, we may be too late to save the princes."

"Are they in the palace?" An anxious pair of green eyes fixed on his face.

He shook his head. "They're in a military camp just north of Kadesh under heavy guard. Jerolin plans to move them to Ishkahl at first light tomorrow. If that happens, they're dead."

Arien wasted no time but began shoving things into a leather pack with Illari's help.

Beryle stepped in front of Jothan, hands planted on her hips. "And we're to go to Eshtaol alone? Two women, with no one to protect us?"

Jothan sighed. "I'd go with you if I could, but just now I've got two princes to rescue."

"We'll be fine," Illari told Beryle over her shoulder. "I've traveled there often enough with Lord Arien, on the way to his country house. There's always people going that way. We'll find some to travel with and will be as safe as if we were with an army."

Beryle narrowed her eyes at Jothan. "You wouldn't be much protection anyway. Just get yourself coshed on the head again, no doubt."

He started to take up the argument but shut his mouth. Beryle was frightened and worried. Instead he put a comforting hand on her shoulder. "I'll watch out for Arien, I promise. But everything counts on you getting there safely and getting a message across the border to King Hubert. If you fail, the king may be killed, and Hamlin will be left alone to fight eighteen-hundred Oteran soldiers."

Beryle gulped, then jerked a nod. Jothan slipped through the door and into his own room. He rummaged in Jerolin's satchel and extracted a copy of the map he'd sketched earlier, along with a note he had written to Quinn. When he'd stored the few personal items he possessed in the satchel, he returned to Arien's room.

"Here." He handed the documents to Illari. "See that Quinn gets these."

"And you take this." The large woman pressed a pouch into his hand. "You may need to buy food or supplies or bribe your way out of a mess."

Jothan squeezed her hands in thanks. He turned to examine Arien. Dressed in her boy clothing, she'd twisted her hair in a long, thick braid and tucked it into her shirt collar. A boy's cap on her head hid most of the red and would do well enough at night. She must have bound her chest, for it was almost as flat as a boy's. At first glance, they might be taken as older and younger brother.

"Are you ready?" he asked.

Arien nodded, then turned to Illari. The older woman enveloped her in a hug, and tears shone in both sets of eyes. "I hate to think I've lost you again after such a long time."

Arien swallowed and shook her head. "Not lost. We'll see each other soon, I hope in happier circumstances. Stay safe."

She then turned to Beryle, who wept openly. They embraced, Beryle wetting her shoulder with her tears.

"I never thought I'd be crossing that damn Pass without you," the girl sobbed.

Arien laughed through her tears. "At least this time you know what to expect. Take care of Illari, and yourself." She straightened, and with a final smile for the two women, faced Jothan. "I'm ready."

Jothan nodded his farewell to Illari and Beryle, and then led Arien out of the room.

Sixteen

They made their way out of the city. On the eastern outskirts of Kadesh, Jothan led Arien north. He'd Perceived a fairly accurate idea of the location of the military camp in Jerolin's mind. The road, flattened by the marching of many soldiers and their mounts, made for fast travel.

They walked quietly, their only conversation an occasional mental exchange. Jothan spared a moment of concern that Arien hadn't fully regained her strength, but what could he do about that now? She kept his pace, and she seemed as determined as he to free the princes. Maybe even more so.

They marched for close to an hour before Jothan sensed the presence of other minds ahead of them. He guided her off the road, aware of the sentries posted just this side of the camp. Slipping through the sparse trees, they drew near enough to Perceive. Jothan sent his mindsense to probe the thoughts of the two guards stationed on this side of the camp.

Alert, but not alarmed. Neither expected trouble, and both were eager for tomorrow's mission. He glanced at Arien, who'd also Perceived the men. They exchanged a nod.

The camp consisted of no more than a few barracks and officers' quarters enclosed within a wall of tall wooden posts sharpened to a point at the top. A wide swath of cleared forest land around the camp made a surprise approach impossible. Jothan Perceived four more sentries stationed at various places outside the stockade, six more mounted on the wall watching the razed field, and another forty or so soldiers inside, most of them asleep. He had no trouble locating Lucian, his natural mindshield unmistakable in the midst of all those unshielded minds. He also found Thaine and Millard, both asleep.

Jothan glanced at Arien. Her pale face shone white in the moonlight, her eyes dark and unreadable.

It would be a simple matter to send Commands to render the two closest sentries unconscious, but their fall would be observed by those on the wall. Of course, when the sentries on the wall fell, that, too, would be observed. Timing would be of the essence. He bit his lip and decided to disable the sentries on the ground first. Then they would proceed to those on the wall, and then to the alert soldiers inside the camp. After that, they'd finish up with the sleeping men.

"We'll disable them with the Command I used on Jerolin's soldiers," he told Arien. *"They should sleep until Lord Jerolin gets here in the morning."*

"Will Otero still attack when we have the princes?"

"I'm sure they will. Nothing can stop that attack now. We'll do no more than irritate them by taking their hostages."

She fell silent. They were about to throw all their training to the wind. But what choice did they have? *What do you want me to do?"*

"I'll start at the east end and you start at the west. But first let me wake the princes."

When he had hidden Jerolin's satchel in a hollow log, he sent a thought. *"Your Highnesses, wake up. Jothan and Arien are here. You'll be free soon. We need you alert."*

He sensed their sleepy responses and saw Arien wince as

she, too, felt the pain from the abuse they had suffered at the hands of Kuriel's soldiers. Then Jothan turned his mind toward the sentries at the eastern edge of the camp. He glanced at Arien—and nodded.

Jothan sent the first Command. The sentry toward whom it was directed crumbled to a heap on the ground, and even before he had finished falling, Jothan moved on to the next. He sent one Command after another, Perceiving his success when his eyes could not see his targets. In a corner of his mind he knew Arien was working quickly through the soldiers at the other end of the camp.

Someone cried a warning inside the walls, but he ignored it. Arien would silence that man in a moment. A few more calls sounded, all of them swiftly silenced. Let them sound their alarms, for the only people to hear them would soon suffer the same fate as the rest.

In no time at all, they finished. Jothan let his Perception sweep across the unconscious minds, searching for signs of awareness.

"Lucian," Arien whispered, just as Jothan encountered the shielded mind of Arien's brother.

"That shield is strong." Jothan stifled a curse. "I can't get a Command through. And look where he's headed."

Jothan took off at a run toward the high gate, aware that Arien sent a warning thought to the princes as she ran. The locked gate stopped him for only a few moments. He Perceived the wooden board barring the gate from the inside. A grim smile took his lips. How many drills had he practiced while still a trainee at the Hall of the Brotherhood? He Moved the particles that made up the wood and watched as their lazy dance became frenzied in response. The board burst into flames at the same moment Jothan and Arien threw their combined weight against the doors, crashing into the camp.

He spared less than a moment's glance to orient himself before running toward the structure where Thaine and Millard were imprisoned, Arien close on his heels. He leaped over the bodies of unconscious men littering the ground and sprinted to the door of the building in the center of the camp. He threw the door open—

—and stopped.

A frustrated curse burst from his lips.

On a narrow cot to the left of the door lay Thaine, First Prince of Creighton, heavily shackled. Dried blood and fresh bruises covered his face. His clothing consisted of nothing but tattered rags. Though gagged by a dirty rag, a pair of alert eyes stared at Arien. Jothan spared him a glance, but his gaze fixed on the figure before him, back pressed against the rear wall.

Lucian held Prince Millard in a strong grasp, a knife blade pressed to the prince's throat. Millard looked worse than Thaine, one side of his swollen face so covered with half-healed cuts and dried blood as to be unrecognizable. Like Thaine, blood matted his hair and covered his ragged clothing. His eyelids drooped, with a quick scan of his thoughts, Jothan winced. Crippling pain wracked his body. The man was only half conscious because of it.

Lucian's mouth twisted into a mocking smile of welcome. "I see you've managed to outsmart the king's soldiers, and my father's as well. I must say I'm rather disappointed in myself that I haven't guessed at your abilities before now. It never occurred to me that someone trained in the Powers of the mind would demean himself to become an anodyte seller."

Jothan forced himself to respond with a calm voice. "What's wrong with making a profit?"

Lucian's smile faded. "You should have stuck with peddling anodyte. Your latest occupation will prove much less profitable." Lucian's head tilted as his gaze switched to Arien. "Did you dislike our father's hospitality so much that you had to leave without a cordial farewell?"

Behind Jothan, Arien didn't answer. He heard her swift intake of breath and sent a quick thought.

"Don't let him confuse you. Don't think about families or children or anything like that. If you are tempted, look at what he's done to the princes."

"Don't worry." Her thought might have been made of steel. *"I won't fall for the same trick twice."*

Lucian moved the knife at Millard's throat. "It seems we are at an impasse. You cannot attack through my shield, thanks to Zadornin's instruction."

"We didn't need to get through Zadornin's—or Addison's if we use his real name—shield to disable him." Jothan smiled as he delivered the reminder.

Lucian paused, his eyes narrowing. "He was struck from behind. I am not stupid enough to let that happen. And I have no intention of letting you have the princes. You'll have to kill me, and I doubt my dear sister is up to it."

Arien spoke, her voice low. "Don't be too sure about that, brother. You were ready enough to have me killed."

Lucian shrugged, the knife still pressed closely against Millard's skin. "That was self-preservation. You've learned of the prophecy?" Behind Jothan, Arien must have nodded because Lucian went on. "Then you can see that Father had no choice. To stand by and watch the downfall of our House would be madness."

"If I'm supposed to be comforted by that," Arien's voice rasped dry behind Jothan's ear, "I'm not."

"We've got to disarm him," Jothan sent to her.

"I know, but how?"

"We're going to have to strip him."

A sneer curled Lucian's nostrils. "If nothing else, we can sit here all night and wait for Father to come in the morning with a fresh company of soldiers."

"If you do," Arien answered, "we'll do the same thing to them that we've done to the rest of your soldiers. We can do it from right here, you know. We don't need to see them to disable them."

"Good," Jothan sent toward Arien. *"Keep talking to him. I've got to find a chink in that shield of his."*

Jothan Perceived while Arien continued to talk to Lucian.

Arien swallowed against a desert-dry throat and gathered her strength to keep her tone mocking. Thaine shifted on the cot, and she mustered the strength not to look in his direction. Her gaze dipped from Lucian's eyes to Millard's. Alarm zipped through her body. The prince had been severely beaten. She needed to get him away from Lucian to determine the extent of his injuries.

Her voice took on a superior tone. “Can you do that, Lucian? Did Addison teach you how to send Commands? Or are your only talents shielding yourself and lying?”

Her brother’s eyes narrowed. “I learned everything I needed to know. It was enough to fool you.”

That hurt, but Arien mustn’t let Lucian know how much. How *could* her training have failed her? How could she have failed to see Lucian’s illusions for what they really were?

Her mindsense tracked Jothan’s searching presence near Lucian’s shield. If he found a way to breach the mindshield, her brother may not survive. She steeled herself against a wave of guilt that accompanied that thought.

“Yes, but I set myself up for it. I won’t be so stupid next time,” she promised. “You know, Lucian, I do pity you, after a fashion. How horrible it must have been, being raised by a man cold and uncaring enough to order the death of his own child.”

That barb struck its target. She saw the signs in an almost imperceptible tightening of his lips.

“You’re getting a response,” Jothan told her. *“His shield just tightened in one area, which weakened it in another. Keep it up.”*

Oh, how she wished she could find another way. To use a person’s deep-seated pain against them sent daggers of agony to pierce her own soul. This man was, after all, her brother. Lisette—their mother—must have loved him.

Still, she had no choice. She kept her tone razor-sharp. “I was raised in an orphanage, you know. All through my childhood I longed for my father. I knew my mother was dead, but my father, well, he could be anyone. I dreamed that one day he would find me and take me away from there, take me home.

“What did you dream about, Lucian? Did you dream that your mother, the woman who left you as a defenseless babe with a cold, uncaring man, would come back for you? Did you wonder what had happened to her? Did you lay in bed at night, wondering if she ever thought of you?”

This time he winced. “My mother was a weak woman, without vision or ambition.” But she detected a change in his tone. Hesitation softened these words, rendered them less biting than as a moment before.

At the same time, Jothan told her, *"I've found it. Just a little more, and then be ready to jump in with me. He's very strong. It may take both of us to pull down his defenses."*

"Our mother was *not* weak." Arien took a half-step forward, her voice loud. "She was strong enough to defy the tyrant she married. She was strong enough to take a newborn infant across an impassable mountain range to find a safe place where her baby wouldn't be murdered. And she was strong enough to leave behind her other baby, even though she had to know the pain that would cause, and how her husband would twist that child to his own ambitions."

"The witch," Lucian screamed, and Arien gasped as the knife pressed into Millard's skin.

"Now!" Jothan shouted, both mentally and audibly.

Arien threw all her Power toward Lucian's shield.

She Saw Jothan's attack against the thick, scarred surface. Saw also Lucian gather his defenses. She added her efforts to Jothan's and together they rammed Command after Command toward her brother's mindshield. One part of her briefly called to memory her own trial, and she knew that as she had succeeded then, so might Lucian now. But even as the thought occurred to her, she felt his control slip, and Jothan pressed their advantage.

Arien enjoyed the benefit of years of Petro's training. Lucian did not.

A break appeared in the shield, and Jothan dove through it, Arien less than a heartbeat behind him. At the same moment Jothan rushed forward to wrest the knife from Lucian's hand. Her mind whirled in a moment of disorientation as she saw Millard slip through Lucian's weakened grasp and fall to the ground. At the same time, she Saw Lucian's shield collapse.

With lightning speed, she withdrew and shielded herself from the agonized suffering her brother broadcast now that his mindshield had been breached. Panic and chaos radiated in waves from him, terrible to behold, and Arien turned away as he slid slowly down the wall and toppled over.

Jothan laid Millard on the dirt floor and inspected his neck. His hand came away sticky with blood.

"It's just a scratch," he said, "but he has a lot more injuries that aren't."

Arien stood still, looking down at her brother. "Is he…"

She couldn't finish the question. Nor could she force herself to Perceive him. Jothan reached toward Lucian's motionless body and pressed bloody fingers to his neck. He looked up at Arien. "He's alive. But you felt his hold on that shield. He couldn't let go. I'm afraid he won't have much of a mind left when he wakes up. *If* he wakes up."

Arien stood silent, staring at her brother. Her cruel words had done this to him, her Commands had weakened him. What would happen to him now?

Jothan watched her closely. "I'm sorry."

Arien licked dry, cracked lips. "So am I."

Behind her Thaine moaned, and she hurried to his side. She untied the knot in the gag and threw the filthy piece of cloth away. Thaine took a deep breath, turning his head toward hers.

"You're safe now." Somehow, she mustered a smile.

He struggled to sit up. "Where are we?"

Arien helped him into a sitting position, and then examined his chains. Metal cuffs shackled them to his wrists and ankles. She Perceived, and then Moved air between the iron particles at the clasp. The metal colored and weakened enough that she could snap it apart with her hands.

"How did you…never mind." Thaine rubbed his wrists as she broke the cuffs around his ankles.

"How are you?" She reached a gentle hand toward a swollen cut above his right eye.

He caught her hand and brought it to his lips, his eyes holding hers in an intimate grasp. "Never better, now that you are here."

Behind them, Millard groaned. She reclaimed her hand and hurried to Jothan's side. Millard's chains had been removed as he lay on the dirt floor, his eyes open and watching them.

"Arien, bring that lantern closer." Jothan pointed toward

a lantern hanging on the stockade's outside wall.

She brought it and held the light so Jothan could examine Millard's injuries.

"Where is the pain, Your Highness?" he asked.

Millard took a deep breath and let it out slowly. "My arm, mostly. The rest is just sore."

"It's probably broken." Jothan tested it with gentle fingers. "And I'll be surprised if you haven't suffered other injuries as well."

"Can't you do something?" Thaine looked at Arien, his gaze full of meaning.

She shook her head. "I wish we could."

Jothan looked up at Thaine. "How are you?"

A brave but decidedly weak smile appeared. "Nothing that won't heal. They were rougher on Millard. Lord Lucien didn't like his attitude. But how did you get here, when we left you in Eshtaol?" He turned to Arien. "And what did you mean about your father's hospitality?"

Arien shook her head. "Later. Right now, we've got to get out of here. My father will be here in a few hours."

Jothan and Thaine found the stables easily enough, while Arien brought clean water and bandages from one of the barracks. She did her best to clean and wrap Millard's wounds, and when Jothan and Thaine returned, they had found a military medical kit. Thaine splinted Millard's broken arm and checked him for other injuries while Arien gave him a pain powder mixed with water.

Thaine continued to work on Millard as Arien stretched Lucian out on the floor and covered him with a blanket. He weighed too much for her to lift him to the cot, but she rolled a second blanket and put it beneath his head. Tears blurred her vision when she stood and gazed down on him. How she had hoped they could love each other. If only he'd wanted the same.

Then they mounted the horses Jothan had saddled. Millard hissed as he climbed onto the animal's back. Arien watched him for a long moment. Had he sustained serious injuries they couldn't see?

"Prince Millard, how do you—"

He shook his head with a jerk. “Not now. Let’s put a safe distance between us and this place.”

How he had changed since leaving Kirklin Castle.

Outside the walls of the camp, Jothan retrieved Jerolin’s satchel from its hiding place. He consulted the map of Otero’s coastline, holding it open to the moonlight, and then handed it to Thaine. “I’m sure you’ll find this interesting.”

Thaine whistled, and then glanced at Millard. “We were right. They plan to sail to Kirklin first. Then they’ll march across the kingdoms to Tadmoure.”

Jothan nodded. “I’ve got all the physical proof in this satchel, plus what I’ve picked out of various minds. We’ve sent Beryle and Illari to—”

“Who is Illari?” Thaine looked up from the map.

“We’ll explain later.” Arien nodded for Jothan to continue.

“—to Eshtaol with a message for Quinn to take to your father, along with a copy of that map. I hope they’ll be in time to help King Mendel.”

Thaine studied the document. “What have you planned?”

“Nothing,” Jothan admitted. “We need to get you both out of Otero as soon as possible. All three of you, in fact,” he amended, indicating Arien. “We thought we’d try the most direct route by going over the Jalapas.”

Thaine and Millard both stared at him in surprise.

“But they’re impassable,” Millard said.

Jothan shook his head. “For an army. But Arien’s mother made it, weak from childbirth and with an infant. I think four of us, on foot, will be able to make it. It won’t be easy, but the terrain should be more level if we keep to the coast.”

During a moment of silence, they considered the task before them. No one spoke, and no one looked at Millard. Arien didn’t need to Perceive anyone’s thoughts to know them. Would the prince be able to endure the rugged terrain of the mountains?

Millard himself must have had similar concerns. “Maybe I should try to get to Eshtaol with Beryle.”

Arien shook her head. “By mid-morning King Kuriel will have everyone in Otero searching for you, probably with enough money on your head to tempt even the most kindhearted person. We don't dare leave you in Otero a day longer than necessary."

"She's right," Jothan agreed. "If we leave now and ride hard, we can be south of Kadesh by morning and into the Jalapas by dark."

Millard nodded and suppressed a wince. Arien squeezed her eyes shut against the obvious pain on his face. Hopefully he'd sustained nothing more serious than a broken arm, but she doubted it. Still, his life was in danger every minute they tarried in Otero. The Jalapas were the best way to quickly ensure his safety. Once they arrived in Hamlin, they'd get him to the first healer they could find.

Jothan and Thaine led them double file down the road. Jothan used his Power to keep the dust from the horses' hoofs stirred behind them, effectively covering any sign of their passage.

Millard was not disposed to talk, and Arien became more and more alarmed at the sound of his labored breathing. Jothan did not set a hard pace, but Millard suffered with each step. Finally, the powder took hold of him, and his breathing eased. Then he became so drowsy, Arien worried he would fall off his horse.

She strained her Perceptive senses ahead and behind, watching for any sign of approach.

Beryle sat in the common room of the Bed and Bitters Inn and decided that Quinn Parkin was not as ugly as she'd initially thought. Big, but not fat. His bulk was more of a kind with blacksmiths than gluttons. The grey in his dark hair made him look older than he really was, and though she didn't normally like to see jewelry on a man, his silver earring gave him a rakish appeal.

Of course, she had a tendency to be attracted to whatever man she found in front of her. She'd noted and accepted the fact long ago. Men were so much more interesting than women. Consider Hassin, who'd turned out to be an Oteran spy. True, it galled her to think she'd been used by someone who wanted only to get information about Kirklin Castle, but she'd certainly enjoyed at least one aspect of their relationship and knew he had as well. Some things a man could not feign, or a woman would know.

Take Lady Arien. A wave of affection and loyalty warmed Beryle at the thought of her employer. Arien could take a lesson from her and begin to enjoy men instead of holding herself so aloof.

Beryle forced her attention across the table, on Quinn.

"Leaving Eshtaol won't be easy." His gaze slid from Beryle to Illari, who sat beside her. "Lucian left a guard, and while they haven't bothered much with us, we're being watched. Good thinking to disguise yourself when you came into town with that trade wagon. I doubt any of them recognize you as Lady Arien's attendant."

She preened at the compliment. "But when we march out with Thaine's guardsmen—"

He waved her comment off. "We won't march anywhere. That'd be asking for a fight, and Thaine only left five guardsmen here to Lord Lucian's ten. Our only hope is to create a diversion and sneak across the border." He eyed Illari's large frame with doubt. "Then we'll have to move fast. It's not easy, traveling the Pass."

Illari raised her chin. "I can move fast when I need to."

Beryle nodded, quite sure that Illari would keep the pace Quinn set more easily than she herself. She had gained a certain measure of respect for the woman during the past few days, fueled in large part by her obvious devotion to Lady Arien.

"We'll keep up," Beryle assured Quinn. "Just tell us what to do."

He fell silent, his lips pursed. *Sensuous lips*. She straightened and forced her attention to the task at hand.

"I'm not sure yet," he told them. "Let me talk to the guardsmen and show them this map. Be prepared to move in an instant when I give the word."

All day, the women kept themselves ready to run at a moment's notice. Beryle dared not venture out into the town for fear of being recognized, so she spent a long, boring day closed away in the tiny room she shared with Illari. Quinn seemed to trust Skelly and his wife, so at least she could talk with them—so long as no one else was around. Skelly's wife even went so far as to produce men's clothing for them both.

Illari heaved a resigned sigh as she held the trousers up to her ample waist. "If we're expected to climb over mountains of rocks, we should at least not have to worry about showing our private garments to the soldiers."

Beryle inspected the clothing laid out for her. Many things had changed since that conversation with Lady Arien back in Tadmoure Castle, when she refused to dress like a boy. Tears blurred her vision. Would she ever see her mistress again? Swallowing hard, she donned her men's clothing.

Full dark had fallen before they received news. At a soft rap on the door, Beryle opened it to a travel-garbed Quinn.

"Get your things," he whispered. "Meet me downstairs as fast as you can."

He retreated down the narrow corridor before she could do more than nod. She closed the door and turned to find Illari had already grabbed a leather pack and was securing the straps across her shoulders. Beryle caught the second pack Illari tossed her way and strapped it on her own back. All it contained was a loaf of bread, a slab of cheese, and some cold venison, along with a skin of water and a pair of tough goatskin gloves. Not heavy, but Beryle didn't relish the idea of carrying it over the Pass anyway.

At the bottom of the stairs, Quinn waited with the five southern guardsmen. Two peered through a crack in the front door while the rest stood whispering near the rear exit. The fire in the room had burned low, and the scent of roasted venison lingered. Skelly and his wife hovered near the kitchen entrance. The woman's wringing hands betrayed her nerves.

Quinn gestured for the ladies to join him. "Our diversion will begin soon, and we'd best move quick-like. We don't want anyone to see us leaving Eshtaol or risk putting them in danger of Lucian's wrath." He glanced toward Skelly, his concern apparent.

The wait seemed to go on forever. Beryle's nerves

stretched tight as time wore on. Finally, when she was sure something had gone wrong, a commotion began outside. Distant shouts grew louder as others took up the cry. The noise approached the inn, and Quinn nodded to one of the guardsmen. The man opened the door and stepped outside. Behind him, Beryle glimpsed people emerging from the surrounding buildings to discover the reason for the shouts.

"Fire," Beryle heard someone scream. "The alchemist shop is on fire!"

"That's our diversion," Quinn whispered behind Beryle.

Skelly took his wife by the arm and hurried toward the door. Before he left, he turned to Quinn. "Good luck, my friend."

"And to you," Quinn replied.

The door closed behind them. Through the window she watched Skelly and his wife hurry down the street with their neighbors to help put out the fire.

Quinn eyed them. "Now we'll just give everyone a few minutes to get there and get involved."

This time the wait lasted only moments. The fire drew everyone, from child to ancient. A fire left unchecked could destroy the entire town in an hour. The alchemist shop was situated at the north end of Eshtaol, next to the only dry goods store. If that store were to burn, the town would suffer immediate want.

"Now."

At Quinn's whisper, the eight of them slipped out the back door.

Fear gripped Beryle's throat, and her breath came shallow. Did the shadows hold unfriendly eyes?

The street behind the inn was deserted. Quinn led them south at a blistering pace, and within a few moments they had left the southernmost buildings behind them. Beryle soon had only one thought on her mind—to keep her feet moving, though her breath came in ragged gasps and a stitch in her side threatened to cripple her. They halted just inside the tree-line of the forest that grew between Eshtaol and the entrance to the Pass.

"Why are we stopping?" asked Illari, as Beryle collapsed

against a sturdy tree trunk, gasping to draw air into her laboring lungs.

Quinn put a finger to his lips.

Beryle sank to the ground. The forest around her lay in shadows, but a glow from unseen flames lit the distant darkness. The strong odor of smoke stung her nose. Had the townspeople managed to stop the fire from spreading?

When at last she felt that her lungs might not burst, one of the guardsmen whispered, “Here he comes.”

A dark shape dashed toward the cover of trees. Quinn stepped out, waving his arms as a beacon, and the shape veered toward them. Inside the cover of the trees, Kerman Sein collapsed against Quinn, much like Beryle had against the tree. The difference in Quinn’s gigantic frame and Kerman’s slim one would have been comical under different circumstances.

The little man’s breath came hard, and for a moment he couldn’t answer Quinn’s urgent questions.

“Yes, all Lucian’s soldiers were there and taking a hand in extinguishing the fire. They’ll stay busy for a while. I’ve rigged several chemicals to ignite, and they’ll be hard to put out.”

“They’ll be busy unless one of them notices we’re not helping,” commented one of the guardsmen.

Quinn nodded. “Exactly right. We’ve got to move. If we’re lucky, we’ll be well into the Pass before they notice, but I don’t put much store in luck lately. Let’s go.”

Beryle stifled a groan as she fell in behind Illari. At least Quinn wasn’t running this time, but the quick jog he assumed wasn’t much easier. She forced herself to keep up, her eyes fixed on Illari’s back.

Seventeen

Millard lay awake on the cold ground, shivering even though the heat from the campfire warmed his back. He knew he wasn't well. Pain radiated from internal organs weakened by repeated beatings. He hadn't told anyone, but he'd passed blood since yesterday.

That day had been the most miserable of his life. At times the pain was so fierce he didn't know how he'd managed to keep his legs moving after they'd left the horses behind. They'd climbed hills so steep he used his one good hand almost as much as his feet. His lungs protested every move, and the resultant cough sent agony racing through his body from several broken ribs. The minute Thaine called halt for the night, he collapsed to the ground.

His condition didn't worry him nearly as much as another realization. Thaine called more rests than he should. The others deliberately slowed their pace for him, stopping more frequently than they needed to give him time to catch his breath. *We can't waste time on another stop,* he had wanted to cry, but his abused body would not let him.

He closed his eyes. His friends stood at a distance, on the other side of the fire they'd built to warm him. Though they whispered, their voices carried. Hopefully Arien would not Perceive his thoughts and know that he heard.

"I don't know how much longer he can go on." The concern in her voice made him wince. "His injuries are obviously far worse than a broken arm. He's passing blood."

Millard gave a sour grunt. *So much for privacy.*

"I know," Jothan agreed, "but what else can we do? We're going as slow as we dare as it is. If we don't hurry, there's no chance at all we'll arrive before the Oteran fleet."

"I could take Arien and go ahead," Thaine suggested. "That way maybe the two of us could—"

"No." Arien spoke loudly, and then lowered her voice again. "I can't leave him here. He's the First Prince of Hamlin. Let me stay with him, and the two of you go on."

Thaine's voice was not loud, but the tone left no room for argument. "I am not leaving a woman and a sick man stranded in a wild mountain range."

Jothan seemed to be the only one of the three able to remain calm. He pitched his voice almost too low to be heard, but Millard strained to make out his words.

"We're going to kill him if we keep pushing him as we have. Arien, Thaine's suggestion makes sense. You go and send back a healer with a litter."

"You don't have enough food to last more than a day or two." Stubborn woman. He managed a weak smile at the argument in her tone. "Besides, a litter won't make it over those cliffs ahead of us. He'll get help sooner if we push on."

"He won't make it over them without one." Millard shut his eyes in the certainty of Thaine's reply. "And you're right. He *is* the first prince. King Mendel will not be happy if we kill his son trying to get him home."

Arien stood firm. "If we must leave him, I'm staying."

Pain shafted through his gut, and his ears roared with suffering, drowning out their voices. He wanted to think, wanted desperately to come up with a solution, but just now he could not. He curled into a tight ball, his mind unable to focus on anything but pain, and eventually fell into a fitful sleep.

When he awoke, the fire burned low and his companions had fallen asleep around it. Millard lay still a moment, taking stock of the pain in his stomach, his chest, his ribs, his arm. He felt the need to relieve himself and struggled to his feet. With an unsteady pace, he staggered away from the warmth of the campfire, and lurched from tree to tree to support his weight.

The moon burned bright above him, and by its light he saw that the liquid he passed was almost black with blood. He smothered a cough and reeled farther from his sleeping companions.

Within a few moments, he came to a cliff and dropped to his knees. He was so unsteady on his feet he didn't want to take a chance on falling over the side, but he did have an urge to look. Creeping toward the edge on hands and knees, he peered over. Below him lay a true precipice, with jagged overhanging rocks giving onto a steep bluff and ending in an uneven pile of sharp boulders far below.

Millard heaved himself up until he was sitting. He set his gaze southward. Those peaks there, barely visible as a black line in the moon's white light, separated him from his home. He'd never thought he would long for Kirklin Castle, for his father, even for Sarana. Was there news of their child? Had it been born, and he too far away to be told? Or maybe the message had been intercepted by King Kuriel, never delivered. He might be a father even now.

A smile crept over him. What would his child look like? A son, surely. Would he have dark hair, like him, or fair like his mother? Would he be tall and well-built, or short and pudgy like his grandfather the king? Either way, he would be kingly, and in line for the throne of Hamlin.

And sooner, rather than later.

He was dying. The knowledge didn't upset him greatly, not in the face of so many other items of import. His home being invaded, his kingdom in jeopardy, the lives of hundreds of his father's subjects at risk. What was dying next to those?

If only he could do something to help before he passed.

He gave a silent laugh, wincing at the pain the small movement caused. Wouldn't his father be shocked to hear that thought? Millard, his selfish son, wanting to help the kingdom? Unlikely.

But he did want to help. Yet as things stood, he hurt more than helped. His condition slowed the pace of those in possession of that all-important message, the one chance his father had to prepare for the disaster about to befall them all. His vision blurred with a rush of tears as he admitted this to himself. All his life he had put himself first—before his father, before the kingdom, before everything. But here, at the end of his life, he wanted to do something more, something noble. Not for himself, but for his father. For Hamlin. For the child he would never live to see.

Thaine was right. Leaving him behind was the only course of action that made sense. But Arien would never leave him. She was too loyal to his father, to King Mendel, and would see it as an act of betrayal. Arien would be wasted here with him. He would never again lay eyes on Kirklin. But with her Power, she could help his father defend the kingdom.

He knew what he had to do. What choice had he? He must ensure that Arien, Thaine, and Jothan reached Kirklin Castle before the Oterans. At best, traveling as fast as they possibly could, they would only beat the Oterans by a day or two. But even that would be better than having an enemy arrive on their doorstep unawares, cannons blazing and arrows flying. Thaine, he knew, would go for the Creighton Guard the moment they were out of the Jalapa Range and would bring them to Father's aid. It might, it just *might*, be enough to hold off the Oterans. If nothing else, it would give Father time to get Sarana and their baby out of danger.

But that would never happen if Millard continued to hamper their progress.

Millard stood. Wind whipped up from the canyon, blowing cold dust in his face. He glanced downward, and then closed his eyes against the jagged rocks spread out below him. Not the most pleasant of deaths, but certainly faster than passing his life's blood drop by agonizing drop over the next several days. If only he had pen and parchment to leave a note for his father. Regardless, he must at least leave a message, a sign of some sort. His rings were long gone, taken by the Oteran soldiers who had beaten him. His royal seal was gone, too, packed in the belongings he'd left at King Kuriel's guest house.

Sighing, he removed his cloak. It was ragged and filthy, but it was all he had. He folded it carefully and placed it on the ground at his feet.

Drawing in a deep breath, First Prince Millard of Hamlin stepped forward, off the edge of the cliff.

Arien awoke early, before the sun had risen, yet late enough that the sky showed the promise of a beautiful, cloudless day. The fire had died out. She stretched, then sat up. Wrapping her blanket around her shoulders against the morning's chill, she glanced to her left—

—and gasped. Millard was gone. She Perceived, searching through the sparse trees that grew around their camp site.

Nothing.

"Get up!" She leaped to her feet and woke Jothan and Thaine with a kick. "Millard is gone."

Both men awoke instantly. She watched Jothan Perceive, silently begging him to find something she'd missed. Dread gnawed at her insides when he shook his head.

"I can't find him anywhere."

"Maybe he's traveled out of your range," Thaine suggested.

Certainty struck her then. Sorrow gripped her. "It's more likely he was sicker than we realized. We should search for his…for him."

They combed the area. Arien ran through the trees, her desperation growing with every step. She'd all but given up hope when she heard Jothan's shout.

"Over here. I've found something."

Arien Perceived his location and ran there. As she neared the cliff, her heart began a desperate beating.

"Look at this." Jothan pointed toward something on the ground.

Millard's cloak.

Thaine stood dangerously near the cliff's edge, peering downward. He turned to Arien, his face full of pain. "He's down there."

Arien sank to the ground beside the cloak.

Jothan stretched his neck to peer over the cliff, winced, and then turned away. "He must have been delirious with pain in the night and wandered too close to the edge."

Arien picked up the cloak, so neatly folded, and placed it in her lap. "No," she told them quietly. "Delirious men do not fold their clothing. He did it on purpose, so he wouldn't slow us down."

Neither answered. The three of them stayed by the cliff, silent. Arien ran a hand over the garment. How would she ever be able to tell King Mendel of his son's sacrifice?

Beryle stepped off the last boulder onto the dirt-packed ground with an exaggerated sigh. It was past supper time, and she had never been so hungry and exhausted in her life. Her hands were raw even with the gloves, her men's breeches ripped, and her legs scratched, scraped and cut. She collapsed to the ground, leaning against the boulder she'd just crawled across, and closed her eyes.

They'd climbed the rock barrier far enough last night to be out of sight of anyone who might choose to follow them, and then posted sentries to watch for signs of approach from the direction of Otero. Beryle had been relieved, fearful that Quinn and the guardsmen expected to cross the Pass in the dark. Instead, they waited the night out perched among the giant boulders, terrified to spy signs of pursuit. Toward dawn Beryle had fallen asleep leaning against Illari, only to be awakened before the sun was properly up and told they must get started.

What followed was the longest day of Beryle's life. Crossing the Nephtali Pass the first time was bad enough. This time she had the added anxiety of wondering if soldiers would climb up behind her at any moment and drag her back to Otero. Or even throw her to her death on the very rocks over which she struggled.

But they'd made it. And now she was going to rest, whether they liked it or not. Nothing could move her from this spot for at least an hour.

"We can't stop now," Quinn's voice announced somewhere over her head. "Every minute we waste means those ships are sailing closer to Kirklin Castle."

Beryle winced. Nothing except that. She sighed again and opened her eyes. Quinn stood in front of her, hands on his hips, staring down with a sympathetic grimace. To Beryle's right, a guardsman helped Illari down from the barrier as two more leaped to the ground behind her. The sun barely dipped behind the western peaks, casting cool shadows over them all.

Beryle sighed again and held up a hand toward Quinn. "Help me up, then. I don't know how much longer my legs will move, but I'll push them as far as I can."

"It's not far." He pulled her to her feet. "We'll be at the guard post within an hour."

"We'll run into sentries before then." One of the guardsmen handed her a skin of water. "Prince Thaine left word that the Pass was to be patrolled, watching for our return."

She sipped the lukewarm water gratefully before returning the skin with a tired smile. "Well, let's be finding them, then."

Illari fell in beside her as they walked. "I've never been so tired."

Beryle patted her shoulder. "The same with me. But soon we'll be in Arnath, and I intend to stop off at that inn where we stayed before. It's run by a woman with her husband to help, and a nicer woman you never met. No matter what anyone says, I'm going to sleep in one of her soft beds and eat some of her good cooking and not move until next week."

They'd only walked a quarter of an hour when they were approached by two sentries on horseback. The guardsmen and Quinn hurried forward to talk to them, and Beryle took the opportunity to sink to the ground and rest her tired, aching legs. Illari joined her. She watched, only half-listening, as Quinn unrolled the map and Brother Jothan's letter, showing it to the sentries.

But the guardsman's words drew Beryle to her feet before she realized she intended to stand.

"The king is dead, and little Prince Roddy, too." Grief carried the man's tone across the distance.

The weary group stared, open-mouthed, silent with shock.

"It was at the funeral for Princess Lianne," the man told them, his voice sorrowful. "A pair of assassins hid in the top floor of a shop. During the funeral parade through Tadmoure, they shot them both with arrows. The little prince was killed instantly, but the king lived a full day before he died. The queen has taken ill because of it. They say she lays in her bed all day, refusing to eat or speak."

"Were the assassins caught?" asked Quinn, while everyone else stared in horror.

The man shook his head. "By the time the guard got into the shop they had killed themselves with a fast-acting poison. There's talk that they were from Hamlin, sent to take advantage of Creighton's grief over the princess."

"No." Beryle shoved her way forward to plant her feet in front of the guard. "No one can believe that."

The sentry flashed a comfortless smile at Beryle. "Most of us don't, but there's such suspicion of Hamlin that it's no surprise the people hurry to toss blame there."

Quinn gestured toward Jothan's note. "We know better. It was the work of Oteran spies."

Fulton clutched the parchment. "We'll get this to Commander Norval."

"Wait." Beryle whirled, eyeing the company. "If King Hubert is dead, that means the new king is…" Her voice trailed off as she looked toward Quinn, her eyes wide.

The guardsman nodded. "Prince Thaine is now our king."

Quinn gave a low whistle. "And he's a prisoner in Otero."

Illari shook her head and spoke firmly. "By now Lady Arien and Brother Jothan have rescued them."

Beryle wished she could be as certain.

Eighteen

Stepping off the last peak in the Jalapa Range and onto Hamlin soil proved almost anticlimactic for Arien. After the dangers they'd braved over the past three days, she almost expected to have to fight her way into the kingdom. But the mountain range ended in a long, grassy mound sloping gently toward the small village of Draper.

Dirty, ragged and exhausted, they became the center of attention within minutes. A mill town, Draper supplied most of the dark, sturdy wood prized throughout Hamlin. Because of its remote location, the villagers didn't receive many visitors. Their appearance drew a crowd. Arien followed wearily as Thaine, who seemed to have received a jolt of energy, shouted to those on the sides of the street.

"Where can we find horses? We carry an urgent message for King Mendel."

Skeptical stares met his request, but one man stepped

forward and pointed to the southern end of town. "The blacksmith has one or two he might part with."

"We need three." Thaine peered at the faces up and down the street.

Whether due to the urgency in his voice or the wild look in his eyes, another man lifted a hand. "I have one you can use, sir, if your message is urgent."

A woman hurried after him, pulling on his arm. "Don't be a fool, Hurlee. He's all you've got to get you to Winthrop. How will you sell your bows without it?"

The man waved an impatient hand toward the woman, as Jothan stepped forward, digging in his belt.

"Here." He held a silver toward the man. "This should help."

The man held the coin up to the sun, his eyes wide.

"It's Oteran," Jothan told them, "but I promise it is the same silver that goes into ours. Any coin broker will honor it."

Suspicion colored the man's eyes while a murmur rose from the onlookers. "Be ye from Otero, then?"

Thaine shook his head. "We've just escaped from there. Has news reached this town of the envoy sent by King Mendel and King Hubert of Creighton into Otero?"

Blank stares met his question, but at last a man in the back of the crowd spoke up. "I heard something about that, last time I was in Winthrop. The first prince went, they say, and the First Prince of Creighton too."

Thaine drew in a breath and glanced toward Arien. From the look on his face, she knew he was preparing to cast off caution and tell these people his identity.

"That's right. We went into Otero under the guise of establishing a trade agreement, but in reality, we needed to determine the truth behind rumors of an Oteran invasion into Creighton. I am Thaine, First Prince of Creighton."

An unencouraging silence met his words. Arien felt disbelief wafting from most of them, though those didn't concern her. Here and there she sensed active dislike, suspicion and even downright hatred.

Thaine held up his hand. "This is Brother Jothan, a

member of the Brotherhood of Power, and our guide into Otero. And this," he gestured toward her, "is Lady Arien, also trained in the Brotherhood's ways of Power."

"Now we know you ain't being straight with us," someone shouted. "Ain't no woman with Power."

Jothan stepped forward. "It is true, I assure you. Lady Arien and I trained with the same teacher, Master Petro, who is now an advisor to King Mendel at Kirklin Castle."

"Good people of Draper," Thaine hurried to say, "while in Otero we discovered an Oteran invasion plot. The target is Hamlin, your own kingdom. That is the message we must take to King Mendel, and soon. Even now, Oteran ships have set sail with eighteen hundred soldiers on board. They're due to land within a few days in Kirklin."

"He's lying," shouted the same suspicious voice. "No ship can get through the barrier reef."

Thaine pulled a document from the satchel he carried and waved it in the air. "This is a map with the way through the reef marked clearly. It was stolen from Kirklin Castle by an Oteran spy."

The people drew shocked breaths almost in unison. Arien admired the way Thaine took control, looking somehow royal and princely even in ragged, filthy clothing. His earnest manner and urgency were beginning to win the people over, even amid their hatred of anything from Creighton.

"If you're Prince Thaine," a woman standing directly before him asked, "then where is Prince Millard? Wasn't he with you?"

Thaine bowed his head, his eyes closed. Would he bear the terrible news to these people? They were sure to treat him with suspicion then, and perhaps even hold him responsible.

No. The news must not come from one they already suspected of being an enemy.

She took a fortifying breath and stepped up beside him. "That is the other news we must deliver to King Mendel." A hush fell on the villagers as her low voice carried to them all. "Prince Millard was severely injured by Oteran soldiers. He was not strong enough to make the trip over the Jalapas. When he realized that his injuries were slowing us down, he…" She swallowed, tears welling in her eyes. "He took his own life so that our message could reach King Mendel in time."

Shock radiated toward her from the assembled, followed with deep sorrow. Arien felt it like a wave washing over her. Surprising, in a way. While in Hamlin she had viewed Millard as self-focused and even foppish. Obviously, the people of the kingdom did not share the same opinion.

"It was nobly done." Thaine spoke in a subdued voice. "The action of a true prince to save his people."

"Then that means the new little prince is now the heir to the throne," someone said from the back of the group.

"New prince?" Arien exchanged a glance with Thaine. "Then Princess Sarana has delivered a son?"

Heads nodded, and the man who had offered Thaine his horse said, "Five days ago. We received word yesterday."

Thaine scrubbed a hand over his unshaven chin. "We must hurry to Kirklin. There may be time yet to get the prince away to safety before the fleet arrives." He turned back to the crowd. "We need two more horses."

The mood of the townsfolk shifted. At the mention of saving their new prince, Thaine made the leap from enemy to friend. Arien still sensed suspicion, but not active distrust or hatred. Half a dozen men stepped forward, offering their own animals.

"I'll come, too," the first volunteer spoke. "I make bows, and have arrows aplenty. They'll be needed in Kirklin."

Arien sagged, her legs weak with relief. She had been so intent on weighing the numbers of soldiers against one another that she had forgotten the people of Hamlin. Of course, they would defend their country.

Thaine stepped forward and grasped the man's hand. "We will need every man we can find, and every weapon." He lifted his head to address the crowd. "We'll ride ahead so King Mendel has time to ready the guard, but you, men of Draper, must spread the word. Send messages to every town and village and tell everyone who is able that they must get to Kirklin with as much haste as they can muster. Tell them to bring anything they can use as a weapon."

At that, people began to move, to run toward their homes,

shouting to their neighbors as they went. Within moments three horses were led into the main street, men trotting along beside them to secure the saddles.

The first man, the weapon-smith, directed Thaine as he handed over the reins. "Follow the stream just east of town until you come to Winthrop. From there ride due south. That's the most direct route, and you can change horses in Winthrop. We'll send a group to Stitzer and Kenley, and I'll take a group to Corral and then down to Walbridge. How long before the fleet arrives in Kirklin?"

Thaine shook his head. "I wish I knew. One of the documents we obtained estimates the voyage at five days, given good weather. They set sail three days ago. The best we can hope for is stormy seas."

Jothan looked up from checking the straps on his saddle. "And another thousand or so soldiers wouldn't hurt either."

Exhaustion hit Arien. When she found herself being lifted into a saddle, she fought to keep her eyes open. Sitting felt good, though she would far rather have collapsed into a soft bed. Or even on the ground, at this point.

A gaunt woman appeared beside her horse and pressed a mug of cool water into Arien's hands. "Drink this. And take this, too. It's not much, but a bit of food will do you good."

At the sight of a thick slice of bread and a wedge of cheese, her stomach twisted with hunger. "Thank you. I can't even remember the last time we ate."

The tall woman patted her on the arm. "There now, dear. You've had a hard time, what with being in that barbarian land and losing the prince and all. But it will come out right, you'll see."

After draining the mug, Arien handed it back with a tired smile. Mounted and ready, Thaine and Jothan verified their directions with the weapon-smith once more. When they set off, the people of Draper halted a moment from their own preparations to call after them, "Godspeed to you!"

They repeated their message in Winthrop. When Arien again spoke of Millard's death, she did so with a true admiration for his sacrifice. If anything, the people of Winthorop, once convinced, were even more determined to help. Though the distance between Draper and Winthrop had not yet taxed their horses, they were given fresh mounts and an escort of a dozen men.

Not long after leaving Winthrop, the sun set, and darkness fell. Though a sense of urgency gripped her, she struggled to stay awake. How much longer could she remain in the saddle without falling asleep?

The next three hours were horrible, and she nearly toppled from her horse several times. A peek inside Thaine's mind showed that he, too, suffered from near exhaustion, but a steely determination possessed him and kept sleep at bay. Jothan's mindspeech, when Arien queried him, was tinged with fatigue. The men from Winthrop fought drowsiness as well. Occasionally the party acquired new members, farmers and woodcutters and those living in outlying areas, as the towns of Winthrop and Draper worked to spread the word. Their group numbered close to four dozen, the newest ones awake and alert.

When they neared Kirklin, they encountered a river that widened as they neared the capital city. The road ran alongside the water, weaving inland and out again. When the sun rose, Arien cast anxious glances at the eastern horizon. Were the Oteran ships, even now, coming into view from the shore? Perhaps the ships' sails would be spotted from land while still far away. She queried Jothan, whose answer did nothing to reassure her.

"If they are counting on a surprise attack, they certainly aren't going to sail near the coastline."

The desire to sleep didn't plague her so much in daylight. Especially since, the closer they drew to Kirklin Castle, a sense of urgency to deliver the message overtook all other concerns. She sensed that urgency in the others as well, and they rode the poor horses to near exhaustion.

Late in the morning, the grassy riverbank became sandy. In the distance she spied the blue haze of the southern sea. Kirklin Castle lay in that direction, protected within its walled fortress. Before them lay a long stretch of open beach. Thaine pushed the horses to a gallop. Arien rode a white animal, and the journey had worked up a lather across its strong neck. She entwined her fingers in the horse's mane. The fast-moving river roared in her ears on her left, and her horse's hooves kicked up a spray of wet sand behind her as they galloped.

A strong sense of familiarity struck her like a slap

It's my dream. I saw this in a dream, long ago as a child, but I didn't know what I was running from. Now I do. I was running away from the Oterans and toward Kirklin. And if we don't hurry, something terrible will *happen.*

The closer they came to Kirklin, the more people they encountered along the way. Small riverside villages existed in abundance, but the message party did not take the time to stop in each one. Instead they shouted the news of the impending invasion to those they encountered along the way and kept their noses pointed south.

Finally, Kirklin Castle loomed before them. They had traveled the entire road from Draper in just over half the time it normally took, and Arien felt it. A glance at Thaine made her look down to examine herself, and she grimaced. Dust and grime from the road covered every inch of her. The men's clothing Beryle had purchased in Otero were now an unrecognizable color, indistinguishable from the skin of her arms, hands, and probably her face as well. She smelled stronger than her horse. Amazing that anyone they'd encountered had taken them for anything but beggars. Her body ached so that she thought her joints would never be without pain again.

She forgot all that as they approached the castle.

By the time Thaine led his ragged company across the causeway, the guardsmen in the turrets had spotted them. When they neared the island, they found the gates barred. They lost precious time while Thaine attempted to identify himself. Arien scanned the minds inside the gates, skipping over those in the town and going directly to the center, the castle, where King Mendel would be hearing grievances at this time of the morning. Focusing on that one room inside the castle, she quickly found Petro's mind, and spoke to him.

"We have returned and are being held at the gate. We must speak with the king without delay."

What a relief, what a comfort, to hear Petro's mindspeech in return. *"And your mission? Is all well?"*

In answer, Arien let him see the thoughts as they jumbled through her mind—her brother and father, the captivity of the princes and her own, their rescue, the fleet of soldiers, and finally, Millard's death.

Petro's thought, when it reached her, was leavened with sorrow. *"The king has sent word that you are to be brought to his private council chamber immediately."*

Within a few moments the guards on the walls received the king's command, and the gates opened. Arien followed Thaine and Jothan as they galloped through the streets toward the castle. They leapt from their saddles to follow the courier sent to escort them to the king.

The people they passed drew back to stare at the filthy strangers hurrying through the castle corridors. Arien recognized a few but didn't have time to do more than notice that they didn't seem to know her. And no wonder.

The guardsman led them directly to the council chamber. Their entire party would not fit inside, so Thaine motioned for everyone but Jothan and Arien to remain in the outer corridor. He stepped through the doorway, Arien following close on his heels.

They were alone. The room contained a small oblong table with a dozen chairs and a steward's chair near the door at the rear wall. The guardsman closed the door behind them, still completely unaware who he'd just let in. Thaine and Jothan paced the length of the room, impatient to deliver their news.

They had been waiting only a few moments when the door at the far end of the room opened. King Mendel stepped through, followed by Master Petro. When she caught sight of her teacher, Arien ran forward to embrace him. Tears blurred her vision as such a powerful rush of relief, tinged with sorrow at her own failure, threatened to overpower her. Strong arms circled her at the same moment his mental touch reached out to her, encompassing her within a barrier of comfort.

"There is no time now for thoughts of yourself," he told her gently. *"There are things you and the prince do not yet know. The king will need your counsel and advice."*

Arien drew a shuddering breath and turned to face King

Mendel. He stood in the center of the room, looking down at Thaine's kneeling form. He glanced toward Jothan, confusion clear on his face, then turned to Arien. Without Perceiving his thoughts, Arien saw the moment he realized that Millard was not with them. While she watched, his features gave way to grief.

"Your Majesty," Thaine said in a tortured voice, "I bring terrible news."

Mendel stumbled backward and sank into the steward's chair situated against the back wall, his gaze never leaving Thaine's face. "My son is dead."

He stated it as fact, without question, though his eyes begged Thaine to tell him otherwise.

Thaine bowed his head. "He is."

King Mendel closed his eyes, took a deep breath. "At the hands of the Oterans?"

"No, Your Majesty. By his own hand."

Mendel's eyes opened and fixed on Thaine's face, unbelieving. "Tell me."

Thaine recounted their journey, beginning with their arrival in Eshtaol and ending with their discovery of Millard's body. The king listened without comment, nodding occasionally, wincing at reports of the beatings Millard and Thaine had taken. His gaze lifted occasionally to fix on Arien or on Jothan as the story included them, but he did not speak a word until Thaine's voice came to a halt.

Silence reigned in the chamber. No one had moved while Thaine spoke. Then Mendel rose and began to pace the room. Thaine moved to a spot near the table, next to Jothan.

When King Mendel spoke, his voice sounded old and tired. "My kingdom is about to fall to the Oterans, and all I can think of is my son. It used to be easier to clear my mind."

"Your Majesty." Arien approached to place a comforting hand on his arm. "The prince gave his life so Hamlin could be saved. He chose his fate so you would have a choice about yours. That is the act of a hero."

King Mendel smiled, a sad, tired smile, and patted her hand. "Thank you, my dear."

"But you must hurry, or his sacrifice will be for nothing."

Jothan executed a quick bow, and then continued, his voice urgent. "The Oteran fleet is not far behind us. The towns of Draper, Winthrop, Stitzer, and Kenley have been mobilized, and soon men and women will pour into Kirklin to help you defend this kingdom."

Mendel glanced toward Thaine, who nodded. "Wherever we went we told the tale of Prince Millard's sacrifice. The people of Hamlin rallied to our side. A few came with us and are waiting in the corridor outside this room. The rest have gone to collect whatever men and weapons they can find and will be here soon" Thaine dipped his head low in a respectful bow. "I beg leave to go to my father immediately. He will honor our commitment and send his guard to augment your own."

King Mendel's head shot up, and his gaze pierced Thaine's. Alarm stabbed through Arien at the look in his eyes.

"You haven't heard," he said in a low voice.

Thaine, instantly on guard, took a step forward. "Your Majesty?"

Mendel rose and stood before Thaine, placing a hand on either shoulder. "Your father and your son are both dead, Thaine."

Thaine staggered backward out of the king's grasp, his eyes widening. "But..."

"They were murdered at Princess Lianne's funeral. Assassins, we assume from Otero, hid in the upper room of a tannery shop and shot them during the procession."

The agony wafting off Thaine hit Arien like a blast. He groped for one of the chairs, and Jothan rushed forward to pull it out for him. The new king of Creighton sank into it, unseeing, while Arien clutched Petro's arm in horror.

"There's more," Petro warned, at the same moment King Mendel's voice continued.

"I am afraid that is not the last of the evil tidings. A courier arrived yesterday with news of your father and asked if we'd had any word from you. When your sister heard the message, she was distraught. Her personal attendant found her late last night, dead." His head dipped even lower, and his voice held an agony even more vivid than the emotions Arien felt.

"She took her own life."

Arien drew in a quick, horrified breath. Too much death, too much tragedy, on top of a sleepless night and an exhausting ride. Before she realized she intended to, she had stepped forward. "How could she? She has a new son to think of."

King Mendel shook his head, his shoulders slumped. "Perhaps she was weak from the birth? A weakness of soul as well as body. The grief of her father's death was more than she could bear."

Thaine sat with his forehead resting on his fist, eyes closed. He spoke without raising his head. "And the child?"

King Mendel smiled, a quick gesture soon erased, but one which spoke of a man's love for his grandson. "He thrives. He is under constant guard. I am taking no chances with the heir to two kingdoms."

Thaine's head rose quickly and he shot a look of shock toward King Mendel. Then the shock faded, and he nodded.

"My sister's son. He is my heir, with Roddy—" He swallowed, his pain evident to anyone with Power or without. "—gone. And your heir as well."

"Your Majesty." Petro stepped forward. "We must take steps immediately to insure the little prince's safety. He must not be here when the Oterans attack."

Thaine stood, determination cemented onto every feature. "Once the child is hidden away, we must prepare ourselves for the arrival of the Oteran fleet."

King Mendel nodded. "But where can we send the babe where he will be safe?"

No one had an opportunity to answer the question because at that moment a soft rap on the door announced the entrance of Commander Jarvis.

"Your Majesty." The man bowed before Mendel. "Excuse the interruption, but I've received word from a runner stationed at the coast. Sails have been spotted, a day's journey due east. They are still too far at sea to identify the colors, but in light of the princes' mission I thought it prudent to inform you without delay."

"You were right, Commander." Mendel turned to Thaine, who made a visible effort to suppress his pain as he focused his attention on Mendel. "As rulers, we do not have the privilege to grieve at leisure. We must put aside our grief and act immediately if we are to save my kingdom, and yours."

Thaine nodded and rounded the table to stand at Mendel's side.

The king addressed Jarvis. "Assemble my council in the large chamber and also those men in the corridor who have arrived with His Majesty, King Thaine of Creighton. Call your captains so they might hear what is decided first-hand—the plans we will make concern all of Hamlin and Creighton. We will not have time to relay messages about."

"Yes, Your Majesty."

Jarvis bowed first to King Mendel and then to Thaine before exiting. Arien heard him shouting orders to the guardsmen posted outside the door, his voice fading as he ran down the corridor to do the king's bidding.

Nineteen

Arien took advantage of the few moments before the council meeting to bathe and change clothes. Donning a fresh, comfortable robe of the Brotherhood revived her. A tray of fruit, bread, and cold mutton sent up by the castle chamberlain tempted her, but she ate only a small loaf of bread. A full stomach would put her to sleep. She ignored the wine decanter for the same reason but did ask for a large pitcher of teaspice and sugar sticks. The drink delivered a welcome spurt of energy.

As she entered the large council chamber, she was reminded sharply of the last time she attended a meeting in this room. She had been about to embark on the journey to Otero, by way of Tadmoure Castle.

The room had not changed, though this time a greater number of people crowded inside. No chair around the oblong table remained empty, and extras had been placed along the south and west walls to hold the overflow. The villagers who had accompanied them were seated there. Several smiled toward Arien as she entered, and she nodded in response.

Jothan's thought reached her. *"I've a chair for you here."*

She found him near the center of the table, seated next to Petro. As she made her way toward her seat, she greeted the various lords and nodded at Commander Jarvis where he sat speaking in a low voice with his captains.

"You look better." Jothan grinned as she seated herself.

"You, too, though I hardly recognized you without the coat of grime I've become accustomed to." She returned his smile and caught Petro's tolerant expression.

"It is good to see that the two of you have become friends."

"Oh, Master Petro," she replied, *"I have so much to tell you, so much I've learned."*

Jothan inserted a thought. *"I've filled him in on Addison."*

Petro nodded. *"I'm sure the Brotherhood will find that bit of information interesting."*

Mendel and Thaine entered the council chamber side by side. They spoke in low voices as they walked. All conversations ceased and everyone rose. As the two kings approached the table, she noticed a second large chair placed next to King Mendel's. The two sat simultaneously.

After a respectful moment, everyone took their seats. King Mendel's gaze circled the room, holding every eye he encountered. The corners of his mouth twitched upward when he looked into her eyes, and she returned the smile.

He spoke in a calm, even voice. "By now you will have heard why you were called to this council. Though time is precious, I want to state our position clearly so there are no misunderstandings, no misconceptions at the outset. Our envoy to Otero encountered disaster in many respects, but success in others. The first prince, my son, is dead." He paused, drew in a deep breath, and then continued. "We are being invaded by a fleet of Oteran soldiers some eighteen hundred strong. Among the documents recovered from the Oterans was a copy of our map detailing the only safe route through the barrier reef, obviously stolen by spies who have infiltrated this castle. Sails have been sighted on the eastern horizon, and

Commander Jarvis tells me they could land on our beaches as soon as tomorrow."

The king held up his hand to forestall Jarvis' interruption. "Yes, Commander, I know you have told me a day and a half is more likely, but I want to plan for the worst possible circumstance. Our guard numbers three hundred twenty-seven men, and couriers have been sent to all outposts, calling them here. We have every hope that they will arrive before the Oterans."

Lord Aldon cleared his throat. From the shock apparent on his face, he had not heard the numbers before this moment. "Even so, we cannot possibly hope to hold off an army of eighteen hundred soldiers with only three hundred twenty-seven guardsmen."

Thaine addressed the distressed lord. "Creighton's Guard is over five hundred strong. I have dispatched a message to Commander Norval and his captains, and I will ride west to join them as soon as this council ends. I assure you that the first of them will arrive in no more than four days, and the rest will be but a day or so behind."

"But, Your Majesty," stuttered Lord Cranston, his eyes fixed on Thaine, "we will still be outnumbered by a thousand men."

"Not quite." Mendel nodded toward the villagers seated at the rear of the room. "The people of Hamlin have determined that they will not give our kingdom away without a fight. These fifty are representative of what we hope will be hundreds to come, bringing whatever weapons they can find."

Glancing at the villagers, Arien noted several determined nods.

"Plus," interrupted Commander Jarvis, unable to contain himself any longer, "we have the advantage of home soil and a brief but vital warning period. We know they are coming. If we can meet them on the beaches, we may be able to stop them from advancing further into the kingdom."

King Mendel glanced toward Jarvis, slightly annoyed, and then Arien saw him give an almost imperceptible shrug. He sat back and let the conversation take life around him.

"Can we destroy their ships before they land?" Lord

Curran asked.

Jarvis shook his head. "Our ships are trade vessels, not equipped with the weapons necessary to sink heavily armed fighting ships. A sea battle is out of the question."

"But with only three hundred-odd men, can we defeat them even with the advantage of being on our home soil?" Lord Cranston's entire face folded into worried wrinkles.

One of the captains seated next to Jarvis spoke up. "We don't have to defeat them. All we have to do is hold them off until the Creighton Guard and the villagers arrive. We are moving all our long-distance weapons to the beach at this moment."

Lord Fuller, looking puzzled, leaned forward to speak. "I thought you said we couldn't attack them at sea."

Commander Jarvis smiled, a humorless gesture. "I said we can't attack their sailing vessels because they are too heavily armed. But at the moment we are burning the only dock on the coastline, the trade dock. They have no place to land."

Shocked silence met that bit of news. The dock was the kingdom's only one, built recently, when the route was found through the barrier reef to accommodate Hamlin's growing island trade. Hamlin's economy would suffer from losing it.

Finally, Lord Curran spoke in a quiet voice. "I'm sure the merchants aren't happy about that."

Thaine laughed, a humorless sound that drew all eyes to him. "Happy or not, they'll have to live with it. What other defensive move could we take? We do have the advantage of the stolen barrier reef map. We know exactly where they will come through, the only place deep enough for their warships. If there is no dock, the sailing vessels will not be able to land. They will have to send their soldiers to the beach in smaller boats, or swim. Either way, we have the advantage of being able to pick off a good number of them before they ever reach land."

Lord Cranston, his expression slightly relieved, sat back in his chair. "Then we will win after all. If we kill them all in the water, they will never make it to land."

Commander Jarvis shook his head. "We won't get them all. We don't have the weapons, the long-distance launchers, or the men. The men we do have are untrained. If I were the commander of that fleet and spotted the dock burning, as we know they will, I'd launch all my men at once, as many as I could, and hope that a good percentage get through." He shook his head, his expression dour. "Knowing our strength, I guarantee most of them will."

The commander of that fleet. Acid rose in Arien's throat when she realized the man they were discussing was Lord Jerolin Arien, her father. By now he knew of his only son's fate. The Seer had spoken the truth at her Foretelling. Because of her choice—the choice for Hamlin over Otero, for Thaine and Millard over her own twin brother and father—Lucian had been left with no mind. The name of Arien would cease to exist with her generation.

How must he feel, her father? What must he be thinking now, as they neared Kirklin? Of course, he had no way of knowing his daughter was here. No doubt he thought her back in Otero somewhere, either captured or trying to avoid capture. But she knew and was aware of his presence on one of those ships in an intense way that had nothing to do with Power.

King Mendel stood, and the room fell silent. "As you can see, Commander Jarvis already has the situation well in hand. We are extremely grateful to him for his quick thinking and brilliant mind." He bowed toward a flustered Jarvis. "Commander, I hereby grant you the authority to act in my name as you command the Hamlin Guard. You answer to no one. Do as you see fit to protect our kingdom from invasion." He turned to the villagers seated along the wall. "And you, people of Hamlin, I owe you my deepest gratitude. I have always striven to remember that, as your king, I serve you with my life. It moves me deeply to know that you, too, are prepared to serve with yours."

More than a few eyes grew wet on hearing the king's words.

King Mendel went on. "But there is one important detail to which we have not yet attended. As some of you know, the princess Sarana passed away late last night." A gasp from the back of the room told Arien that some of the villagers had not heard this sad bit of news. "Her death creates an interesting situation concerning her son, the unnamed prince. With the death of my son, the child is now First Prince of Hamlin, my heir and first in line to the throne."

Thaine stood beside King Mendel. Emotion dragged at his features, rendering them ragged. "And, since the child is the son of my sister, and since I have no other living relatives—" Thaine took a deep breath, and Arien suspected that only she and perhaps Jothan knew what it cost him to utter those words. "—he is also my heir."

A hush fell over the assembled as the impact of this declaration hit home. Arien heard whispers of *the reunion* and experienced a sudden and vivid recollection of the dinner conversation around Kalinda's table, when she'd first learned of the hoped-for reunion between the divided kingdoms.

King Mendel raised his hands, and the whispers fell silent. "We must take steps to see that the babe is kept safe through the coming conflict. For certain, he is not safe here. And with the recent discovery of assassins in Creighton, I will not assume his safety in Tadmoure Castle either. So, I put the question to you, my councilors and my friends. We must have a safe place to send the little prince. Where shall it be?"

Beside Arien, Petro stirred. All heads turned toward him as he rose. He'd maintained an unusual silence throughout this meeting.

"I have an idea." His warm baritone boomed the length of the council table.

King Mendel nodded permission for him to continue.

"I agree with Your Majesties that the child is not safe here, nor in Tadmoure. Both castles are most certainly seeded with spies. Probably the larger towns throughout the Twin Kingdoms as well. In puzzling over this problem, I first considered an orphanage I know of." A flush of warmth shot through Arien when he smiled toward her at the mention of her childhood home. "But I am afraid if my first thoughts were of such, the Oteran king might think the same. No, I think there is only one place where the little prince will be safe." He straightened to his full height. "At the Hall of the Brotherhood of Power."

Whispers, louder than any yet, began around the room before Petro's voice had fully stopped.

They quieted when Thaine spoke. "In my experience, the men of the Brotherhood prefer to remain apart from anything which might connect them with either kingdom. Will they accept the child?"

Petro dipped his head. "It is true that since the time of the Split, the Brotherhood has taken the official position of non-assistance to either kingdom. But the time for hatred in the Divided Kingdom is at an end. All men must recognize that fact, including the men who belong to the Brotherhood. I believe we can convince them that now is the time to end their policy of non-assistance."

Lord Theobald half-raised his hand and interrupted, his manner hesitant. "We can assume that the Oterans are aware of the existence of the Brotherhood. If their king's first thought of the prince's location is an orphanage, the second most assuredly will be the Halls of the Brotherhood. Will the child be safe there?"

The smile Petro turned on the man held an undeniable confidence. "Let me assure you, good Lord Theobald, that if the Brotherhood agrees to protect the prince, no force on earth will be able to get to him. Our only task will be to convince them to commit themselves to his protection."

The Powers yielded by members of the Brotherhood were legend. Arien Perceived that no one in the council chamber doubted Petro's assertion. She, however, recalled vivid memories of Master Parnell's inflexible attitude. Did Petro know what he was doing to propose such a thing?

Mendel glanced around the chamber. "Are there any other suggestions?"

No one spoke.

"Then it appears we have little choice. Master Petro, I will leave it with you to arrange. I remind everyone that the little prince's safety may rest upon whatever spies have been planted in our kingdoms not hearing of his whereabouts, at least until he is safely within the protection of the Brotherhood." He cast a stern glance around the room. "Do not speak of these plans outside this room, to anyone. We will come together again as the need arises."

With that, King Mendel left the table and the council chamber. Thaine, after a brief smile at Arien and Jothan, followed. No doubt he was eager to be off to find the Creighton Guard. She probably wouldn't see him before he left. She stared at the door after he had gone through it, wishing…for what she did not know.

She didn't have time to puzzle it out, for at that moment Petro plucked at her elbow. "How are you faring?"

His eyes searched hers, and she felt his mental probe.

With a pat on his arm, she smiled. "I am fine, or I will be after I've had a good meal and about twelve hours' sleep."

"The meal, yes, but I can only allow you half that much sleep."

He pitched his voice low, so that only she and Jothan could hear his words. He switched to mindspeech and addressed them both. *"You must leave before dawn, and I suggest you stay clear of the larger towns. You'll have to hurry, but I'm afraid the goats will slow you down."*

Arien glanced to her left, where Jothan wore the same astonished expression she knew was apparent on her own face. *"Goats?"*

"For the baby's milk. He's only a few days old, not nearly old enough for travel rations. We can't risk a wet nurse, or that will mark him immediately. Better that you appear to be poor and the child's parents. You won't be able to travel fast with an infant, either. It is not safe to bounce a baby around on a galloping horse. It will probably be best if you take a wagon."

Arien narrowed her eyelids. *"Why do you keep referring to this trip as though you won't be there?"*

"I won't. The two of you will take the prince to the Brotherhood."

Arien laughed out loud, but Jothan stood still and silent.

Petro awarded Arien with a stern look. *"I assure you, my dear, this is not a laughing matter. Weren't you listening? The safety of the prince is of utmost concern to both kingdoms. And besides, I have an even more important task for you."*

Arien glanced at Jothan, who bit his lip. His mind-voice

was subdued, even a little fearful. *"You want us to convince the Brotherhood to come here, to fight for Hamlin, don't you?"*

Petro nodded. *"I knew you would see the need right away. Mendel and Thaine cannot hope to be victorious, not with eighteen hundred trained soldiers against eight hundred-odd guardsmen and a few handfuls of untrained villagers. The Brotherhood must intervene, or all is lost."*

Arien shook her head, trying to picture herself relaying that message to Master Parnell. *"Then you must come. You can convince them."*

"I am the king's advisor. I cannot leave him now. He would not allow it. He has more need of me at this moment than ever before. No, it must be the two of you."

"We will be able to explain ourselves easily on the road." Jothan spared a vacant smile toward the villagers, who vacated the chamber. *"A young couple traveling with a baby is not so unusual. Especially trailing goats and packing a few chickens, perhaps. We could spread news of the invasion on the way, by saying I am taking my young wife and child to safety before returning to fight against the Oterans."*

"Exactly."

Petro beamed at Jothan, while Arien glared. But she was too tired to think straight and could not come up with anything close to a persuasive argument. In fact, now that the council meeting had ended, someone appeared to have attached weights to her eyelids. This might be her only chance to seek Thaine out, to wish him luck, but she was too tired. In fact, if the entire castle were falling to the Oterans right then, she wouldn't have the energy to cry out for help. Instead, she allowed herself to be led back to her room, where she collapsed into bed.

She woke to a gentle shaking.

No, she wanted to moan, *I'm too tired to move. I can't open my eyes. My arms feel as though there are boulders on them. I can't even remember where I am.*

But she did remember, as soon as Petro whispered in her ear. "Arien, wake up. You must leave now. Everything is ready. Here, sit up and drink this teaspice."

She whimpered but did open one eye. Petro's face loomed inches above her. His silver hair caught the light from a nearby lantern like a halo.

"That's good," he said, a little louder. "Now sit up. Here, I'll help you."

She was lifted, not very gently, into a sitting position and propped against the headboard. The rim of a cup pressed against her lips, and she sipped automatically. The warm liquid had been liberally sweetened. She drank again, more deeply this time, and even managed to lift her hands to take control of the mug herself.

"Good. Finish that, and then put this on."

She drank, using the time to remember exactly why Petro was waking her at this terribly early hour when she wasn't nearly slept out. He held her traveling costume draped over his arm. A common villager's skirt and blouse, with a brown starched apron and a knitted shawl. On her travels, she'd seen hundreds of women dressed similarly. Disappointment dragged her spirits down. Would she ever be able to wear her Brotherhood robes for more than a few hours at a time?

She sighed, then drained the brew. "I suppose Jothan is ready to go."

He nodded. "He is waiting in town. He left with the wagon a few moments ago."

"In town? Why isn't he waiting at the palace stables?"

Petro's eyebrows arched. "Apparently you've discovered at least one spy in the stables. Though he is no longer here, we thought it best if the two of you were not seen leaving together. In fact, we hope no one will notice you've gone in the confusion of battle preparations. One spy may lead to more, though I've searched every mind I encounter and haven't found any yet. You will take the child and meet Jothan at the blacksmith's near the gates." He narrowed his eyelids. "Do you know where it is?"

She nodded, then slipped behind the changing screen. The clothes were loose, but wearable. Upon emerging, she looked around and found the boots she'd worn during their escape from Otero. They were worn enough to be comfortable, and common enough to escape notice.

"Any suggestions as to what we should say when we get there?" She laced them snugly on her feet.

"Be persuasive. And honest. You'll think of the right words."

I hope so. The sentiment remained confined within her own mind. She wasn't sure she'd be able to strip the bitterness from her thought and didn't want him to know how unsure she was of their ability to persuade the Masters of the Brotherhood to even let them through the doors with the infant prince. To lend their aid in battle? They'd need a miracle to pull that off.

A soft rapping at her door announced the delivery of a tray of steaming food. Her mouth watered when she caught sight of broiled fish and spiced vegetables drenched with butter.

"Left over from last night's supper," Petro explained as she devoured the food. "I thought it best not to wake you."

She nodded without taking the time to answer. The meal tasted delicious. Even as an orphan in a poor village, she'd never gone hungry as often as she had the past few days. When the plate sat empty before her, she unashamedly used her finger to clean the last of the juices.

Petro watched with an amused expression. "We've loaded plenty of food on Jothan's wagon, so you can eat your fill along the way. But now you must leave."

Sighing, she stood and faced her master. She'd been so focused on her own worries that she'd given no thought for what he must be going through, preparing for the battle that would soon be thrust upon him. Fear stabbed a sharp dagger at her insides. He would be fighting against her birth father, this man who was the only real father she had ever known.

She grabbed his hands. "Please take care of yourself, Master Petro. These Oterans are ruthless."

He drew her to him in a warm embrace. "My dear, Jothan has told me something of your struggles in Otero. When you return, after we've defeated the Oterans, we'll take the time for a long talk, and you can tell me everything."

She returned his embrace, hoping they would have that

opportunity.

They left the bedchamber and slipped through the castle corridors. Arien scanned the thoughts of every guardsman they passed and knew Petro did, too. She heard many questions in those minds, but nothing subversive.

The wet nurse, whose thoughts were all of concern for her charge and sorrow at the parting, thrust a small, warm bundle into Arien's arms. "He's just eaten, the poor mite, and isn't taking well to the pouch at all. But he was so hungry he finally gulped down enough milk to put himself to sleep. Here." The woman handed Arien a leather bag that sloshed as she slung it over her shoulder. "That will last only a short while, and if he doesn't drink it all soon, you'll have to get him some fresh. He'll probably cry when you first offer him the pouch, but maybe it won't be so bad, since he's had it twice."

"How often should I feed him?" Anxiety washed over Arien. She'd cared for younger children often enough in the orphanage, but never a babe this tiny.

"He eats five or six times a day, a little at a time."

Astonished, she cast a disbelieving look at the wet nurse. "Five or six?"

The woman eyed her with something close to alarm, and Arien realized she'd somehow given herself away as a novice.

"But how will I know when to feed him?"

At that the nurse smiled. Arien took no comfort from her expression.

"He'll let you know," the woman assured her. "You and anyone else within earshot."

Petro interrupted. "We must hurry. Is there anything else she should know?"

The wet nurse shook her head, sad again. "His changing cloths are in this bag, and here are extra clothes."

She handed a second, larger bag to Petro, who eyed it suspiciously. "Nothing to mark him as a prince?"

The woman assured them the bag included only ordinary baby clothes. Then she folded back the soft woolen blanket in Arien's arms and gazed into the face of the sleeping infant. "Goodbye, little prince."

Arien looked at the tiny face. The prince's skin was pink,

with blue veins lining the miniature eyelids. His cheeks were round, and his tiny lips drawn into a rosy pout. They moved as he made slow sucking motions. She searched for something she could recognize, features reminiscent of Millard or of Sarana, but saw nothing familiar. He didn't look particularly regal, either. He looked like a sweet baby, not a prince.

She covered the infant's face and followed Petro through the twisting castle corridors. They finally emerged into the main courtyard. Night still gripped the sky, not even a hint of sunrise in the blackness above them. Guardsmen were stationed about, both on the ground and high up on the walls. An inky shadow near the gate became a horse as Petro steered her toward it.

As he secured the baby's bundle to the saddle, the man holding the animal's reins stepped forward and smiled at Arien. She caught sight of the face hidden inside a deep hood and bent her knees in an awkward curtsey. "Your Majesty."

King Mendel's hand pulled her up. "I'm disguised so that anyone who might be watching will have no reason to think I'm me." He tossed a patronizing grin toward Petro. "I thought it best to go along with the master on this one. Let me say goodbye to my grandson."

Arien handed the baby to him, and then allowed Petro to help her into the saddle as the king uncovered the tiny face. When she had the reins firmly in hand, King Mendel reluctantly handed the infant up to her.

"Take care of him." The emotion in his whisper struck her to the heart.

"I will."

From his expression, her promise was as important to the grandfather as to the king.

Petro stood looking up at her. "We've posted guardsmen inconspicuously along the streets of Kirklin and for a short distance on the shore. When you leave them behind, you'll be on your own. The guard has orders to make sure you are not followed, but to follow you themselves would be to announce your presence to anyone who might be watching."

"We'll be fine." For the king's benefit, she instilled her voice with more confidence than she felt.

Petro raised a hand in farewell. "Send word as soon as you can."

Arien nodded, then prodded the horse into motion with her knees.

She traveled through the town at a walking pace, conscious of the sleeping infant in her arms and Petro's warnings of the danger of galloping with her fragile bundle. Her mind, fully awake and much more alert than she could have hoped a short time ago, scanned the area around her. As Petro warned, she spotted guardsmen stationed in the shadows, but no one else was awake.

Jothan waited near the blacksmith shop, the wagon hitched and ready to go. She waved at him, even as she identified herself mentally. He lifted her and the baby from the horse's back and silently untied the packs from the saddle.

A guardsman stepped out of the shadows beside the smithy building and took the horse without a word. Jothan grinned toward Arien.

"Master Petro certainly instilled his instructions well. I've located six guardsmen within whispering distance and haven't been able to get a word out of any of them."

The baby clutched in her arms, Arien circled the wagon, examining it. A small, two-wheeled arrangement hitched to a sturdy animal that would have looked more natural pulling a plow. That would lend credence to their story of escape. Bundles and bags, and even a small chair, had been roped onto the wagon, as though they'd packed all their worldly possessions for the journey. She spied a plain but sturdy cradle near the front bench, well padded. Tied to the rear were two goats, both ready to be milked. Arien shook her head. One would have been plenty. Two would produce more milk than this tiny prince could possibly drink. Apparently Petro was willing to take no chances. She sighed and gave a little shrug. The Brotherhood would welcome the extra goat, no doubt.

She placed the sleeping prince in the cradle, padding him with a rolled blanket to keep him from being jostled against the sides, and then climbed up on the bench. Jothan leapt up beside her and grasped the lead. With a flick of his wrist, he prodded the animal toward the gate. They were on their way.

Twenty

Thaine, uncrowned King of Creighton, pushed his horse to near exhaustion. He had attempted to sleep at Kirklin Castle, but though his body had dutifully shut down, his mind refused. The resultant half-night of unconsciousness proved more draining than restful. The five guardsmen who rode with him cast looks at one another behind his back, but he didn't care. He ignored their whispers during the brief stops they convinced him to take, because he didn't care to hear their opinions. They probably thought him possessed.

I am *possessed.*

The pounding of his mount's hooves kicked up clouds of dust from the road. The royal banner, proclaiming him to be on an urgent errand for the king, fluttered wildly above him. An overwhelming urgency to find his guardsmen possessed him. He *must* get them back to Kirklin Castle. Though he could not possibly return before the Oterans landed, not one more man than necessary would fall in the attempt to hold the northern soldiers to the beach. If he had to drive himself to the brink of death, he would do it.

Behind the urgency, feeding the exhaustion with one agonizing memory after another, lay the grief he did not have time to express. He must not remember the pride on his father's face when Thaine was awarded the rank of Captain of the King's Guard. He must fight against visions of Roddy as a baby, giggling when he threw a ball that hit his father square in the nose. He must ignore the pain that threatened to overwhelm him when he realized that he would never teach his son to hold a shield or shoot a bow or wield a sword.

Instead, he rode, his thoughts focused on the sweat that poured from his body and the dust that choked him.

They thundered through the villages bordering the road running from Corral to Kirklin, halting only when they needed to change horses if the village was big enough to provide that service. Fear lay heavy on the few villagers they encountered. News of the invasion had spread quickly. Fresh mounts were scarce, for most had been ridden east carrying the men that seemed to pour toward Kirklin in droves. They passed countless numbers on the road without stopping, their banner announcing to everyone that they must not be delayed.

Because of their midnight start and their madcap pace, they neared Corral just after mid-day, before the sun had attained its full, stifling heat. Thaine's eyelids drooped, and his arms could barely hold the reins. If he didn't stop here, he would collapse. What use would he be in a battle if he drove himself to exhaustion? Yet the fear and grief that clutched at his belly were real and gripped him in fists so firm he despaired of ever breaking loose.

When he saw the multitude of men approaching, Thaine thought his eyes had failed him at last. He must be hallucinating. They wore blue uniforms, the colors of his own guard. For a moment, despair nearly bested him. He reigned in his horse and stopped dead in the road, staring through bleary, blood-stained eyes.

But the sounds of their approach were real, and within a moment, his own men surrounded him. His old friend and fellow Captain, Niall Teodor, leapt from his horse to kneel in the dust before Thaine.

"Your Majesty."

Thaine almost fell off his own horse dismounting and immediately Niall rose to lend a strong arm for support.

"Niall, Niall." Thaine nearly collapsed against his friend. "Were you there? Did you see my father, my son, as they died?"

Niall closed his eyes and gave a slow nod.

Thaine drew a shuddering breath and was about to speak again when someone ran up beside him and grabbed him roughly by the sleeve.

"Where is she?" a loud, female voice demanded of him. "What have you done with Lady Arien?"

Confused, he focused on a large, broad-faced woman upon whom he had never before laid eyes. Behind her another female approached, vaguely familiar, but his mind had stopped functioning and he couldn't remember where he'd seen her. When he attempted to answer the one who still held his arm in a tight grip, the world began to swim. He felt a flash of irritation when he realized that he was about to pass out, just when he needed to talk to these people. But he couldn't help himself.

His knees buckled, and King Thaine succumbed to darkness.

"Is he awake yet?" Thaine heard someone ask.

"Shh," answered a deep female voice. "He needs sleep."

His eyes flew open as memory pressed in on his groggy mind. He tried to focus, but darkness surrounded him, broken only dimly by the light from a distant lantern.

With an effort, he wrenched his head sideways and found himself staring directly into a very large female posterior.

Great heavens, he must be hallucinating!

"Where am I?"

Not a very original question, but the best he could come up with at the moment, and the one most pressing on his mind.

The posterior turned, and a woman bent over him. Her face loomed in giant proportions above his own, vaguely familiar. The same woman who had approached him on the road.

"It's too soon." She frowned, her tone scolding. "You should sleep until morning, maybe longer."

Another voice intruded. "Your Majesty."

The woman turned to glare at someone, but Niall sidestepped her and came to kneel beside Thaine. Thaine struggled to sit up and take stock of his surroundings. He lay upon a pallet on the ground, surrounded by the thick canvas walls of a guard command tent. The distant light came from a lamp in one corner, and beyond the open tent flap he glimpsed a pitch-black sky.

He dug at his eyes in an attempt to make them focus properly. "How long have I been sleeping?"

"It's just past the first watch," Niall replied, while the woman backed up to stand, glowering, in a corner.

"Too long!" Thaine grabbed Niall's arm, squeezing. "We must get to Kirklin, Niall! The Oterans are attacking by sea, may be landing even now."

Niall nodded. "We know, and Commander Norval has sent the bulk of our forces there already. Justen and Barthel were with me when his orders came, and they've gone to assemble their companies. If they haven't arrived in Kirklin already, they will soon. We have only a handful of men here with us."

Thaine's grip tightened. "Every man counts, Niall. Every man. We must go."

Thaine tried to struggle to his feet, but the woman in the corner stepped forward and, with one shove, pushed him back onto the pallet. "Not so fast, Your Majesty."

Though she addressed him with his royal title, he detected no hint of softness in her tone.

He looked up into her stern face. "Who *are* you?"

She drew herself. "My name is Illari, recently in the employ of Lord Jerolin Arien, of the Oteran House of Arien."

Ah. Of course. Now everything made sense. Thaine relaxed back onto the pallet. "Arien and Jothan told me about you. So, you and Beryle made it safely to Eshtaol and met with Quinn there. You warned my guard, got them marching toward Kirklin before I could even give the order." He smiled up at her. "I owe you a debt of gratitude, as does King Mendel of Hamlin. You may have made it possible for us to save our kingdoms."

"Lady Arien is safe?"

Thaine nodded, and her expression softened.

"Is she there, at this Kirklin Castle?"

"No, at the moment she is on the road somewhere north of here. But she's safe enough, for she's traveling with Brother Jothan." He rubbed a hand over his mouth, the seriousness of Arien's situation pressing in on him anew. "At least, I pray she is safe. She has the first prince of two kingdoms in her keeping."

"Your Majesty?" Niall's voice, startled, held a dozen unspoken questions.

Thaine shook his head, and clapped Niall's shoulder, a curiously light feeling suddenly sweeping over him. For the first time in many days, he spied a glimmer of hope in the dark horizon that stretched before them all.

"It's a long tale, Niall, and one yet without an ending. But, thanks to the two of you, I have hopes it will turn out well. If you will have someone bring me something to eat, we'll talk." He looked from the man to Illari. "And you, Madame, along with the good Beryle, must prepare to leave again. At the moment, the best place for someone of your obvious, uh, protective abilities, is the Hall of the Brotherhood of Power."

The baby's cries pulled Arien out of a deep sleep, and she groaned. Hungry again? She Perceived the infant's thoughts, and sensed waves of discomfort and intense hunger. Arien groaned and shoved at Jothan's sleeping body.

"Get up," she said, her voice irritable. "I'll change him, you milk the goat."

Jothan struggled to his knees and crawled from beneath the wagon, more asleep than awake. Still groaning, she pulled herself out of her coverings and into the pre-dawn chill. They had camped beside a seldom-used path in the middle of a wide, open plain. She reached for the baby, and his cries stopped the moment she touched him.

Though he had not yet been named, his Naming Day having been delayed in order to save his life, Arien and Jothan found it awkward to refer to him constantly as "the baby," and had begun calling him Milo. It wasn't a princely name, but it *was* taken in part from his dead father, and he seemed to respond to it.

Milo had thoughts, strongly tainted with emotion and physical desire, but without logic or any real form. Arien fought the impulse to do a little mental "teaching," aware that any tinkering on her part would influence the little prince's developing mind. Jothan was fascinated with him, and Arien kept a close watch on them, certain that Jothan would attempt to test him for Power the moment she fell lax.

"But this is so interesting," Jothan had told her enthusiastically. "I've never believed the old masters when they said Power was something we are born with. I've always thought it could be taught, if we just got a child early enough. This one is perfect."

Arien leveled him with a stern look. "You are not going to experiment on the first prince of two kingdoms. I won't allow it."

He agreed, though with obvious reluctance.

She got to her feet, holding Milo tightly against her chest to keep him warm, and pulled out a clean set of changing cloths. When she exposed his bare skin to the cold air he whimpered, but apparently wasn't uncomfortable enough to wail.

By the time she'd cleaned him and wrapped him in a fresh blanket, Jothan had his milk in the pouch. Milo sucked with energy at the flexible nipple while Jothan added fuel to the dying fire.

"We should arrive by midday." He arranged a pan of water over glowing embers.

Nerves fluttered in her stomach. "Are you worried?"

He tilted his head as he skewered a piece of rabbit left

from last night's supper and propped it on the spit.

"A little anxious," he admitted. "I remember the old masters being a pretty rigid bunch. I haven't been to the Hall in a long time, but I doubt they've changed much."

"Believe me," Arien sourly assured him, "they haven't. Especially Master Parnell."

His shoulders heaved in a laugh. "I was always half afraid of Master Avram."

Arien smiled. "I know what you mean. But when he tested me, I realized he wasn't as bad as I'd always thought."

He straightened. "Avram tested you?"

Arien nodded, and Jothan whistled. "Then maybe I'm not anxious after all. If old Avram actually loosened up enough to pass a woman, things have changed."

"Not that much," she told him.

Milo slept again, and Arien set the pouch aside. She laid him back in his cradle while Jothan dished out a pan of grain for the goats.

"How do you think it's going back there?" Arien sprinkled teaspice leaves into the warming water.

"The fighting's started, for sure. The Oterans couldn't have been a day from landing when we left, and that was three days ago. Even if your father chose the diplomatic route and sent messages ashore first, and then waited for King Mendel to respond, that would have only taken another day. I hope Commander Jarvis is able to hold them off until Thaine's guardsmen arrive."

Arien did her best to ignore a stab of discomfort at the mention of her father. "Do you think Thaine has made it back to Kirklin yet?"

Jothan shook his head. "Don't see how he could. His Guard is probably spread out all over the kingdom, and it will take a while to round them up. Jarvis's best hope now is the villagers."

Arien stirred the steaming liquid in the pan. "I wonder if Beryle and Illari made it to Eshtaol."

"I hope so."

They fell silent, each of them lost in their own thoughts. They ate their breakfast quickly, then worked together to clear the camp site with the ease of two people who have become accustomed to one another's company. The sun rose to find them on the path, heading northeast.

The rest of the journey passed quickly. Before Arien realized how close they were, the wagon rounded a bend in the forest, and she caught sight of the Hall. Its four stories towered over the closest trees, the Brotherhood's encircled triangle standing out clearly above the huge double doors.

As they drew near, the doors burst open and two women ran out, followed more sedately by an old master in the usual black robes. Arien recognized Illari and Beryle. But how could they be here? In the next moment, she was pulled off the wagon and smothered in Illari's fleshy embrace.

"You've made it at last. We were ready to send out searchers," Beryle informed her.

Her brain numb, Arien could only shake her head. "You knew we were coming?"

Beryle nodded. "We'll tell you all about it inside." She lowered her voice. "And this is a strange place, don't you think? Men and boys everywhere, not a woman in sight, and most of them acting like they're scared to death I'll speak to them. And speaking of speaking, they don't. It's like a death house in there."

Arien laughed. "There's plenty of talking going on, Beryle, just not the kind you can hear. And I've no doubt you're the subject of most of it."

Arien turned to Illari, who had found Milo and wasted no time in retrieving him from his cradle.

"The little darling!" The big woman unfolded the blankets and checked his changing cloths, then leveled a disapproving stare on Arien. "He's wet."

Arien held up her hands to ward off the verbal attack. "The child wets constantly. *You* try and keep up with him."

Illari re-wrapped Milo and, cuddling him close, headed into the Hall. As she crossed the threshold, she addressed Jothan over her shoulder. "Bring me his cloths and other things. Right quick, too."

Jothan gazed after her retreating back, bemused. "Nice to see you, too."

He leapt off the wagon as Arien hurried forward to greet Master Thaddeus, who'd been standing to one side during the reunion. She hugged the old man warmly.

"You are exactly the same," she told him, smiling.

"I am. And I'm eager to hear why you've returned, and with the grandson of King Mendel."

Arien drew back to look at him, startled. *"You know who he is?"*

"Of course. Your friends arrived yesterday and told us to expect you. They also brought news of the invasion, and I can tell you that the idea of harboring a prince within our walls has caused much debate around here."

"Get ready for more," Arien warned.

"Master Thaddeus!" Jothan's enthusiastic shout preceded him as he ran around the wagon to grasp the old master in a bone-crushing embrace. Arien feared for Master Thaddeus's frail frame, but he thumped Jothan's back with energy. They stood beaming at one another, conversing mentally, but to all appearances simply looking at one another in silence. Thaddeus gave a burst of laughter, and thumped Jothan again, then they started toward the Hall.

"See what I mean?" Eyeing them, Beryle shook her head. "It's like that everywhere. Spooky, that's what I think."

Arien laughed and looped her arm through Beryle's, guiding her toward the Hall.

They were met by a quickly gathered assembly of black-robed brothers and masters. To Arien's intense pleasure, Sinclare and Dorian greeted her with an embrace.

Master Avram awarded her a warm smile. "Welcome home, my dear."

"Thank you, sir."

Arien detected Master Parnell watching from the doorway and directed a smile his way. But he turned his head. She sighed. At least he didn't scowl at her.

Jothan, handing the baby's bag to Illari, raised his voice and spoke to the rapidly swelling group. "We have urgent business to discuss and no time to waste."

Master Thaddeus nodded toward Beryle and Illari. "We've had some warning of your news with the arrival of our guests. I suggest we convene a meeting immediately."

In answer, Parnell marched toward the large meeting room beyond the dining hall. A stream of black-robed men followed.

Illari, her gaze circling the assembled, issued an order in a voice that brooked no argument. "You there, boy. Get outside and see to the wagon. And you, bring the child's cradle to my room and see that the goats are fed and watered."

Several boys leapt up to do her bidding, and Arien suppressed a grin. Many of these young men could barely remember their own mothers. Clearly Illari made an impression on them. The looks they gave her as they hurried by were tinged with awe.

Illari turned to her. "I'll take the babe to my room while you have your talk. We'll catch up later." Her gaze softened. "I'm glad you're safe, child."

She mounted the stairs, cooing at the living bundle in her arms.

"Will they be talking in that meeting?" Beryle gazed after the backs of the disappearing brothers. "Or just thinking at each other?"

Arien laughed. "Some of both, probably."

The maid shook her head, lips twisted in disgust. "Then I'll be in the kitchen until you're finished. I've been trying to teach that Brother Bayard a thing or two, but a more stubborn man I've never met. Now he'll be busy, and I can have the place to myself. I'll show him what a decent meal is like."

She scooted off toward the kitchen, and Arien, grinning, joined the others.

Jothan had seated himself at the head of the long table and motioned for her to take the chair beside him.

As she slipped into her seat, she performed a quick tally of the faces around the table. Thirty-one masters and brothers present, probably everyone in residence at the Hall. Most she recognized, while some were new faces. Possibly masters recently returned with new trainees.

The moment Master Sinclare shut the door, Jothan wasted no time. Every eye focused on him, and Arien sagged against her chair-back. Letting him be the primary speaker and persuader suited her just fine.

"Thank you, members of the Brotherhood, for allowing us to address you on such short notice," he began. "I don't know what you've heard already, but apparently you know some of the events which have brought us here."

Master Avram answered. "We know of the deaths of the king, the princess and Prince Roddy of Creighton. Brother Federk, who makes his home near Tadmoure, brought that news a few days ago." He glanced toward a man Arien didn't know. "And yesterday our female guests arrived in the company of two guardsmen, with news of the death of Prince Millard and Princess Sarana, and of the impending invasion. The ladies have described your journey into Otero."

A pang of anxiety niggled at her. She'd hoped they could break the news of the invasion. The initial shock might have rendered them more easily persuaded to lend aid.

Jothan appeared undisturbed. "Then you've heard the most important news, though there is one interesting tidbit which you may not have heard. While in Otero, Brother Arien and I met a man trained in the ways of Power."

That grabbed their attention. Spines stiffened around the table.

"They have an organization like ours?" Master Calder asked.

Jothan shook his head. "No, he was trained here. His name was Addison."

Shock registered on every face. Many of them would have known and worked with Addison.

"So that's where he went," Master Parnell mumbled.

Jothan nodded. "He went to Otero, where he made himself available to the Oteran king. In fact, he claimed to be the mastermind behind this invasion. He planned to rule the Twin Kingdoms through the Oteran lords he influenced."

Anger darkened several expressions, while others looked pained or even ill. To prevent such a misuse of Power was the reason the Brotherhood existed.

"He must be stopped," someone halfway down the left side of the table muttered.

"Oh, he has been." Jothan issued a humorless laugh. "He

died of a cracked skull while preventing my attempt to rescue Arien from her father's house."

"You attacked him?" Master Sinclare queried.

While at the same moment Master Avram burst out with, "Her *father's* house?"

The weight of many eyes fixed on Arien, and she suppressed the urge to squirm. Obviously Beryle and Illari had not told them *everything* that happened in Otero.

Jothan glanced down at her, and she raised her eyebrows. He winked before continuing.

"I didn't attack him. It was one of your guests. Illari, it turns out, was also Arien's nurse as an infant before her mother fled Otero to save her life. And Illari was not about to let anyone harm Arien, Power or not. But please don't tell her Addison died. I didn't want to burden her with the knowledge she'd killed someone, so she is under the impression we left him unconscious." He glanced down at Arien. "I'll let Arien tell you about her family later."

"My dear," Master Thaddeus said privately to Arien, *"what a time you've had."*

"You have no idea," she replied with a shudder.

"Let us get on to King Mendel's request concerning the babe."

Master Parnell's voice did nothing to comfort Arien. He glared the length of the table at Jothan, his expression stern. Must the man disagree with everything?

Sinclare leaned forward and rested an arm on the table while addressing Jothan and Arien. "The ladies and the guard who escorted them here have told us why you travel with the infant prince. We've discussed nothing else since their arrival." He glanced at Parnell. "Our opinions are mixed."

Master Thaddeus stood and surprised everyone by pounding his fist upon the table. "We cannot turn away a helpless child. Especially not this child."

"We can't interfere with affairs of state," Tirrell insisted. "The Brotherhood must remain impartial, as we have been since the beginning."

"Don't be an idiot," Thaddeus snapped. "This is a special circumstance."

Their arguments had the feel of having been repeated often, and as far as Arien could see, no one looked close to convincing the other.

"We should bring up Master Petro's request," she told Jothan.

"Get ready for some real fireworks." He raised an arm to attract attention.

"I sense the issue has been discussed at length. But there is another, more pressing matter at hand. Brother Arien and I were asked by Master Petro to present a second request." He cleared his throat in the first sign of nervousness he'd displayed thus far. He glanced down at her, and she smiled her support. "Documents we obtained in Otero list the number of soldiers on those fighting ships at eighteen hundred."

Judging by the shocked expressions, the number of attackers had not been previously given to them.

Jothan continued. "Hamlin's Guard numbers just over three hundred men. By now we hope they've been joined by Creighton's five hundred." He paused for a breath, letting his audience absorb the numbers.

Brother Medwin raised a tentative hand. "I understood the guardsman who escorted the ladies to say that villagers are also joining the battle."

Jothan nodded. "We picked up thirty or so on our way down the eastern coast, and word is spreading. I think we may be able to add another few hundred at the most."

Watching their faces, she was satisfied with the deep concern she saw on most of them.

Good. It's a serious matter, about which they should *be concerned.*

"But that's only a thousand men," Brother Simon said, stating the obvious.

Jothan nodded. "It is. And most not trained or even properly armed. Of course, there is the benefit of familiar territory, but only half our men will have that advantage. I think it's obvious any effort the Twin Kingdoms put forth is doomed to almost certain failure."

Jothan was not given the chance to continue. An outraged Master Parnell stood, drew himself up to his full height, and interrupted. "I know where you're going with this. That… that reprobate, Petro, wants us to join the battle! He wants us to use Power against the Oterans."

All eyes turned toward them, and Arien dared not look up at Jothan.

"*Quick, isn't he?*" Jothan sent to her. "*Feel free to jump in any time. I agreed to do this, but I didn't agree to do it alone.*"

"*Sorry,*" she replied, "*but you've done splendidly thus far.*"

Resigned to setting herself up as a martyr, Arien stood and faced Master Parnell with what she hoped was a calm expression. "That is the request we've brought." The man drew breath to cut her off, and she raised her voice. "We are the only chance Hamlin has of surviving this attack."

Master Sinclare spoke next, and his tone, though apologetic, held no sympathy. "We understand the difficulty. But both of you know as well as anyone in this room that the reason for the existence of the Brotherhood is to control Power, not to misuse it."

Jothan stomped a foot. "We are not suggesting a misuse of Power. We are suggesting that we use every option available to defend ourselves. And be warned that if the Oterans take Hamlin, the Brotherhood will fall to them sooner or later."

"Not a misuse of Power?" Master Dorian shook his head. "You are asking us to kill people and that's not misusing Power? It goes against everything the Brotherhood stands for."

The statement settled on the group.

Drawing a breath, Arien voiced a quiet argument. "If you don't, those same people will kill innocents by the hundreds." She looked around the table. "Don't think you'll escape, either. I'm sure Addison has given their king plenty of ideas about what can be done with the Brotherhood. You'll become slaves to him, or more likely be killed yourself."

"No one without Power can kill us or force us to do anything we don't want to do," Master Avram said, with just a touch of conceit.

Arien rounded on him. "Oh, so it is permissible to use

Power to defend yourselves, but not to defend innocent people from certain slaughter." She lifted her chin. "How very *humanitarian* of you."

The master had the grace to look embarrassed and would not meet her eye.

She regained control of her irritation before speaking again. "The Brotherhood has always kept itself isolated and for good reason. But it's time to change that. I know some of you don't like change." She purposefully did not look toward Master Parnell. "It's hard to break away from the things we've always done, the things that are comfortable. It's even harder to break away from ideas or beliefs we've always held. And it's frightening to realize that you've spent your whole life believing in something, wanting something, and then watch that thing slip away from you. I *know* it is." She poured conviction into her tone. "There comes a time when you must face those beliefs, and consider the possibility that maybe, just maybe, they need to change."

She gazed around the table. This was not going at all as she planned. How could she ever convey to these men the depth of her feelings? And how could Petro have thought they would listen to anything she, a mere girl, had to say?

Jothan placed his hand over hers and gave a comforting squeeze. She sent him a sideways grimace.

Every eye around the table focused on her. She drew a fortifying breath. "Sometimes change is forced on us, and now is one of those times. Change *is* in store for the Brotherhood, like it or not. If we do nothing, it will come to us in the form of a ruthless Oteran king. Or we can meet it head-on and choose to change in a way that will protect the lives of innocent people." She rested both hands on the table and leaned forward. "Isn't that what we're supposed to do? Protect innocent people?"

She stopped, looking desperately around the room. Were her words reaching anyone?

"That was very good," Jothan told her.

"I don't know. No one is jumping up to pack their travel bags. Uh oh. Look whose turn it is now."

Master Parnell stood slowly, his expression thoughtful.

Arien braced herself for a verbal attack, but at his first words her jaw slackened with surprise.

"I agree with the girl." He looked not at her but at Masters Sinclare, Avram, Dorian, and Thaddeus, one after another. "Let us all remember for a moment, the reason our founder established the Brotherhood. Was it not to protect innocents against the inadvertent misuse of Power? Is that not the reason we place such emphasis on control, so that innocents will not be harmed?"

Nods all around, but no one interrupted.

"We have focused on Power of the mind, because that is what Olney Devland focused on. But is it not the intent of our organization, the underlying goal, to protect people against the misuse of *all* power?" He looked down at the table, his features fluid. "It seems to me that this Oteran king is misusing the great power he has available—military power—and innocent people will die because of it." His hands clenched into fists as his expression hardened. "We cannot, in all conscience, allow that to happen. We must use whatever resources we have available to stop this slaughter."

He sat, a satisfied smile curving his lips.

"Well!" Jothan leaned back in his chair, his thought flooded with surprise. *"I must say, I never expected that."*

"Me, either. Having him on our side helps."

"True, but it's not a sure thing. I still see a lot of unconvinced expressions."

She smothered a sigh. When they arrived, she'd anticipated an early night in a real bed, without having to worry about being killed in her sleep or awakened to feed and change a crying baby. But with one glance at the stubborn expressions worn by many of the influential masters, she resigned herself to yet another late night.

Twenty-One

Master Petro wiped the sweat from his forehead. If only he could change into dry clothes. His shirt dripped with perspiration, and his breeches clung to his legs. This attack had lasted far longer than the others, and he neared the end of his endurance. If he didn't sleep soon, he wouldn't be able to Perceive anything, much less issue a Command.

A volley of blazing bits of oil-soaked wood sailed overhead, drawing his gaze upward. They had gotten another catapult working. He sent a Movement to squelch as much of the fire as he could, leaving the rest to be dealt with by the townspeople who ran in that direction. Then he shifted his Perceptive sense outward, toward the Oteran troops on the eastern shore from which the fiery blast had come. He located the catapult by the thoughts of those soldiers piling a new load on the sling and sent another Movement. Their anger, flooded with frustration as the weapon collapsed before their eyes, gave him a moment of grim pleasure.

The Oterans held the shore circling all sides of Kirklin. They had attempted to raise blockades, but Petro simply reduced each one to a pile of rubble as soon as it neared completion. While this had frustrated the attack somewhat, they now used the piles of ruined blockades as shelter and the siege continued. The southerners, those from both Twin Kingdoms, had been effectively trapped inside the walled town for a day and a half.

"Release!"

Commander Jarvis' voice rang in the air, and Petro looked up in time to see the return volley of fire sail from the parapet. Another trebuchet sat atop the castle's keep, also active at the moment. Petro watched a double load soar over the wall. The larger winch gave the weapon a greater range, and he hurried to a window slit to see if the load hit its mark. A cheer went up from the keep as a handful of Oteran soldiers scattered mere seconds before the flaming load hit their shelter—a pile of wood and debris on the wide street at the end of the natural causeway, leading from Kirklin across the lake to the shore.

The Oterans' single-armed catapult's aim was just as accurate, and Petro winced as screams from soldiers ablaze reached him.

Jarvis lay an arm across the shoulders of the guardsman controlling the weapon and whispered a few quiet words before he climbed down a ladder. Petro walked over to him, taking advantage of a lull in the fighting.

"It's never easy, killing a man," Jarvis told him, shaking his head.

Petro sighed. "There's not a man, woman, or child here who hasn't learned that lesson in the past few days. Those of us who are left."

Jarvis' lips tightened at the reminder of the hundreds of fallen guardsmen and villagers. Petro closed his eyes, a pang of regret striking him anew. How many men had he personally killed since the Oterans landed? True, he had not killed anyone by direct mind-to-mind attack, but the weapons he'd guided had caused their deaths just as surely. If he could bring himself to kill individuals with Power, it might be a kinder death.

He shuddered. Nothing could persuade him to do that. Nothing. His first attempt, after being called to the initial battle on the beach, had been enough to teach him that. The soldier had been a young Oteran, barely more than a boy, terrified and following his orders blindly. His arm moved mechanically, battling a Creighton guardsman with a sword, but his active thoughts had been saturated with longing for his home, his parents, and a girl with dark curls and a dimpled chin.

Petro had turned away, unable to watch while the guardsman's sword found a break in the boy's defense and accomplished what Petro could not bring himself to do.

Since then, his assistance had been in the form of attacks on objects of war, not people. True, people died just the same. He had Moved the wood in the bottom of a skiff carrying soldiers and a large projectile weapon to the beach and watched as the boat sank. Some of those soldiers made it back to their ship and some to shore, no doubt.

But not all of them.

At least he hadn't had to Perceive their thoughts in the moment of their deaths.

"Any news of King Thaine?" Jarvis' hopeful question broke into Petro's gruesome memories.

Petro shook his head. "I've not sensed even a glimmer."

"I hope he can get what's left of his guard regrouped soon. We can wait out a siege, but I don't know what the rest of those Oterans are doing to the surrounding towns and villages. Maybe they've already started marching toward Corral."

"I haven't caught news of that in any of the soldiers I've Perceived." Petro glanced over his shoulder, toward the wall and the shore beyond it. "Their thoughts tell me their commander has set up a command post in an area unknown even to them, though it's not far from here. Far enough to be safe from me, evidently. Perhaps by now he has fallen back to the beach."

The Commander, Petro knew from those minds he had Perceived, was none other than Arien's father, Lord Jerolin Arien. Lord Jerolin had recognized that someone was destroying their weapons and sabotaging their plans from a distance.

He obviously possessed knowledge of Power and had been prepared for its use.

Thanks, no doubt, to Addison.

Jerolin had quickly retreated with the bulk of his army and all his captains to a distance where Petro could not sense their presence.

"Incoming arrows."

The warning shout came from the parapet, and everyone in the vicinity dove for the nearest shelter. Petro followed Jarvis around the back of a small inn which had been commandeered at the beginning of the siege, as had the rest of the town's buildings near the wall. He slumped against the wood and shut his eyes.

"I was about to remark that the attack appeared to be slowing down." His voice sounded tired, even to his own ears. He looked up with a wry grin and saw Commander Jarvis watching him through narrowed eyelids.

"You're exhausted," the man announced.

Petro shrugged. "A few hours' sleep yesterday hasn't gone far, but it's more than some have gotten."

"Take a rest, man. The king did, a few hours back, and well-deserved, too. If you wear yourself into exhaustion, we'll have a hard time defending ourselves against those catapults they keep putting back together. You're my best weapon."

Petro tried to laugh, though he was too tired to generate a sound. Jarvis was right. If he didn't rest soon, he'd fall unconscious, and then it would be days before he could be useful again. A few hours now, while this battle was surely winding toward an end, would be prudent.

His thoughts were interrupted by another shout from the parapet.

"Commander! There's smoke from the north, and the Oterans are leaving!"

Petro and Jarvis ran for the nearest window slit. Jarvis arrived first and shoved his face as far into the slit as it would go. Petro, being the taller of the two, rose up on his toes to see over Jarvis' head.

The last of the Oteran soldiers disappeared into the northern tree line at a run. In the distance, a huge cloud of smoke billowed upward. Petro attempted to Perceive the cause of that smoke, but the source lay too far away to Perceive. Both men drew back from the slit to look at one another. Then Jarvis started toward the ladder, clouting Petro on the arm as he did so.

"Get some sleep while you can," he said, then shouted upward. "Owen, get me four scouts. I want to know what's going on over there. Maybe King Thaine has rallied."

Sleep? Not likely now. He followed Jarvis to the ladder.

He placed his foot on the bottom rung, and then another shout from above stopped him.

"There's someone coming from the trees, leading a horse. He's headed this way."

Petro sent his Perception toward the shore. Relief washed over him like a tidal wave when he encountered a mind he knew, and knew well.

"Master Petro!" came Arien's thought.

"Thank goodness you're safe child. But did you bring help?"

Arien's answering thought reached him, flooded with satisfaction. *"We did. Plenty of it. Twenty-six masters and forty-seven brothers."*

"Forty-seven brothers?" Had lack of sleep and strain affected his mind? *"Where did you find—"*

"Everywhere. Many in Corral and every other village or town within a distance to travel quickly. Master Parnell has been wonderful, gathering support wherever we went."

That settled it. His abilities *were* failing. *"Did you say Parnell?"*

"Yes. And we met Thaine and a company of Creighton guardsmen, and they've been watching the Oteran camp. The attack has started. Come on! I don't want to miss anything!"

Above him, the guardsmen were discussing the possible identity of this strange, lone man on the far shore.

A voice drifted down to him. "... a trap, Commander. We should shoot him."

"No," Petro shouted. "Jarvis, you fool, that's Lady Arien. She's brought help, and King Thaine is attacking the Oteran camp even now. Come on, man. It's time to move."

Jarvis turned to squint over the wall, shielding his eyes with a hand.

"Wave at Commander Jarvis, my dear. He thinks you might be a trap."

Jarvis gave an exclamation, and Petro leaped from the ladder toward the nearest window slit. He grinned at the sight of Arien's slim figure, dressed in her boy's clothing once again, waving her thick braid above her head while the sun glinted fiercely off the fiery red. A cheer rose from the guardsmen on the parapet.

"What's all the noise about?"

Petro turned to see King Mendel coming down the center of the street. He was flanked by his guard, his hair waving wildly about his head and his eyes still more than half asleep.

"It's Arien, Your Majesty," Petro shouted over the cheers. "She's just returned from the Brotherhood and has brought seventy-three men of Power to fight the Oterans."

Petro ran toward the gate, eager to join Arien and find the others. Then he stopped, whirling back to the king. "Oh! And King Thaine has returned with his guardsmen. He's fighting the Oterans now."

"Jarvis!"

Petro didn't wait to hear what the king said to his commander. He arrived at the gate and pounded, shouting for someone to open it and let him out.

He lost precious moments convincing the gatekeeper that it was safe to open the gate, and by the time the giant doors swung wide, a company of guardsmen had assembled in the street. Jarvis approached leading two horses, followed by the king mounted on his own chestnut bay.

"You might need this." Jarvis tossed a set of reins to Petro.

Petro lost no time mounting and following Jarvis and King Mendel through the gate and over the causeway to the far shore. Arien waited, still mounted, on the other side.

"You look tired," she said as he neared.

"I am *tired, but I wouldn't miss this for all the gold in the Twin Kingdoms. Do you know where you're going?"*

Arien nodded.

"Then lead on, my dear."

Arien prodded her horse forward, giving a half-bow from the saddle as she approached the king.

"Your grandson is safe, Your Majesty. I left him in the care of a capable nurse and a watchful master."

Petro raised his eyebrows. Who had stayed behind to guard the little prince?

She answered his unspoken question. "They drew lots to see who would stay, and Master Dorian lost. He wasn't pleased about it, either."

She turned again in her saddle and kneed her horse forward. Petro fell in behind her, with the rest of them strung out in a line, following. She set a pace as fast as the sparse forest would allow. While they rode, she fed his ravenous mind with details about the meeting at the Brotherhood.

"...and if Master Parnell hadn't spoken up in our favor, I don't know how matters would have turned out. The discussion went on most of the night, but at last everyone agreed. Once they reached that decision, protecting the prince was never even discussed again."

Petro shook his head. If only he could have been there to witness that meeting.

They rode for a quarter of an hour before sounds of the ongoing battle reached their ears. Petro sent his Perceptive sense ahead and detected a cluster of people, all of them extremely active. The Brotherhood had joined the battle, and their presence was evident. Thoughts darted here and there, dancing between one another like sparks spraying from a forest fire. Afraid any attempt at conversation on his part would distract someone at an inopportune moment, Petro resisted the urge to announce his presence.

Following Arien's lead, they came upon a camp site, smoke still billowing into the sky. The remnants of a hastily constructed fort lay in burning embers, and the smell of scorched flesh bore witness to the gruesome sight of what Petro estimated were no less than a hundred half-charred bodies within the burning wooden structure. He squelched the remaining flames before the surrounding forest caught.

The battle had shifted a surprising distance to the east. Commander Jarvis, now easily able to follow the visible signs of combat by a trail of dead and dying bodies, urged his horse and his company in that direction, leaving Arien, Petro, and King Mendel to follow.

"My father is there," Arien told him as they turned their horses to follow the guardsmen.

"I know. I've Perceived him."

An ache in the vicinity of his heart thudded at the pain clearly displayed on her face. If only there were something he could say to comfort her. But what that may be, he didn't know. They rode in silence.

The noise of the fighting grew louder as they neared the battle, but the beach took him by surprise. He hadn't realized how far east they'd come in the forest, but suddenly the ocean lay in front of him, and a vicious battle raged between him and the salty waves.

The fighting here was too close for horses. Swords clashed, knives sliced, shields deflected deadly blows. Dead or wounded soldiers littered the ground, so many that those still on their feet were in constant danger of tripping. Everywhere Petro looked, he spied villagers interspersed with the blue uniforms of the Creighton guardsmen, the grey ones of Hamlin, and an abundance of red-clad Oterans.

And black. Scattered here and there throughout the fighting were the black robes of the Brotherhood, their silver medallions flashing in the sunlight. Compared to the number of guardsmen and soldiers, their number appeared small. But their work bore evidence to their presence. Wasted weapons covered the ground, swords gone dull with rust, maces with wooden handles splintered into pieces, armor in shreds.

As Petro watched, a blue-clad guardsman raised his shield to deflect a blow, and the Oterans' heavy steel sword shattered upon impact. The look of surprise on both faces might have been comical in less gruesome surroundings. The guardsman recovered, made effective use of his own weapon, and the Oteran soon joined the others oozing blood onto the sands beneath the feet of the combatants. Sensing the use of Power, Petro turned in time to see a vaguely familiar brother turn away from the sight. The young man wore a sickened but determined expression as he searched for another place where his Power could be used to advantage.

An answering stab of repulsion assaulted Petro as his nose registered the smell of freshly spilt blood. His nostrils flared and he fought a wave of nausea. He turned at a choking noise from behind and saw that King Mendel also appeared similarly affected.

"Your Majesty," Petro said, "you shouldn't be here. It's not safe."

In answer, Mendel nodded toward the center of the fighting. Following his gaze, Petro caught sight of King Thaine surrounded by four Oteran soldiers. The battle raged thick all around him, his movements hampered by the press of soldiers and guardsmen.

As Petro watched, the sand gave way beneath the feet of two of the soldiers. The Oterans went down, startled and thrown off balance, their feet sunk suddenly to the knee in a rift of soft sand barely an arm-length wide. Thaine seized the advantage and slayed them both as he leapt over the rift to a place where relative freedom of movement was possible.

Beside him, Arien gave a satisfied grunt, and Petro looked toward her, startled. *"That was you?"*

She didn't waste time responding but nodded as her eyes swept the battlefield.

The battle was shifting again, toward the north where the ground was clear of the fallen. As the fighting men edged sideways, they left behind them a chaotic mess of bodies, both dead and dying. Moans, sobs, and the occasional curse rode atop the sounds of the waves breaking on the shore and the clash of steel on steel. Petro's gaze fell on an Oteran soldier, blood pumping from the wound in his chest as he tried to grasp the handle of a knife wedged between his ribs. His hand wouldn't cooperate, and he gave up with a heavy sigh.

His last.

Arien uttered a cry and slid from her horse's back. Horror stole over him as she ran across the battlefield, dodging bodies while her feet trampled the red-stained sand. He dismounted and overtook her as she crouched over a bleeding form. A thinning thatch of bright orange hair left no doubt as to the man's identity.

Arien knelt in the bloody sand and placed a hand on her father's sweaty forehead. His chest barely moved to draw shallow breaths. She blinked away tears and took stock of his injuries. A sword had slashed through his armor in a powerful blow to the collarbone, slicing the metal as though it were no more than soft cheese. The only way a blow could cut through armor like that was with the help of Power. Blood saturated his uniform and soaked the ground around him. Using her sleeve, she attempted to wipe the blood from his face. Sobs threatened to rise from a chest as tight as though bound by metal bands, but she suppressed them.

His eyes opened, and he looked up into her face. Cracked lips parted but could produce no sound.

Arien Perceived and sensed Petro's mental presence with her. She found two active thoughts in her father's mind. Only two.

"She looks like her mother with red hair." And the other. *"That damned witch was right. I should have killed her in her cradle."*

His chest rose one last time, and as he expelled his last breath, his thoughts died with his body.

Arien closed his eyelids and then got to her feet. She turned blindly toward Petro. His arms came around her. She tried to draw comfort from his tight embrace, but what comfort could he give her? Her own had father hated her right up until his end.

"I—I hoped maybe if he saw me…" No more words would come. What had she hoped? That he would realize he loved her after all? That he regretted the years they missed? Something, *anything* nice that she might take away as a comfort in the years to come when she remembered this moment.

"I'm sorry."

In Petro's thought she felt so much sorrow and helplessness and disgust for the dead man at their feet. She leaned back enough to look up into his face. *"I'm no more an orphan now than I was an hour ago. You've been my father, far more than he ever could have been."*

He pulled her to his chest again, hugging her fiercely.

When he released her, she drew in a breath and tilted her chin high. "Let's go see if we can help finish this."

Together they headed in the direction they'd come. Petro froze, his gaze fixed on the edge of the forest.

"The king!" he shouted. "Where is he?"

Arien scanned the battlefield, and then pointed. "There."

The fighting had moved a good distance up the beach in a short time. She spotted King Mendel easily because he sat atop his horse, the only figure still mounted. He held a sword aloft, ready to defend himself from the Oterans who tried to advance toward him. But several black-robed figures had positioned themselves between the king and the soldiers. As Arien watched, the advancing Oterans found themselves suddenly holding swords that glowed bright red with heat. Their screams reached her ears as their weapons hit the ground and soldiers scattered toward the ocean to cool their blistered hands in the surf. She allowed herself a grim smile. The king was protected.

"What's going on there?" Petro pointed toward a small cluster of black-robed men huddled together on the eastern edge of the fighting, where the waves lapped up around their feet.

Arien recognized Masters Thaddeus, Parnell, Sinclare, and Hugh among them. She started to suggest joining them but then looked closer at Petro. Exhaustion showed in his drooping frame, the sagging skin beneath his eyes.

"You should leave. Go back to the castle and rest." She waved a hand. "Let those who are fresh finish this."

He looked offended. "You can't be serious. I won't stop now, with so many exciting things happening. I'm not going to miss the end of the battle."

Together they picked their way through the fallen toward the group. Jothan stood there, dressed once again in the robes of the Brotherhood, his expression proud. Petro greeted several brothers she'd met along the way, many of whom had passed their trials some years back and had not returned to the Hall.

Parnell clouted Petro on the shoulder. "Ah, Petro, about time you showed up to help." The stern master actually wore a grin, something Arien had never seen.

Thaddeus nodded agreement. "Yes, we said earlier it took gall to invite us to participate in this war and then not show up to help." The old man's eyes twinkled with humor.

Petro's lips twitched. He drew himself up, his chin high. "I'll have you know I've been handling things *on my own* since the attack began."

Jothan clapped him on the back. "Not doing a bad job of it, either." He turned to look out at the ships anchored this side of the barrier reef. "We think we've found a way to end this, though it won't be pleasant."

Lorin shuddered. "Has any of it been pleasant?"

Parnell, his gaze straying toward the still-raging battle, shook his head. "It has not. But the sooner we end this, the sooner the killing will stop."

"What is the plan?" Arien asked.

Sinclare nodded toward the ships. "Those. The remaining soldiers are there. If we sink them, the soldiers will have no chance to get to shore."

Arien Perceived the ships. Five were still heavily populated, and the other thirteen had no more than a dozen people aboard. She scanned the battle and estimated maybe two hundred red-uniformed soldiers still fighting. Considering that the Oterans had come with eighteen hundred, a thousand men had fallen on the Oteran side alone.

Apparently, Petro's thoughts followed the same track. "*For how many of those deaths am I responsible?*"

The comment arrived to her alone. She poured comfort into her answer. "*And how many lives have you saved by stopping the advance before their army got to Hamlin's towns and villages?*"

He started and gave her a searching look.

"*What?*" she asked.

He gave no answer other than narrowing his eyes.

"Surely we needn't sink them all." She fixed a beseeching glance on Master Thaddeus.

"That's what we were discussing." Sorrow darkened his

liquid blue eyes. "Callous as it sounds, we believe we should sink one of the full ships and two of the nearly empty ones."

Arien fixed her gaze on the closest ship. A hundred mind-lights glimmered within the wooden vessel. "Couldn't we only attack the empty ones?"

Petro shook his head. "If we don't devastate the army, King Kuriel may try this again."

"That's part of it," Jothan said. "We know from the documents in Jerolin's satchel that another thousand soldiers remained in Otero. We must make sure Kuriel knows we won't tolerate a second invasion attempt. And that we have the ability to prevent it."

Master Hugh spoke up. "The Oteran captains are ruthless. The thoughts we've Perceived…" A shudder rippled his body. "If we display a hesitancy to match their callous actions, they will view it as a sign of weakness."

Sinclare gestured toward several ships in the distance. "We want to keep a few ships intact. They will make an excellent start for a Hamlin fleet, along with the money Kings Thaine and Mendel will get when they ransom the Oteran survivors."

"But we don't want to have to go through this again," Parnell concluded.

With that Arien agreed wholeheartedly.

"Then we're agreed?" Thaddeus asked.

No one spoke, but several nods answered him.

Petro had remained silent during the discussion, his expression pensive. He held up a finger. "Before we act, I have an idea." Everyone looked his way. "We all know that females with Power possess an ability no brother ever has."

"Empathy," Thaddeus agreed. "That has proven to be their downfall." He smiled at Arien. "Until now."

Her cheeks warmed, but she watched Petro. "What are you thinking?"

"A moment ago, you bespoke me and included such emotion I felt it as my own."

"I've felt that too." Jothan's eyes took on a gleam. "You can imbue emotions in your thoughts."

The center of attention, her face heated even more. "I

suppose so."

"How do you do it?" Petro's question held a note of urgency.

"I—" Arien stopped, her mind busy. "I've never thought about it. It just...happens."

"But not all the time." Now Thaddeus, too, fixed an intense stare on her. "Your mindspeech with me is as plain as Parnell's."

She drew in a breath and concentrated. "That's true. When I want to share my feelings with someone, I blend them with a thought. It's kind of like issuing a Command."

"*That's* what I wanted to hear!" Petro jabbed a finger so close to her face she jumped. "Can you manufacture an emotion? One you don't feel?"

Parnell's mouth gaped open, and then he rose on his toes, excitement apparent in his tense stance. "I see where you're going, Petro." He rounded on Arien. "If you can project fear, or even terror, to the Oteran soldiers, they will flee. The ships will turn around and leave."

Jothan looked stubborn. "That won't prove to King Kuriel that we aren't afraid to be as ruthless as he."

"It will be even better," Petro said, his grin wide. "Imagine what tale the retreating soldiers will tell upon their return. They'll talk of ships sinking for no reason, of swords melting in their hands, and of nameless terror overtaking them."

Thaddeus caught the excitement. "He may think he can overcome us physically, but he'll realize he can't fight against us mentally."

A wave of enthusiasm swept through them all, while a nearly overwhelming insecurity attacked Arien. She swallowed against a dry throat. "I've never done that. I don't know if I can."

"Try it." Parnell turned and scanned the battlefield. He pointed at an Oteran soldier occupied in a hand-to-hand battle with a blue-garbed Creighton guardsman. "Do it to him."

Her hands trembled, and she shoved them in the pockets of her boy's trousers. She fixed her gaze on the soldier. How could she project an emotion she didn't feel?

Wait. She may not feel fear now, but as a child she'd

experienced terror that stole her breath and left her screaming. Night terrors, Mora had called them. So powerful were those feelings they'd stayed with her, hidden in the back of her adult mind. With a little effort…

She shut her eyes and searched her memory. In one particularly horrible dream, her mother had come to the orphanage to claim her. But when she answered the door, a horrible monster snatched her into slimy arms. The creature loomed in vivid detail still.

Her pulse pounded in her ears as she drew the long-buried emotions to the surface. A violent trembling attacked her limbs, and someone slipped an arm around her waist to support her. When she felt the terror grip her heart with an iron fist, she located the Oteran soldier and sent a single thought his way.

"Run, or die a death too horrible to imagine."

Murmurs of approval reached her ears, and someone applauded. She opened her eyes in time to see the soldier dive head-first into the surf and swim with a frantic pace toward his ship.

Still clapping, Jothan grinned at her. "I don't know what you did, but if you can do that to them—" He jerked his head toward the ships. "—you might just save their lives."

Still trembling, she leaned hard on Petro's arm. "I—I can't do it to a whole ship load of people. I can't broadcast a thought any more than you can."

"You won't need to," Parnell assured her. "Just to the captains and officers of each ship. They'll issue the orders, and their crew will obey. We'll help you locate them."

The others nodded.

Disappointment carved even deeper crevices in Thaddeus's forehead. "We'll still get to sink a ship or two, won't we?"

Petro laughed. "I think two or three might be a perfect demonstration. And we'll select ships close enough to others that the survivors can swim to safety."

The older man heaved a relieved sigh. "Then let's get on with it. Parnell, you, Petro and I will take that one." He pointed toward the northernmost ship. "Sinclare, Hugh, and

Lorin the one behind it. And for the third…"

Jothan pointed to one right in the center of a cluster of five. "What about that one? The others will see the destruction up close."

Thaddeus nodded. "Good thinking. You, Cleon, and Rand take that one."

They outlined the timing. The attack on the three ships would occur simultaneously. Immediately afterward, Arien would terrorize—she shuddered at the word—the commanders of the farthest ship. That one lay at the edge of her Perception range. Would a Command be effective that far away? She hoped so. The other four would follow in sequence, with the masters and brothers at her side working to identify the officers for her.

They all turned to face the ocean, arranging themselves in a line. Though she had not been assigned a ship to sink, Arien Perceived, and felt the Perception of those around her as well. She focused on the hull. From this distance, it took a moment to see the dance of the particles, but soon enough they caught her up in their swirling activity.

"Is everyone ready?" Parnell asked.

No one answered. Arien glanced at Jothan and saw him swallow convulsively. Petro wore a dismal but determined expression. Hugh remained stoic, Sinclare, sorrowful.

Thaddeus rubbed his hands together. "All right, then. Let's get it over with."

Arien closed her eyes. The nightmare hovered on the edge of her consciousness, ready to attack her when she let down her guard. Her heart pounded at the thought. She watched as Petro sent a Movement speeding toward the ship. The particles just below the water's surface changed their dance. Their grip on one another slackened and the wood splintered. Water rushed in. The force cracked the weakened wood and a large area of the hull collapsed.

A distant explosion echoed over the water. She opened her eyes to see a huge ball of flame erupt on the deck. A quick Perception in that direction showed her someone had located several barrels of flammable oil. Tiny figures leapt from the sides of the quickly sinking ship.

Barely a breath later, the second ship burst into splinters.

When the third vessel sank, the sounds of the battle behind them dwindled to near silence. The fighting stopped. Oterans and southerners alike stared, many mouths agape, as the last of the three ships sank rapidly beneath the salty waves.

Petro placed a hand on her shoulder. “Now, Arien.”

She closed her eyes and received a thought from him. Following his trail, she located the commanding officer of one of the five battleships that still held a full complement of soldiers. Though she wasted no time Perceiving his thoughts, confusion emanated from the man. She mustered her dream forth, her breath coming in gasps as childhood terror washed over her. When panic gripped her, she sent forth her thought, imbued with all the emotion that held her in its grip.

“Now the next,” Parnell said, and sent her the location of the second-in-command.

She repeated her thought four times on that ship, and then proceeded to the second. And the third. And the fourth. By the time she reached out to contact the confused mind of the fifth warship’s commander, the first two ships had already begun their withdrawal. Rapidly hoisted sails caught wind, and oars plunged through the water.

Soon all five vessels joined in rapid retreat.

On shore, an Oteran soldier not far from them looked out at the remaining ships. He threw his sword to the ground, dropped to his knees and placed his hands on his head in a gesture of surrender.

Several near him did likewise, and within a few moments not one red-clad soldier stood upright on the beach. A cheer went up from the guardsmen and villagers.

“It’s over.” Parnell’s voice trembled with relief. “I hope we never have to do anything like that again.”

Arien sank into the strength of Petro’s arms. She heartily agreed.

Twenty-Two

Arien stood beside the rest of the black-robed Brotherhood delegation, their medallions gleaming in the twinkling candlelight of the ballroom. Millard's son slept on the dais, unaware that in moments he would receive his name and his official investment as first prince of two kingdoms. Arien smiled as Illari, hovering anxiously to one side, frowned at Petro when he lifted the baby from his cradle. Petro seemed not at all perturbed. His face fairly shone with pride in having been selected as a representative of the king's council at the prince's investment.

The rest of the council and their families lined the wall opposite the Brotherhood delegation. Next to them stood the council from Creighton. Besides the three official groups, the room overflowed with those invited to attend this all-important investment ceremony. Arien spied Beryle, her hand resting lightly on the arm of Quinn Parkin, her dimpled face turned toward the dais. On Quinn's opposite side, looking like a dwarf beside a giant, stood Kerman Sein. She hadn't yet spoken to those two since Thaine's first official act as king, declaring the sale of anodyte by anyone but a licensed chemist illegal.

She glanced to her left at Jothan. *"Was Quinn upset at Thaine's new law?"*

"Yes, for a while. But he's decided to finance the building of a new chemist laboratory for Sein in Arnath. He's sure Sein will pass whatever licensure exam they come up with, and with Quinn's contacts, their partnership is sure to make them rich."

Arien grinned. *"I have no doubt. But why Arnath?"*

"It's approximately the same altitude as Eshtaol, and close to the Nephtali Pass. Quinn is convinced King Kuriel will want to open a trade agreement with the Twin Kingdoms, now that we've sent his army limping home."

"Thaine and King Mendel think the same," Arien told him.

The little prince let out a squeal. She turned her attention once again toward the dais in time to see Petro hastily bounce the bundle in his arms to soothe the fussy infant.

Smiling, King Mendel rose from his throne and extended his arms toward Petro and his grandson. Once again, he wore robes of state. A rich purple cape edged with gold flowed elegantly behind him. Arien hid a wistful smile. She much preferred him in his gardening clothes.

Seated in the throne beside Mendel's, Thaine also rose. He, too, wore formal robes. Though he would not be officially crowned for another six days and was therefore not entitled to wear the heavy, jewel-studded crown of his father, he looked no less kingly with the gold circlet of a first prince encircling his head.

In Arien's biased opinion, he looked magnificent.

Petro released the child into his grandfather's arms, and then retreated to the rear of the dais to stand beside Illari. King Mendel stepped forward, the baby in his arms. The tender expression on his face as he gazed at his grandson broadcast pride even to those in the back of the room. Arien's heart twisted within her chest. No father could be prouder of a son. Had he looked upon his own son this way, when Millard was an infant?

Mendel turned the baby in his arms and lifted him toward the watching crowd. The little prince gazed out over the assembly with blue baby eyes already beginning to darken.

Jothan's thought reached her. *"He looks as if he's about to say something intelligent."*

At that moment, the baby's mouth did open, in a huge yawn that ended with a tightly clutched fist being shoved into its toothless depths. The crowd tittered, and Mendel smiled.

"I present to you Jasper Millard Hubert Roderick, First Prince and heir to the throne of Hamlin."

"Yikers, what a name they've stuck poor little Milo with."

Jothan's irreverent thought reached Arien as Mendel turned to hand the baby to Thaine. She leveled a narrow-lidded glare on Jothan and placed a finger across her lips before focusing on the ceremony.

Thaine also held the baby in his arms. He peered down into the little face for a long moment. What was he thinking? Was he remembering the naming another baby named Roderick?

Whatever his thoughts, they remained un-Perceived.

Thaine addressed the assembly. "And I also affirm Jasper Millard Hubert Roderick as First Prince, and heir to the throne of Creighton."

A cheer rose to fill the ballroom, and Arien could not stop from lifting her voice with the others. Thaine turned toward Illari, and with one more tender glance at his nephew's face, handed the child to the eager nursemaid.

King Mendel held his hands up to request silence. "Please join the rest of the assembly in the outer courtyard, where a feast has been prepared to honor our first prince."

As Illari disappeared through a door to the rear of the dais to take the guest of honor back to the nursery, Thaine and Mendel stepped off the dais toward the crowd. People pressed them from all sides to express congratulatory sentiments. Arien waited for Master Petro to join her, and then walked with Jothan and Masters Parnell, Thaddeus, Avram, and Dorian toward the exit at the rear of the ballroom.

"Well, that's done." Jothan rubbed his stomach. "Now we can eat."

Master Thaddeus scowled. "You ate like a pig as a trainee. I see that hasn't changed significantly. I'm surprised you're not as big as Brother Bayard by now."

"I may have the chance one day, if his cooking is as good as it always was," Jothan responded in an off-hand manner. "After the crowning in Tadmoure, I think I'll find myself a suitable trainee and return to the Hall."

Master Parnell stopped in his tracks. "You, a master?" He threw up his hands in mock disgust, all the while grinning.

Arien leveled a disapproving stare on Jothan. "Just you make sure that your trainee is of a suitable age, and not an infant."

His grin bore all the charm of a boy's. "Someday I'll prove that theory. But what about you? What are your plans after the crowning? Ever consider becoming a master yourself?"

Arien opened her mouth to answer, but at that moment Thaine came up behind her. He placed a warm hand on her back, which sent delicious thrills through her body.

"Hasn't she told you? She's coming to Tadmoure, to be my advisor."

Watching Jothan's face, she saw his gaze drop to take in Thaine's hand before it returned to her face. His eyebrows arched high on his forehead.

"Like that, is it? I'd wondered. Well, as Kerman Sein said, your family is part of the royal Oteran line. If this situation develops, maybe that bloodline of yours will do you some good after all."

A furious blush burned in her face. She turned away from him. Still, her thoughts had traveled along similar lines in the past few weeks. Thaine's hand, warm and firm against the small of her back, threatened to rob her of the ability to speak intelligently.

She thrust those distracting thoughts from her mind and turned instead to Petro. "Are you sure—"

He cut her off with a gesture. "Absolutely. Much as King

Mendel and I would like you to stay, you're wasted here. I can handle whatever comes up in Kirklin. Don't worry about me. We'll stay in touch."

"Yes, we all will." Master Parnell dipped his head in Jothan's direction. "Brother Jothan has some very interesting ideas concerning the Brotherhood. We need to strengthen our fellowship. And as someone told us recently—" He smiled toward Arien. "—every now and then, change is necessary."

Petro nodded agreement. "Isn't it nice to be able to choose the direction of change, instead of having it thrust upon you? Life is so much more pleasant that way."

They turned into the short corridor that would lead them to the feast. In the years since Master Petro took her from Mora and Guy's orphanage, she'd experienced more change than most people in two lifetimes. With her new role as Thaine's advisor—and whatever else developed when she settled in Tadmoure—more changes loomed on her horizon. Good changes, she hoped.

They reached the end of the corridor and halted to gaze at the celebration in the courtyard. Everywhere she looked, people laughed and talked and lifted goblets to toast not only the new prince, but the victory they'd won together.

"You've no idea how much I'll miss you." Petro's comment drew her eyes to him. *"But your decision is a good one. It doesn't take a Seer to know your future is full of promise. If your life were a story, I believe you've found your happy ending."*

Arien cast a quick glance at Thaine, soon-to-be-crowned-King of Creighton. She looked back at Petro, unable to suppress a smile. Nor did she attempt to temper the joy that saturated her thought.

"I have a feeling I've found a happy beginning."

When Petro laughed aloud, she looped her arm through Thaine's and dragged him into the celebration.

About the Author

Ginny Patrick is the pen name for Virginia Smith, award-winning author of nearly forty novels. Though she loves to write fiction in all forms, with *Sister of the Brotherhood* Ginny returns to her literary first love – epic fantasy. She and her husband live in her home state of Kentucky. Get to know Ginny online at www.VirginiaSmith.org.

Made in the USA
Monee, IL
24 February 2020

22053619R00215